# Deadly Curiosities

First published 2014 by Solaris
an imprint of Rebellion Publishing Ltd,
Riverside House, Osney Mead,
Oxford, OX2 0ES, UK

*www.solarisbooks.com*

ISBN: 978 1 78108 233 1

10 9 8 7 6 5 4 3 2 1

A CIP catalogue record for this book is available
from the British Library.

Designed & typeset by Rebellion Publishing

Printed in the US

# Deadly
# Curiosities
## GAIL Z. MARTIN

WITHDRAWN

SOLARIS

For my wonderful husband Larry
and my children, Kyrie, Chandler, and Cody,
and all of the extended family who rallied to
help with the events that inspired this story.
Much love and gratitude to you!

# Chapter One

"HAVE YOU EVER seen something you can't explain?" The woman peered at me anxiously, looking to me for validation.

"Sure. Hasn't everyone?" My answer was meant to put her at ease, but it was a dodge. If I answered her question directly, she definitely wouldn't rest easy, now or maybe ever again.

I'm Cassidy Kincaide, owner of Trifles and Folly, an estate auction and antiques shop in historic – and haunted – Charleston, South Carolina. On the side, we're also a high-end pawn shop. I inherited the shop, which has been in my family since 1670. Most people think we deal in antiques and valuable oddities, and we do. But our real job is getting dangerous supernatural objects off the market before anyone gets hurt. When we succeed, no one notices. When we don't, the damage usually gets blamed on some sort of natural disaster.

It's the perfect job for me since I'm not just a history geek, I'm also a psychometric. I read the strong emotions connected to objects, and often I get bits of memories, voices, and images. So when my customer asked if I'd ever seen anything I can't explain, I was certain she didn't really want to know the truth, because I had seen some very scary stuff.

"Maybe it's the lenses," the woman said, bringing me back to our conversation. "In the opera glasses. When I look through them at home, or in my yard, they seem to be fine. But when I take them to a show, there are... shadows... and the images get blurry."

I was willing to bet that there was more to it, but it didn't take a psychic to see that my customer was being careful with what she said, worried I would think she was imagining things, or worse.

"That can happen in old pieces like this," I said, allowing her to save face. "Lenses are delicate things. Over the years, if they get bumped or jostled too much, they can get out of alignment."

In front of me on the counter lay a beautiful set of opera glasses, the kind refined ladies of a bygone era took to the theater for a better view of the stage. They were finely crafted, with mother-of-pearl inlay and brass trim, and I could imagine them being tucked into the beaded handbag of a well-to-do patron of the arts. Without even touching them, I could also sense that they were not entirely what they seemed.

"Are you interested in purchasing them?" The woman seemed antsy, like she was ready to be rid of the item and be gone.

I smiled at her. "They're lovely," I said. "We'd be happy to purchase them." I paused. "Can you tell me a little about their history? Buyers love pieces that have a story to go with them."

Now that the opera glasses were no longer her problem, the woman seemed to relax a little. She was dressed casually, but I knew enough about clothing to know that her silk t-shirt, designer slacks, and tasteful-yet-expensive shoes probably cost more than the current balance of my bank account, and that was without adding the real gold earrings, Swarovski crystal bangle bracelet, and elegant (and large) diamond wedding set. Although she obviously took good care of herself, I saw a few tell-tale clues that made me guess that she was older than I had originally guessed, probably in her early seventies.

"They belonged to my great-grandmother," she said, giving the opera glasses a wary look. "She came from a well-to-do family up North, and moved to Charleston when she married my great-grandfather around the turn of the last century," she added. "According to family legend, she was quite a patron of the theater. She saw all the greats of the day, actresses like Lillie Langtry and Sarah Bernhardt, and actors like the Barrymores and Eddie Foy, Sr."

I nodded, and although the names sounded vaguely familiar from a long-ago college theater history class, I couldn't remember any details.

"So early 1900s?" I asked, but the opera glasses had already given me the answer. From their materials, finish, and workmanship, I knew they came from a time when craftsmen took their work seriously.

The woman nodded. "Of course, I never met her. But the opera glasses have been handed down through the family, and when my aunt died, she left them to me because I always loved going to plays." She sounded wistful, and I followed her gaze to look at the beautiful glasses that had made her so wary. It was a shame that whatever supernatural qualities they possessed had made her unable to enjoy the gift.

I looked over to the other counter where the register sat. "Teag will take care of you," I said, catching the eye of Teag Logan, my assistant manager. I knew Teag read my look for what it really meant, and that he would be certain to get the name, address, and phone number of our visitor in case the object turned out to be more of a problem than it appeared.

I waited until Teag paid the woman and she had left the store before I ran my hand just above the opera glasses. Teag came over for a closer look. "Do we have a spooky or a sparkler?" he asked.

That was our short-hand way of describing the items that came into the store that had a supernatural element to them. 'Mundanes' were regular items that didn't require special handling. 'Sparklers' had a little something extra about them, but nothing dangerous. 'Spookies' had a darker edge, maybe even a malevolence. They go into the back room until my silent partner, Sorren, can safely get rid of them.

"It's got some kind of juju," I said, "but I'm not sure what just yet." I gave Teag a sidelong look. "I thought I'd wait until the customer left before I pick it up, just in case I put on a show." I tucked a stray strand of strawberry-blonde hair behind my ear. Late spring in Charleston meant it was already hot and humid, and although I was twenty-six and possibly ready for a more 'grown up' hairstyle, most of the time I wrestled my hair into a ponytail and hoped for the best. With my green eyes and pale skin, I often felt light-headed from the Southern heat, even when I didn't handle an item with a questionable supernatural past.

Teag chuckled, but it sounded forced. Sometimes, when I handle an object, the emotions and memories are overwhelming and I get pulled in to its energy. When that happens, I can end up flat on my back – or unconscious. Teag isn't just my assistant store manager. He's also my assistant auctioneer, archivist, and occasional bodyguard, with his own powerful magical gift.

"What do you make of it?" I asked Teag. I was stalling before touching the opera glasses, and both of us knew it.

"Without looking them up, I'd say mid- to late nineteenth century, possibly imported, definitely expensive," Teag replied.

Once upon a time, Teag had been studying for his doctorate in history at the University before Sorren and I recruited him to work at Trifles and Folly. The history and the mystery of what we do got him hooked, and now he's ABD (All But Dissertation) and in no particular hurry to finish his degree. He's good looking, tall, and slender, with a skater boy mop of dark hair, and a wicked sense of humor. And right now, he looked worried.

"Let's see what I see," I said, working up my nerve to pick up the glasses. Teag moved a little closer, the better to keep me from falling to the floor if things went wrong.

My fingers tingled when I picked up the opera glasses; a sure sign there was some supernatural juice flowing through them. I picked up a jumble of feelings: confusion, fear, sadness. Then I took a deep breath and held the glasses up to my eyes. It was like looking through a miniature pair of very ornate binoculars. I could see the other side of the store very clearly, and when I turned toward Teag, I could see the pores in his skin and the stubble from his morning shave.

"Well?"

I set the glasses down and sighed. "Nothing unusual. But that's what she said – strange things only happened when she took the glasses to the theater."

"There's a production of *Arsenic and Old Lace* at the Academy Theater," Teag said, naming one of Charleston's many wonderful refurbished old theaters. "Are you doing anything tomorrow night?"

Since my love life at the moment was also ABD (All But Defunct), the chances of me having big plans on a Saturday night were slim. And since Maggie, our part-time helper, had called off sick, I'd be spending the weekend working at the shop anyway. I checked the calendar on my phone, just to make sure I hadn't forgotten anything. I hadn't.

"Sure," I said. "It's been a while since I've seen the City Players, and I'd love to go." I frowned. "Don't you and Anthony have anything planned? I don't want to mess up date night."

Anthony was Teag's other diversion from finishing his Ph.D. With his blond hair, blue eyed boy-next-door good looks, and his Battery Row charm, I could definitely see the attraction. Anthony had just finished law school and taken a position with the family law firm. He and Teag had been a couple now for over a year, and the three of us often went out together, or double dated when I was seeing someone.

"He's got a couple of big cases going right now," Teag said, shaking his head. "I've barely seen him all week, and he warned me that he'd be working late all weekend. So I was resigned to spending the night alone with a movie."

"In that case, let's see the show," I said. I don't mind a quiet evening at home, but the idea of an impromptu night out was sounding better and better.

"How about if I slip over and see if I can get tickets?" Teag suggested. "I'll be right back."

"Sounds good," I agreed. "Did you get a name for our seller?"

Teag nodded. "Trinket Ellison. Of the Battery Park Ellisons. Don't you ever read the social page? Her family has been in Charleston as long as yours has; in other words, practically since the first ships dropped anchor."

"I don't pay a lot of attention to that kind of thing," I said, and it was true, although in Charleston, the old families all knew each other socially. "The real mystery is, how did a woman from up North – no matter how wealthy – end up marrying into an old Charleston family like the Ellisons back in the day?" I shook my head. "Some folks in these parts hadn't gotten over The War by then."

Truth be told, even now, some folks hereabouts still weren't over The War. That would be what folks up North called the Civil War and what Charlestonians were more likely to call the War Between the States if they were being polite and the War of Northern Aggression if they weren't.

Teag shrugged. "Beats me. I'll ask Anthony. He usually knows everything about everybody."

*Trust a lawyer from an old established family to know all the dirt,* I thought.

While Teag went out for tickets, I went through my email. One of the messages caught my eye. The sender was 'Rebecca@GardeniaLandingB&B.com' and I was almost ready to hit 'delete' expecting a sales pitch before I read the message.

*We're having some problems with several antique décor pieces we recently acquired. Maggie told*

*me that you're good with this kind of thing and
I was hoping you could please stop by. She says
you have a knack for dealing with haunted items.
I'll be happy to comp your stay for a night or two
if you would come. I don't know who else to ask,
and I can't put up with things the way they are.*

I sat back and stared at the screen. At first, I thought
maybe she had purchased some items to decorate her
bed and breakfast and changed her mind about them.
It happens. Several local interior decorators shop at our
store on a regular basis (of course, we only show them
the mundanes or the tame sparklers).

But it didn't sound like the problem had to do with
a decorator's style. Maggie didn't know the full story
about what we do at Trifles and Folly, but she did know
I had a gift for recognizing haunted things. She was
discreet enough to only mention that if the client raised
the issue first. Rebecca's last line sounded desperate,
and scared. I frowned. If Rebecca was correct, how on
earth had she gotten her hands on a sparkler without
my knowing about it?

I thought for a moment, then hit reply. *I'll be glad to
help,* I wrote, *but can you please tell me more about the
problem?* I hit send and went back to my email, deleting
a few spammy messages. I figured Rebecca probably
wouldn't get back to me until tomorrow, but just as
I was getting ready to step away from the computer, a
new message popped into my inbox.

*You really need to see for yourself,* Rebecca had
written. *Please, please come – soon.*

Well, that was interesting. The desperation was
unmistakable. Although it was Friday, I wasn't quite

spontaneous enough to consider packing up and heading out to her B&B.

But come to think of it, I was due to have some work done on my house next week. I live in the house my parents inherited from my great-uncle Evanston, the same one who left me Trifles and Folly. It's what folks in Charleston call a 'single house', a two-story brick house from the 1880s that's only one room wide, with a porch (called a piazza) that runs along one side. It's a lovely house, but its age means there's a lot of upkeep. My parents happily sold the house to me for a token payment when they moved to Charlotte, leaving me the proud owner of a home I absolutely loved and couldn't possibly afford otherwise.

I was getting the hardwood floors refinished, and between the mess and the smell, that meant that Baxter, my little Maltese, and I were going to have to find another place to stay for a few days. I'd already booked Baxter into the local puppy spa, and I'd made reservations for myself at a chain hotel, but Rebecca's invitation could turn necessity into a mini-vacation – depending on just how much of a problem Rebecca was having, and how easy it was to fix.

*How about next Tuesday and Wednesday*? I emailed back.

*THANK YOU!!!* Rebecca replied, and I figured from the all caps and the extra punctuation that she was very happy.

TEAG WASN'T BACK yet, so I plugged Gardenia Landing into Google and did a little online sleuthing. A tasteful web page popped up, with images of an idyllic old home that looked both restful and expensive. The bed and breakfast looked charming.

I read through the home's history. The house dated from the 1850s, practically qualifying it as new construction in a city as old as Charleston. That meant it had seen a lot of history, and stood a good chance of having a few resident ghosts, like many of the older homes in Charleston.

Heck, if you believed the guides on the nightly ghost tour carriage rides, every house, garage, and alleyway was haunted. Some of that made for good fun for the tourists, but there was an uncomfortable undercurrent of truth. Charleston was a beautiful city, but it had been built on the blood, toil, and misery of African slaves. Pirates had been tried and hanged here, duels were once common, and the plagues, earthquakes, and hurricanes that claimed thousands of lives over the years left restless spirits aplenty. In nearly four hundred years, Charleston also had more than a few sensational murders. Stories of the taverns and brothels of long ago – and the inevitable fights they spawned – still made good gossip. Charleston might prefer its nickname of 'the Holy City' for its many churches, but it was one of the most haunted places in the country, for good reason.

So Gardenia Landing might have a few resident ghosts, I mused. I'd have to do some digging into its history. Beneath many a charming façade lay tawdry tales of mayhem and murder. Some places played up their checkered history, while others tried all the harder for respectability. Gardenia Landing wasn't hawking ghost tours, so I guessed that its owner wasn't viewing supernatural activity as being good for business.

"Got them!" Teag sang out as he burst into the shop, sending the strip of sleigh bells on the front door jangling. "Two tickets, Grand Tier. So we're in the first balcony, but up against the railing with a good view of the stage." He was grinning ear to ear.

"Technically, the show is sold out, but the theater manager is a friend of mine, and I wheedled a favor out of him, for old times' sake," Teag added with a conspiratorial wink.

"What's it going to cost us?" I asked with a smile. Teag could work social connections – real or online – better than anyone I know, but there was usually some *quid pro quo* involved.

Teag shrugged. "I might have said we would consider loaning a few pieces for one of their upcoming plays – with proper credit in the program book, of course, so it's almost like free advertising."

I chuckled. In my opinion, Teag had been wasting his talent on a Ph.D. in history. He had the instincts of an impresario coupled with the social finesse of a master fundraiser. Turns out it wasn't just his magnetic personality: some of it was magic. Fairly recently, Teag discovered he had a supernatural gift as a 'Weaver', someone who could work spells into woven goods – and into the 'web' of the Internet. Teag had an uncanny talent for following information strands, either offline or online, to find and piece together bits of data and weave it into valuable intel. Now we knew it wasn't all luck.

"We'll need the insurance paperwork and receipts, but that's easily done," I said. "I'm excited about the play."

"You need to get out more, Cassidy," Teag said, sounding like a big brother.

I shrugged, afraid to answer because it was true, and switched subjects. "Have you ever heard of Gardenia Landing?"

Teag frowned, thinking. "Bed and breakfast?"

I nodded. "I just got a rather desperate email from the owner begging me to come stay – for free – and help her with a problem with an item she got here."

Teag scratched his head. "I don't remember selling anything to a B&B owner."

"She may have gone through a decorator."

"Okay. I can go through our list of regulars and see which designers have made purchases lately."

"Please. I'd like to have a clue about what I'm walking into before I go out there."

Teag raised an eyebrow. "You're going? Just like that?"

"Baxter and I need to get out of the house for a couple of days while the hardwoods get done over – remember?"

"What about the owner's 'problem'?"

I shrugged. "If she bought something here, it couldn't be more than a sparkler. Maybe the B&B has its own ghosts, and they amped up the new piece so it's acting out. At best, I find it and figure out how to neutralize it. At worst, I offer her store credit and a replacement and bring it back for Sorren to deal with."

Teag fixed me with the kind of stare my grandmother used to use if she caught me in a fib. "You know, and I know, that 'at worst' can be a whole lot worse than that. Be careful, Cassidy. Sorren's not going to like you going out there by yourself when we don't know what you're up against."

I grimaced. "I'll figure something out," I muttered.

What Teag said was true. Sorren was the mastermind behind Trifles and Folly, from its beginning nearly four hundred years ago. He had been the silent partner with the shop's owner – always a relative of mine – down through the centuries. Sorren was also one of the early members of the Alliance, the group that got rid of dangerous magical items.

"Maybe you should let Sorren know about this before you go," Teag said, raising an eyebrow.

"It's probably nothing," I said. "I don't want to bother Sorren until we know for certain." When I inherited the store from my Great-Uncle Evan, I inherited the 'real' family business: protecting Charleston against supernatural danger. Sorren was part of that package. The Alliance was the other piece.

Sorren's maker had brought him into the Alliance in the 1500s when Sorren was a century old. The Alliance has been busy since then. When we make a mistake, lots of people die. Plagues, floods, earthquakes – fewer of them are natural than people think. Often, there are supernatural or magical fingerprints all over them, because someone very powerful made them happen. I didn't want that on my conscience. On the other hand, the Alliance included some very powerful magic users and immortals. They didn't get involved in routine hauntings.

"Speaking of Sorren," Teag said, "This came for you." He held out an overnight mail sleeve and I ripped it open to find a letter in Sorren's distinctive handwriting. "Hasn't he heard of email?"

I chuckled. Sorren used email just fine, and we both knew it. But with my gift, a letter carried far more information than what it actually said, information that couldn't fall into the wrong hands if it were intercepted.

"Let's see what he has to say," I said, and sat down before I touched the envelope. But as soon as my fingers touched the crisp paper, I knew we were in for trouble.

"He's worried about something," I said. In a nod to the old ways, Sorren still used a drop of sealing wax embossed with the imprint of his signet ring to seal the envelope. It wasn't an artistic flourish: there was magic in the wax that kept the letter eyes-only for the recipient.

I broke the seal and pulled out the short note. "*On my way*," I read aloud. "*Be careful. Something's up – not sure what. Big players involved. Details soon – Sorren.*"

But the paper told me much more. Death and danger had gotten the Alliance's attention, and Sorren was worried. His warning was clear. Something very bad was heading our way.

Sorren took his commitment to my family – and to me – very seriously. And if I thought Teag was overprotective, he couldn't compete with a six hundred year-old vampire.

# Chapter Two

I FELT RUSHED and flustered as I bustled to answer the front door. It was Saturday evening, and I'd spent the day rushing around. Baxter scampered back and forth underfoot, and barked up a storm when he knew we had a visitor.

"Ready to go?" Teag asked, stepping inside. He looked good in a sport coat and slacks. His dark eyes held a hint of mischief, and he was wearing his trendy glasses instead of contacts, which added to the dashing young professor look. For once, his hair was tamed enough to stay out of his eyes. Since Teag tended to favor jeans and t-shirts, I suspected Anthony might have had a hand in selecting his wardrobe for the evening. He was more dressed up than I'd ever seen him, and I grinned. He bent down to scoop Baxter into his arms and tousled Bax's ears.

"Anthony's going to wish he'd joined us," I said. "You clean up well."

Teag laughed. "So do you."

I was wearing a sundress and heels, a tribute to the spring weather. A light wrap was slung across my shoulders, in case the theater was cold. Given Charleston's hot and humid weather, odds were good that the difference between the outside air and the A/C on the inside would be enough to fog my sunglasses.

"Here's hoping that the opera glasses don't pack much of a psychic wallop, so we can both enjoy the show," Teag said.

The small binoculars were tucked in my purse. I had handled them several times, and even tried using them to view a television show, thinking that might activate whatever our client had seen. Nothing happened. That meant that either the opera glasses only did their thing for live theater, or perhaps our client had an overly active imagination.

Although technically our outing was work-related, I was excited. Maybe that said something about my social life, but the truth was, when I wasn't working late at the store, I socialized with a small group of friends, or savored a quiet evening with a good book, a cup of tea or a glass of wine, and my little Maltese. Charleston offered one soiree after another, many for charitable causes, but the constant social swirl seemed more obligation than recreation. So I had to admit my excitement included looking forward to the play itself, not just figuring out what was going on with the opera glasses.

"Did you know this play was originally produced in 1939?" Teag asked as we headed to the theater. He became a theater-geek fountain of information, keeping me entertained until we reached our destination.

"I've got to admit, I'm as interested in the theater itself as the play," I said, pausing on the other side of the street to take in the grand marquee that jutted out, retro-style, over the sidewalk and rose like a tower along the front of the building. We had to walk a few blocks since parking tonight was at a premium. "The theater's a drama queen in its own way."

Teag chuckled. "The Academy has been a Southern belle, a movie star, a spurned lover, a bag lady, and a dowager queen. This was the biggest vaudeville theater in the South back in the day. Even after movies came out and many of the old theaters were converted to show motion pictures, the Academy remained the place to see a live performance in Charleston."

I felt a rush of excitement as we walked into the Academy. The theater lobby had been painstakingly refurbished to its glory days. From the big, retro lit-up marquee outside to the old-style concession stand, plush red carpets, and velvet-upholstered seats, the Academy Theater was quite a showplace. It had taken a major effort from the community and the city's theater lovers to pull off the fundraising and renovation, but the results were stunning. Everything screamed Victorian abundance, from the lush burgundy velvet curtains and the plush carpet to the crystal chandeliers, gilded decorations, and huge mirrors.

"But the movies won out, didn't they," I said.

"For a while," Teag replied. "It closed in the 1970s, and it was empty for a long time. The local arts community managed to keep it from being torn down. Some well-heeled investors finally put the Academy back in business."

Those investors must have had pretty high heels and deep pockets, I thought, looking around at the opulent decor. Every detail had been lovingly restored, a nod to an era that believed too much was never enough.

"We're in the Grand Tier," Teag reminded me as we climbed the sweeping marble steps. Even the railing was an ornate masterpiece, and each step seemed to bring us closer to the huge, sparkling crystal chandelier that was the centerpiece of the lobby. "So we should have a great view of the stage as well as the theater itself."

We found our seats. The view was amazing. Once we were settled, I pulled the opera glasses from my purse. The mother-of-pearl inlay glistened in the lights. The opera glasses consisted of a petite set of adjustable magnifying lenses on a single inlaid vertical handle. I could hold the lenses up to my eyes with the handle like a carnival mask, without having to take a two-handed grip like a crazed bird-watcher. It all felt very glamorous in an old-fashioned movie-star kind of way.

Yet as I touched the opera glasses, I felt something that had not been present in the store; I felt uneasy, as if something were about to happen.

"Are you getting any vibes from this place?" I asked.

Teag was trying to eavesdrop on the couple sitting in the row ahead of us. My comment startled him. "Vibes? Just awe in the presence of this much bling," he replied.

I had to agree, the Academy reminded me of a wealthy woman who had decided to wear her entire diamond collection – and perhaps all of Tiffany's – at the same time. But I didn't think the feeling I was getting from the opera glasses was a fashion statement.

I lifted the glasses to my eyes, and looked around the theater. No one was on stage yet, but with the lenses, I felt as if I were right in the footlights. Something moved off to the side, but when I turned my head, I saw no one. I continued to pan the theater, spying on the people in the box seats, admiring the outfits and jewelry of other theater-goers. From somewhere, I heard a child crying. I froze. It wasn't the sound of a baby fussing or a testy toddler. The sound was faint, but it was a howl of fear and anguish that made my blood run cold.

"Cassidy, are you okay?" Teag looked at me anxiously.

"Did you hear that?" I struggled to keep my voice down.

"Hear what?" Teag's expression was sincerely confused.

"I swear I just heard a child screaming for his life, and before that, I thought I saw a black shadow to the side of the stage."

Teag shook his head. "I've been staring at the stage for the last several minutes, and I didn't see anything. I didn't hear anyone screaming, either." I must have looked unconvinced. "Look around, Cassidy. If a child were screaming bloody murder, don't you think people would be restless, trying to figure out what was going on?"

The other patrons were engrossed in conversation or studying their programs. I eyed the opera glasses with suspicion and a little trepidation. "I'm beginning to get an idea of what Trinket saw," I murmured.

The orchestra was just warming up. I closed my eyes and let my thoughts float free. Now, as I sat in my comfortable velvet seat, I began to get snippets of images that seemed utterly out of place.

A pirate. Dancing girls. The old woman who lived in a shoe. I shook my head, wondering where the images were coming from, but more flickered in my mind. I saw a building that looked like a Greek temple on the outside, and a lavish Victorian palace on the inside. On a busy street, snow lay banked along the sidewalk, and I shivered as if a gust of winter wind had suddenly swept past me.

"It's starting," Teag murmured, jostling me out of my vision. Shaken by what I had seen, I was glad to be brought back to the present. I opened my eyes, and for an instant, the Academy Theater I had entered was gone. I saw a stage set with scenery like a castle, and heard the faint strains of a waltz played by an orchestra. In front of me were a row of women in fancy velvet and silk shawls and men in dark coats with stiff white collars. I glanced down at my lap and saw the opera glasses as well as the long satin sleeves and full skirt of my dress, my high-button shoes just peeking their toes from beneath the hem.

I blinked my eyes and everything was as it should be. Gone were the castle sets, the old-fashioned clothing and winter wraps, and the waltz. My pastel cotton sundress was as cheery as ever, my arms were bare and my hem ended above my knees. I resisted the urge to bolt from my seat, and tried to stop shaking by taking several deep breaths.

"Cassidy?" Teag's voice was a low stage whisper. "What's going on?"

I swallowed hard. "I don't know yet, but I have the feeling I'm going to find out."

I tried to regain my composure. The opera glasses remained on top of my evening purse, not touching my skin. On stage, the classic play unfolded just as I remembered from high school. The audience loved it, but I couldn't shake a growing sense of doom.

The brightly lit exit signs caught my attention. They suddenly seemed far away. Panic tightened in my chest. *How long would it take to reach the doors?* I wondered. *Could I climb over the seats if I had to? What about all the children in the aisles?*

*Children in the aisles?* I thought, shaking myself out of my reverie. The aisles were empty.

Teag was watching me with a worried expression. The woman on the other side of me glanced away quickly when I looked in her direction. She was probably wondering if I had forgotten to take my medication.

I let out a long sigh and got up the courage to lift the opera glasses once more. At first, the binoculars gave me a bird's eye view of the play we'd come to see. But the longer I watched, the more often I caught glimpses of shadows crossing the stage. I was about to put the opera glasses down when a spark of light near the catwalk caught my eye.

I peered through the glasses, scanning the rigging that moved the scenery. A light flared, then disappeared. A few seconds later, I saw it again. Was that a flame? Before I could grab for Teag's arm, a new onslaught of images overwhelmed me.

*Fire billowed above the stage. Voices began to shout and the people around me pointed toward the curtain, which had now burst into flames. A man on stage shouted for us to remain calm and begged the orchestra to keep on playing, but people were already climbing out of their seats, running toward the doors. Doors? Where were the doors? I grabbed my son's hand, dragging him over the seat in front of us, as he cried and whimpered, knowing we had just a few moments before the smoke made escape impossible.*

*Smoke filled the theater. The lights went out. Nothing but darkness and flame. I held tight to my son's hand, and pushed toward where I had seen a door. I'd never felt a press of bodies like this, and I gathered my son into my arms, knowing that if we fell we would be trampled. An elbow caught me in the ribs, but I kept on, maneuvering into the places between people where there was a little space. I could hear shrieks behind us, and it felt as if an ocean wave was building, set to carry us out or roll us under. The doors gave way and cold winter air hit us. We stumbled out into the snow, pushed from behind. I was gulping in great lungfuls of cold winter air but everything still smelled like smoke...*

"Cassidy? Cassidy!" I could hear Teag's voice from a distance, but I couldn't stop shaking long enough to answer. I was shaking from remembered cold, from a long-dead woman's mortal terror, and from grief, because I knew in my heart that so many of those in the vision had not made it out alive.

"Does she have seizures like this often?" A stranger's voice was matter-of-fact.

"Sometimes she forgets her pills," Teag replied in a confidential tone. "It's not as bad as it looks. I'm sorry for the disruption."

"Maybe we'd better take her to the hospital, check her over," the stranger, a security guard, said. I was coming back to myself, and embarrassment replaced terror. I had a vague idea of what must have happened, and if I was right, I'd probably never be able to show my face in this theater again.

"Really, she'll be fine," Teag protested. "Just let me get her home, let her get some rest, and she'll be better by morning."

"I'm fine," I managed groggily. "Really."

Teag and the guard helped me to my feet, one man under each arm. The patrons next to me had already vacated their seats, giving me one more reason to want to sink into the earth and disappear.

"Keep your head down and lean on us," Teag

whispered. "That way fewer people can see your face and people will feel sorry for you because you're sick."

I groaned, but kept my face averted and let my rescuers half-carry me to the lobby.

"If you change your mind about the ambulance –" the guard said.

"She's going to be fine," Teag said, with his friendliest puppy-dog grin. "Her color is coming back already. I can get her out to the car from here. Thank you so much."

The guard grunted something I didn't quite catch, then retreated. Teag scooped an arm under my shoulders and helped me stand, then steered me toward the ladies room.

There was a lounge area in the rest room, and I sat for a few minutes to catch my breath, then went to the sink and splashed cold water on my face. I stood up straight and squared my shoulders as I walked out to the lobby. Teag was waiting by the door.

"Let's get out of here," he said, leading me toward the side entrance, into the alley. "I'll tell you all about it in the car." By the time we reached the outside, I had my wits about me once more. We walked the few blocks to his car in silence.

I waited until we had paid the attendant and Teag had pulled out onto the street before I spoke. "Did I –"

"Yes."

"You don't even know what I was going to ask," I said defensively.

Teag rolled his eyes. "You had a full-blown vision, right during the second act. You started shaking, and you pointed toward the top of the stage. If I hadn't clapped my hand over your mouth, I'm betting you would have yelled 'fire!' in a crowded theater, which would have gotten you – and probably me – thrown into jail." He shook his left hand. "As it was, you bit me."

"Really?"

He turned his palm so I could see it and sure enough, teeth marks were already causing a vivid bruise. I felt my cheeks get hot. "I'm so sorry."

"It beat spending the night in lock-up," Teag replied. I could tell from his voice that he was more concerned than angry.

I told him about the vision. Teag had seen enough of my talent to know that I didn't make this stuff up. At the moment, I was seriously re-thinking my chosen line of work.

"You saw the theater catch on fire," Teag repeated. "Somewhere it snowed, so it was winter."

"It was around the holidays," I said, then stopped. "I'm not sure how I know that, but it's true. Just before or after Christmas." I searched my memories. "Some of the performers were in holiday outfits."

"Did you see anything else?"

I recounted the images I had glimpsed before the vision overwhelmed me. Teag frowned. "A pirate? At a holiday play?"

I shrugged. "It didn't make sense to me, either. And I kept hearing a waltz." I shook my head. "Do you have any ideas?"

"Trinket said the opera glasses came from her great-grandmother, who came from the North, right?"

"Right," I replied.

"Okay, so if Trinket is seventy, her great-grandparents might have been born around 1880 or so, give or take a few years," Teag said.

"Sounds about right." I thought for a moment. "The woman in the vision had a small child with her, and I had the distinct feeling that I was seeing her thoughts, not the boy's," I said, trying to focus on my memory of the images. "I'm guessing from the clothing that whatever it was happened right around 1900." I looked over at Teag. "Where are the opera glasses?"

"They're in my pocket," he said. "And no, I'm not giving them back to you today."

"Fine with me."

We pulled up in front of my house, and Teag parked by the curb. I was recovered enough to walk up to the piazza by myself and let us in. As with most Charleston single houses, the side of the house faces the street and so the door opens into the piazza, not the main house. The real front door looks out onto a little private garden enclosed by a brick wall with a wrought-iron gate.

We walked into the house, letting the air conditioning revive us, and Baxter skittered up to greet us, dancing on his hind feet until I picked him up to nuzzle him. Once I had said hello, Baxter insisted on being handed off to Teag for acknowledgement, and then wiggled to be put down.

"Would you like a soda?" I asked, resolved to be polite although I was beginning to feel the aftereffects of the visions.

Teag rolled his eyes and sighed. "I can find the fridge. Go sit down. I'll get something for both of us."

Relieved, I collapsed onto the couch, and Baxter pranced beside me until I picked him up. He settled on my lap, and I leaned back against the cushions and closed my eyes. A few moments later, Teag returned with two sodas.

"Mind if I switch on your laptop?" he asked.

"Go ahead. You're just lucky I brought it back from the store."

Teag powered up the computer. "All right, let's see what we can find," he said. He actually sounded excited about tracking down what I had seen. "Let's start with famous theater fires," he mused, typing the information into the search bar.

I stroked Baxter's silky fur and tried to relax, but every time I closed my eyes, I saw flashes of the vision. Although I knew it was only my imagination, the smell of smoke lingered, not the pleasant smell of a campfire, but the acrid smoke of burning fabric, and a faint scent of burning meat. I tried hard not to think about that. My stomach twisted.

"Anything?" I asked to get my mind off the memories.

"There's a pretty long list," Teag replied, "but if you're right about the time period, that narrows it down some."

"Just because it was snowing doesn't mean it was in the United States," I said. "It could have been somewhere else, like London, Toronto –"

"Chicago," Teag supplied. "How about Chicago?"

I opened my eyes, but I couldn't see past him to the computer screen. "Maybe. They get snow in Chicago. What did you find?"

"December 30, 1903. The Iroquois Theater caught on fire. Over six hundred people died."

I caught my breath. "What else does it say?"

"There are a lot of articles," Teag mused, and I saw him clicking on links and scanning down through the information. "The theater had only been open for a few weeks. They did a special holiday performance on

December 30, and had a standing room only crowd. It was so full, people were sitting in the aisles."

"Children," I murmured. "There were children in the aisles," I said, remembering the vision.

"Here's why you thought of a pirate," Teag said grimly. "The play was called *Mr. Bluebeard*. It seems to have been a mish-mash of rather forgettable songs and scenery including a castle, and partway through, a spark from one of the spotlights caught the scenery and curtains on fire."

"People couldn't get out," I said, reliving the horror of what the opera glasses had shown me.

"Says here that's because some of the doors were locked to keep out gate-crashers, and other doors were hidden behind curtains," Teag said, reading down through the articles. "They had even put locked gates at the bottom of the stairs to the upper levels, I guess to keep people from switching to more expensive seats than what they paid for."

"They locked them in?"

Teag nodded. "The theater was supposed to be fire-proof –"

"Yeah, and the Titanic was supposed to be unsinkable," I muttered.

"But apparently, the owners skimped on fire extinguishers, and some of the fire escapes weren't even finished," he said. He paused long enough that I looked at him, worried.

"What?"

"The fire broke out while the orchestra was playing a waltz," Teag said quietly. "One of the actors, Eddie Foy, Sr., tried to keep the people from panicking so they could make an orderly exit, but it didn't work."

"Eddie Foy, Sr." I repeated. "Trinket said her great-grandmother had seen most of the famous actors and actresses of her time. He was one of the names she mentioned. I'd never heard of him before."

"He survived," Teag said. "And everyone hailed him as a hero. They even made a movie about him, and it included the fire." He drew a deep breath and leaned back in his chair, staring at the screen. "It says here that some of the cast were dressed in holiday costumes," he added. "And here's a picture of what the Iroquois Theater looked like before the fire."

He scooted the chair aside so I could see. The grand facade of the doomed theater had pillars in front, a Victorian version of a Greek temple, just like I had seen in the vision.

"Wow," I said. I took a sip of my soda. My heart was racing. Baxter seemed to sense that I was uneasy, because he gave me a curious look with those little black button eyes and snuggled closer.

"You're good, Cassidy," Teag said, shaking his head. "Sometimes a little too good."

I stared at the old photo on the screen in silence for a moment. "What I want to know is why Trinket was able to see the images," I said. "I didn't get the feeling that she had any clairvoyant abilities. She seemed too freaked out for that." I was quiet again, mulling things over.

"The fire was certainly horrific," I said slowly, working it out as I went. "That kind of trauma can leave a residue that even people without a 'gift' can sense – that's why normal people see ghosts."

"The opera glasses have been passed down for several generations," Teag said, turning his chair to look at me. "You'd think if they were so blatantly haunted, someone would have gotten rid of them by now."

I nodded, having had the same thought. "I think we need to talk to Trinket again. Maybe she's heard stories about her ancestor and the fire. She might not have mentioned that the glasses had a tragic past if she thought that would hurt the sale. She really wanted to get rid of them."

Teag leaned forward and rested his elbows on his knees. "Which makes me wonder – if they freaked out the people who owned them, why hang onto them?"

"And if they didn't cause a problem before, what changed?" I said, my thoughts racing. "Did something... activate them... somehow?"

Teag met my gaze. "We'd better find out. It's bad enough if the glasses were always that powerful. That makes them definite spookies and something Sorren will want to deal with."

"But if something charged up their hauntedness, then we're dealing with more than just the opera glasses," I said. "Because whatever – or whoever – it was could juice up something else."

"And in this city, with all its haunts, that would be a real problem."

# Chapter Three

By the next morning, I had recovered from the trauma if not the embarrassment. Fortunately, being Sunday, we didn't open until noon, which meant that I could spend the morning in the back going through some of the more benign pieces. Teag handled the mundanes. Right now, we didn't have any spookies in stock except for the opera glasses, and I was grateful. Still, the tragedy of the fire stuck with me. I hadn't slept well. My dreams had been dark, lit only by flames, and once I had woken with my heart pounding and my palms sweaty.

I was mostly recovered by the time Monday morning rolled around, although I hoped that none of our customers had attended the play on Saturday.

"You doing okay, Cassidy?" Teag stuck his head in the back room.

"A little tired, but that's all. The coffee is definitely helping. Thank you." Teag had come in early and had the coffee pot in the shop's small kitchen already chugging out liquid wakefulness before we opened for the day. It was exceptionally thoughtful of him, since he didn't drink the stuff, but he probably figured I'd need it more than usual today. Teag had a large mug of tea, his beverage of choice.

"I put in a call to Trinket," Teag said, standing where he could keep an eye on the front of the store. "I got her voice mail, and I asked her to give me a call."

"Maybe she caught wind of what happened at the play and decided to high tail it out of town for a while," I said with a lopsided grin.

"Maybe," Teag replied. "But she has to come home sometime, and I doubt she's skipped town just because of you. In the meantime, I'll check the Darke Web."

Teag's gift with information makes most hackers look like newbies. If it's anywhere online, no matter how well hidden, he'll find it. That goes beyond the Dark Web, used by mortal criminals, and into the currents of information shared by the supernatural, magical, and immortal communities, the Darke Web. Law enforcement can't break the enchantments, and Teag wanders those digital pathways like a native son. If it was out there, I knew he'd find it.

I'd felt like skipping town after what happened, but I figured it would blow over faster if I just faced the music. Although the physical effects were gone, the embarrassment lingered on. Even now, two days later, I'd settled for toast and peanut butter at home instead of my usual muffin at the bakery down the block, not quite willing to answer questions yet or dodge curious gazes.

The front door opened and the bells clanged against the glass. "Cassidy? Teag?"

Andrea Andrews, owner of Andrews Carriage Rides, was one of my best friends, and one of the most connected business owners in Charleston. I took a swig of my coffee for sustenance, and squared my shoulders. "Hi, Drea," I called.

Drea gave me the once-over when I stepped up front. She was a dark-haired whirlwind, a petite bundle of energy who could rival a hurricane for sheer force of nature. She had built her family's carriage ride company from one carriage to a fleet of twelve, and expanded into specialty tours, including one of the top ghost tours in the city.

Clutched in her hand was a bag from the Honeysuckle Cafe, my favorite bakery. I could smell the fresh blueberry muffin, my usual breakfast selection, all the way across the store. "I brought you something," she said with a grin. "Somehow, I figured you'd skip your morning muffin."

"You're an angel," I said as she handed off the bag and I could feel the still-warm muffin through the paper.

"Trina said today's muffin was on the house," Drea said, watching with a satisfied smile as I took a bite of blueberry-packed goodness and closed my eyes, savoring the taste. "She thought it might cheer you up."

"You two are fantastic," I said, and I meant every word. Not only were Drea and Trina good friends, but we also referred a lot of customers to each other.

"So let me guess," Drea drawled. "You had a problem with one of your latest acquisitions."

Drea didn't know the full truth about what we did at Trifles and Folly. She didn't know about the Alliance, or that Sorren was an immortal. But she did know about my ability to read objects by handling them, and she believed in my gift, and me, without reservation. Drea didn't have any clairvoyant abilities of her own, but she accepted that there were things in this world that operated outside conventional wisdom, and truth be told, she thought what I could do was kinda cool. Right now, I didn't share her sentiment.

"Yeah. I decided to try out a new piece I got." I gave a wry, self-conscious smile. "It didn't go as well as I had hoped."

Drea's snort confirmed my opinion. "Ya think? Fortunately, everyone who mentioned it to me thinks you had the flu, except for Mrs. Monroe, who wondered if you were pregnant."

I almost choked on my muffin. "Did you tell her I'd need a boyfriend for that to even be a possibility?"

Drea grinned. "I didn't think it was any of her business, so I just told her that I was pretty sure it was just the flu."

I had wolfed the muffin in record time, proof of just how stressed I still felt over the incident. "How many people make up 'everyone'?" I asked.

Drea's fingers moved as she made a mental count. "Four or five," she said. "Most of those were in the bakery and Valerie asked about you when she came in to pick up her paycheck." Valerie was Drea's leading ghost tour guide, and another good friend.

Out of the dozens of people who ran shops and restaurants in historic downtown Charleston, I guess four or five wasn't as bad as it could have been. "Do you think they'll lose interest any time soon?" I asked.

"In the flu?" Drea chuckled. "They might avoid you for a week to keep from catching anything, but that's about it. You won't be ostracized."

That was a relief. "So how's business?" I asked, eager to change the subject. Drea's carriages were beautiful and her horses were pampered. Her tour guides shared interesting information on their rounds, as well as legends, scandals and unsolved mysteries. It was a profitable combination.

Drea made a face. "We've been booked solid with conventions and tourists. But if the news people keep talking up those murders, I'm afraid visitors will stop coming out at night."

I frowned. "You mean the homeless men?" Charleston's temperate climate attracted tourists, conventioneers and retirees, as well as some folks who were down on their luck.

She nodded. "The body they found makes two so far," she said, and shivered. "I don't know why anyone would do something like that; robbery certainly isn't the motive." She dropped her voice. "The police aren't saying, but there's a rumor that both of the dead men were torn apart."

"Ugh," I replied. Her description pinged a warning in my mind. That kind of killing could be mundane, but the brutality of it made magic suspect as well. "Anything else?"

Drea browsed the shelves where Teag had put out new stock. "Actually, yes. Valerie took a tour past Gardenia Landing two nights ago, and she got a little more than she bargained for."

"Oh?" I asked. "Spill."

Drea grinned. "It was one of the late night ghost tours. You know what they're like."

I did. Charleston is a marvelously atmospheric city, and even more so after dark in the Historic District. Ghost tour guests ride in a horse-drawn carriage listening to Valerie spin tales of murder, mayhem and unrequited love, all ending in death – the more gruesome, the better.

"Valerie was filling them in on all the duels and suicides and star-crossed trysts and it all went well until they came to Gardenia Landing."

"And?"

"When they came up in front of the B&B, she noticed that the shadows near the building seemed strange. At first, she thought that maybe someone was hiding there, so she made sure she kept the carriage in the light." She shook her head. "She swears that she saw men come out of the darkness toward the carriage, but there were only shadows – no real people."

"Did anyone else see them?"

"Just one guest, and it turns out that person has seen ghosts before." Drea said with a 'how about that' expression. "Valerie said she left as fast as she could, and was afraid to look back."

"Wow," I replied. "Has Valerie ever had anything like that happen on her other tours?"

Drea shook her head. "Not with Gardenia Landing. She's had enough encounters with strange things down by the Old Jail that she won't do a late night tour there unless Mrs. Teller rides along." Mrs. Teller was well-known in Charleston as a sweetgrass basket weaver and also as a 'root' woman, someone with powerful magic.

"The shadows Valerie saw seemed to glide rather than walk," Drea added. "And they vanished in plain sight." She met my gaze. "And you know how hot it was last night? Valerie said that the street felt colder than a winter night."

Valerie, like many Charlestonians, felt rather possessive about our neighborhood ghosts. After all, they were part of the lore that brought crowds of tourists to the Holy City season after season. But more than that, Charleston's many ghosts were the warp and the woof of the city's history, and their tragic stories felt like family heirlooms, handed down from generation to generation. I had never known her to make up a story about a sighting.

"How did the guest react?" I asked.

Drea chuckled. "She felt like she got a bonus, and left a big tip."

"How's Valerie?"

"Once she got over the jitters, she called that spook hunting group she goes out with and told them all about it. They were all excited, so she's right as rain." Drea glanced at her cell phone. "Oops! I need to get back to the office."

We said goodbye, after promising to get together for lunch later in the week. I was about to go back to my workroom when the sleigh bells rang and Trinket Ellison walked in. She looked a little nervous, and glanced around for Teag. "Did someone from the shop call my house this morning?"

"I did," Teag said, turning from where he was dusting the shelves. "Thanks for dropping by."

"Your opera glasses are lovely," I said. "We were hoping you might share a few more details about the family member who first owned them." I paused. "Would you like a cup of tea or coffee?"

Trinket looked like she wanted to turn around and leave, but after a few seconds, she took a deep breath and seemed to gather her resolve. "Tea would be lovely. Thank you."

Teag showed her to the small table and chairs in the back.

"You took the opera glasses to the play on Saturday."

I was busted. I felt my cheeks flush.

"If it's any consolation," Trinket went on, "I discovered their ability at a Broadway play." Her face reddened at the memory.

"Oops," I said, realizing that her experience was probably even worse than mine. I leaned forward, hoping to inspire her to confide. "I'd really like to know what you saw. To make sure we got the same impressions."

A range of emotions flickered across Trinket's features: fear, sadness, and regret. Teag and I listened in silence as she told us what she had seen and how she had reacted. When she finished, I told my tale, and we compared details. The stories were remarkably similar.

"Teag thinks what we saw was the Iroquois Theater fire from 1903 in Chicago," I said. "Do you know if your great-grandmother was a survivor of that event?"

Trinket took a sip of her tea, and nodded. "It wasn't something she liked to talk about, for obvious reasons, but the stories that have been handed down through the family have enough details to confirm that somehow, what we saw through those damned glasses was what she experienced when she and her son almost died."

"What do the family stories say?" I asked.

Trinket sat back in her chair, staring down into the tea. "Great-granny Eugenia came from a very wealthy Chicago family. She met my great grandpa Daniel when he went North to college." She sighed. "I know there was a lot of bitterness between the North and South in those years not long after the War, but not everyone down here thought the War was a good idea, even if they didn't say it out loud, and that included Daniel and his family. Afterwards, they saw that there was money to be made serving a reunited country, and so Daniel went to Chicago to school."

She paused. "They moved back to Charleston when Daniel finished school and they married. Daniel's parents were so much a force in the city at that time, no one dared say anything about Daniel's Yankee bride, at least not to their faces. Everyone 'made nice' and life went on."

"Until 1903," Teag added.

"Eugenia and Daniel took their three children up to visit her parents during the holidays. The children wanted to see real snow," Trinket said, with a faint smile. "But the younger two caught cold. Eugenia had already bought tickets to a show at the Iroquois Theater for the whole family as a holiday treat. It had just opened, and it was supposed to be quite the place. Daniel stayed home with the younger children, while Eugenia took Todd to the play."

She paused, remembering the story. "At the time, Eugenia was a bit put out that they couldn't be in the Grand Tier for the view, but they bought the only tickets they could get – in the very back of the Orchestra section, on the first floor." She gave a sad smile. "Ironically, those bad seats saved their lives." This time, she paused again, so Teag jumped in.

"There were over two thousand people in the audience that day," Teag supplied from his research. "Most of the ones who survived were on the main floor."

"That's awful," I murmured.

"It was awful," Teag agreed. "Everything that could go wrong, did go wrong. And when someone in the backstage area opened the big loading doors to get the actors and crew out, the gust of wind sent a fireball out over the heads of the people in the Orchestra section and incinerated the folks in the upper balconies." He made a face. "There was so much outrage about the fire that it changed safety regulations for public buildings to this very day."

"Yikes."

"Eugenia and Todd were lucky. They got out. In the chaos, they wandered around in the cold, until a policeman found them," Trinket said quietly. "You can imagine, they were both in shock although they weren't injured. Eugenia was never quite right afterwards – they called it 'nerves' back then. Todd was young enough that he outgrew the nightmares and seemed to be fine. Oddly enough, the opera glasses were passed down through the family as a lucky charm, since they had been a Christmas gift from Daniel to Eugenia that year."

"Were the glasses always haunted?" I asked, leaning forward.

Trinket frowned. "No. That's what's so odd. Eugenia left them to Todd, and they came down through his family along with the story. I remember seeing them at my grandmother's house, and when she died, she left them to my mom. Mom kept them on a shelf for years, until we had to box up her stuff when she went into the nursing home.

"Last year, I moved mom's boxes out of storage and into my garage, so I could go through them more easily. I found the opera glasses and thought it would be cool to take them on a trip to New York City when my husband and I went a few months ago." Trinket sighed. "That was a mistake."

"Do you know if anyone else tried to use the glasses at a play since the tragedy?" Teag asked.

Trinket nodded. "That's what makes this so strange. Eugenia was a strong woman. Even though she never completely got over the tragedy, she refused to let it take away her love of the theater. She willed herself to go back to plays after a year or two, and was a patron of the theater for the rest of her life." Trinket's expression showed that she was just as baffled as we were. "Todd kept up the patronage, and down through the years, it's been a family tradition to support local theater groups. My mother and grandmother used to dress up to go out to the theater, and I remember seeing them take the opera glasses with them.

"I always thought they were so beautiful. That's why I wanted to take them to New York, once I found them again in Mom's things."

Teag and I shared a look. "Did anything happen to the glasses between when your mother used them and when you inherited them?"

Trinket shook her head. "There was no chance for anything to happen. We boxed everything up when we sold her house, and I'm just unboxing things now."

I wasn't any closer to figuring out why the glasses had suddenly become a menace, but I felt a little better about what had happened to me at the play. I managed a smile. "Thanks for telling us, Trinket. We'll make sure no one else has a bad experience with the glasses."

After Trinket left, I stayed at the table for a few moments, finishing my coffee and going back over the tale Trinket had told. *What would make the opera glasses suddenly get haunted?* I wondered. Something had changed them. Maybe, because of the tragedy, they had always been imprinted with strong emotions, but it wasn't powerful enough to manifest. What could have possibly happened to juice them up? I didn't know, but I figured Sorren might.

The shop door opened, and a bike messenger leaned into the shop. Teag signed for a package, and he brought the small box over as I finished my coffee.

I frowned. "I wasn't expecting anything. Who's it from?"

Teag looked at the return address. The handwriting was barely legible and the ink had smudged. "I can't read the name, and I don't recognize the address."

That wasn't unusual. Trifles and Folly had a whispered reputation as the place that would take haunted heirlooms off your hands. Once or twice a month, we would get unexpected packages in the mail or find boxes dropped off by the front door, and most of them contained items their owners no longer wanted to deal with.

"Let me open it – just in case," Teag said. He cut open the packaging to reveal a plain cardboard box. "I've got a bad feeling about this one, Cassidy. You getting anything?"

I nodded, holding my hand several inches above the box. "Definitely a spooky – maybe more. Be careful."

Teag used a pencil to flip up the lid of the box. Inside was a man's plain silver wedding ring. Reflexively, I backed up a step.

"Well?" he asked.

"If you could smell magic, that thing would be a tuna sandwich that had been locked in the trunk of a car during a heat wave," I said. I swallowed hard. "There is no way I'm touching that – not without Sorren." But I did let my hand hover over the open box. Even at a distance, the images were so powerful they threatened to overwhelm me.

*Whoever wore the ring had been terrified, running for his life. Only he couldn't outrun the shadows, and something in the shadows was bad. Very bad. Even though he wasn't completely sober, he could feel the evil. It let him run, for a while. Like a cat with a mouse, it toyed with him, enjoying his fear. And when it moved in for the kill, there was nothing he could do about it. It started tearing his skin off his body, then pulling off limbs, knowing all the while just what to do so that he didn't die too quickly. It liked his screams.*

"Cassidy!" Teag's voice wrested me away from the vision. I realized that he had physically moved me away from the box, putting himself between me and the table.

My breath was ragged and I wanted to throw up. "That's got to be from one of the murdered men," I said, trying to stop my stomach from lurching. Teag guided me to a chair. "Why would anyone send us something like that?"

Teag brought me a fresh cup of coffee and then typed the return address from the package into his cell phone. "Nothing," he reported. "Probably an empty lot." He paused. "I can talk with the messenger service. Someone ordered that delivery, and it must have been paid for. I'll see what I can find out."

I drank the last swallow of coffee, just as the phone rang. Teag went to answer it, and held up the receiver. "It's for you."

I drew a deep breath, set aside my mug and took the receiver. "Cassidy?" the caller asked, so breathlessly I couldn't quite place the voice.

"It's Debra Kelly," the caller said. Debra was one of several interior designers who sourced unusual items from Trifles and Folly for their clients. She sounded flustered. "Cassidy, you've got to help me. I'm in a heap of trouble."

# Chapter Four

MY SURPRISE MUST have shown in my face, because Teag looked at me questioningly, and all I could do was shrug.

"What kind of trouble, Debra?" I asked.

"Rebecca's blaming me for making her B&B haunted. I sold her a number of items that I bought from your store, and now she swears she's being overrun with ghosts." She rattled off a list of items. I remembered all of them and none were even sparklers, let alone spookies.

I frowned. "What makes Rebecca think the inn is haunted?" Drea's story about the shadow men came to mind immediately.

"I swore I wouldn't tell you, because she wants you to come and see for yourself."

"Okay. Give me that list again." Teag shoved paper and pen in front of me while I wrote down the items.

"I'm sorry, Cassidy," Debra said. "Some B&B owners would love to be able to claim that they're haunted. In fact, I thought Rebecca would actually have liked to have a resident ghost from some of the things she said."

She paused. "I think something scared her enough to change her mind."

"Sounds like it." Teag was looking at me with his head turned to one side like a confused puppy. "What does she think I'll be able to do by coming out there?"

"I don't know. But I think she's hoping you can make her problem stop."

"Why not just return all the items?" I said, cringing as I spoke. That would be a big hit to this month's revenue. Bye-bye eating out; hello macaroni and cheese for supper. Every night.

"She likes the items," Debra replied. "She would just like the bad ghosts that came with them to leave her alone."

"I promised her that I would come, and I'll be there," I said. "But I'm not sure what I can do other than remove the items. We could offer her store credit." At least store credit wouldn't take money out of my bank account.

"Keep that as Plan B." Debra was beginning to sound perkier. "I'm glad you're taking this seriously. Good luck going out there."

I didn't doubt that the ghosts were real. I figured I'd need all the good luck I could get. "Thanks. I'll let you know what we come up with."

I hung up the phone and stared into space for a moment, trying to figure out how the shipment for Rebecca had gone so wrong. Then I realized that Teag was standing in front of me, snapping his fingers, waiting for me to come back to myself. "Cassidy? Are you in there? Yoo-hoo, Cassidy?" He was grinning, but I could see the concern in his eyes.

"Rebecca must really be freaked out to have gotten

Debra that upset." I pushed the list of items toward Teag, and he frowned as he examined them.

"None of these were spookies," he said, glancing down the list. "I remember selling these to Debra. I packed them myself. You and Sorren had already been through them and cleared them."

I chewed on my lip as I thought. "Do you remember where any of the pieces came from? Did they all come from the same seller?"

"I'll check the records, but I don't think so. I know that the vase came from an estate sale, and the lamp was from a nice couple who downsized to a smaller house. I'll see what I can find out about the others." He headed off like a man on a mission.

I went to the back and poured myself another cup of coffee, thinking as I added the creamer and stirred it into the dark liquid. Somehow, perfectly normal items were turning into ghost-attracting menaces. Someone had mailed us a ring from a man who had been gruesomely murdered. Shadow men were turning up outside old houses. This sort of thing just wasn't normal, even for us, and we stretched the definition of normal way beyond the limits of the dictionary.

*It's just like with the opera glasses,* I thought. *Almost as if something activated their spookiness like turning on a light switch. But how?* I went back through the list Debra had shared with me, wondering how such normal pieces could possibly generate a dangerous supernatural vibe.

A tea set? Well maybe, if the previous owner had choked to death on a scone. I remembered at least one of the vases Debra had bought. If someone had used the vase as a murder weapon, it would have shattered, so that was out. I came up with even fewer ideas for the lamp, and none at all for the picture frame.

One of the items on the list was a mirror. I'd heard of haunted mirrors, and they seemed to have a reputation for being especially nasty. By the time I considered the linens I was getting a little punchy from the stress and the caffeine. We didn't sell blood-stained sheets, so I pictured a particularly hideous tablecloth my grandmother had always used for holiday gatherings. Remembering its ugly awesomeness made me chuckle. Memorable, but hardly haunted.

"Glad to see you haven't lost your sense of humor," Teag said from the doorway. "Something you want to share?"

I giggled. After all the stress, laughter felt good. "Just trying to figure out the mystery of the terrible tablecloth," I said. I told him about my grandmother's grapevine monstrosity.

Teag just shook his head. "I guess you had to be there."

"Oh, come on! Don't tell me your family didn't have any strange holiday customs when you were a kid."

"My family was strange enough without needing odd holiday customs," he chuckled. He sobered. "I'm working on a list of original owners for the items at the B&B. None of my notes indicate any interesting stories about the pieces at all. They were all normal purchases: estate sale, auction, family member, even a couple of yard sale finds."

I sipped my coffee. "There's got to be something that ties everything together. The people who sold us the pieces could have lied about them being haunted, but I would have picked up on it when I handled them. We wouldn't have resold them if they had bad mojo."

"Maybe it's like the opera glasses," Teag said, leaning against the door frame. "Maybe they have to be in a certain setting to be affected, or be used in a particular way."

"We'd better figure this out quickly, before the whole store gets freaky."

"That would be bad," he said, glancing around at the multitude of items on our shelves.

I repressed a shiver. "That would be very bad."

AFTER WORK, I headed home with my thoughts still focused on the bed and breakfast dilemma. When my key turned in the lock, sharp, high-pitched barks welcomed me home.

"Hello, Baxter!"

Baxter bounced around like a crazed cotton puff, pouncing and running in circles. I grabbed a treat from the bowl next to the door, and he danced on his hind legs. He seemed to know that cuteness was a sure-fire antidote for a stressful day, and I couldn't help chuckling at his antics. It's hard to resist anyone who is that happy to see you.

I put my purse down and scooped Baxter into my arms, getting a lick on the chin and then a play-bite to the tip of my nose. I blew a puff of air in his face, and he pulled back, only to return with more licks and wiggles.

Reluctantly, I put Baxter down and went through the mail. It, too, was gloriously normal: a few bills, a couple of catalogs, and a magazine. I snagged the magazine out of the pile and carried it with me into the kitchen, promising myself some reading time later.

But first, it was time for Baxter's walk. Baxter might

weigh in at under six pounds, but he walks with a hustle that proclaims to the world that he has things to do and places to go. It was after five, and past the heat of the day, although in Charleston, that didn't mean it was cool. I tried to get my mind off of the B&B problem. Baxter can move surprisingly fast for a little dog, and he takes his nightly rounds seriously. He sniffed his way along the garden walls, tried to peer beneath the gates or look through the wrought-iron fences, and wagged a greeting to everyone we met.

"Hello, Cassidy!" I looked up to see Mrs. Morrissey heading my way. Baxter saw her too, and began to dance on his hind legs.

"Hello, Mrs. Morrissey," I replied with a smile.

"How's Baxter today?" she asked in that tone people reserve for babies and small animals. I had never seen Mrs. Morrissey looking as if she wasn't on the way to or from a dinner at the Country Club. Her hair was perfect, despite Charleston's constant humidity. St. John suits looked as if they had been made with her slim frame in mind, and her minimal jewelry was all the more notable because the gemstones were, indubitably, real. Rumor had it that her late husband had left her quite well off, both monetarily and in the currency that really mattered in Charleston, social connections. And somehow, she had decided to take a shine toward me and Baxter.

"You know Bax. He's up for an adventure," I replied. Baxter had finished wiggling all around Mrs. Morrissey's stylish pumps. Now he sat looking up at her, blinking his black button eyes, expecting a treat.

Mrs. Morrissey did not disappoint. From her small purse, she produced a single dog biscuit, which she ceremoniously held out to Baxter. He knew the drill, and jumped to his feet, happily dancing in a circle before she handed the biscuit to him.

"How are things at the store?" Mrs. Morrissey asked. She had been a good friend to my late uncle, and even now, she occasionally stopped in when the mood struck. I enjoyed our conversations, because she moved in the rarified air of Charleston's old elite and usually knew everything about everyone.

I sighed. "There've been a few problems lately," I said, as Baxter crunched his biscuit. "A couple of customers made purchases and then had second thoughts."

"I see." She gave me an inquiring look. "By the way, how are you doing? I heard you weren't feeling well."

I felt my face flush red. "I think I've been skimping a little too much on lunch lately."

Mrs. Morrissey nodded, but there was a twinkle in her eye. "Of course, dear. Your Uncle Evan had spells of that, too, on occasion."

I fought the urge to do a double-take, mostly at her use of the word 'spells'. *Could Mrs. Benjamin Taylor Morrissey, doyenne of South of Broad, have an inkling about what really goes on at Trifles and Folly?* She looked amused as I recovered.

"Maybe it runs in the family," I replied. "I need to remember – less coffee, more food."

She smiled. Unlike so many older ladies of her social standing, Mrs. Morrissey had not removed all evidence of a life well lived with Botox and cosmetic surgery. Her skin crinkled around her bright blue eyes, and the fine lines around her lips hinted that perhaps in younger days she had been a smoker. It made her look real, and I respected her for her courage. "You haven't been down to the Historical Archive for a while," Mrs. Morrissey said, her tone gently reproving. She gave me a sly smile. "We could have told you about Trinket's ancestor and the Iroquois Theater fire."

I stared at her, open mouthed. "You know?"

Mrs. Morrissey chuckled. "Historians are the worst gossips, my dear. We gossip about the dead as much as we do the living. And, as they say, we know where all the bodies are buried."

Her grin was positively impish. "Trinket had been down to see us not long before she sold the glasses to you. She wanted to validate a family story about her great-grandmother and a rather miraculous escape from a very famous theater fire, which was quite the scoop for the papers down here at the time, even if it did happen up North."

Teag had Weaver magic, but I had my sources, and one of them was Mrs. Morrissey. She was one of a dozen older women whose blood was as blue as the rinse in their hair, and who spent their many volunteer hours serving as the keepers of Charleston's long and sometimes salacious history. They could be the icy guardians of propriety, but if they liked a researcher, they could point the way to old and juicy scandals.

"I imagine she was horrified," I replied. "I've read a little about the fire online. It was awful."

Mrs. Morrissey nodded. "I've known Trinket for years, and she seemed genuinely distraught," she said. "It's no wonder she wanted to be rid of the glasses once she knew the story. I imagine it haunted her dreams."

"I'm sure that made it impossible for her to enjoy using them, once she knew about it," I agreed.

Mrs. Morrissey adjusted her necklace. "Ah well,

so long as you and Trinket are both well, that's what counts." She narrowed her eyes. "Aren't you getting your floors redone soon?"

I nodded. "The work starts tomorrow. Baxter is going to the dog spa, and I'm going to stay at Gardenia Landing."

"I imagine you've heard about the ghosts?"

*Did everyone know?* "I didn't know Gardenia Landing was haunted," I said, hoping I could feign surprise.

"Hmmph," Mrs. Morrissey said. "I'd be more surprised if it weren't. What with all that's happened there."

I raised an eyebrow. "Oh?"

Mrs. Morrissey nodded. "For all their wealth, the Harrison family had more than their share of tragedy. Several children died young, including a daughter who came down with what used to be called consumption. It's said that the babies were buried in the home's garden because Mrs. Harrison couldn't bear the thought of them being far away from her. Then the wife of one of the sons went mad. She drowned in the garden fountain."

She frowned. "But the worst of it was when Mr. Harrison got caught up in the unpleasantness about those smugglers and that awful Jeremiah Abernathy," she said, as if it were a story everyone had heard.

Mrs. Morrissey checked the tasteful, diamond-studded watch on her thin wrist. "Oh dear, I'd better run. Stop down sometime at the Archive and I can tell you more. Gardenia Landing's address has been well-known in Charleston for a long time."

With that, she bade Baxter and me good night and headed off toward her next social engagement.

I watched her go for a moment, then turned back to Baxter, who was eagerly pulling toward the remainder of our route. "I'm coming, I'm coming," I said, letting him take me down the sidewalk.

I was glad Baxter knew the route, because Mrs. Morrissey had given me several new things to think about. *If Gardenia Landing had a sordid past, could that have made the items we sold Rebecca 'come alive'?* I wondered. Obviously, I needed to do some digging, and Mrs. Morrissey seemed quite willing to take me on a tour of the B&B's dark side.

It was late afternoon, and in Charleston's picturesque narrow streets and historic alleys, the shadows were lengthening. Only when we were halfway down a pretty little cobblestone sidestreet did I realize that the shadows seemed to be a lot darker than they should be for this time of day. I picked up my pace, but the shadows felt like they were closing in.

Baxter has the heart of lion in the body of a guinea pig. He wheeled on the shadows with a snarl and began to bark a shrill alarm. I scooped Baxter up in my arms and started to run, feeling like Dorothy in the *Wizard of Oz*, except instead of flying monkeys, we were being chased by shadows.

I only dared one glance over my shoulder. Shapes were stirring in the shadows, things with long, outstretched arms and grasping hands. I managed a burst of speed, and we ran out into the light of the cross street, right into the path of a Toyota Corolla. The driver slammed on the brakes and laid on the horn.

I was quick to put the Corolla between me and the alley, but the shadows did not venture past the sidewalk. I pantomimed apologies to the driver, and scooted away, glad we were only a block from my house. That's when I spotted a tall, thin man in a broad-brimmed hat, standing on the corner. I might not have paid any attention, except that he seemed to be staring at me, and although the hat hid much of his face, what I could see looked not just wrinkled, but withered. Something about his silent regard gave me the creeps, and I walked off in the opposite direction as quickly as I could.

No one was around as I unlocked the door, and I let the wash of cold air revive me. Baxter went straight to his water dish, lapping thirstily. I locked the door and pulled the curtains back to look at the street again. I spotted the tall, thin man again. He was slouched so I couldn't make out his features. Baxter distracted me for a moment and when I glanced again the man was gone.

After I checked the deadbolt again, I went to the kitchen for some ice water. I poured some kibble into Baxter's bowl, then opened the fridge to figure out what to make for dinner, and decided I wasn't hungry.

Trying to get my mind off the attack in the alley and the man outside my house, I flipped through the magazine. One paragraph in an article on organizing closets caught my eye. "Many people hold on to items because they're really using them as 'memory anchors'. They're afraid that if they get rid of the item, they'll lose the memories they're reminded of by the piece."

*What if you wanted to get rid of bad memories that a particular item brought to mind?* I wondered. *What if certain pieces soaked up memories and events more than others?*

Normally, I could tell right away whether or not a new item had any kind of supernatural residue, good or bad. That's what was baffling me about the B&B

problem. *Did something happen after we sold the pieces that turned regular objects into dangerous items?*

Soon enough, I'd get the chance to see the Gardenia Landing ghosts up close. The more I heard about the B&B's new haunting, the more it looked like trouble.

# Chapter Five

I WAS READY for the floor refinishing crew when they knocked on my door bright and early. I'd already dropped Baxter off at the puppy spa. As much as I hated to be away from him for a few days, I knew he would have fun at the dog resort. And while Baxter enjoyed his occasional visits to Trifles and Folly, he wouldn't like being there alone at night, especially since dogs are sensitive to supernatural activity. Even I didn't want to be there overnight. I'd lived in the apartment over the shop when I first inherited Trifles and Folly, but being that close to some of the sparklers and spookies was just too much.

Once I'd gone over the instructions for refinishing the floors with the workmen and handed off my keys, I tossed my laptop and luggage into my little blue Mini Cooper and headed for the shop. Thankfully, there were no new reports of perfectly normal old items suddenly turning into haunted horrors. I basked in the boredom, compared to the unsettling events of the last few days.

"I've got a list of contacts for the people who sold us Gardenia Landing's items," Teag said. "I made a few calls yesterday evening, and some this morning. Want to know what I found out?"

"Sure," I said, pouring a cup of coffee to fortify my resolve.

Outside, a steady rain deterred shoppers, giving us the chance to talk undisturbed. Teag leaned against the counter with his cup of tea.

"The tea set came from Avery's Auctions," he said. "Belinda Avery remembered it. G.R. Collis silver. She wasn't aware of anything unusual in its background, but she said she'd call the former owner and ask."

"I had to leave a message for the mirror lady," he continued. "Helen Butler used to own the tablecloth. She was pretty hesitant about talking at first, but I finally got her story. Seems the tablecloth belonged to her grandmother, and it was used for holiday dinners. One holiday, Mr. Butler's grandfather had a heart attack at the table and died."

"Oh my," I said. "Still, lots of linens and furnishings are present when someone dies, and they don't become haunted."

He nodded. "Unless there's something else at work. The vase originally held funeral flowers and was used for special occasions for fifty years or so. The owner's daughter sold it because she didn't like the style."

I remembered the vase, a heavy cut glass piece, early 20th century – not very old by Charleston standards. I had thought it was pretty. "No hints at all?" I pressed, disappointed.

"I even asked her about the funerals where the vase was used," Teag said. "Most were deaths from old age or natural causes, nothing dramatic. But the first funeral, when the vase came into the family, was different."

"Oh?"

Teag nodded, and his grin slipped away. "Pretty tragic, actually. Back in the 1920s, the owner's great aunt and uncle lost two young children to scarlet fever."

"So funerals, but no ghosts, huh?" I said, chewing my lip as I thought. "I guess we'll have to see who – or what – the vase conjures up at Gardenia Landing." I set my coffee aside. "How about the lamp and the picture frames?"

"They came from a moving sale. The people who live at that house now aren't the ones who sold the picture frames."

"So a dead end."

"Yeah," he replied. "As for the lamp, the couple who sold it are out of town until the end of the week."

I glanced toward the door to make sure no one was likely to disturb us. "Baxter and I had a little more excitement than we wanted last night," I said, and filled him in on what had happened.

Teag looked worried. "I don't like the sound of that. First, shadow men at the B&B, now in an alley where you've never had any problems before." He took a sip of his tea. "We really need to get Sorren in on this."

I nodded. "We also need to figure out who the guy in the hat is."

"Tall guy, wide-brimmed hat?"

"Yeah. He was on the corner near where the shadow men came after me, and then again, outside the house."

"I thought I saw him outside the shop right after I opened up, but then he was gone when I looked again," Teag said.

"I don't know about the shadow men, but I think the man with the withered face is real. He seems to be following us or watching us, and I don't like it."

"Oh and I forgot," Teag said. "Maggie called when you were talking to Mrs. Butler, she's still not feeling well. She won't be able to work tomorrow or Thursday. But, not to worry. I can cover."

"You sure? It's not going to put you in a bind or make you miss anything important?"

"No, I didn't have anything scheduled," Teag said, and sighed. "Anthony's really tied up with those cases. You can make it up to me later."

"Should I be worried about Maggie? She doesn't usually call in sick." I had inherited Maggie with the store and she had been working with us ever since. She was a retired teacher, quite knowledgeable about antiques and how the store ran.

Teag shook his head. "No, I asked. She thinks she got a touch of food poisoning. She just needs some time to recuperate." He hesitated, and the look on his face told me that he had something on his mind.

"Cassidy?" he said. "Be careful."

"Count on it," I replied. "If it looks dangerous, I'm outta there." I didn't want to admit it to Teag, but the whole idea of suddenly spooky antiques was making me very nervous. "I left a message for Sorren on his cell phone, but he hasn't called me back."

Yes, a nearly six hundred year-old vampire uses a cell phone, and email. As Sorren has told me many times, vampires who can't adapt with the times don't survive long. Problem is, Sorren's work with the Alliance often means he falls out of touch for days or weeks at a time. Then again, his letter gave me hope we'd hear from him soon.

It wouldn't be soon enough.

# Chapter Six

GARDENIA LANDING WAS a Victorian 'painted lady' with a two-story colonnaded piazza, an intriguing garden wall and an elaborate wrought iron gate to a garden with lush greenery and a fountain. It was exactly the kind of place I would have picked if I had wanted to indulge and pamper myself.

I parked and hefted my backpack and overnight bag out of the trunk, along with a small pack filled with some 'special' tools to help me tackle whatever was causing the problems at the B&B. Since I deal better with haunted antiques on a full stomach, I'd stopped for a quick dinner on my way over. I was even wearing my favorite agate necklace and earrings, gemstones I trusted to help protect me from bad supernatural mojo. With a deep breath, I squared my shoulders and resolved to take on the worst Gardenia Landing had to throw at me.

Gardenias were in season, and so was honeysuckle and Confederate jasmine. The burble of a fountain promised cool respite from the warm Charleston evening.

As I opened the door into the foyer, the smell of freshly brewed coffee and warm sugar cookies welcomed me and enticed me inside. I was greeted by a room done in period wallpaper and antique furniture with a large crystal chandelier. Off to the left, I got a peek of a dining room, and to the right, what I guessed was a parlor or library. I'd explore both later, I vowed.

Straight back down the hallway was the kitchen with modern, stainless steel appliances. A door under the stairs was likely a powder room. The place managed to feel homey and upscale without pretension.

"You must be Cassidy!" A trim woman in her mid-forties rushed from the kitchen at the sound of the door. Her very wavy brown hair fell shoulder length, setting off tasteful gold earrings and a discreet – yet expensive – gold necklace. She wore a blue t-shirt and jeans that looked as if they had been pressed, over Sperrys without socks. Everything about her exuded warmth and welcome, except for the look of worry in her blue eyes.

I smiled. "Are you Rebecca?"

She nodded. "Yes. And thank you so much for agreeing to come."

I still wasn't convinced it was a great idea, but I was resolved to see this thing through. "Your B&B is lovely," I said sincerely.

Rebecca's good cheer dimmed. "Thank you. I really love this place. But if we can't figure out what's going on, I don't think I can stay here. Maggie said you had a talent for dealing with these things. I don't have a whiff of ESP, but unusual abilities do run in my mother's family, so you're not going to shock me."

"How about if I put my bag in my room and then we sit down and talk?" I suggested. "I'd love a cup of that coffee; it smells amazing!" I paused. "Unless you've got other guests waiting."

"Unfortunately, no." She gave a sad smile. "It's just you and one other couple for the next few days. I'm afraid word might be getting out about the problem." She gestured for me to follow her. "Come on. I'll show you to your room."

I climbed the stairs, looking around at the foyer with its dark wood, beautiful balustrade, and antique furniture. A lovely cut glass vase was filled with hydrangea blossoms, and I recognized it as the funeral vase Teag researched. I resolved to come back for a closer look once I settled in.

Upstairs, I counted four rooms plus another set of stairs. "I live on the third floor," Rebecca said as she led me down the hall. "It was originally the maid's room."

She stopped in front of the last door on the right. "This is your room," she said, opening the door for me. "Every room has its own bathroom with a shower. It's a little tight, but you don't have to share."

The room was charming. The walls were painted a pale blue with a stenciled border. The large brass bed was the focal point, with its plump throw pillows and chenille bedspread. A small white night stand with a lace doily stood to one side, complete with a brass reading lamp with a stained glass shade. *Is that the lamp she bought from Trifles and Folly?* I wondered, suddenly a little disquieted by the idea of having it next to my bed.

At the foot of the bed was a dresser with a tall mirror and a marble finish on the top. A fluffy white bathrobe was draped invitingly over the arm of a comfortable chair with an ottoman, below a perfectly-angled floor lamp. I loved every piece, and the combined effect made me wish my stay was truly for rest and relaxation.

I set down my luggage and turned back to Rebecca. "The room is beautiful. Can you show me around the rest of the B&B, please? Then let's talk about what's been going on."

Rebecca smiled, but I could tell she had a lot on her mind. I tried to set her at ease. "I always love to hear stories about old homes like this," I said warmly. "And if you know the stories of any of the pieces that aren't from our shop, please fill me in!"

"Most of the furniture in this room came from my grandma's house near Savannah," Rebecca replied. "Everything except the lamp, which is from Trifles and Folly."

"Your grandmother had good taste," I said.

Rebecca's smile grew reflective. "She got a lot of the furniture from her mother and grandmother, so it's authentic Victorian. When I was a little girl, I loved sleeping in the big brass bed."

"The linens look period, too," I said. Later, I would risk touching pieces, when I was alone. But Rebecca didn't know much about my talent, and I didn't want to give her an impromptu demonstration.

"Oh yes," she agreed. "Though the table cloth Debra bought from you is in the dining room. The bedspread was also my grandmother's, as are the pillow shams. But the pillows and sheets are all brand new!"

I wanted nothing more than to cozy into that inviting bed with a good book and a cup of tea, but relaxing would have to wait. "It all goes together perfectly. Do you have a different theme for each room?"

That was Rebecca's cue to lead me back into the

hallway. She handed me a key on a pretty keychain, and I recognized the fob as the handle from an ornate silver plated fork or spoon. Lovely.

"The house itself was built in the 1850s as a wedding present from James Harrison to his bride, Clarissa," Rebecca told me as we walked down the narrow, dimly-lit hall. "The light fixtures were originally for gaslights, although of course, everything was remodeled for electric years ago." The wall sconces had bulbs that replicated the warm glow of gas, which made the hallway a little eerie.

"The Harrisons raised their family in this house," Rebecca continued. "They had three sons and a daughter, all of the sons rose to prominence." She frowned. "Unfortunately, they also lost two infants, something that was far too common back then."

"Did the house stay in the family?" I prompted. Mindful of the haunting, I was listening to validate the tragedies Mrs. Morrissey had mentioned, events that might have primed the house for paranormal activity if the right catalyst was introduced.

Rebecca paused with her hand on the molded brass door knob to one of the other guest rooms. "It did, for a while," she replied. "The oldest of the Harrison sons, Joseph, took over the family shipping company, and brought his new wife here. The other two sons eventually purchased homes nearby."

"And the daughter?"

"Arabella Harrison did not fare as well as her brothers, I'm afraid," Rebecca said. "She had what they called back then a 'delicate nervous condition'. Today, I guess we'd say she was given to bouts of depression or worse. She died young."

"Did she pass away here in the house?" I asked. "I'm looking for clues about what might be going on," I said apologetically, feeling like a ghoul.

"Actually, she did die in the house," Rebecca said. "From consumption – the old name for tuberculosis."

I shivered. "Do you know where she died?"

Rebecca shook her head. "I've never found anything that says exactly. Family letters just say that she spent most of her time in the garden, and that she died 'in bed'." She pushed open the door and turned on the light to the second guest room.

"We do have guests in this room, so I can't let you do more than look." As if she could guess my thoughts, she added, "None of the items we bought from you are in this room, and neither this room nor your room have had any problems."

From the doorway, I peered into the room. It had a masculine feel, with a dark walnut bedroom set that had all the Victorian ornamentation. The bed's high headboard nearly reached the ceiling. There was a huge armoire, a comfy chair and ottoman, and brass lamps with brass shades that reminded me of ones I'd seen in big city libraries. The dresser was the same dark walnut, with a white marble counter and an ornate mirror that must have been almost eight feet tall, crested with a carved medallion. Small antique pieces gave the room a lived-in look: old tintype photos in silver frames, a watercolor of a dog on the wall behind the chair, and white antimacassars on the backs of the chairs.

Two duffle bags lay to one side. Obviously, the other guests hadn't unpacked, either. I wondered if I would run into them later on. The web site said that guests were invited to gather nightly for cocktails.

"I'll show you the other two rooms," Rebecca said, as we stepped back from the doorway and she locked it up again. We turned toward the opposite side of the hallway, where the doorways were staggered so that one room wasn't directly across from another.

These doors weren't locked. The first room was shadowed, and although I knew that, outside, dusk had fallen, something about the darkened room made the hair on the back of my neck stand up. Rebecca turned on the light, but the faux gaslight glow didn't dispel the feeling that something was not quite right.

"This room was the first place we got reports of problems," Rebecca said. She nodded toward the large oval mirror with a broad bronze ribbon-like frame. I was certain it came from our shop.

"What happened?" I asked.

Rebecca looked chagrined. "Guests said they felt uncomfortable in the room, as if they were being watched. A few reported waking up to see a shadow moving across the wall."

*Shadow men, again.*

"Could it be car headlights from the street?" I asked. "That's given me a start now and again."

"Not up here," Rebecca replied. "The angle's wrong." She sighed. "This is one of the places guests and cleaning staff have reported cold spots and small items moving around on their own."

"Were there problems before you bought the mirror?"

She shook her head. "We brought all the pieces from Trifles and Folly in at the same time, so it's hard to say whether it's all of them, or just some of them." Rebecca gestured toward the room. "You can see why I don't want to return the pieces. They're just perfect for the décor – if we can get them to stop scaring the guests."

The furniture in this room was oak, with a bed, dresser and old-fashioned washstand. The bed still had the very tall headboard and footboard, but lacked the ornamentation of the last room's furnishings. Other than the troublesome mirror, there was an oil portrait of a pretty young woman, and a seascape that seemed a bit moody and dramatic for a bedroom. A Chinese Foo dog statue and a pewter lamp sat on the nightstand. The room had the requisite overstuffed chair, and also boasted a small fireplace.

"Do the fireplaces work?" I asked.

Rebecca nodded. "Several of them were bricked over before we bought the property, and the contractor advised against opening those back up. But the ones you see all work, and in the winter, guests like to cozy up to a fire even though as you know, it never gets all that cold here."

I was glad when we left the room. I wondered whether my imagination was running away with me or whether I really was picking up the vibe from the mirror, but there was no way I would have been comfortable sleeping there.

"This is the last guest room," Rebecca said, opening the door wide. She turned on the light, and I found myself looking at an imposing bed that had a small wooden half canopy protruding from the very high headboard, a detail that made it look like a throne. A vintage quilt covered the mattress, along with needlepoint throw pillows which made the bed only slightly less intimidating.

I spotted another set of silver picture frames on the dresser, ones I immediately recognized from our store. The pictures were old tintypes of a man and woman, authentic and completely unremarkable, yet instinctively, I wanted to draw back from the frames in unaccountable sadness.

"What happens in this room?" I asked.

"It's odd," Rebecca said. "The last room gives guests the willies, although no one has reported being hurt – thank heavens! But in this room, it's almost as if something gradually drains the happiness out of the guests who stay here. Guests have cut their trip short, saying that they just didn't feel like vacationing anymore. One woman told me that she broke down sobbing for no reason. My cleaning lady says the same thing."

"So the problems have been witnessed by people other than just guests?" I asked. It had occurred to me that an unscrupulous guest might be tempted to concoct a story to get a discount or a refund.

Rebecca nodded. "Since the problems began, I've had to replace the cleaning position twice. The woman I have now, Cecilia, wears several charms around her neck, but then again, she's Gullah, and says her people have ways of making peace with the spirits." She drew a deep breath. "Sometimes when she's cleaning, I hear her chanting to herself, but honestly, I don't care what she does as long as she doesn't quit!"

The Gullah people were descended from runaway or freed slaves who settled in isolated areas along South Carolina's coast, the area most people call the Lowcountry. Gullah folks are known for their distinctive language, a combination of African and Caribbean languages borrowed from the cultures of the original settlers. One of their old traditions involves 'root work', a powerful form of folk magic and healing. The magic is real, and root workers deserve the high degree of respect – and awe – they are accorded. If you're wise, you take root work very seriously.

I looked around the hallway as Rebecca closed the bedroom door and followed her back downstairs. The parlor had a magnificent Victorian single-end sofa, with a curving back that was higher on one side than the other, and rich red velvet upholstery edged in dark wood. Fringed lampshades glowed on the table lamps with their elaborate molded bronze stands. Rebecca laughed as she showed me how the big armoire hid a large screen TV and stereo system. A pair of comfortable chairs sat near the fireplace with an end table between them, inviting me to curl up and read.

"It's lovely," I said sincerely. "Any incidents in here?"

Rebecca grimaced. "Now, we seem to have incidents everywhere. At first, it was just in the bedrooms. Then, guests and staffers started experiencing strange things down here as well. And last week, we had a couple of unusual things go on in the garden."

"Like?"

She sighed. "There was damage to one of the flower beds, but everyone denied doing it, and frankly, I can't really imagine one of our guests tearing out the geraniums."

I couldn't either. "How about your room? Do you have any antiques I should look at up there?"

Rebecca shook her head. "Everything in my room is modern – I brought it from my old house and I've had it for years. I put all the good pieces where guests could use and enjoy them." She looked sheepish. "As much as I love the antiques, having only modern furniture in my room is a nice break, and it helps me feel like I've left work, if that makes sense."

I nodded. "It does. Any disturbances up there?"

Rebecca hesitated, and I figured she was deciding just how much to trust me. "Not at first," she said quietly. "But then 'he' started showing up."

She had gone quiet and pale. "He?" I asked gently.

She nodded, and exhaled in a rush, as if summoning her courage. "I see a shadow of a man, but it's too dark to be a regular shadow." Her eyes pleaded with me for understanding. "Imagine if you cut a silhouette out of black construction paper. No light goes through it. Sometimes, I see him on the stairs. Sometimes, I wake up in the middle of the night and see the shadow slide out the door, like he's been watching me."

"Has your shadow man actually tried to harm anyone?"

"No, but I'm afraid it's heading that way. A few days ago, I fell on the steps. Only I didn't trip. I definitely felt someone push me from behind, but there was no one here. One of my guests took an evening walk in the garden, and she said a vicious black dog growled at her. It chased her into the house, but of course, when we went searching for it, the gates were closed and there was no dog."

"Have you had any reports of strangers loitering near the place?"

Rebecca frowned. "The day I fell, I happened to look out the front window and I saw a man in black clothing with a broad-brimmed hat near the gate. It stuck in my mind because his clothing seemed odd for the season. I saw him again, the day the shadow dog chased my guest."

She paused. "At first, I thought he might be new in the neighborhood. But I saw him just a few moments before you arrived, and I tried to catch up with him, but by the time I reached the sidewalk, he was gone."

*That definitely did not bode well,* I thought. *Shadow men, and now the man with the hat.* Not to mention the fact that the incidents seemed to be getting more dangerous. Someone was going to get hurt. Maybe that was the point.

I followed Rebecca into the dining room, and gasped. Dominating the room was a massive mahogany table and an ornate sideboard that gave the bedroom sets real competition when it came to carved ornamentation. The table would easily seat sixteen, and the chairs had leather upholstery and graceful, curved backs.

A huge, heavy server table sat up against one wall. No doubt many a Thanksgiving turkey and sides of sweet potatoes and okra had once waited their turn from that fine piece of furniture. But it was the equally massive sideboard and matching china cupboard that were the stars of the room.

The china cupboard stood at least seven feet tall, with a fan-shaped, intricately carved wooden frill at the top that probably added another foot or so to the height. The back of the cabinet was mirrored, with glass shelves to set off treasured china and decorative objects to their best advantage. The sideboard was probably four feet long and over five feet high, with a wide counter for holding tureens and platters. The tea set from Trifles and Folly sat on the broad counter, ready for use. The sideboard had a mirrored back above the counter, with carved wooden pillars at each end and another delicate but big wooden frill at the top. Drawers below would have held linens, flatware and other necessities, making it a very solid piece.

"It's absolutely magnificent," I whispered.

Rebecca grinned. "We've got some nice furniture in the house, but this is the showstopper," she acknowledged.

"My father's great-great-grandfather was a sea captain, and he did well for himself. When he brought his bride to their new home, he wanted to make sure its furnishings made a statement to the neighbors that Captain Harrison and his wife were people of quality."

"I imagine this did the trick," I said. Part of me longed to run my fingers over the beautiful carvings, but I held back, unsure what kind of psychic image I might receive.

Rebecca nodded. "By all accounts, the captain and his wife were very happy for many years."

"Until?" Something in her voice told me that the Harrisons' happiness did not last forever.

"Shipping is a dangerous business, especially back in that time. When Captain Harrison was in his late fifties, he decided to retire from the sea and planned to enjoy his later years with his wife. Unfortunately, his ship was lost on his final voyage, and he never made it home."

"That's awful," I said.

Rebecca ran a hand lovingly over the table's beautiful wood. "Mrs. Harrison lived into her nineties and never remarried. She was twenty years younger than her husband, so it was a long widowhood. The story that was passed down through the family was that she set a place for the Captain every night, just in case fate brought him home to her." She looked at me conspiratorially. "And according to family legend, it did. But not in the way she expected."

"Oh?"

Rebecca gave me an impish grin. "According to family legend, Mrs. Harrison was walking down by the Battery and spotted something bobbing in the water next to the sea wall. She had a servant fish it out." Flotsam wasn't unusual down by the harbor, but most of the time it consisted of obvious trash.

"The item turned out to be an oilskin pouch that had been sealed with wax. Inside were papers from Captain Harrison himself, along with a fine silver chain necklace. An unfinished letter in the pouch in the captain's handwriting indicated that the necklace was a gift for her, and that he looked forward to being home as soon as they completed this last trip, and that he would bring her a fresh pineapple to celebrate."

There was a reason so many houses in the Charleston area used carvings of pineapples in their decorations. Once upon a time, the fruit had been quite rare, and many a sea captain brought them home as highly desirable gifts.

Rebecca shook her head. "Of course, his ship never made it home, but somehow, the sea brought her his last gift and letter."

"What a great story!" I said, although as a historian, I had my doubts about its authenticity.

"Oh, that's not the end of it," Rebecca said. "The story says that great-great Grandma Harrison put the chain around her neck and went home with the letter. She was giddy with excitement, and told the servants that the Captain was coming home that night."

"The poor old dear," I murmured.

"In fact, she told the servants to serve dinner for two, and then leave her uninterrupted, because she and the Captain had a lot of catching up to do," Rebecca said with a gleam in her eye.

My scalp began to prickle. "What happened?"

"According to the story, they found her dead at the table later that evening, slumped in her dining chair. But listen to this: the servants said that the food had been eaten at both place settings and that the room smelled of Bay Rum and pipe smoke, as it did when the Captain was in port." She met my gaze. "And there was a fresh pineapple in the middle of the table."

I eyed the table once more. *With all these stories, I'm more surprised that the inn wasn't haunted before this. Both the house and the furnishings are prime spook material. So the real question is – why now? What set off the haunting?*

"Their second son, Benjamin, also went into the shipping business with his brother, and was also lost at sea," Rebecca added. "Good story, huh?"

"Very good." I paused. "What about the linens from our shop?" I asked.

Rebecca crossed the room and opened the door beneath the huge sideboard. She took out a folded tablecloth and unfurled it over the dining table.

"I fell in love with this as soon as Debra showed it to me," Rebecca said wistfully. "For its age, it's in excellent condition, and the embroidery is just beautiful," she said, caressing the old stitches between her thumb and finger. The stitching was as white as the cloth itself, but it formed a complicated tracery border that was a work of art.

"We only use it for show," Rebecca said. "I don't serve meals on it, because I'm afraid of stains. But I enjoyed putting it out at other times, until *she* showed up."

"She?"

Rebecca hesitated. "Actually, people have seen two old women in this room, but not at the same time. One of them seems angry about something, and the other one has a darkness about her that has made people uneasy."

*Grumpy old lady ghosts*, I thought. "No idea who they are?"

"I think one of them might be Mrs. Harrison," Rebecca said. "I've only glimpsed her once or twice, but the way she had her hair made me think of an old photograph I saw as a child." She looked sheepish. "Of course, there were probably thousands of women in her day who wore their hair like that. I could be wrong."

"But no clue as to why one is angry and the other is out of sorts?"

Rebecca shrugged. "No idea. But one night, I heard a sound like china breaking, and when I came downstairs to see if something had fallen, there was nothing broken, but the doors to the sideboard were open, and I'm certain I had shut them before going to bed."

I followed her to the very modern kitchen, where she poured us each a cup of coffee and we settled down at the breakfast nook.

"You're sure there weren't any sightings of ghosts or strange happenings before you bought the items from Trifles and Folly?" I asked, sipping and savoring my coffee.

Rebecca shook her head. "After everything I've told you, you'd think we'd have had a spook-a-palooza here, right?" She made a face. "Truth is, I used to envy the inns that claimed to be haunted. They always get mentioned more in the tourist brochures, and between the ghost tours and the annual Halloween Haunt write-up in the *Post and Courier*, it seemed to be good for business."

"If that's the case, why change it?" I asked. "You've got some great stories to tell, and Andrews Carriage Rides would probably be thrilled to have some fresh tales." Some of our ghosts are famous enough to be celebrities in their own right. A new story with evidence to back it up could be valuable marketing.

Rebecca sipped her coffee, staring into the liquid like she might see an answer in the swirl of her cream. "I thought so too, at first…" She shivered.

"Tell me," I urged, reaching out to touch her arm.

"The 'sad' bedroom upstairs certainly isn't good for business, or staff turnover," she said with a grim smile. "The mirror room is unsettling, and the spirit in that room has a habit of playing pranks that have gone from funny to creepy."

"Oh?"

Her dark hair bobbed as she nodded. "At first, it was just little things like moving a guest's glasses or sliding a key from one side of the dresser to another. Then later, items went missing, even when no one had been in the room."

"You're sure it wasn't a member of staff playing a prank?"

Rebecca shook her head. "It's usually just me and one assistant who helps out in busy times, plus a part-time cook and the cleaning lady. At the times guests reported the incidents, there was no one here but me."

"Could the guest have staged it themselves for attention – or a refund?"

"I don't think so," Rebecca replied. "The guests didn't ask for their money back. Two of the others asked for a change of room. But they were all really spooked by it. I don't think they were acting."

"What else?"

"The ghosts have gotten more vocal," she said with a sigh. "We've heard children in the hallway when there weren't any kids staying here, and a woman's voice when the room was empty."

"Anything else?"

Rebecca met my gaze. "I'm worried, Cassidy. In the last week, the activity's gotten worse. Doors slamming and locking. Damage to the flower beds outside. That incident on the stairs. And in the mirror room, I found one of the feather pillows ripped to shreds." She shivered. "These aren't the fun type of ghosts."

"Do you think the ghosts are angry about something?"

Slowly, Rebecca nodded. "That's exactly what I think." She paused. "I told you about the shadow man in my room. But there's someone else up there as well."

"Who?"

"I don't know her name, but I think she might have worked in the house a long time ago. Maybe that was her room. She's a middle-aged woman with her hair in a top knot, and she looks like she should have a rolling pin in her hands, if you know what I mean. I think she shows up to protect me."

"How?"

A smile touched her lips. "One night when I saw the shadow man, I thought he was going to come closer. That was the first time I saw Greta."

"Greta?"

Again, the sheepish grin. "That's my name for her. Greta was standing between the door and the foot of my bed. I could almost see through her, but her figure was very clear. She had her hands on her hips, and she looked like she meant business. The shadow man disappeared, and didn't come back for several nights."

I leaned forward. "Do you know anything about James Harrison being involved with smugglers?" I asked. "Have you ever heard of a man named Jeremiah Abernathy?"

Rebecca frowned, thinking. "Smuggling wouldn't surprise me. That was practically the official industry in Charleston for a long while." She paused. "I don't know anything about Jeremiah Abernathy, but there was some talk about the pirate loot that James Harrison and his crew brought back on their last trip."

"Oh?"

She nodded. "Their ship, the *Lady Jane,* was just coming back from Barbados. Rumor had it, they had picked up some of the treasure of a pirate ship that had sunk in a freak storm, and James brought it back to Charleston. A couple of days later, they sailed out again never to return." Rebecca paused.

"Mrs. Harrison's diary made it sound like the treasure they had picked up brought trouble. Some of Captain Harrison's sailors thought it was cursed, and wanted to throw it overboard. They were all relieved to set out again and leave it behind in Charleston. Maybe they should have left it floating where they found it," she said with a sigh.

A chime sounded, and Rebecca looked up suddenly, glancing at the clock on the wall. It was quarter to eight. "Yikes! I've got to get ready," she said, draining her coffee cup. "I offer light hors d'oeuvres and cocktails in the dining room at 8:30, so I'd better get a move on."

I finished my coffee and stood. "Can I help?"

Rebecca made a tsk-tsk sound. "Thanks, but no. You're my guest! Relax a little – I think you'll enjoy meeting the other couple."

With that, I left the coffee cup by the sink and headed up to my room, which was just as I left it. *So far, so good.*

I had less than an hour before cocktails, so I unpacked my overnight case and laid out a fresh blouse. *Time to see what kind of a read I'll get from these pieces,* I thought. I wanted to be able to sleep tonight, so I was hoping none of the objects in this room were too highly charged with supernatural juice.

I picked up the kit we used on investigations and pulled out a small package of salt, and another bag with some charcoal pieces in it, good for neutralizing negative energy. I didn't want to damage any of Rebecca's lovely antiques, but I didn't want to be damaged by any of them, either.

Gingerly, I touched the footboard of the large brass bed, and waited for my gift to kick in. The images were faint, but pleasant. I caught a whiff of lemon verbena, and saw an image in my mind of a plump older woman, her gray hair in a bun and apron strings tied over a work dress. Running my hand across the chenille bedspread reinforced the same mental picture. *Rebecca's grandmother?* I wondered. Whoever she was, the old woman was a comforting presence.

I felt a little more hesitation when I approached the lamp. I remembered handling it in the shop without any strange effect. This time, I felt a tingle that had nothing to do with loose wiring. But like the bed and bedspread, the feelings and images were safe and comforting. A few notes of a lullaby sounded in the distance, and murmured good-nights. I pulled my hand away, and the vision disappeared, but not the sense of being wrapped in a warm embrace.

None of the pieces in my room needed to be cleansed or neutralized, so I put my items back in the pack and set it near the door for later that evening. Relieved, I settled into the chair with my book for the remaining time, figuring that I'd prowl the inn this evening after my fellow guests retired for the night. Before I knew it, the time had come to spruce up for cocktails.

I brushed my hair, washed my face, and then pulled on my new blouse and put on some lip gloss. *Much better,* I thought, appraising my reflection.

As I went down the stairs, I could hear low voices in the dining room and Rebecca's laugh. When I reached the doorway, I stopped in my tracks, and my mouth may have fallen open in astonishment.

Teag and his partner Anthony stood leaning against the large sideboard, each holding a glass of wine, with Teag's arm draped across Anthony's shoulders.

"Hello, Cassidy," Teag said with a cat-that-ate-the-canary grin. "Fancy meeting you here. Isn't this a lovely place to get away for a couple of days?"

# Chapter Seven

"YOU KNOW EACH other?" Rebecca said, confused. She looked from me to Teag and back again, as Anthony walked over and gave me a hug.

I chuckled, realizing I'd been set up. "Teag and I work together at the shop, and Anthony is a dear friend," I said.

"We're your back-up," Teag explained, pressing a glass of wine into my hand. "I told Anthony about the email you got and about you coming here by yourself –"

"And I asked what he thought about getting away for a couple of evenings," Anthony finished the sentence. He grinned broadly, flashing me a smile that no doubt was part of his stellar ability to woo juries and broker successful contract negotiations. Usually, I saw Anthony in a suit looking like he had just stepped off the cover of a men's fashion magazine. Teag, with his skater-boy hair and jeans, was *Rolling Stone* to Anthony's *GQ*.

Tonight, Anthony had traded in his suit and tie for a collared polo shirt and crisp khakis over boat shoes, a popular upscale Charleston look. Other than changing into a fresh t-shirt from the one he had worn all day at the shop, Teag looked the same as he had a couple of hours earlier. They made a cute couple.

"Honestly, Cassidy, I didn't think you should tackle this by yourself," Teag said.

Rebecca looked abashed. "I'm sorry," she said. "I didn't mean to cause a problem."

I patted her arm. "You haven't. We sold you the items. So we've got a responsibility to figure out what's going on."

She put on her game face and managed a smile. "What can I do to help?"

"You've already given me the tour, and gotten me thinking," I said. I gave her my best gung-ho smile. "We'll take it from here. Why don't you go up to your room if you feel safe there and stay put for the night?" Rebecca looked relieved. Now that I'd had time to study her features, I could see that there were dark circles under her eyes. If living in a newly-haunted house wasn't wearing her down, then worrying about the ghosts' impact on her livelihood certainly couldn't help, especially if the haunts were becoming more active – and dangerous.

Teag and Anthony and I hung out in the dining room enjoying our wine and the plate of appetizers while Rebecca cleaned up the kitchen and made a tray to carry up to her room. At my request, she also put on a fresh pot of coffee, since it was likely to be a long night, and set out cups. We promised to rinse out our wine glasses and put the hors d'oeuvres plate back in the kitchen and bade Rebecca good night.

"I can't believe you two came to help me out," I said when Rebecca was gone.

Teag put his hands on his hips and cocked his head,

giving me his best stern schoolteacher look. "Really? After what's been going on, you think I'm going to let you come to a whole house full of spookies by yourself? If the haints don't scare Rebecca, seeing you go into a dead faint with one of your visions is sure to!"

I had to smile. 'Haints' was a local term for ghost, and it even had its own paint color, 'haint blue', named after the vivid shade some people painted their doors to keep away nasty spirits.

"I even brought an extra kit, just in case," Teag said, and nodded toward the leather messenger bag he had placed next to the door. I knew it would contain everything that was in my own pack upstairs in my room.

Our kit for investigating questionable objects included several common, but supernaturally powerful items: salt, for protection; chalk, sometimes needed to mark an area to protect or avoid; charcoal; a small bundle of sage, and an abalone shell, to cleanse an area after a working. We usually carried several other useful items, including a wind-up flashlight (supernatural creatures tend to wreak havoc on batteries), and a pouch with dried fennel, hyssop, marigold, and rue, also useful for banishing negative energy. Just for good measure, we usually also threw in a couple of pieces of turquoise, agate, and onyx.

"I even made sure Anthony and I have our lucky agate stones with us," Teag said with a grin, and held up a smooth polished small agate disk which he had hidden in his pocket. "We're ready."

"What can we do to help, Cassidy?" Practical as always, Anthony was the perfect foil to Teag's unbridled enthusiasm. "Short of breaking and entering, I'm with you."

I chuckled, knowing that with Anthony's family and legal connections, he could probably get away with B&E in this town, but I wasn't going to ask that of him. "Well," I said. "We're already inside, so no breaking necessary.

"I thought I'd start by trying to 'read' the objects room by room. After that, I figured on a stake-out to see some of this ghostly activity. Something changed these pieces. If we can figure out what made the difference, we should be able to make it stop."

Anthony frowned. "Can't we just remove the objects?"

I shook my head. "Now that it's started, I don't think just taking the pieces away is going to make it stop." Briefly, I filled them in on what Rebecca had told me earlier in the day, and the sightings of the man with the broad-brimmed hat. Teag glanced out of the front windows, but no one was in sight.

"Let's go," Teag said, finishing his wine and setting the glass aside.

Touching the wood of the table and sideboard gave me a fleeting image of dinners and happy conversation. I reached out to touch the tea set, but got only a vague, pleasant aura and the distant scent of Earl Gray. "It's got some resonance, but the energy is positive."

I bent down and opened the doors below the sideboard. "Would you please pull out that tablecloth?" Anthony carefully removed the folded tablecloth and set the bundle on the mahogany dining table.

"I recognize that," Teag said. "I still don't get any vibes of magic woven or embroidered into the piece."

I moved to touch the tablecloth, but Anthony pulled out a chair for me. "Why don't you sit down to handle the objects, Cassidy?" he said, in his best lawyer-advisory tone. First, I let my hand rest on the wood of the table itself. As with the sideboard, the fleeting images were of happy times, making me feel safe and reassured. I took a deep breath and laid my right hand on the tablecloth, then closed my eyes and waited for the show to start.

It didn't take long. There were images of family gatherings, mostly happy, crammed together like a super-fast slide show.

*I saw an elderly man sitting at the head of a table set for Thanksgiving dinner. Relatives of all ages were busily talking and laughing. At the other end of the table sat a tall, handsome woman with high cheekbones and intelligent, dark eyes. She was presiding over the meal with quiet pride. Judging from the clothing, the year was around 1940.*

*The images shifted so fast I grabbed at the table to steady myself. I saw the older man straighten suddenly, saw him clutch his chest in pain, trying to call out. Family members rushed from their places to help him out of his chair, easing him to the floor as the tall woman ran to his side and held his hand. Another spasm of pain wracked the man's body and he wheezed, then fell still. Dinner sat forgotten, and the celebration turned to mourning.*

*I sensed the passage of time in the vision as the images blurred like someone had hit fast-forward. The table with its holiday covering now hosted a funeral dinner for the mourners.*

*The next image was the strongest. The dining room was dark, the mourners had gone, and the tall woman sat in her seat at the table, looking down to the empty seat at the end. I could feel her heart breaking. And I knew what she was going to do next.*

*"No," I whispered. "Don't." But the actions had been taken long before I was born, and nothing would change them now. I watched in horror as the woman left the room and returned with a stout length of rope. She slipped off her shoes and then climbed onto the table, looping one end of the rope over the heavy chandelier. She had already fashioned a noose. Eyes fixed on the empty seat at the end of the table, she took a breath, closed her eyes, and stepped into oblivion.*

I came back to myself lying on the floor, the tablecloth clutched in my hands, gasping for breath. Teag was kneeling next to me, and Anthony was staring at both Teag and I as if we had lost our minds.

"This is what the two of you do for a living?" he asked, wide-eyed.

Teag had the good grace to give a nervous laugh. "Not always. But yeah, sometimes."

He helped me sit up. It took me a moment before I could speak. "I think Mrs. Butler left out some of the story." Teag and Anthony helped me up, and I took a deep breath. "The linens have a powerful psychic imprint," I said, and recounted what I had seen. "I think the other woman is old Mrs. Harrison, the wife of the man who built this house," I ended. "But we still don't know what made the ghosts show up now."

Teag sprinkled a few grains of salt onto the tablecloth. The salt wouldn't damage the fabric, but it would put a damper on the negative energy. That should help us narrow down which piece or pieces were the real troublemakers.

Anthony watched as Teag sprinkled the salt. "Why

don't you do whatever you're doing before Cassidy touches something? It would certainly spare her a lot of distress."

"The problem is, if we dampen the energy, we don't really know what we're dealing with," Teag explained. "The only time we put out the protective materials in advance is if the item has been known to actually harm someone."

Nothing else in the dining room had any hint of supernatural power, so we headed to the entranceway. I touched paintings, doilies, the antique rug, and a set of candlesticks and got nothing, but when my fingers skimmed the funeral vase, images lit up in my mind.

*I heard women weeping and men clearing their throats in grief. I saw the vase, and two small coffins in a sparse parlor. The weight of the onlookers' sorrow fell heavy on my heart, and I began to sob.* Teag gently reached over and separated my hand from the vase and the vision winked out.

I dragged my sleeve across my eyes. Anthony handed me a tissue. "I saw the funerals," I said when I could speak again, with a nod to Teag. "It's a strong vision, but not powerful enough to energize the whole place." Teag dropped a bit of charcoal into the vase.

The parlor held no sparklies or spookies at all. Even the vintage couch was completely mundane. It was a relief after the last two rooms, and gave me a little break to catch my breath. I suspected that the upstairs would be exciting, and not in a good way.

Since I had already checked out the items in my room, we went to Teag and Anthony's room.

I received some images from touching the bedframe, and blushed. The bedset resonated with sensual satisfaction, and I guessed it had witnessed some memorable reunions in its time. Embarrassing, yes. Dangerous, no. Teag must have guessed as much from the way my face reddened, because he chuckled but did not ask questions. I touched the other objects in the room and got sparks from a few of them – brief, fragmentary images, most of which were positive. Nothing in this room held bad mojo.

I knew we weren't going to be as lucky with the next room. "Let's do the sad room first," I said. I was putting off the mirror room.

With more confidence than I felt, I swung the door open. This room had an impressive – and expensive – suite of furniture. Once again, I started with the bed, but this time, there were no strong emotions at all. The quilt gave snapshots of ordinary lives, nothing dramatic or tragic.

None of the rest of the bedroom furniture gave up any secrets to my touch, so I turned my attention to the decorations. The still life paintings had no resonance at all, nor did the silver bowl on the mantel or the elegant hurricane lamp. But the pair of silver picture frames drew me, filling me with a sadness beyond words even before I touched them.

A handsome young man and pretty young woman looked back at me from the photographs. I guessed that they were in their late teens or early twenties. They looked happy and full of life, dressed in their best finery.

"I'm going to sit down," I announced. "I think this is going to be intense." I settled into one of the chairs by the fireplace, and Teag brought the frames to me. Mustering my courage, I let him place the frames on my open palms.

*Black despair washed over me, unreasoning and limitless. The world around me dimmed. Nothing intruded on the grief. Voices called to me, but I could barely hear them. If I were still breathing and my heart still beat, it happened without my knowing it. I felt as dead as my babies, as cold as their pale skin, lifeless as their still bodies.*

*My babies? A rational corner of my mind argued, but I was too far gone to notice. If the grief of the old woman in the dining room had driven her to suicide, this overwhelming sorrow led to madness. Dimly, I heard a woman screaming as the picture frame tumbled from my hands...*

"Cassidy! Cassidy, snap out of it!" Teag's voice sounded from a long way away. In my grief, I lacked the power follow it. I was being swept away on a dark, cold tide that was sure to draw me under.

Icy water hit my face and I came up sputtering. "What the hell was that?" I asked, coming back to myself in a rush.

"Sorry," Anthony said, giving me his most endearing smile. "You were screaming. It seemed like the fastest way to bring you back."

I shook my hair like a wet dog and looked down at my damp shirt. Anthony handed me a towel, and I dried off, trying to regain a shred of my dignity. "Well, I was right. It was intense," I said ruefully.

"I think I've found something," Anthony said. He was kneeling beside where the pair of picture frames had fallen. The shock had broken the glass, and knocked the backing off the frames. I winced, sorry that I had damaged the antique. But Anthony's attention was on something behind the pictures, and I watched as he gingerly teased out two completely different photographs underneath the frame's backing.

"That might explain it," Teag said, coming around to stand behind Anthony and looking down on the new photos.

"Let me see!" I said, turning in my chair. Anthony ducked, remaining beyond my reach.

"No way! I'll hold them up for you, but I'm not handing them over," he said.

I caught my breath. "Those are death pictures," I said softly. I stared at the antique prints. In the years after the Civil War, when photography was still new, family pictures were an expensive luxury. Sometimes, the only photo that might be taken was after death. Ghoulish as the thought was to modern sensibilities, Victorians did not find the idea shocking or disturbing, and a whole photographic specialty sprang up to give bereaved families a memento of their lost loved ones.

*Memento mori.*

The photos that had fallen out were of the same man and woman I had seen in the frames, perhaps a little older, wearing the same clothing, but with a crucial difference. They were posed in lifelike positions, seated upright in high backed chairs, eyes open and hands clasped on their laps. A second look revealed an unnatural stiffness in the limbs, and that the 'eyes' had been painted onto closed eyelids. They were very definitely dead.

I swallowed hard. *Was it a mother's grief I felt?* It was clear to me that the deaths of these two young people had caused a third tragedy, the complete breakdown of someone who loved them more than life itself.

"We don't have to finish this all in one night," Teag said quietly. He had gone to the door, to reassure

Rebecca that all was well, and a moment later, she came back with a glass of sweet iced tea before she returned to her upstairs hideaway.

I drank the sweet tea with gusto. In Charleston, sweet tea is brewed strong and loaded with sugar. It was just what I needed. While I drank the tea, Teag set the picture frames image side down on the table and placed a small piece of charcoal on top of them. I felt the bad vibes calm almost immediately.

"I'll be okay," I said resolutely. "I still don't think we've found the key."

On the way over to the mirror room, I made a mental note to give Teag a well-deserved raise. For combat pay. And I resolved to take him and Anthony out for dinner at the nicest restaurant I could afford. I couldn't imagine doing this on my own, and I was immensely grateful for their support.

I thought that Anthony might have balked at the idea of ghosts, supernatural phenomena, or my psychometric talent. But falling for Teag meant learning to accept his Weaver magic. And since he and Teag had already jumped that hurdle, I guess seeing my abilities in action was no longer much of a shock. So far, I thought he was coping rather well.

Anthony opened the door to the last bedroom and flipped on the light.

"I don't think I'd want to sleep here," he said, glancing around. "I can't put my finger on why, but something's not right."

*Then again, perhaps Anthony's a sensitive,* I thought to myself. *That would certainly explain a few things.* Teag had hinted as much, though I suspected Anthony might still be chalking up his insights to intuition.

I started with the furniture again. It radiated moodiness. Anthony walked over to the window and looked out.

"This room looks down on the garden," he said. *The garden that was mysteriously vandalized,* I thought.

I picked up a vague longing from the seascape painting. The oil painting of the young woman, to my relief, gave no impression at all. That left the pewter lantern and the Chinese Foo dog statue, plus the mirror.

The lantern held a candle inside a small glass globe. It wasn't one of the pieces that came from Trifles and Folly, and neither was the Foo dog statue. The lantern didn't seem to have any supernatural juice, so it wasn't what was causing our problem.

This was one of the rooms with a working fireplace. The opening was covered with a metal curtain, and a vintage poker and tongs sat in a holder next to the hearth. Two chairs were arranged facing the fireplace, and if weren't for the damned mirror, I bet the room would have felt charming and cozy.

The mirror hung over the mantel. It was the focal point of the room, and the piece I had been avoiding. Anywhere else, I would have thought it was a handsome piece with its ribbon-like bronze frame. For its age, the silver backing on the mirror was in very good condition, and I remembered thinking how lovely it was when we had it in the shop. Now, it seemed sinister.

As I stared at the mirror, I caught a glimpse of a shadow behind me. I wheeled, and saw nothing, feeling foolish as Teag and Anthony stared at me.

"Something wrong?" Teag asked.

"I thought I saw something," I murmured, turning my attention back to the mirror. I decided to leave the Chinese Foo dog statue for last.

I took another step toward the mirror, fighting my fear. As I stared into it, I felt turmoil, as if beneath the placid silver surface wild seas roiled. Just in case, I took one of Teag's pouches of salt and shoved it into my jeans pocket. When I got within arm's length, I saw that the mirror was gray, not silver, and at this distance, I could make out ghostly images sliding across it.

I touched the mirror, and tumbled into its depths.

*Someone – something – was in the mirror. I could see motion out of the corner of my eye, but every time I turned nothing was there. I felt like Alice, gone through the looking glass, adrift in a silvery world. A world where I was not alone.*

*Claws skittered against a hard surface behind me. I wheeled, but the silver room was empty. I could hear muffled voices in the distance. Some were chanting. Others screamed in terror.*

*A shadow slid across the silvery surface of the walls, but like a hall of mirrors, it was impossible to know what was real and what was reflection. I was cold, disoriented, and afraid. The shadow man skirted the edge of my vision, and I had the sense the spirit was enjoying my fear, feeding from it. I was afraid to move, fearful that I might get lost in this reflective realm, unable to find my way back.*

*Then I saw him. The shadow man loomed ahead of me. The image was more solid than a normal shadow, its form elongated, not quite human. Although I couldn't make out any features, I knew it was watching me, making up its mind. Malevolence radiated from the image and my heart thudded. It was the predator. I was the prey.*

*The shadow rushed at me, impossibly long arms outstretched, claw-like fingers grasping. It came at me like*

*the wind. With one hand, I grasped my agate necklace,
and with the other, I grabbed a handful of salt from the
pocket of my jeans and threw it at the shadow. Just for an
instant, it wavered, but I knew it would come at me again.*

Strong hands grabbed me from behind, hauling me
backward. My hand lost contact with the mirror. Only
then did I realize I was screaming. I came back to myself
caught in Anthony's tight embrace and, fresh from the
horror of the vision, I fought him, possessed with sheer,
primal terror. His strong hands gripped my wrists.

"Take it easy," he coaxed. "You're back now. You're
safe."

I was shaking, and I felt sick to my stomach. Anthony
eased me into the chair by the fireplace. It was several
more moments before I could give even the briefest
account of what I had seen. In the meantime, Teag had
already sprinkled a line of salt beneath the mirror and
had begun blowing a fine dusting of charcoal powder
over the reflective surface, which reduced its powerful
energy to a dull, distant roar.

"You were screaming bloody murder," Teag said,
looking utterly unnerved. "Good thing we're the only
guests at the inn, or someone would be calling the cops."

One thing was undeniable – the mirror had not possessed
the power to draw me into it at Trifles and Folly.

"I saw the shadow man in the mirror," I told them,
once I caught my breath. "It's become a gateway, a
portal. It was looking for me, and it attacked. Thanks
for getting me out of there."

"Do you think the mirror is the key?" Teag asked.

I thought for a moment, then shook my head. "No.
It's dangerous, and whatever spirit was inside it is
malicious, but I don't think it's the focal point."

Just for good measure, I touched my palm to the agate necklace on my chest. Then I turned to look at the Foo dog statue.

*When you have eliminated the impossible, whatever remains, however improbable, must be the truth,* Sherlock Holmes had said. I had the feeling that I was staring the 'truth' of Gardenia Landing's haunting in the eyes as I looked at the Chinese sculpture.

I put out my hand, and let it hover above the shiny blue glaze that covered the stylized little dog. "I think I've found the problem," I said.

# Chapter Eight

"YOU THINK THAT dog statue is bringing everything else to life?" Teag asked incredulously.

"It's giving off really strong energy, and right before the mirror drew me into the vision, I felt a spike in power from the direction of the Foo dog," I said, eyeing the blue sculpture warily.

"It's not one of our pieces," Teag said, moving closer for a better look. He frowned. "You know, these dogs never look friendly, but this one looks meaner than usual."

I peered at the dog and had to agree. The dogs – some people called them lions – were intended to be fearsome guardians with bared teeth and long claws. Some of the statues veered more toward cute while others tended to be more authentic, looking like watchdogs you didn't want to cross. This Foo dog was about the size of a real Pug, and it had a particularly nasty expression and a mouthful of jagged teeth. "Why not just neutralize it and destroy it?" Anthony asked. I had to admit, it was a logical question. And unfortunately, I had a fairly logical response.

"We could, but then we might never know what set it off," I replied. "I doubt anything with such a strong energy vibration would have attracted a buyer. Rebecca seems to have good instincts." I shrugged. "A lot of times, people bring us objects that they can't sell or give away because no one will take them. Even if they can't say exactly why, they know something about the piece is wrong."

"Why do you care what set it off?" Anthony persisted. "If you can get rid of it, then the rest of the pieces in the inn should settle down and behave themselves, right?"

"The problem is, we're starting to see a pattern," Teag replied. "First the opera glasses, now the Foo dog, items that might have witnessed an event that made an imprint on their energy. But neither item seemed haunted until something set them off. So what turned them 'on'?" he asked. "We need to figure that out because whatever happened to them might have happened to other items we haven't found yet."

"That's a lovely thought," Anthony replied. He looked to me. "It's up to you, Cassidy. What do you want to do next?"

"Let's hedge our bets," I said. I pulled out another bag of salt and the small bag of charcoal from Teag's bag and shoved one bag in each of my jeans pockets. Then I took out the handful of protective gemstones and tucked them in also, just to be safe.

"How about we assume that the dog is going to do 'tricks'," I said, keeping my eye on the statue as if it might move. "I'm hoping that having the protective items on me instead of on the sculpture will keep me safe without smothering its energy so much that we can't get a reading."

"What do you want us to do, Cassidy?" Teag asked. I smiled, because I had an answer ready. Both men nodded as I laid out my plan, and got into position. I swallowed my fear, and reached out toward the statue.

Behind me, with no one near it, the door to the hallway slammed shut.

We all flinched. I lunged forward before anything else could happen, and grabbed the statue's head with both hands.

*The room around me winked out. I found myself in a seedy wooden building that smelled of brackish water, wood, and hemp rope. Lamps barely pushed back the shadows, and from the smoke, I guessed these lights were burning whale oil. Nearby, I could hear waves lapping against something solid, and when I looked down, I glimpsed water through the gaps in the boards beneath my feet. Outside the building, I heard a jabber of languages, but one was more prevalent than the rest: Chinese.*

*"The crates are all here, as you ordered." The speaker was a man dressed in a black frock coat and stained silk vest. A dark cravat was tied at his throat over a tall, fold-over collar. His mutton chop sideburns seemed exaggerated even for their time. I spotted a battered top hat to one side. From his clothing, I fixed the time period in the 1830s. By his accent, I figured him for American.*

*The building appeared to be a warehouse, and in the shadows behind me, I could barely make out stacks of wooden crates, no doubt from the ships in the harbor outside. I glanced overhead, and saw the ropes and pulleys that made it possible to unload heavy cargo from wagons. Oil lamps hung from brackets attached to heavy* wooden beams along the walls. To one side was a worn wooden desk and on it, I saw an abacus, a ledger book, and an inkwell, along with the Foo dog statue.

"We must count." The second man had a heavy Chinese accent, and was dressed in traditional robes. He was an older gentleman, with gray hair and a carefully groomed beard and moustache. He barked an order in Chinese, and half a dozen dock workers sprang into action, taking up crowbars to open the nearest rows of wooden crates. Along one wall stood six men who looked European and were dressed like sailors.

"Don't you trust me, Mr. Tuan?" the American asked. "Fifty crates, as promised."

Mr. Tuan's expression did not reveal his thoughts. "Patience, Captain McCreedy. A good count benefits both of us."

The Chinese workers pried off the wooden lids and tossed them aside. They began to dig through the sawdust that filled the crates, revealing a cargo of what looked like Turkish rugs.

"Tell them to be careful with those," McCreedy said. "That opium's worth a lot."

I struggled to remind myself that I had not left the room at Gardenia Landing, that Teag and Anthony were hovering nearby, no doubt worried and ready to step in if things went too far. But the reality of the sights, sounds, and smells of the vision made it very difficult to believe that what I saw happened long ago.

McCreedy grew impatient as Tuan's workers moved from crate to crate. "Let's get this wrapped up," he said. "My ship is due to sail."

"Patience," Tuan repeated. "Verification weaves the fabric of trust."

*I didn't trust McCreedy, and I wondered if Tuan did, either. The captain looked antsy, and I wondered what he was hiding. Finally, all of the crates had been opened to reveal their cargo of rugs.*

*"See? Just as I promised," McCreedy said, a little too glibly.*

*Tuan nodded. "Yes. The number of crates and packages are correct. Now, we must make certain that what is in the packages is what we have agreed upon."*

*McCreedy made a show of checking the pocket watch that hung on a chain below his vest. "Look, my ship can't wait," he replied, and his voice had lost its congenial tone. "I'll be back in port in six months. If I've given you more than you ordered, we can settle up then."*

*McCreedy turned to go, gesturing to the sailors who waited along the wall. But before he could take more than a few steps, more Chinese workers emerged to block his path. He turned back to Tuan angrily.*

*"What's the problem?" he demanded. His expression was angry, but I thought I picked up a tone of fear in his voice beneath the bluster.*

*Tuan folded his hands in front of him, his face placid. "The problem, Captain, is that I have had reports that some of my customers have been unhappy with the quality of your opium."*

*"That's ridiculous! I only bring you the best of the crop, Turkey's finest," McCreedy huffed.*

*"Nonetheless, as a businessman, I must make sure," Tuan replied, unruffled. "Keeping my customers satisfied is in both our best interests, wouldn't you agree?"*

*McCreedy's eyes darted to the workers who stood between him and the door. I had the distinct impression that he had read a note of threat into Tuan's equanimity. "Of course," he said, but his tone sounded forced.*

An elderly Chinese woman dressed in a traditional silk robe came forward. A man followed her as she moved from crate to crate, indicating with a gesture which rug to unroll in each shipping container. Inside the rugs were bundles wrapped in brown paper and twine. The woman selected a bundle from the box, and the man cut a slit into the paper with a knife he pulled from his belt.

Underneath the paper, I glimpsed a brownish-black brick of what must be raw opium. The man scraped off a small amount of material from the brick and handed the knife to the woman, who touched it to her tongue and nodded.

"I told you, it's good stuff," McCreedy said, in a tone that had become edgy. His earlier deference was gone, and for the first time, I noticed the gun thrust through his belt.

"I'm sure it is, Captain," Tuan replied. His flat tone was neither assurance nor accusation, and I had a growing feeling that something was about to go very wrong.

Silently, the woman and the man with the knife moved from crate to crate, repeating the process. For the first few boxes, the woman nodded her approval. But when she reached the last ten crates, she scowled as she tasted the contraband. I didn't speak Chinese, but I had a fair idea of what was happening. The old woman passed the knife with its most recent scraping to her helper, who also touched it to his tongue, and then spat. A torrent of clipped, angry Chinese followed, to which Tuan responded in his maddeningly placid tone.

The two moved to the next box, and then the next, apparently disappointed with the cargo in each. By the time they had finished the last of the boxes, both the old woman and her knife man looked livid with rage.

"What did he say?" McCreedy demanded. "What's the problem?"

Tuan turned to face the captain. "The problem, Captain McCreedy, is that you have delivered only part of the opium I paid you for," he said, his voice dangerously level. His façade of geniality was gone, and I saw the flat, cold eyes of a killer.

"I don't know what you're talking about," McCreedy said, mustering outrage. Behind him, I saw some of his men try to slip out the door, only to be blocked by what seemed to be a growing number of Chinese workers.

"I believe you know quite well what I mean," Tuan replied. "My taster tells me the blocks in the last ten crates appear to be date paste. Perhaps a match in color, but not what I have paid you quite generously to deliver."

"It must have gotten switched in the port when we loaded," McCreedy said, growing red in the face. "I can't keep my eye on every box all the time."

"Perhaps not, but in this case, a little more caution would have been prudent."

As Tuan spoke, the workers had moved forward until they now formed a ring around McCreedy and his men, forcing the sailors away from the wall. McCreedy was well outnumbered.

"Maybe the boxes were mislabeled," McCreedy said, bargaining now that his escape was cut off.

"I highly doubt that."

"I can fix this. Let me go back to my ship. The right boxes –"

A cold smile touched the corners of Tuan's lips. "Yes,

Captain. I suspect that if you were to return to your ship, you would find ten crates of Turkish opium. But I do not think the boxes were mislabeled. I believe you intended to cheat me."

"No. Of course not. Why would you even think –"

"I'm afraid my mind is quite made up on the matter," Tuan replied. He gestured, and the workers who stood behind McCreedy's sailors lunged forward, then reared back, tightening garrotes around the men's throats and lifting them off their feet as the metal wires dug into their necks and their bodies bucked and kicked.

"To hell with you," McCreedy said, pulling his Colt Paterson revolver from his belt. He managed to get off one shot before Tuan's workers tackled him. The bullet caught the old lady full in the chest, knocking her backward onto the floor.

McCreedy was a fighter. He had four shots left, and dropped as many of Tuan's workers in their tracks. When the others closed in on him, he used the pistol grip as a bludgeon, snatching up a crowbar to keep his attackers at bay. The numbers were against him. Even he must have known how it would end. He backed up, hemmed in on all sides by Tuan's workers, until he was against the desk. Tuan slipped between two of the workers to approach McCreedy, and now the old man carried a long knife with a carved bone handle.

"I make it a point to be clear about shipping terms," Tuan said. "The contract clearly states 'no returns or exchanges'." He gave a predator's smile. "So sorry. Our business is at an end."

Two things happened at once. Tuan lunged forward with the knife, driving it between McCreedy's ribs, and McCreedy snatched the Foo dog sculpture from the *desk with his right hand and brought it down with a sickening thud on Tuan's skull.*

*A cry went up from the workers who surged forward. Somehow, they had all managed to draw knives, and as McCreedy sank to the floor, the workers swarmed over him, their knives rising and falling as he screamed. Blood covered the floor. It pooled beneath the old woman's body, and under Tuan's head where the heavy sculpture had laid open his scalp and crushed his skull. Rivers of blood were running from where McCreedy lay, and the Foo dog's base diverted it into eddies as the blood just kept flowing...*

A crash made my heart thud, and the world swirled around me as I lost my bearings. Another crash, and a spray of sharp splinters peppered my skin. The vision had lost its hold on me, but I was adrift, reeling. The third crash yanked me firmly back to the present.

As usual, I woke up screaming.

This time, I came back to myself on my own. I opened my eyes and saw Anthony standing over the broken remains of the Foo dog sculpture, a fireplace poker raised to strike again. Shards of the statue were scattered across the room, and fell from my skin and clothing.

Teag was throwing handfuls of salt, herbs, and charcoal onto the broken antique. Both men wore grim expressions, as if they had just gone to battle. If I hadn't had such a rotten headache, the sight of them rushing to my rescue would have warmed my heart.

"It's okay," I managed. "I think the dog's dead."

# Chapter Nine

"WHAT DID I miss while I was 'out'?" I asked. By now, I was sitting in one of the fireside chairs as Teag swept up the remains of the Foo dog and placed them in a garbage bag. I had already given them a complete recounting of the vision.

"It was quite a show," Anthony said, in a tone that made me wonder if he would ever consent to help out again. "When you first went into your trance, we just waited and watched. Teag got the things ready from his kit, and told me to grab the poker, just in case."

"And?"

"Then all hell broke loose. We saw ghostly images moving in the mirror. A shadow man appeared on the wall and started to make his way toward us. I could hear wailing coming from the front hall, and a woman's scream from the dining room. There were heavy footsteps coming up the hall, even though Rebecca had locked herself in her room. It was like all the ghosts that were linked to the haunted objects hit full strength at once," he said.

"So even with the salt we scattered, the energy in the

Foo dog could still summon up all that bad mojo," I mused.

"Apparently so," Teag replied.

"And that's when Teag and I decided it was time to do something."

"I threw salt at the shadow man, and it made him back off," Teag said. "Then I poured a salt circle around the three of us so that nothing could sneak up while we were dealing with the statue. Anthony and I worked together so that I poured the crushed herbs and charcoal over the sculpture to weaken it, and then Anthony started whacking away with the poker."

"I have to admit, that was rather satisfying in an afraid-for-your-life sort of way," Anthony admitted sheepishly.

"As soon as the statue broke, the other phenomena stopped," Teag added. "Poof. No wailing, no shadow men, no ghosts in the mirror. End of story."

"That was a little more excitement than I expected," I said, taking a deep breath. "If the Foo dog had been owned by a Chinese drug lord and was present for multiple murders, then it explains why it had acquired so much negative energy. But we still don't know what activated it, or how it got the power to bring the other pieces to life."

"We can work on that later," Teag said. "But first, we should go make sure Rebecca is all right. She's probably hiding under her bed."

I nodded, and mustered the energy to get to my feet. "I'll check," I said, and headed up the steps to the third floor. I was alert for any remnants of ghostly energy, but felt nothing.

I knocked at the door at the top of the steps. "Rebecca? Are you okay? It's safe to come out now."

For a moment, it was silent, and then I heard footsteps coming closer. "Cassidy? Is that you?"

"It's me," I reassured her. "And we think we found the problem and took care of it. Why don't you come out and we can tell you about it." *Because I don't think any of us is going to go to sleep right away,* I added silently.

The door opened slowly. Rebecca gave a sigh of relief when she saw me. "Oh thank goodness you're safe. The shadow man was back, and this time, I think he meant to hurt me. Greta drove him away, and then all of a sudden, they both winked out." She was pale and trembling.

"Come on," I said. "Let's go down to the kitchen. I can make hot chocolate. Then we can all tell ghost stories."


WHEN EVERYONE HAD a steaming cup of hot chocolate, Rebecca slouched in her chair. "Do you think it's over?" she asked.

"You've got a lot of history in this house," I said. "I can't promise that you'll never see another ghost or have an odd feeling from time to time. But yes, I think we took care of what was causing the trouble." *Except we don't know what turned the Foo dog on.*

Rebecca took another sip of her hot chocolate. "I almost forgot," she said. "Right before the shadow man came, I was looking out the window. I saw the man with the hat again, just outside the garden wall."

Teag and I exchanged glances. First shadow men, then our own personal stalker.

"Rebecca, do you know where the Foo dog statue came from?" I asked, deciding to change the subject.

Rebecca frowned, thinking. "I bought it at an estate sale from a lady who was getting rid of her mother's things. She had quite a lot for sale between what was in the house and what they found tucked away in a storage unit."

"And you don't recall anything odd or unsettling about the statue when you saw it at the sale?" Teag asked.

Rebecca shook her head. "I certainly wouldn't have bought it if it made me uncomfortable."

"Did it seem to call you to it?" Teag pressed. "Sometimes, objects 'select' a new owner by becoming irresistible."

Rebecca thought for a moment, then shook her head once more. "I liked the color and I thought it looked nicely done." She paused. "But come to think of it, the owner seemed rather willing to give me a very good deal. She's the one who drew my attention to it and offered it to me for a bargain price."

"Did she say why?" I asked.

"No," Rebecca said, "but she offered to throw the dog statue in with the rest of the things I was buying for an extra twenty-five dollars."

"Didn't she realize it was from the 1800s?" Teag asked. "It would have been worth hundreds."

"She said she really needed to clean the place out and to take it with her blessing."

"And how long after you brought the dog here did the problems start?" I asked.

Rebecca took a drink from her hot chocolate as she thought. "I had the dog statue for a week or so before Debra brought me the things from Trifles and Folly. And it was just after that when the problems started."

"So the Foo dog was already in the house before any of our items arrived," Teag said. "Interesting."

"If the dog statue had some kind of weird energy, it might have eventually activated the ghosts that were present in the house but couldn't manifest by themselves," I mused. "And as luck would have it, the items Debra brought all had histories of their own, but without the Foo dog's energy, no one could tell."

"Which goes back to the main question," Anthony recapped. "What do all the items have in common? And what juiced up the Foo dog to give it so much power?"

I looked back at Rebecca. "Would you happen to remember who the lady was who sold you the Foo dog?"

Rebecca sighed. "I can give you directions to the house, but it won't do you any good. The woman who lived there was moving to Georgia."

"I have a feeling there's something we're missing, a common thread," I said, finishing my drink. "But I'm too tired to figure out what it is." I yawned. "It's way past my bedtime. Let's see what we can come up with in the morning."


WHEN I WALKED to Trifles and Folly the next morning, I was afraid that I'd find the man with the withered face watching at the street corner or that Teag would tell me that the rest of our items had gone haywire. Instead, Teag gave a merry wave when I entered, and went back to his phone call, scribbling notes as he murmured encouraging sounds to the person on the other end of the line.

I put my purse away, powered up my laptop, gave the puppy spa a quick call to check on Baxter, and then checked phone messages. Two of the people I had phoned the previous day returned my call, and while the shop was quiet, I took the opportunity to ask questions. By the time I was finished, Teag had wrapped up his conversation, and was chatting with a customer who had wandered in.

I checked the rest of the messages, and found one from Sorren. *"Expect me at 9 p.m. A situation's come up that you and Teag need to know about. I'll explain when I get there. In the meantime, be careful."*

I stared at the phone after the message finished, pondering. Sorren, my silent partner, had bankrolled the founding of Trifles and Folly back in 1670. Sorren came and went on his own schedule, stopping in to alert us to a new danger, staying long enough to help face down some of the nastier haunts. He owned a home outside Charleston, one of many around the world. Sorren had the charm of a thief and the instincts of an assassin, and for more than three hundred and fifty years, he had proven an unwavering loyalty to my family.

Centuries had come and gone. Wars, hurricanes, and financial panics had left their mark. Trifles and Folly had occupied several buildings over its long life. Yet two things remained constant. One was our true mission, to find and neutralize dangerous magical objects that somehow found their way into unsuspecting hands. And the second was Sorren.

Much as I hated to admit it, I was stumped. We had shadow men, our stalker with the withered skin and broad hat, and haunted objects that seemed to be getting more dangerous every day. I really needed Sorren's advice, and after what we had faced at Gardenia Landing, I was ready for some Alliance back-up.

Until now, in the time since I had taken over Trifles and Folly after Uncle Evanston died, nothing we had done quite prepared me for the kind of threat we were facing. Oh, Sorren and Teag and I had handled some nasty haunted or magical objects, but we had been able to tackle them one at a time. Now, it felt as if every haunted object in Charleston was ganging up on us, with a shadowy someone behind it all. I really didn't like the sound of that.

I started to pace. My office is small, and I never really got around to cleaning out Uncle Evanston's books and knick-knacks. Manuscripts and leather-bound volumes filled the bookshelves that covered three of the small room's walls. I had left things where they were when I took over the office. We had been so busy since then, I had never even had the chance to go through the books and trinkets. I winced at how dusty the shelves were.

And then something caught my eye. It was a feeling, really, that directed my attention. I looked around the packed shelves and found myself in front of Dante's watch. The watch was one of Uncle Evan's favorite pieces, carefully kept under a glass dome. He was especially fond of pieces that had belonged to family members who had worked with Sorren in years gone by. I reached out to pick up the glass cover and touch the pocket watch. It was very old – from the late seventeen hundreds. Before I had given it thought, the watch pulled me into its story.

*Two young men were fighting for their lives. One of the men, skinny with straw-blond hair, struggled to keep a shadow man at bay, slashing and poking at it with a lit torch. The other, a broad shouldered young man with lank, dark hair, held a sword two-handed, staring down a creature that was straight out of nightmares. Somehow I knew that the pocket watch belonged to him, my ancestor Dante.*

*The creature they fought had slick, greenish skin, the color of the film on rotting meat. It towered over Dante. Elongated arms and legs ended in sharp talons, and the creature's bulbous head had a maw of wicked looking teeth, set row on row like a shark. Nothing about it was natural, but my mind supplied a word for the thing: demon.*

*The two young men were in the courtyard of a large home that looked abandoned, and between the dark-haired man and the demon was a large, brass-bound trunk, its lid thrown open. The red velvet lining was streaked with ichor and blood. From behind the demon, four dead men staggered forward. Their eyes were dull and their ashen corpses bore wounds no mortal could have survived, but still they came, bound to the demon's will.*

*From the look of them, the young men had been fighting hard for some time. Their clothing was torn and stained red. They were dirty and bruised, soaked with sweat. Now, they were fighting almost back to back, and from the grim looks on their faces, they expected to die here, soon.*

*A streak of white light, like a lightning bolt, crackled across the dimly lit space, striking the demon full in the chest. It roared, and fell back a step as its smooth skin blistered and sloughed off. The dead men kept moving forward, heedless to anything around them.*

*I saw a blur of motion, and the dead man on the right was lifted off the ground, its head ripped from its rotting body as if it were made of paper. Another* blur, and the second dead man was hoisted into the air and bent backwards, its spine making a popping noise as it snapped, and the still-twitching corpse fell to the ground. A boot came down hard on the skull, shattering it.

Whoever had sent the streak of light was approaching from behind me, but in this vision, I was rooted to the spot. The demon howled and gave a mighty leap, ignoring the two young men, soaring over my head to land behind me, facing down this new threat.

I saw a slender, blond man grab the third corpse by the shoulder, tearing the arm from the decaying body, and with a movement almost too quick to see, thrusting one fist through the dead man's rib cage as the other hand tore the skull from the neck. Sorren stood victorious, covered in dark blood, ready for the next attack.

Behind me, another blinding flash of light flared and the demon shrieked. My view shifted. I saw a woman with an ornate walking stick grasped in her hands. Its tip still flickered with light. She was dressed in ruined finery, as if she had just come from a ball. Her skirt was torn and her sleeves were ripped. Dark hair clouded around her face, come loose from an elaborate upsweep. A crystal necklace glowed with harnessed energy, and I knew this woman was a wizard of considerable power.

Everything seemed to happen at once. Sorren motioned for the dark-haired man to throw him his sword, catching it like an expert. The vampire then lunged toward the demon, striking it through the spine with the sword as the woman sent another searing wave of light. The dark-haired man raised his hands. For a few seconds, nothing seemed to happen, as the woman struggled to keep up the barrage of light and Sorren *kept stabbing the demon with his sword.*

*From a cistern in the courtyard, a tide of water rose, then split into thick tendrils. The tendrils snaked toward the demon, moving rapidly. The woman was chanting now, words I did not understand. Sorren thrust his sword one more time and leapt free as the water tendrils smashed into the shrieking creature. Its smooth skin had been burned away by the woman's magic, and it was bleeding from dozens of gashes where Sorren had done damage with his sword.*

*Scorched by fire, bound by water, the demon screamed its fury. As the woman's chant grew more insistent, the demon began to tremble, its remaining skin splitting and peeling away, until the creature suddenly exploded into a rain of gobbets that sizzled against the water and burned where they hit exposed flesh.*

*Abruptly, the vision ended, and I collapsed against the bookshelf, still clutching the watch in my hands.*

I had no idea how long my vision had lasted. Only minutes, probably, though I felt as if it had gone on forever. My hands were shaking as I replaced the pocket watch on the shelf. I hugged myself, trying to get warm.

I wasn't sure who the woman was, but Sorren had told me stories about Dante and his friend Coltt, his partners from long ago. I had never seen Sorren fight like that, and the utter ruthlessness in his eyes gave me pause, though I reminded myself he had saved his human comrades.

But now I had a name for the power behind the corrupted objects and the shadow men. I recognized the feel of the magic as soon as I saw the hideous shape of the creature in the vision. The same feel and taste of the magic I had from the Foo dog. And while the evil behind the dangerous magic we faced had not yet shown its face, I knew what to call it.

"Holy hell," I muttered. "We've got a demon on our hands."

# Chapter Ten

WHEN EVENING CAME, I closed the shop, and Teag and I went down the street to Jocko's Pizzeria, run by Giacomo Rossi, 'Jack' to his friends.

"Cassidy! Teag! Long time no see!" Jack Rossi stood behind the counter. He wore an apron that was smudged with flour and olive oil. There was even a dusting in his dark black hair.

"Hi Jack!" I replied. As always, Jocko's smelled of fresh tomatoes, basil, and cheese, along with the scent of a wood fire and baking crusts. It was a little bit of Italy near the heart of Charleston, and one of my favorite places for a quick bite to eat.

"You want the usual?" Jack asked, spinning a crust as he talked. Jack was in his late forties, with a touch of gray in his temples that couldn't be blamed on flour.

"Sure," I replied, and my stomach growled just thinking about it. Teag and I probably stopped in to Jocko's at least once a week, sometimes more. I breathed deeply, relaxing into my chair and allowing the familiar, comforting smells to ease away the tension of the day.

The walls of the restaurant featured a hand-painted

mural in vibrant colors, telling the story of the Rossi family's history and Jack's journey from New York to Charleston. Jack's portion of the mural began with the World Trade Center as the towers had once stood, tall and proud. Jack had been a stock trader in the North Tower on September 11, 2001. He had been one of the lucky ones, and within a year he had resigned from the brokerage business, moved to Charleston and opened up Jocko's, a move that left him more time to spend with family.

Jack brought out a pale ale for Teag and a glass of red wine for me. It was Wednesday evening, and the restaurant was quieter than usual. "How's the shop?" Jack asked, returning with plates and silverware.

"Doing well," I answered. "Thanks for asking."

"Hey Jack," Teag said. "Do you have any of your world-famous antipasto tonight?"

Jack shook his head. "Sorry. I didn't get my shipment this week. So no artisan-cured salami and none of the specialty marinated Kalamata olives you love."

"Damn," Teag replied, brushing his lank hair out of his eyes. "What happened? Did New Yorkers suddenly get peckish?"

Jack dusted off his hands. "Unfortunately not. Police found a dead guy behind the specialty food warehouse, and they closed down the whole place until they figure out what happened."

I sipped my wine. "Was it a robbery?"

Jack shrugged. "Dunno. My guy at the warehouse says the police have been cagy about the details. Made him wonder if it might be gang-related or something like that." He shook his head. "I heard whoever did it made a real mess of things."

"Was the dead man someone who worked at the warehouse?" Teag asked.

Jack shook his head. "No idea. The warehouse is over by the abandoned Navy yard. The whole area is a little down on its luck, gets a lot of vagrants. "

Jack brought the pizza, and stood by like a proud papa as Teag and I praised his work. He went back to the kitchen while Teag and I dug into our meal.

I checked my phone for messages. There were none, but I glanced at the time. "Oops! We'd better get back to the shop."

"Inventory?" Jack asked, bringing a small box for leftovers.

"Out of town supplier," I replied. Sorren kept a low profile in Charleston out of necessity. It wouldn't do for people to notice that he never seemed to age. His involvement with the store was something known to only a few trusted associates.

"Well, send your supplier this way and I'll make sure he gets the royal treatment," Jack promised. "Anything for a friend of yours."

"He usually eats before he comes by the shop, but I'll let him know you offered," I said. That was true. Sorren always made sure he had fed before visiting Trifles and Folly. How he fed, I wasn't sure I wanted to know.

We got back to the store just as I heard the bells of St. Michael's church toll nine times. Before the echo of the ninth ring had faded, a voice startled me.

"Nice to see you again, Cassidy."

Even though I was expecting him, I jumped. "I swear I locked all the doors," I said, one hand over my thudding heart.

Sorren grinned. "You did. And you've invited me

129

inside in the past. Don't forget, I was once the best jewel thief in all of Belgium, and I do have a key."

Sorren looked to be in his twenties, but I knew for a fact he was turned in the late 1400s. His hair was an unremarkable shade of blond, with features that were pleasant enough without being noteworthy; something Sorren told me had been a good thing back in his days as a master thief. But his blue-gray eyes always captured my attention, eyes the color of the sea before a storm. And while most mortals would do well to avoid making eye contact with a vampire for risk of being compelled to do their will, apparently I had the immunity to compulsion that seemed to run in my family.

"Nice to see you, too," I said, catching my breath. I double checked the lock on the door then led the way to the back room. Teag emerged from the stock room with a wave.

"I got your message," I said, sitting down at the table. "And your warning. So I'm curious about your news, because, boy oh boy, do we have news for you."

Tonight, Sorren was dressed in khaki slacks, a casual collared shirt and Sperrys without socks. Nothing about his appearance would have drawn a second glance from anyone who met him on the street. A slight flush to his skin told me that he had fed before visiting.

On some visits, when there were no pressing problems, we had gotten Sorren to talk about the centuries he had survived. Talking to someone who had personally experienced most of the last six hundred years was a dream come true for history geeks. But with everything that was going on, I was sadly certain that tales of the old days would have to wait for another time.

"Something is very wrong," Sorren said. "There have

been some odd spikes in supernatural activity around the Charleston area. The last time we saw these kind of energy fluctuations –"

"It was a demon," I finished for him. He looked at me, surprised.

"Yes," he replied. "It was."

Sorren had a network of informants that would put government or law enforcement intelligence to shame. Although his visits to Charleston were sporadic, he always arrived knowing more about what was going on in the dark corners of the city than we did.

"Could those surges – and a demon – cause slightly haunted objects to suddenly turn malicious, and set nasty things wandering… say, shadow creatures?" I asked.

Sorren looked worried. "Yes to both. I think you'd better tell me your news."

We took turns filling Sorren in, first on the unfortunate incident at the Academy Theater, and then on the eventful night at Gardenia Landing.

"We traced the history of the items as best as we could," I said. "The pieces all have some tragedy associated with them, but none of the former owners will admit to knowing that the items were haunted or even unsettling." I turned my palms up in a gesture of resignation. "We haven't found the common thread."

Sorren had listened intently. Now, he began to pace. "My contacts believe the spikes in supernatural energy near Charleston have something to do with a series of murders. That would also be consistent with demonic activity. The question is, how did the demon get loose, and what does the person who summoned it want?"

I thought about the death near the warehouse that Jack had mentioned, and the ring that had arrived in the box. Teag brought the box out to show Sorren, and he handled the ring gingerly.

"I think this was sent as a warning," Sorren said. "Someone's aware of your gift, Cassidy, and whoever it is, is trying to make sure you don't get involved."

I met his gaze. "Do you have any idea who's behind this?"

Sorren hesitated. "Maybe. But if I'm right, he's someone who should be dead."

I raised an eyebrow. "Death isn't permanent for everyone."

He nodded. "For some more than others. And in this case, I was certain that we had been able to destroy him."

"Destroy who?" Teag asked.

"He goes by the name of Corban Moran," Sorren replied. "You might think of him as an arms dealer, only he deals in dangerous magical objects, not guns and bombs. He's rogue, so he's not really part of any group, but more often than not, his ventures align with whatever the Family is up to."

The Alliance tried to get malicious supernatural objects off the market. The Family did their best to get their hands on dark magic artifacts and use them to further their own purposes. Both groups recruited immortals and mortals in a worldwide network that was off the grid of conventional security agencies. It was like a paranormal arms race, with the world up for grabs.

Teag had grabbed his laptop, and he was already delving deep into the Darke Web to see what he could find.

"You thought Moran was dead," I said. "Why?"

Sorren leaned back in his chair. "Because I killed him, or at least I thought I did."

He ran a hand back through his hair. "It's probably easier to show you than to tell you," he said, and withdrew an envelope from his pocket. Inside was a photograph of a man and a woman.

The man was tall and thin, with a build that could well be the man I'd glimpsed following us. If so, then time had not been kind to him. The picture looked to be about ten years old, but the man's face was very different from the wrinkled, withered skin of our stalker. Moran had an intelligent look to him, though his features were not striking, except for the utter coldness of his dark eyes. I glanced at the woman who stood next to him. I didn't think I'd want to meet her. She had the same cold look to her as Moran, but there was something in her expression that made me think she enjoyed her work a little too much.

From the same envelope, Sorren withdrew a charred button that looked like it came from a man's coat. "Take it," he said.

Drawing a deep breath to steady myself, I let Sorren drop the button into my outstretched hand. The vision took hold immediately.

*I was in the mechanical room of an old building, and from the signs in English and French, my bet was somewhere in Canada. Large boilers, dark with age, filled the space amid brick pillars and twisting pipes. The whole place stank of dark magic, and the air crackled with power. I spotted Sorren in the dim light. He was dressed in a dark sweater and jeans, blending into the darkness.*

*"The building is warded. You can't get out," Sorren shouted into the shadows.*

*"You're assuming I need to leave the way I came in." Corban Moran stepped out from behind one of*

the brick pillars. In his right hand was a box made of human bones, decorated with yellowed teeth. In his left hand was a wizard's staff of twisted and gnarled willow.

Sorren lunged for him, but Moran was faster. He leveled his staff at Sorren and an invisible force sent the vampire sprawling. In the same instant, Moran spoke a word of power and fire erupted from the box in his right hand, splintering the bone box and shooting up toward the old wooden beams in the ceiling.

Sorren climbed to his feet, and Moran's staff blasted one of the boilers, sending scalding water flying and shaking the foundations of the building. Sorren rushed at him, and two more boilers exploded. The beams in the ceiling were beginning to catch fire and the blasts had jarred the brick columns enough that some had begun to collapse.

Moran was chanting a guttural litany, and as Sorren ran at him once more, the flames surrounded Moran without burning him. As I watched, a figure appeared in the flames, and while it was not exactly like the monster I had glimpsed in the vision with the pocket watch, I had no doubt that this creature was some kind of demon.

Sorren threw an object that looked like a crystal orb into the heart of the fire. There was a blinding flare of light and a burst of energy from within the flames, sending out a halo of fire and splintered glass. Inside the column of fire, Moran began to writhe.

With a deafening, thunderous roar, Moran disappeared and the ceiling came crashing down.

"Moran can summon demons," I said, coming back to myself.

Sorren nodded. "He's a nephilmancer. He can call on outcast spirits, like demons. But it takes a great deal of power, and demons always want something in exchange."

"You were in that boiler room when the roof collapsed," I said, meeting Sorren's gaze.

He nodded. "Yes. It's difficult to kill a vampire, but not impossible. That came closer than I would have liked." He paused. "Recovery was… unpleasant."

"And for Moran?"

"The glass ball I threw into the demon fire was spelled," Sorren replied. "It should have drained Moran of his life and magic, leaving him a withered, dead husk."

"But it didn't?"

"Apparently not. Although from what you've reported, the incident took its toll." He shook his head. "If Moran's here, then there's something he wants very badly. But what is it, and why does he want it?"

"What happened to the woman in the picture?" I asked.

Sorren looked away. "She was a powerful witch. For a while, she was Moran's partner in crime. Then he killed her. Sacrificed her, to gain the power of the demon he called."

Teag looked up. "That's all very interesting, but I think I've got something."

We looked over to see him grinning in triumph. "You never know what you're going to find on the Darke Web," he said. "It's a wretched hive of scum and villainy."

I wrinkled my nose at the *Star Wars* quote. "Get on with it."

"There's always the usual: traders in black magic services, banned dark magic potions, poisoners for hire," he said. "Most of the sites have all the usual onion routing plus ensorcelled encryption." He cracked his knuckles. "Makes it fun to hack."

"And?" I prodded.

"Someone's been looking for a cryptomancer," Teag said. "They want to hire someone who's magically gifted with codes and secret writing."

"Is that like being a Weaver?"

Teag shrugged. "Related, but not the same. I can weave data bits together to find information. Cryptomancers excel at hiding information, or breaking into hidden data. We probably all fall under arithmancy, which is magical math."

"What makes you think the posting is related to our problem?" Sorren asked.

Teag smirked. "I hacked the encryption on some of the Darke Web exit nodes, just enough to set a flag if any of the traffic can be linked to Charleston."

"I thought the Darke Web masked the origin of users," I said.

"It does. I can't get user information, but I can tease out a little location info if the person posting isn't careful – or savvy. The cryptomancer posting definitely came from the Charleston area, and it's fresh – just two weeks old."

"Can you tell if whoever did the posting found someone?" Sorren asked.

Teag shrugged. "I would guess so. The posting is closed to new submissions and the contact information has been scrubbed."

I really didn't know what to say to that, so I changed the subject. "Did you find anything out about the murders?"

"I can ask Anthony to find out what his friends in the police department discovered for the official scoop,"

Teag said. "He's got pretty good connections." He grinned. "And I can hack into the police database." We waited while he tapped a few instructions into his computer.

"I think our boys in blue have been covering up," Teag said quietly. "This doesn't look good." He bit his lip. "There've been at least five murders in the past year that are unsolved. All homeless men, all found ripped to shreds." He grimaced.

"They started off looking for a wild animal, and finally decided they have a serial killer," he said, shaking his head. "But from the autopsy reports, I'd say it's magic-related. Skin flayed and stripped, bones shattered from the inside out, fingers and toes missing." He let out a long breath. "There's a very sick bastard running around out there."

"That could be Moran," Sorren said.

"The police withheld news of two deaths from the public," Teag said, scanning down his illicit search results, "probably trying to avoid a panic." He paused.

"Now that's interesting." He looked up at me. "An entire salvage team went missing six months ago off the South Carolina coast."

I inched my chair back to see what he was reading. A picture of five smiling young men on a boat took up much of the screen. "'The five-member crew of the *Privateer* were reported missing and presumed lost at sea when they failed to return from a salvage mission'," he read. "'The wreck was said to be somewhere between Charleston and Bermuda, and the team was keeping details a secret, but they had told friends they were searching for a pirate ship that sank with a treasure from Barbados.'"

"Barbados," I said. "Rebecca said that the man who built Gardenia Landing was lost at sea under very mysterious circumstances, right after he had returned from Barbados, bringing with him some salvaged pirate treasure."

"Barbados is home to quite a lot of dark magic," Sorren said quietly. "It might interest someone who can call to demons."

"When did the first unsolved murders begin?" I asked.

Teag checked his computer. "Six months ago."

"Any pattern to where the bodies were found?" Sorren asked.

Teag shook his head. "All over the city."

"See what you can find out about the dive team," Sorren directed. "I have a feeling they're connected somehow." He was silent for a moment. "I'm hoping it's not what I think it is. Let me see what our contacts in the Alliance can turn up. I'll also ask if we have anyone who has abilities or powers for dealing with demons, but there's no guarantee they can get here in time." He shrugged. "We will have to make sure we are prepared... either way."

He leveled a look at Teag and me. "This mysterious man watching you is not to be discounted," he said. "And if it is Moran, he's throwing down a gauntlet for me by threatening you." The same ruthlessness I had seen in the vision flashed in Sorren's eyes. "I don't take such a challenge lightly."

He paused. "I don't like this," Sorren said. "Either there's someone with powerful – and dark – magic playing a dangerous game, or something is upsetting natural limits on supernatural power – or both. It's just the kind of thing Moran would be hip deep in. It's a bad business."

"What can we do?" I asked.

Sorren gave me a stern look. "Until I know more about this, you're to do nothing except follow up on the phone calls you've made, and wait for me to gather more information. Whatever's going on is dangerous, and I have no desire to see either of you get hurt."

"How can we make sure that the pieces we're selling don't suddenly go wacko?" Teag asked. "I mean, the items Debra bought for Gardenia Landing were perfectly ordinary when we sold them. What's to stop whatever-it-is from doing that to other pieces?"

It was a good point, and it made me cringe to think about it. If we had to stop selling items until the problem was resolved, it wouldn't be good for the bottom line.

Sorren considered the question for a moment. "The spikes in supernatural energy are fairly recent," he said. "As far as we can tell, they began about six months ago. And from what Teag's found, so did the deaths."

"But we haven't had pieces we've sold go crazy for six months," I countered. "In fact, we've only begun hearing about problems in the past few days."

Sorren nodded. "Bear with me. If something was altering the energy six months ago, perhaps the changes affected people near the area first, then built up its effect in inanimate objects," he mused. "It's only a theory – we'll need to do some investigating – but for now, it's my best guess."

"How does that affect our inventory?" I asked. "I'm guessing that we need to quarantine all our sparklers until this is over, and expect our spookies to be more disruptive – maybe even dangerous. But what about pieces that don't seem to have any supernatural energy at all?"

"I don't have a good answer for you yet," Sorren said. "But I will. I just need to poke around a little more." He grinned, exposing the tips of his long eye teeth. "And if Moran's behind everything that's happened, I assure you, we'll know."

"Where do we start?" I asked.

"I'm waiting to hear from several of my contacts," Sorren replied. "That may shed some light on things." He looked concerned, and that gave me pause.

*What worries a vampire?*

"You know I can't compel you to stay safely on the sidelines until we know what we're up against," Sorren said, looking at me with an expression that mingled fondness and mild exasperation. "But this is dangerous business. Please, don't go off on your own investigating until we have a better sense of the problem."

It was odd having someone who looked my own age show fatherly concern for my welfare, but I nodded. "I promise not to go poking around abandoned buildings without you, if that's what you're fishing for," I replied with a grin. "But there shouldn't be any harm in Teag and me putting out feelers for information to our networks, or doing some Internet sleuthing."

"How long before you hear back from your people?" Teag asked.

"Soon, I hope," Sorren said. "One problem with immortality is that it discourages urgency. There always seems to be enough time. I shall, however, push for answers with a mortal's definition of 'quick'."

"In the meantime, we'll pull the sparklers out of the front of the shop and keep looking for that common thread," I said, resigned. "Sooner or later, we'll get a break."

Sorren glanced over to Teag. "Getting used to your magic?" he asked.

Teag sighed. "Trying to. It's all a bit much to take in. I'm taking it slow. Just the basic knots and some weaving for now – nothing dangerous, I promise."

Teag had discovered his own latent magic fairly recently. But his gift went beyond yarn and fabric. Teag's magic included 'data weaving', which accounted for his amazing research skills. Teag was still trying to wrap his head around both parts of his gift.

"I need to get the two of you home," Sorren said.

"Anthony's probably waiting outside," Teag said. "He insisted on coming around to drive me home." That was unusual. Teag normally enjoyed biking or walking to work, even after dark, and the constant foot traffic in the Historic District made such trips safe even late in the evening. He glanced at me. "We can drop you off at Gardenia Landing and then pick you up in the morning."

"If you wouldn't mind, I'd like to escort Cassidy back to the inn," Sorren said. "I may be able to glean some information just from walking the grounds." He smiled, showing just the tips of his long eye teeth. "I promise to be discreet."

I had the feeling that, at least for tonight, Sorren's investigation might involve an all-night vigil to assure my safety. Many people might not feel protected by a vampire on watch, but I felt some of the tension ease from my shoulders.

"Thanks," I said. "Maybe you'll be able to figure out what caused the damage to the garden. My money is on a ghost from the Harrison family, but since getting rid of the Foo dog seemed to get rid of the haunting, we never made it out there."

"Tomorrow, expect a visit from Lucinda, a Voudon friend of mine," Sorren said. "She'll refresh the wardings on the office and on the safe room in the basement, and I'll also have her stop by and renew the wardings on your houses."

"You had wardings put on our houses?" Teag asked. A smile spread across his features. "Cool!"

Sorren chuckled. "Lucinda is quite good at the Craft," he said. "Her protections will repel most negative energy, as well as ill intent."

"Most?" I asked. "What doesn't it cover?"

Sorren's smile slipped away. "The unknown," he said. "That's always the most dangerous part."

# Chapter Eleven

FORTUNATELY, THE NIGHT was quiet and restful and the next day, I resolved to leave the problem of the haunted objects behind and keep the day as normal as possible. Sorren had not yet contacted me with news, and I took that as an indication that he was exploring information from his own channels. I really needed a break, and decided to give myself an easy day.

I went to the martial arts studio in the morning and worked up a good sweat. Uncle Evan had surprised me ten years ago with an offer to pay for my classes, and I enthusiastically took him up on it. Now, I knew why. Being able to defend myself had come in handy with some of our prior cases, and I was afraid it might be useful once again. I wasn't as good as Teag – he'd won mixed martial arts championships in Brazilian and Filipino-style fighting – but I could hold my own. It was a great way to work out some of my frustrations, and I left the training hall feeling pretty chipper.

I poured myself a cup of coffee, and spent the morning on chores that had nothing to do with haunted objects. I caught up on doing the bookwork, and then

I rearranged the front window display, something that always feels more like play than work. Then to cap it off, I added some new really nice pieces to the Trifles and Folly web site.

By lunchtime I was feeling pretty good about things, so I didn't protest when Teag offered to watch the store while I grabbed lunch and ran a few errands. It was a beautiful day, and even though it was hot and muggy, the air seemed to carry the scent of flowers wherever I went. For a while, I managed to put strange ghosts, unsolved murders and old tragedies completely out of my mind as I went for a walk down King Street.

Valerie passed me with a carriage load of tourists. I waved to her and all of her passengers waved back. A trip to the post office went off without a hitch. I made a quick call to the work crew about my floor as I walked, and was thrilled to discover that despite the muggy weather, the floors were done and almost dry, so Baxter and I should be able to move home the next day. We might have to keep the windows open to deal with the smell, but at least we'd be home.

That last news gave my mood a huge boost, and I decided to celebrate with a walk through the Charleston City Market. It's a top tourist attraction in Charleston, filled with lovely crafts and art, as well as fresh produce and baked goods, and I feel lucky to have it within easy walking distance. It's a wonderful place to people watch. I found myself smiling as I mingled with the locals and tourists, making my way through the rows of crowded stalls. Fresh vegetables tempted me on one side, while hand-made soaps and lotions seduced from the other. The smell of sweetgrass from the basket weavers at the entrance mingled with the scent of freshly baked cookies.

"How are things going, Niella?" I asked one of the women with the sweetgrass baskets.

Niella and her mother were a fixture at the market, setting up their spot by the outside of the lower doorway in the shade every morning just after dawn for nearly twenty years. Watching their fingers fly as they twisted and wove the narrow strands of grass made it look easy, but I knew it was a craft passed down from parent to child for generations within the Gullah people, and that Niella and her mom were two of the best.

Niella gave an expressive shrug. "Today won't be scorching hot, so there should be more tourists. That makes me happy." Her fingers never stopped moving, and I knew it took decades of practice to be able to weave the complicated designs without looking.

I knew what she meant about tourists making her happy. More tourists equaled more income for most of Charleston. If the weather became stifling hot, even by Charleston standards, people stayed in air conditioned hotels or went to tour historic homes and plantations instead of wandering the Market and the downtown streets.

"You get your floors done yet?" Niella's mother asked. I had to think for a moment, because I didn't remember telling Niella or her mom about the refinishing. Then again, Mrs. Teller was a root woman with a way of knowing things. I was pleased that something as trivial as my floors popped up on her sixth sense radar.

"They'll be done tomorrow. Thanks for asking," I said. "I've had to put Baxter in a dog spa and I miss him." In the evenings, I often brought Baxter for a walk along the outside stalls of the Market, and he was a favorite of both Niella and her mother.

Mrs. Teller nodded. "Good. Good you're not staying long. Nice place for other people, not so nice for you." She was looking down at her basket, so she didn't see me startle. "But last night, you were safe. Very safe." Her voice was thick as roux and sweet as cane syrup, heavy with the song-like Gullah accent.

Sorren had made sure that I was safe, but how Mrs. Teller knew, I wasn't going to ask.

"Yes, I slept well," I stammered.

Mrs. Teller nodded. "Good."

Niella rolled her eyes. "Mama's telling stories out of school again, isn't she?" she chided, but her voice was fond.

Mrs. Teller gave her daughter a dismissive look. "When the Good Lord and the Old Ones speak to me, I gotta say something," she said, as her fingers moved at lightning speed.

"Thank you," I said. I'd had enough dealings with Mrs. Teller that I trusted her instincts. And if she suspected what kind of business I really ran and who my 'night watchman' really was, it didn't seem to run afoul for her by either the Old Ones or the Good Lord, for which I was grateful.

"I'm playing hooky," I said with a conspiratorial grin. "But I'd better make my rounds and get back to the shop before Teag figures out I'm truant."

Niella laughed. "I hear you, girlfriend. Get going. Time's a wastin'." I waved good-bye and headed into the market.

Over the time since I'd moved back to Charleston, I'd been such a regular at the Market that I counted many of the vendors as friends. That meant that a visit wasn't just about shopping, it was a time to catch up on news, gossip and the latest jokes. It made for a very pleasant outing.

I lingered for a moment at a stall selling silver jewelry, and stopped to finger a nice pashmina shawl in another booth. Ruth, one of the produce vendors, recognized me as a regular customer and let me know what she had brought fresh today. A quick glance at my watch told me I needed to pick up the pace, and I scouted the rest of the market in record time, managing not to get snarled in other conversations. I had one more stop before I headed back to the shop, and I didn't want anything to get in the way of a fresh latte at Honeysuckle Café.

"See you soon!" I called to Niella and her mother as I walked out of the market.

I walked down the street and turned the corner, looking forward to my coffee. I was about halfway down the block before I realized that the alley was unusually quiet for this time of day. I caught a glimpse of a reflection in an office building window and spun on my heel. Coming up fast behind me was the man with the withered face. *Corban Moran?*

"Stop following me!" My voice had more bravado than I felt. It was daylight, but there was no one around, no one to interfere.

His broad-brimmed hat shaded most of his features, but even at a distance, my magic was screaming warnings, telling me to run. I glanced around. This side street was flanked by office buildings whose front doors faced the main thoroughfare. Short of running through a plate glass window, there was no doorway to duck into.

I crossed the street, putting a patch of torn up sidewalk between us, using the barricades and rocky patch of dirt as a buffer zone. "Who are you?" I asked. "What do you want?"

He didn't answer me, but the cold smile told me more than I wanted to know. I eyed the distance to the next main street. I might be able to make it if I ran, but that depended on whether my pursuer was fast, or not quite human. One hand went to the agate necklace, but I didn't know whether the man with the withered skin was supernatural. Creepy as hell, yes.

Hat Man was closing fast. I decided to swallow my pride and run. He hurdled the sidewalk barrier, ran through the mud and caught up to me in the shadow of a tall office building, grabbing me by the arm. I swung around, ready with an arm block and a low kick, but he didn't flinch. I shoved him, hard with the flat of my right hand, getting a staggering mental image from the touch.

"Stay out of my business," he warned.

"Let go of me!" I was still reeling from the brief vision I'd gotten from touching his clothing, but I was scared and angry enough to fight. My training should have enabled me to take down someone bigger and stronger than I am, and that told me something I didn't want to know. Moran wasn't entirely mortal.

"What do you think you're doing?" Mrs. Teller shouted from behind us. She and Niella stood with hands on hips in the middle of the side street. Niella was holding up a small flannel pouch, something I recognized as a mojo bag, a conjure amulet.

But my attention was on Mrs. Teller. A glow surrounded her entire form, faint at first, but growing brighter. "You let go of her right now!" Mrs. Teller commanded.

I took the momentary distraction to land a sharp kick between Moran's legs and wrench free. He fell back several steps. Even immortals are tender in the stones, it seems. I ran toward Niella and Mrs. Teller, although I wasn't sure what magic Hat Man could muster or whether anything Mrs. Teller could do would be enough to keep all of us from getting killed, especially if Moran had anything to do with those flayed bodies showing up all over town.

Mrs. Teller's glow was as bright as if she had a spotlight behind her. She gathered some of the light in the palm of her hand and hurled it down the shadowed alley at Moran, who vanished in the blink of an eye.

"Thank you," I said, still jumbled from the vision and from seeing Mrs. Teller in a whole new way.

"Humph," Mrs. Teller said, lifting her chin. "The nerve of some people. Niella and I saw him hanging around the marketplace, and when he followed you, I knew he was no good."

"I wanted to call the police," Niella said dryly.

Mrs. Teller shook her head. "Police ain't going to do anything about his kind," she said, and I knew immediately what she meant. *His kind. Magic.*

I had more questions, but Mrs. Teller was already heading for the place where the sidewalk was missing. The barricades had gotten knocked over, and in the middle of the red clay dirt was a clear impression of a man's boot. *Not much to tell the police there, other than his shoe size.*

I was surprised when Mrs. Teller squatted down by the patch of dirt and dug in a woven cloth bag she wore on a strap across her body. She took out a small pouch and sprinkled some gray, odd-smelling dust into the shoe print.

"What's that?" I asked, bending down to see.

"Kufwa dust," she said without looking up.

"Folks around here call it 'goofer' dust," Niella replied. I had heard of that. Part of a root worker's tools, especially if that practitioner also ventured into what some called 'conjure' or 'hoodoo.'

Mrs. Teller took a knife out of her pocket and a small glass bottle from her bag. She mixed the dust into the shoe print, then scraped some of the dirt into the glass bottle and put a stopper in it.

"Here," she said as she rose and handed me the vial. "Up to you what you do next. Keep it in the bottle, and that man'll get mighty sick. Bury in a graveyard, he'll die. Throw that bottle into a crossroads, and he'll leave town." She gave me a pointed look. "He's bad news."

I closed my hand around the bottle. "Thank you," I said, looking from Mrs. Teller to Niella. "Thank you very much."

I was surprised when Mrs. Teller suddenly grabbed my hand. "Bad things comin'," she said, meeting my gaze earnestly. "Watch yourself. Something's riled the dead, and there'll be problems 'til they're quiet. Even your shadow friend, he best take care."

In all the time I had known Niella and her mother, Mrs. Teller had never spoken at such length to me, and certainly not about danger and ghosts. Niella must have misinterpreted my moment of stunned silence, because she gave her mother a look of warning. "Now Mama, you're going to scare Cassidy," she said.

I gave Mrs. Teller's hand a light squeeze. "No, really, it's okay. Thank you. I'll be careful."

Mrs. Teller gave a curt nod without looking up. "Best you take care. Someone's gonna die again real soon."

I got to Honeysuckle Café wishing I dared order an

Irish coffee instead of a latte. A wee bit of whiskey would probably help my nerves, and by now, I was wide awake. With a sigh, I decided to be a good girl and stuck with the espresso double shot. I treated myself to an extra vanilla flavoring, just because.

Rick was the barista on call today, working at the bar for Trina, who owned the café. In a world of twenty-something hipster baristas, Rick was a pleasant anomaly. He was probably in his forties, and carried himself like a man who has seen a lot of living. He had deep brown eyes and a long, hound-like face which seemed to elicit instant trust from his customers. He played it up by favoring vintage jackets, old-time casual wear and fedoras, and he'd hung a sign that proclaimed 'Rick's Place' over the coffee bar, making the nod to *Casablanca* complete.

"Hi Rick," I said. "Got the exit papers?" It was our little joke, homage to our favorite Bogart movie.

"No, but I'm about to get carpal tunnel from pulling espressos if this keeps up. This is the quietest it's been all morning."

I looked around. While the Charleston City Market had been emptier than usual, I could tell from the detritus of cups, napkins and stir sticks that Trina and the bus boy were clearing that the café had been slammed. "Get hit by a tourist bus?"

He shook his head. "Nope. Cops."

Mrs. Teller's warning echoed in my mind. "Traffic problems?" I hoped for the best, but I had the sinking feeling that my optimism was misplaced.

Rick shook his head, expertly manipulating the huge brass espresso machine like an artist. "No such luck. They found another dead guy out by the old Navy yard."

Crap. My good mood plummeted. "Any juicy gossip?"

Rick was the kind of guy who should have been slinging booze in one of the dark-paneled cigar bars that poured expensive scotch and sold the finest smokes north of Havana. I had the impression that Rick had done a stint like that and moved on. Like his namesake, I suspected Rick had lived many lives.

He shrugged. "You know the boys in blue. They talk a lot when they think it's just among themselves." I took his meaning right away. Most people forgot that waiters, bartenders, and baristas weren't just part of the scenery.

"And?" I figured Rick had his secrets. We all do. And I figured he kept secrets for others. But this was likely to make the evening news, so it wasn't exactly like hacking into the Pentagon. I left that to Teag.

Rick glanced around the café, checking to make sure we didn't have an audience. "They're worried," he said quietly. "All the murders have been men, all homeless or vagrants, and they don't seem to have a break in the case yet." He paused. "Bad for business if it gets out. Tourists don't like vacationing where there are unsolved crimes."

I nodded. Tourists are skittish. All it took was a rumor of a flu outbreak or a rash of muggings and people would cancel reservations or decide to take their daytrips elsewhere. And both alternatives were a bottom-line hit for merchants who had nothing to do with the problem and no way to fix it.

"Anything else?"

Rick frowned. "Well, there are several theories floating around. I'm not sure which is worse. Some of the cops think it might be a serial killer. The others think it could be some weird cult thing, or maybe black magic."

*Uh-oh.* "What makes them think that?" I asked, hoping I sounded curious but not too interested.

Rick's gaze darted around the room once more. "The cops all seemed to know the same stuff, so they didn't spell it out, but I got the feeling that all the bodies were 'done to' pretty bad, cut up, that sort of thing."

He gave an expressive shrug. "One cop said something about 'the way they looked' and the others all nodded, then started jibing each other about who threw up when they saw the bodies."

Whoo-boy. That spelled trouble. "Well, let's hope they find a solution soon," I said, trying to sound disinterested. "I'm sure people are looking into it." People that included Sorren, Teag, and me.

I WAS PLEASANTLY surprised to find the shop busy when I got back. Teag flashed me a grateful grin to welcome me, and I went behind the counter, happy to see customers shopping and buying. I pushed my worries aside for the next few hours, glad I'd gotten a jolt of energy from my latte.

The afternoon was almost gone by the time the last of the influx finally left, laden with packages. Between the sales I'd made and what I'd seen Teag close, it was going to be a very good day, which was welcome after how slow it had been.

*Just wait until word of a serial killer gets out if you want to see slow,* a little voice nagged in my head, but I resolutely ignored it.

"How was the Charleston City Market?" Teag asked with a knowing glance. I sighed. He knows me too well.

"Who says I went to the Market?" I bluffed.

Teag cocked his head and rolled his eyes. "I know what your errands are like. They include a stroll through the Charleston City Market and a visit to Honeysuckle Café."

"Guilty as charged," I said with a sigh. I had bolstered my morning latte with several cups of coffee from the coffee maker in the back room, but the last of my cup was cold. "I did pick up some info, so it almost counts as work."

I filled Teag in on what I'd heard from Rick, and then told him about Hat Man and Mrs. Teller. Then I pulled out the bottle with the kufwa dust and clay dirt in it and held it up. "I don't know if Sorren and his friends can make anything out of this, but Mrs. Teller thought we could jinx him at least."

"I'm more interested in what you saw when you touched him," Teag said with a pointed glance.

I had been avoiding thinking about that. "Nothing good," I replied, sipping the last of my now-cold latte. "Not right," I said slowly, trying to wrap words around the images in my mind. "Polluted. Foul. Not really dead but... putrefying on the inside, if that makes any sense."

"Have you ever gotten a read from Sorren? How did it compare since Sorren is, well, dead."

*Undead.* "I've only had a couple of glimpses of Sorren, and it's not the same at all. He doesn't feel dead, not like a real dead person," I said, feeling like the English language was not built for this. "He feels ancient, sad. I get bits of stories jumbled together." I shook my head. "Moran was more like rotting meat."

"Yuck," Teag said with a grimace. "I've got Anthony doing some digging and he promised to call when he wraps up work." He gave a nervous grin. "And I'm flexing my Weaver talents to see what I can shake loose from the Internet."

I nodded. "And whenever Sorren surfaces, we've got some news for him that he isn't going to like."

I breathed a sigh of relief when we finally closed up for the night. Teag walked me to the bank to make the deposit. At first glance, he may look like a skateboarder, but I knew he had just won a national competition in Capoeira, a Brazilian style of fighting, after already mastering several other mixed martial arts. He'd competed at the international tournament level for Eskrima, a weapons-based Filipino fighting style, and he was also an instructor in several forms, which is where we met. Teag was my instructor before he became my assistant manager.

Teag told me once that he had been bullied in school for being gay and decided he wasn't going to take another thrashing. I was sorry for his reason to want self-defense skills, but knowing how to defend himself was one more way he seemed perfect for the job.

Teag said Anthony would join us for dinner, so we headed over to Viva Venice, the best little Italian restaurant this side of Broad Street. I waved at Fioretto, the owner, and pointed toward the back. He nodded, and motioned for one of his servers to escort us to the rear-most table, where we could speak without interruption.

"How are some of my favorite customers?" Fioretto asked, stopping by the table. He was a short, wiry man with bright eyes and a thick head of dark hair.

"In the mood for some good food," I replied.

Fioretto beamed. "Then you've come to the right place. Do you want the usual?"

Teag and I both nodded, and let Fioretto know that Anthony would be joining us. Knowing Anthony could be late, Teag and I dove into our food, and held off discussion until Anthony joined us so we didn't have to repeat ourselves. Fioretto's food was so good I could even approve of Teag's favorite, a pizza with anchovies, sweet peppers, and capers.

"What did I miss?" Anthony said, sliding into the seat next to Teag, giving him a quick peck on the cheek. He set his jacket and tie aside, but it was clear from his slightly rumpled shirt and creased slacks that he had just come from a long day at the office.

"Nothing but the view of us stuffing our faces," I replied, dabbing a bit of sauce from my lips. "We pre-ordered for you."

"Same old, same old," Anthony joked, and Teag gave him a friendly poke in the ribs.

Fioretto must have spotted Anthony, because his food came out at the same time the server refreshed our sodas. While he ate, Teag and I made small talk, mostly about the horde of shoppers who had descended on Trifles and Folly with their credit cards at the ready. Anthony wasn't in retail, but he certainly understood the benefit of having a lot of clients, so he nodded at the appropriate places while he polished off his food.

When the plates were cleared, the server brought us all cups of Fioretto's excellent Venetian coffee along with the light, crispy lemon cookies that were a house specialty.

I drew a deep breath, and launched into a recount of what had transpired at the Charleston City Market with Mrs. Teller. I finished with the news Rick had shared at the café.

On that note, Teag and I both looked expectantly at Anthony. He adjusted his collar, a mannerism I learned long ago meant that he was trying to decide how much he could share of what he knew.

"If I didn't think that your haunted objects might help solve the murders, I wouldn't tell you anything," he said, with an affectionate glower that was meant to be stern. "It's an ongoing police investigation, so you can't blab anything I share."

Teag rolled his eyes. "We don't blab."

I held up my hands, palms out. "Absolute blab-free zone."

Anthony sighed and shook his head. "Okay, here's the scoop. The cops found another body by the old Navy yard. Dead, no sign of theft."

"Natural causes?" I speculated. "Heart attack?"

Anthony shook his head. "Definitely not natural causes. Body was ripped apart. Pretty savage. They're still trying to figure out what it would take to be able to do that in an alley." He made a face. "Think 'mauled by a pack of hungry tigers' and that still doesn't do it justice."

"Could they even identify who he was?" I asked.

Anthony nodded. "His wallet was nearby. Empty, but I don't think he had anything in it to start with. Like the other dead men, he had a record of petty crime: looting, theft, illegal betting, that sort of thing. They think he owed the wrong people money."

Teag frowned. "Did the dead man put up a fight? Any evidence of the attacker? DNA, hair, clothing, blood, footprints, anything?"

Anthony shook his head. "Not that they've been able to identify yet. That's what's started the rumors about monsters and black magic. It just doesn't add up."

Teag and I exchanged a glance. "It doesn't – unless there's some bad magic going on," I replied. That was Sorren's area of expertise, and I was antsy to find out what he had learned from his sources.

"There is one more thing," Anthony said. "On a hunch, I called an old friend who heads up the cold case files. He said that the recent murders got him thinking, so he started to dig up other unsolved killings."

"Did he find anything?" Teag asked, leaning forward, looking utterly innocent.

Anthony nodded. "Charleston doesn't have a huge murder rate. Of the murders that happen each year, if you took out disputes related to criminal activity and domestic violence, the number of truly 'random' murders are pretty few."

"Meaning?" Teag pressed.

"Meaning that he turned up three more deaths that couldn't be explained away by a drug deal gone bad, for instance, or a love affair gone wrong, deaths where the bodies were mutilated in some way." He paused. "Two of the bodies were found near the old Navy yard. They aren't included in the count for the more recent killings."

"I can see why that would look like a serial killer," I mused. "Similar locations, similar type of victim, and a similar style of death." I tilted my head, thinking, and then looked at Anthony. "These old deaths – how far back did they go?"

Anthony shifted in his seat. "The oldest one was a little more than six months ago."

A thought occurred to me. "Anthony," I said slowly as the idea worked itself out in my mind, "did you get any idea of the pacing of the deaths? I mean, are they happening closer together now than before?"

He nodded. "I hear that's what's got the cops so spooked," he said, then realized his own unintentional pun. "Sorry. Bad word choice. They're worried that whoever – or whatever – is behind the deaths has a new sense of urgency, and might be working up to something big, like a bombing or a mass shooting."

"The cops don't think in terms of the kind of stuff we saw at Gardenia Landing," Teag said with a glance toward Anthony. "They might joke about it, but if we tried to actually tell them there was a demon involved, they'd send us to the loony bin."

"Recommend you for psychological evaluation," Anthony corrected with a sigh. "Not very PC of you."

Teag rolled his eyes, but I jumped in. "Moran's got something to do with this, and in the past, he tried to call a demon. So odds are, there's a demon involved again, and Moran or whoever raised it is trying to harness power through the deaths."

Anthony's expression grew grim. "And if you're right, and nothing makes it stop, it's going to be worse than a bomb or a shooting, isn't it?"

I nodded, feeling a sudden chill down my spine. "I'm afraid so. Much worse."

# Chapter Twelve

I TOOK IT easy on Friday, figuring I deserved a little R&R. By the time I packed my bags the following day to leave Gardenia Landing, I felt a little wistful. I now counted Rebecca as a friend, and was utterly charmed by the inn. Picking up Baxter from the puppy spa was a chaotic reunion. Baxter just about wagged out of his silky white fur to see me, and the staff assured me he had been a good boarder. Since it was Saturday, he came to the shop with me. Fortunately, things were uneventful.

Teag insisted on helping me move Baxter and my suitcases into the house. "Anthony and I are considering having the floors done at his place, too. He told me I had to see what kind of job the refinishers did," he said with a shrug. I figured it was his cover story so I wouldn't mind him making sure I got home safely.

We reached my house just after sunset. Teag grabbed my suitcase from the trunk and I took my purse and Baxter's kennel from the back seat. I paused for a moment before heading up the steps to the piazza.

"Something wrong?" Teag asked, picking up on my hesitation.

I shrugged. "Have you ever just been able to feel that someone else has been in your house?" I asked. "I mean, I hired them to come, I saw them working, so it's not exactly a surprise. But still –"

"Someone's been in your private space," Teag finished for me. I nodded.

I opened the door, expecting to be bowled over by the smell of polyurethane. I was pleasantly surprised to find that while the smell was strong it was bearable, and the floors looked fantastic.

"Wow," Teag said. "They did a great job."

Teag set down the suitcase as I put Baxter's kennel on the floor and opened its door. "I promised Anthony I'd help you do a walk through before I left, just in case," Teag said. I was just about to protest when Baxter began a deep-throated growl.

"I've already made a complete check. The house is secure," Sorren said as he stepped from the shadows, coming from the direction of the kitchen.

Baxter went ballistic. Maltese are small in stature, but inside, Bax has the heart of a Mastiff. He barked and growled, sensitive to the supernatural.

Sorren regarded Baxter with affectionate resignation. He knelt down and looked right at Baxter. "What a good dog," Sorren said in a calm voice. "A good protector. But you remember me. I'm your friend."

Immediately, Baxter stopped in his tracks, sat down and began to wag his tail, with a happy expression that looked a little loopy. I still wasn't sure how I felt about Sorren using his vampire mojo on my dog. He can't glamor me (and he says he wouldn't as a matter of honor), but glamoring Baxter doesn't seem to bother his conscience one whit.

"That's cheating."

Sorren shrugged. "In my mortal days, many a dog got a piece of me – or nearly did – as I made it over a fence. Since I learned to make friends, it goes better for both of us."

"Is everything okay?" I asked, with a nod toward the rest of the house.

"Inside, yes. I sense no one except the workmen have been here, which is as it should be. But outside..."

"What?" I asked, feeling fear rise in my throat.

"There is a residue of something supernatural and... unhealthy."

"Unhealthy how?" Teag asked. He had unconsciously fallen into a defensive pose from his martial arts training. But if Sorren was concerned about a threat, even ninja moves weren't enough.

"Bad magic. What people when I was alive called 'bad night air'. A hint of evil," Sorren replied.

I shivered. "How did it find me? And do you think it's connected?"

Sorren frowned. "Yes, I think it's related, but I don't know how. All the more reason to take steps to make sure it causes no harm."

"Is it Moran? The demon?" Teag asked.

Sorren shrugged. "Very possibly Moran. It may be that my arrival scared him off."

"How do I cleanse it?" I asked.

Just then, there was a knock at my door. I looked to Sorren, but he just nodded. Obviously, he had been expecting someone.

"It's Lucinda, the mambo I told you about," he said. "Invite her in. That will grant permission for her to use her magic to project you."

I'd had to do the same when Sorren first visited me. All those stories about vampires not being able to enter without permission are mostly true, it turns out. Mostly. Sorren gave me reason to suspect there are loopholes and technicalities if the vampire doesn't want to be polite.

I went to the door. Baxter, still enthralled with Sorren, never moved, staring at my business partner with a look of slightly glazed admiration.

When I opened the door, I found a slim, vibrant looking woman with a mane of hundreds of tight braids and skin the color of espresso. She wore a simple white shift with a necklace made of onyx disks and carved ebony and she carried a large tote bag. If I had to guess her age, I'd have said mid-forties, but Sorren had taught me how much looks could be deceiving.

"You must be Lucinda," I said. "Welcome."

She smiled, and her dark brown eyes met mine. I felt an instant affinity, and wondered if, like Sorren, she could glamor people. She seemed to guess my thoughts.

"*Non, cherie*. I didn't spell you. We're just likely to hit it off," she said with a chuckle. Lucinda spoke with an accent I identified with New Orleans. Up close, I got a better look at her beads. I could make out complicated traceries carved into the onyx stones, marks I recognized as *veves*, part of the Voudon culture.

"Lucinda has agreed to cleanse your house of evil and strengthen the wardings to protect you," Sorren said. He glanced toward Teag. "She'll be doing the same at the shop and at Teag's apartment."

"Fine by me," Teag said.

"I've known Lucinda's family for quite some time," Sorren said. "She comes from a powerful line of women who are on particularly good terms with the Loa. She's a descendant of Mama Nadege," he added.

I knew that name. And I also knew that Mama Nadege had been dead for over two hundred years. Sorren had told me stories about times Mama Nadege – both dead and alive – had aided him with difficult situations. I was honored and a little scared to be in the presence of one of her descendents. Honored because I knew how much Sorren esteemed Mama's magic. Scared because this sounded as if he were bringing in the big guns, so to speak.

"Thank you for coming," I said.

"Something wicked's come this way," she said, with a smile to acknowledge her play on the old quote. "Searching, I think. Yes. Curious. It wants your measure," Lucinda said, and looked me up and down. "It feels your power. It has a connection to the pieces you've handled. And I think it wants to know how much of a threat you are."

Lucinda eyed the agate necklace I wore to deflect evil. "Let me touch your necklace," she said. I unclasped it and handed it to her.

She shook her head and I heard "Tsk, tsk, tsk," under her breath.

"Is something wrong?"

Lucinda met my gaze. "Your necklace has served you well. Its stones have shielded you. They must be cleansed to... recharge... their power. You'll need them again."

She looked around my living room and found a side table next to a window. Light from the nearly full moon shone in brightly. Lucinda placed the necklace on the table and let the moonlight bathe it. Then she reached into her bag and withdrew a small pouch of powdered herbs with a spicy, pungent smell.

Next to the necklace, on the smooth wood of the tabletop, Lucinda sprinkled a dusting of her herbs and then drew a *veve* with her finger as she chanted quietly. My knowledge of Voudon was limited, to say the least, but I recognized that particular *veve*. Papa Legba, one of the most famous – and powerful – of the spirit guides.

Lucinda turned back to me. "If we had time to do this right, your necklace should sit in the moonlight for a full cycle of the moon to regain its energy. When the threat is gone, that's what you must do. But for now, even a night with the moon so close to full will help."

She turned away before I could thank her. Lucinda laid her large tote bag on a chair and rummaged into it, producing an abalone shell and a cigar-sized bundle I recognized as sage. She struck a match and lit the end of the sage bundle, letting it smolder in the abalone shell as she began to walk counter-clockwise around my parlor.

Lucinda murmured as she moved around the room. Her pace changed, and she began to dance. An ecstatic expression was on her face, a look of total concentration and rapture, and I wondered if she had allowed one of her Loas to possess her to draw on the spirit's power.

Teag, Sorren, and I followed Lucinda at a respectful distance as she danced her way around the perimeter of each room downstairs. A shake of Sorren's head cautioned us not to speak. I felt a tingle of power in the air, something I associated with strong magic. But the power that rolled off Lucinda was very different from my magic, Teag's, or even from the sense of the Dark Gift I got from Sorren.

The magic radiated from Lucinda, but it did not

originate within her, at least, not from Lucinda the mortal. The magic that suffused the cleansing and protection spells Lucinda was invoking was much older even than Sorren, and I thought again about the Loas, ancient spirits whose followers had called on them for blessing and safety – and vengeance – for untold generations. I'd had a brush with that kind of power before, and I was properly in awe.

Lucinda wasn't finished until she had led our quiet parade through every room in my house, upstairs and downstairs, including the tiny attic. Baxter followed us, sniffing the air curiously, as if he wondered about the sage and whether it meant food.

Finally, as if she were closing an invisible circle, Lucinda returned to the place where she had begun her chant. She raised her arms to the ceiling and let her head fall back. I heard words in a language I did not recognize, some spoken in Lucinda's buttery accent, and some in a huskier, strange voice.

Lucinda opened her eyes wide as if looking into some mysterious realm the rest of us did not see, and cried out three times. A tremor shook her whole body, and then she slumped, like a puppet whose strings had been cut.

In the blink of an eye, Sorren was behind her to catch her, although I had not seen him move. His vampire speed always unnerved me, nearly as much as his ability to move in utter silence. Sorren gathered Lucinda into his arms like a child and laid her on my couch.

"Get her food," he instructed. "Bread, fruit, and water. It'll refresh her and also serve as an offering to the Loas to say 'thank you'."

I hadn't been home for a couple of days so I'd skipped going to the store, but I did have a loaf of bread handy as well as an apple, which I sliced and put on a plate next to the bread. Personally, I would have wanted some cheese to go with it, but Sorren hadn't mentioned it and I didn't know how Loas felt about cheese, so I kept it simple.

By the time I returned, Lucinda was sitting up and chatting with Sorren and Teag. She accepted the plate gratefully and took a drink of water, then sighed.

"Everything is cleansed and blessed," Lucinda assured me. "My wardings are strong. Powerful Loas helped me. Not much will break through easily."

*Not exactly an iron-clad guarantee*, I thought. *If I take her literally, 'something' could break through, but it will have to work for it.* Still, it was better than before.

"Thank you," I said, meaning it from the bottom of my heart.

Lucinda reached over to pat my hand, and I felt a slight *zing* that had nothing to do with static electricity. This was one powerful practitioner. "You're Sorren's friend. That's good enough for me."

I yawned, and hurried to cover my mouth, not wanting to look impolite. Baxter, seemingly unfazed by everything that had happened – or at peace with Lucinda's brand of magic – stretched up on his hind legs and scratched at my knees to be picked up. I settled him onto my lap.

"Now that your house is taken care of, Lucinda and I will accompany Teag back to his place and make a similar warding," Sorren said. "Tomorrow night, we'll do the same at the shop. They've all been warded before, but it's best not to take chances."

"Do you think whatever came here will come back?" I asked.

Lucinda frowned. "If it does, it'll know that powerful spirits are watching over you. And if it has lesser spirits in league with it, the wardings I cast won't let them get past the sidewalk."

I glanced at Sorren. "Will it stop Corban Moran? Will it stop a demon?"

Sorren and Lucinda exchanged a glance I couldn't decipher. "For Moran, the warding should cause him more trouble than I think he'll want," Sorren said.

"Loas are jealous spirits," Lucinda replied. "Once they've been invoked, they feel a mite possessive. They won't take kindly to a demon poking about."

In both cases, less than an iron-clad guarantee, but magic didn't come with a warranty. It would have to do. I had a moment's mental image of a bunch of frustrated spirits and demon minions milling around outside my piazza gate.

"Thank you," I said again. "And thanks for doing Teag's place as well."

Lucinda inclined her head. "Of course."

I rose to walk them to the door. Baxter nested happily in the warm cushion I had left behind. "Good night," I said, suddenly feeling the full effect of the last few days. I locked the door behind them, turned off the lights and scooped Baxter into the crook of my arm, and then headed up the stairs to bed. Maybe it was Lucinda's wardings, or sheer exhaustion, but I slept like a log.

# Chapter Thirteen

THE NEXT MORNING was drizzling rain. I muttered at my alarm when it rang. I was supposed to be off today but with Maggie still recuperating from food poisoning, it was just another day. *Teag and I are going to have to hire some additional help as soon as this is over,* I promised myself.

I was running late. Baxter waited patiently while I showered and dressed, then playfully pounced from step to step as we went downstairs, certain that kibble would shortly appear in his dish. He was not disappointed.

I toasted two slices of bread, slathered them with peanut butter and stuck them into a sandwich bag so I could eat at the store. I'd wait for coffee until I got there, too. I liked to have time in the shop before the customers started coming in. Baxter was staying home today. With a quick kiss for Baxter, I slipped out the door, making a mental note to stop for groceries on the way home or I'd be eating dry cereal for supper.

Teag was already at Trifles and Folly when I arrived, and I smelled fresh coffee brewing. He was the best assistant manager ever.

"How did it go with Lucinda last night?"

"She made short work of the apartment," Teag replied, sipping his cup of tea. "Sorren suggested that she also ward Anthony's place, to keep the folks who are out for our heads from deciding to go after him to get to us." He looked as if that possibility had cost him some sleep. "I have a key, so I let her in since he was working late." He sighed. "I don't know how I'll explain the smell.

"I couldn't sleep last night," he confessed. "So I spent some time on the Internet and the Darke Web. Anthony sent me a list of names for the murder victims the police have connected along with the three his friend found out about, so I did some digging and plotted where each body was discovered. I left the map in your office. Take a look when you have a chance. Maybe it can narrow down our search."

"The real question is – search for what?" I said, tucking my things beneath the counter and heading to the back to make my coffee. He followed.

"We're pretty sure Moran is behind things, but what does he want? What's the demon got to do with it? And what's up with the dead men – or the missing salvage team?" I munched my peanut butter toast as I thought about all the important stuff we didn't know.

"I'll watch the front," Teag said. "Why don't you have a look at the map?"

His insistence told me that Teag had already formed a theory and that he was waiting for me to validate it or poke holes, so I headed to my office, where Teag had left a map.

I spread the map out on my desk. The old Navy yard was about a forty-five minute drive from the historic section of the city, over in an area that was mostly used for shipping and warehouses. It wasn't the prettiest part of town, but it also wasn't known as particularly crime-ridden. Many of the murders had either happened near the Navy yard, or the bodies had been left there. Either way, it suggested a connection. Or maybe it was just a good place to dump a corpse and not be seen.

I let out a long breath and picked up a pencil. I drew a line from dot to dot, and it was an amoeba-like, squiggly sort of thing. With the dots connected, I could see what was inside the sort-of-circle. Squinting, I could make out the names of some of the buildings. To my eye, a lot of what was enclosed by the circle was empty space. That might mean that there really were no buildings – possible since the old military yard was being repurposed, and so many of the original buildings had either been torn down or were abandoned. Or it could mean that any buildings that were in use weren't big enough to bother mentioning.

I grabbed a piece of paper and made some notes. First, I wrote down the streets that made a rough border around the area where the murders had occurred. Then I wrote down the names of the biggest buildings along that route that showed up on the map. A couple of them appeared to be warehouses. One spot had a building without a name. There was an office building and something that appeared to be a lab or a research facility. Not much to go on, but it was a start.

When I refilled my coffee, I poked my head out to see if we had customers. One stalwart soul had braved the rain and was browsing, but Teag was taking care of him. I went back to my office and plugged in the names of the buildings I had identified on the map.

None of the places I found screamed supernatural trouble spot. I copied down the names and address of the warehouses, came up completely dry on two of the other buildings, and read the Wikipedia entry about the Navy yard for good measure.

"Made a sale," Teag sang out when I heard the door close behind our customer. "How about you?"

I brandished my notes as well as a printout of the Wikipedia page. "I found out a few things."

"Spill!"

I recapped my results, and then smoothed the print out on the counter. "Here's a tidbit that might be important. The whole Navy yard area has been in use for a long time. During the Civil War, several of the old warehouses were used as hospitals or holding areas for prisoners of war."

"Meaning some bad mojo," Teag supplied. I nodded.

"Caskets of soldiers killed in conflict during World War I, World War II, and Vietnam came through the yard, and the unclaimed bodies were stored there until arrangements could be made." I added. We both knew that could mean restless spirits.

Teag gave me a sidelong look. "Are you thinking what I'm thinking?"

I sighed. "Probably. But Sorren won't be happy."

"Road trip!" Teag crowed. He gave me a conspiratorial glance. "And as for Sorren, we could go after we close up shop and be back before it's dark."

The rain never let up, but despite the weather, a dozen or more tourists sought shelter in the shop, and half of them bought something, so the day turned out pretty well. It was raining harder at five o'clock, so I felt no guilt about locking up right on the dot.

We climbed into my Mini Cooper, and I handed him the map. "Where to first, boss?" he asked with a grin.

I pointed to one of the larger buildings on the map. "Let's start with that one."

Neither of us spoke on the drive over to the decommissioned Navy yard. I wasn't sure this was a smart thing to do for two people who had a guy with a demon after them. Then again, hiding in my house didn't appeal to me, either. Corban Moran couldn't be everywhere, and I was gambling that tonight, he wouldn't be any of the places we were going.

Before long we sat in front of a sorry looking warehouse. The building had no sign, and a chain link fence separated it from the street. The windows were boarded shut.

"You getting any vibes?" Teag asked.

I concentrated, but felt nothing. "Nope," I said. "Next?"

Teag gave directions, but we ended up in front of an empty lot. I went around the block and cruised by again slowly, making certain to check street numbers on the decrepit buildings on either side.

"Guess the building's gone. You pick up anything from the lot?"

I shook my head. "Let's move on."

We went down the street as slowly as the speed limit allowed. I didn't want to miss seeing something, but I also didn't want to arouse suspicion. Teag looked surprised when I stopped at the curb in front of a large old house. "What's up?" he asked.

I stared through the rain at the forlorn old house next to us. It had seen better days. Shingles were missing from the roof, and part of the porch was tilting at an alarming angle. Windows had been broken, and whoever owned the property didn't care enough to board up what was left. Graffiti covered the front door and some of the wall, blurred by the peeling paint.

"I don't know what happened here, but I'm picking up some very strong resonance," I said. "Can you make out the house number?"

Between the two of us, we figured out the address, and Teag marked it down. I couldn't shake the feeling that the house had something to do with our demon problem. "Once we get back, let's see what we can find on the Internet," Teag suggested. "I bet we can turn up a last owner."

I nodded and pulled away from the curb with a self-conscious glance over my shoulder. It didn't look as if anyone was around, but I didn't relish having anyone call the cops. The next several buildings were rubble. Parts of the former Navy yard had been renovated into an office park, but this section looked like it had been bombed.

Nothing set off my senses. Then we turned a corner, and I felt something so strong I nearly stopped the car in the middle of the road.

"What's wrong?" Teag asked, worried. I guess my feelings showed in my face. I felt like I was driving through a curtain of dread. I shivered.

"Is that one of the ones I marked?" I asked, forcing myself to keep moving until I could get to the curb.

Teag consulted his list and nodded. "Yep. Simchak Exports and Freight was the last listed owner, according to what you've got here."

The Simchak building was made of red brick, and from the design, I guessed it was built in the late 1800s. It was a hulking place, with large barn door-sized openings covered with weathered wood. Over the main door, light colored bricks spelled out 'Covington.'

"What does your spidey sense tell you?" Teag asked. Something about this whole area gave me the creeps.

"That it's got juice," I said. "We'll need to do some digging."

I peered through the drizzle, trying to determine what was giving me the heebie-jeebies. The shadows seemed thicker near the warehouse. Something had happened here, but what, I wasn't sure. Despair seemed to roll off the old building like the rain.

"Cassidy?" Teag looked worried, and I figured I had zoned out longer than I intended.

I shook off my mood, and took another deep breath. "How close were any of the bodies found to this building?" I asked.

Teag consulted his map. "Hmm. Three of them were found within two blocks of here."

"I wish we knew where the murders happened, not just where the bodies were found," I said. "Not to mention why Moran and his demon are juicing up objects that should just be minor-league haunted. Let's keep going."

The day was so overcast, it was difficult to see the sun, but my dashboard clock said six p.m. and I thought the day seemed darker than it should be for the time. This time, when we pulled away I felt as if something was watching us. I didn't see anyone around, but I still couldn't shake the feeling.

"You've got one more address listed." Teag said as he looked at the map. "Should be close, around the block."

We headed for the last site. I got a glimpse of several buildings inside a compound surrounded by a chain link fence as we came up on the address from the back.

Even at a distance, the whole place gave me a severe case of the willies. "Definitely bad mojo," I said. "Let's go around the block and get a closer look."

Several large buildings were between us and the cross-street, blocking our view. I turned a corner, and up ahead I saw the flash of police lights. "Uh oh," I said. The cops were between us and the last address, blocking the road.

"Pull over," Teag said. The rain had stopped, and no one else was around. Cars crowded near the flashing lights. "Let's see what's going on."

"You mean, just walk up there and poke our noses in?"

"No," Teag said, reaching into the back seat and grabbing the spare leash I keep for Baxter in the car. "I mean wander up while we're looking for your lost dog."

I parked the car and we got out, calling Baxter's name and looking from side to side. The cops weren't expecting bystanders, so when we approached quietly, it took them a minute to realize we were there.

It was long enough to get an eyeful past the crime scene tape. I glimpsed what was left of a body, big enough to be a man. It looked as if it had gone through a shredder. No skin, face or hair, and what remained of muscle and bone had been ripped apart and broken. I leaned against Teag, trying not to be sick, but even so, one thing stuck out in my mind.

There wasn't enough blood.

If something had done the killing right there, the whole block should have been spattered with gore. I didn't try to look at the body again, but it hadn't been lying in a huge puddle of blood, and the ground underneath it was an old asphalt parking lot, so the blood hadn't just soaked in. He'd been dumped.

The other reason I was so sure the murder had happened somewhere else was that I hadn't passed out from a vision of the dead man's final moments. Even if the victim had been stoned out of his mind, being flayed and ripped to shreds has a tendency to sober someone up. If he had died here, so recently, the images would be impossible to avoid. His terror and pain should have completely overwhelmed me. But there was nothing.

"Hey!" a cop shouted, just noticing us. "You shouldn't be here!"

Teag held up Baxter's leash. "Have you seen Baxter? Little white dog?"

The cop hustled toward us. "No. I haven't seen your dog. Shit, you didn't take pictures, did you?"

"No pictures," Teag replied. "Just figured we'd ask if you'd seen him." He glanced over toward the body and paled. "Wow," he said.

"In case you didn't notice, we've got a murder investigation going on," the cop said, shooing us toward our car. "And if you're smart, you'll lock your doors and head straight home. Whoever killed the guy is probably around here somewhere."

The same thing had crossed my mind as well, and since I was pretty sure Moran and his demon were behind the killing, we had even more motivation than the cop might have expected to get the hell out of there. So I was surprised when Teag stopped to pick something up.

"What?" I asked.

"Later," he said, pretending to tie his shoe. The cop was still watching us, and he kept staring at us until we turned the car around and drove away. The sun was just setting, and I was anxious to get out of the Navy yard.

"What did you find?" I asked, steering for home.

Teag opened his fist. Inside lay a metal button, something you'd find on a pair of men's jeans. It was scuffed with wear, but didn't look like it had been sitting out in the weather for long.

"Think it's from the dead man?" I asked.

Teag shrugged. "That's as good a guess as any," he replied. "There weren't any occupied buildings down that way, so there's no reason for foot traffic. Then again, who knows?"

I'd know as soon as I touched the button, but that would have to wait until I wasn't driving. Teag pocketed the button, and I turned a corner. Finding my way out of the Navy yard was proving harder than going in.

"I'm turned around," I said. We had managed to find a street of even more decrepit buildings than any we had seen. The rain had started up again, and the sun was nearly gone. The diversion with the cops had kept us out later than we planned and it was getting dark fast.

Too fast.

"Hang on," I said. I glanced in my rear view mirror. Darkness was falling like a curtain behind us, inky black and opaque, rushing at us like the tide. Every nerve ending in my body screamed for me to run.

I gunned the engine and floored it, wishing my Mini Cooper was a muscle car. We were out of sight of the cops, and everything around us looked deserted. We roared down the crumbling roadway, and I leaned on the horn, hoping for once in my life we'd attract attention and get pulled over for speeding.

No such luck. My horn made no noise, though I had beeped at a slow driver just fine earlier in the day.

"Uh, Cassidy. All your warning lights are blinking," Teag said.

*No shit.* But Teag meant in the car, and when I looked at my dashboard, it was lit up like a Christmas tree. Even my car was panicking. Or more likely, the dangerous magic that was closing in on us was also playing havoc with our electronics. And that meant that the car might go –

Dead. Just like that, the car engine cut out and we coasted to a stop. Darkness descended over the car, blotting out the light. Normal darkness has stars and street lights and reflections. This was like someone had dropped a black shroud over the car, blotting out the world.

I'd already slammed down the door locks, but I checked again. Teag and I held on as a force began to rock the car. I heard metal ripping. The car lurched to one side as something slashed the metal in Teag's door. It didn't get into the passenger compartment, but the next swipe certainly would. The rear window smashed, and a foul smell seeped into the car. Teag and I were both screaming.

I tried the key but the engine didn't even grind. The car rocked again, not quite tipping over. The darkness was toying with us. Playing with its food.

Inside the car, the temperature plummeted. My teeth were chattering, and ice crystals were beginning to form on the windshield. My left hand was holding onto the agate necklace hard enough that the silver setting drew blood.

Abruptly, the rocking stopped.

*Was it the blood?* I wondered. *Or was the big bad thing outside just getting ready for new tricks?*

Blindingly bright light flared, knifing through the darkness. I saw two things. First, Sorren stood directly behind us, dressed all in black, armed with a very large, very lethal looking sword.

The second thing I saw were monsters.

Maybe I should have been glad that Moran's demon wasn't the thing wrecking our car, but his minions were plenty scary. If Dr. Frankenstein had built a do-it-yourself monster from the rotting parts of big reptiles, it might have looked like the things that surrounded the car. Big teeth. Sharp talons. Powerful legs. Crafty eyes that were utterly cold and looked very hungry.

The car's engine roared to life and I floored the gas pedal.

"You're just going to leave Sorren back there?" Teag asked.

"Nope," I said. I'd been scared, and now I was just plain pissed off. I cut the Mini Cooper in the tightest turn I could manage at high speed and headed straight for the *things* that were closing on Sorren.

Six of them to one of him. Not a fair fight, even though Sorren was laying about with sword fighting moves that would have done a movie blockbuster proud. The sword gleamed an odd blue, and I wondered if he'd chosen it over a Glock because magic is better at fighting magic. Whatever the reason, he'd obviously had practice, and by the time we got there, he had put down two of the creatures.

The other four were closing on him. From the look of it, they'd already scored a few hits. Sorren's left sleeve was slashed and dripping dark blood. The front of his shirt hung in tatters. I revved the car and steered straight toward the monsters.

"What the hell!" Teag screeched. "You're going to hit Sorren!"

"Bowling for bad guys," I muttered, bearing down on the creatures. We hit the first one, smashing the left headlight. The second one bounced into the air, crashed down on the hood of the Mini Cooper and left a bloody streak and a big crack on the windshield. Teag got the third one with his door in a move that was either brilliant or suicidal. I steered toward the last one, which was still battling Sorren.

"For God's sake, Cassidy!" Teag threw up both arms and ducked his head.

We hit the monster square on, knocking him down and running him over. Problem was, I couldn't stop fast enough to take out the creature and not hit Sorren, too.

Good thing vampires are fast.

I skidded to a stop, watching carefully for either the darkness or the minions. The engine was making suspicious coughing noises. My windshield wipers seemed to be stuck on. A nasty streak of black blood was smeared down the cracked glass of the windshield and all the way to the grillwork. My car was a wreck, but we were alive.

Sorren came up behind us, and I saw that he was limping. I unlocked the doors, and he climbed into the back. "Nice driving," he said.

I took it slow on the way home, because that was all my poor, battered car could manage. I doubted demon protection was part of my insurance coverage, and at my most creative, I couldn't for the life of me invent a plausible lie. *You see, there was this rabid, hungry, escaped tiger in rut...*

We took the back streets, because the cops could probably get me on a dozen vehicle violations, and I didn't want to explain all the blood. Sorren didn't say a word for the entire trip, which took longer than usual because the Mini Cooper could no longer cough up speeds above a crawl. Teag and I were silent too, with a sense of doom hanging over us that I haven't felt since I got caught sneaking out of the house as a teenager. We were totally, completely, busted.

Just before I got to the turn that would bring us back to my house, I saw the car in my rear view mirror. "Uh oh," Teag said. "Looks like we picked up some company."

Just then, the police cruiser switched on its strobes. Obediently, I pulled over to the curb and sighed.

A cop stepped out of the car. He was a State Police officer, and his hat had a plastic rain protector over it. He didn't look happy.

"Hello officer," I said, hoping I managed to look harmless.

"Having problems with your car?" he asked. It was dark out, so I prayed that the worst of the damage – and the blood – wasn't apparent. How I would explain the claw slashes escaped even my fertile imagination.

"I think we hit a deer," I said, doing my best to meet his gaze. "It came out of nowhere from the trees, bounced off us and kept going. I hope it's not hurt too badly."

The cop eyed me like he was trying to decide whether or not I'd been smoking something. I did my best to channel Baxter's blinky-eyed innocence. Next to me, Teag was staying very, very still.

Sorren leaned forward and smiled at the officer. "She's been through a lot tonight," he said in a honey-smooth voice. "She really needs to get home."

"You really shouldn't be on the road," the officer said. "You need to get home."

"You won't need to report this," Sorren said with the same tone he used to turn Baxter into his adoring fan. "She can take it up with her insurance."

"Sorry about the deer," the officer said. "Just report it to your insurance company." He slapped the roof of the car and I winced, expecting it to fall off. "Drive safe, y'all."

Teag didn't move a muscle until we were well out of sight. Then he let out a gust of breath and slumped in his seat so quickly I feared he'd been shot.

"What?" I asked, alarmed.

He withdrew the map from its hiding place and fanned himself with it. "Oh. My. God. You and Sorren handled that so well. I was terrified he was going to search the car for drugs or something and find the map."

I gave a shaky laugh. "I was pretty scared of the same thing. Where did you hide it?"

Teag shot me a sly grin. "That cop looked pretty straight to me, so I put it somewhere I didn't figure he'd look. I slipped it in the waistband of my jeans under my shirt."

I chuckled. "Good thinking." I knew Teag had had a run in with some homophobic cops at one time in his life, and I didn't like how pale he looked. I had been afraid of getting a ticket. It hadn't occurred to me that Teag was afraid of getting roughed up, or worse.

"Let's get out of here," I said, turning the car toward home. I thought about cracking a joke about Sorren glamoring the cop, but then I saw the look on his face and reconsidered.

The car sputtered to a stop in front of my house and we got out. I caught my breath. The back window was smashed, and the rear bumper was gone. Three deep slashes had ripped through the passenger door like a can opener. The front windshield was cracked from side to side, and the hood was dented so deeply it looked like a boulder had bounced off it. The driver's front tire was nearly flat.

Sorren had stopped and was talking quietly on his cell phone before joining us.

Teag followed me up the steps to the front door. I could tell that, despite his injuries, Sorren was on high alert, turning around to watch behind us as we entered. Baxter greeted Teag and me joyfully, overdue for his dinner. He took one look at Sorren, stopped barking and sat down with the same glazed look I had seen on my stoner cousin. I wondered if Sorren's glamoring would give Baxter the munchies.

"Of all the irresponsible −" Sorren began as soon as the door shut.

I held up a hand, palm out. My vampire boss could talk to the hand. "*Not* before dinner," I snapped. I had seen a body that was flayed and ripped to shreds, been chased by the black cloud of doom, saved a vampire from a pack of demon-spawn, and had my car totaled by refugees from Jurassic Park. I was hungry and I was *so* not in the mood to be lectured.

Sorren was angry. Well, so was I. And right now, I was angry at Moran for killing homeless guys. I was pissed at the demon for whatever its role was in turning Trifles and Folly's antiques into supernatural C-4. And I was royally ticked off at the hassle I was going to face explaining my damaged car to the insurance agent.

Sorren muttered something in Dutch. His accent, usually unnoticeable, becomes more pronounced when he's angry or hurt. And belatedly, I realized he was both.

"You're bleeding," I said. I stopped to look him up and down. He looked like he'd been to war, and he had been, to save our necks.

"It's only a flesh wound," he deadpanned.

I gave him a 'shut up' look and started to look for gauze.

"Really, Cassidy. I'll be fine," Sorren said. "I'm nearly healed." He pulled back the shredded cloth of his black shirt to reveal a newly healed set of slashes, thin pink scars where, not half an hour earlier, there had been a bone-deep gash.

I uncorked a bottle of wine and sloshed some into glasses for Teag and me. It was that kind of night. By now, I had grabbed one of the frozen pizzas I keep for emergencies and thrown it in the oven. I poured kibble into Baxter's bowl, grabbed my wine glass, and sank into a chair.

"Ok," I said to Sorren, taking a swig of Chardonnay to steel my nerves. "You were about to tell me that going to the Navy yard was irresponsible, reckless, and stupid. Go ahead. Let me have it."

Sorren watched me for a moment, and then he began to chuckle.

"What?" I asked, thoroughly annoyed.

"You are so like your uncle," he said, shaking his head.

"Uncle Evanston?"

"Actually, you take after all of your relatives," he said, in a tone that left me wondering whether or not that was a good thing. "Headstrong, completely heedless of danger – and rather remarkable," he said.

I chanced a look at him. "You're not going to yell at me?"

Sorren sighed, and since he didn't need to breathe, I knew it was an intentional gesture. "What would be the use?" A hint of a smile quirked at the corner of his mouth.

"Yes, what you did was dangerous, reckless and all the rest. But it needed to be done, and daylight was the time to do it," he said. "As for what happened, you could have hardly expected it."

"There's been another murder," Teag said. Sorren listened as we recounted what happened before the darkness fell.

He finished his recap and turned to me. "You never said what vibes you picked up from the murder scene, Cassidy," Teag said.

I took a deep breath and sipped my wine. "It feeds on fear," I said, and I could hear my voice shaking. "It enjoys killing those men, even as it feeds on their blood." I paused, trying to make sense of what I had seen.

"It's not human, the thing that's killing them. It's never been human," I said. "And it killed him somewhere else. There wasn't enough blood."

Sorren nodded. "Anything else?"

I was shaking, but I pressed on. "It's gathering strength for a purpose," I said slowly. "I don't know what that is, but whatever's killing those men isn't at full strength yet."

"God help us," Teag muttered. He refilled the glass of wine in my hand, and I took a gulp, not a sip, trying not to think about that mangled body.

"We didn't get to all of the locations on the map," I added. "But we found several worth going back to."

"And we found this," Teag said, digging in the pocket of his jeans. He held out the button on the flat of his palm.

"You can do this another time, Cassidy," Sorren said, giving me a worried look.

I shook my head. "No. People are dying. There isn't time." I took a deep breath, squared my shoulders, and took the button.

"It's Jimmy Redshoes," I said. 'Jimmy Redshoes' was the name downtown regulars gave to a gregarious panhandler who always wore a beat-up pair of red sneakers. He'd come home from a couple tours of duty overseas in the Army, but part of him broke over there and never got fixed. After that, he slept where he could and raised money the only way he knew how. Sometimes he played his guitar for coins, and he was good enough to draw a crowd before the cops shooed him away for performing without a permit.

Around the holidays and during city celebrations, Jimmy came up with costumes and posed for pictures with tourists, many of whom were happy to drop some money in his hat. At other times, he could be found selling an ever-changing assortment of kitschy junk just out of the watchful gaze of the police. He was harmless and charming, and the knowledge that he had met such a pointless, painful death made me angry.

I frowned, trying to make sense of the jumbled images. Jimmy's thinking was full of angles and sharp corners, and it was difficult to piece the bits together. "He'd glimpsed the danger before," I said. "Something kept bringing him into the area, and he knew it was dangerous. He'd been chased, but he came back anyhow."

"Why?" Teag asked.

I searched the impressions I received from the button, but the answer wasn't there. "I don't know," I replied. "But it was something he thought was important enough to take the risk. And it killed him. He was truly

terrified and running. Whatever it was clawed him...
lots of pain and there it ended. The button must have
popped when he was struck." I loosened my grip, and
the button slipped out of my hand onto the table.

Just then, the timer sounded, and I went to get the
pizza out of the oven. I brought it back and set it on the
table, but I had lost my appetite.

"What were those things that attacked the car?" Teag
asked.

Sorren leaned back in his chair and closed his eyes.
"They are *akvenon*, minions of fear," he replied.
"Dangerous, but not nearly as deadly as their master."

"Who is?" Teag prodded.

"A full Asmodius-level demon," Sorren replied. "The
*akvenon* are just attack dogs, doing their master's
bidding."

"Does Moran control the demon?" I asked.

Sorren opened his eyes. "Moran may think he controls
the demon," he said. "But in the end, demons best their
would-be masters."

"I still don't get it," I said, beginning to pick at the
pizza. Teag had already downed three slices. "Why the
murders?"

"When a demon is first summoned, it's weak," Sorren
replied. "It needs to feed in order to gain power, and it
feeds on pain and death."

"So the murders, you think they've been feeding the
demon?" Teag asked.

Sorren nodded. "Almost certainly."

"How does any of this connect to the opera glasses
and the haunted objects at Gardenia Landing?" I asked.

"I don't know yet," Sorren said. "But I think it all
connects somehow."

"We know that Moran was hanging around the B&B," Teag said. "Maybe he could feel the magic in the haunted objects."

"Captain Harrison, the man who built Gardenia Landing, went down with his ship after delivering part of the pirate's cargo from Barbados," I added. "And now there's another salvage team missing."

"Interesting about the salvage team," Sorren said. By 'interesting' I was pretty sure he meant 'bad'.

I looked at him sharply. "You think they found the pirate ship?"

"It's possible," Sorren said. "The question is: what was onboard that ship that someone wanted badly enough to kill for it?"

"As soon as I get back to my computer, I'll find out," Teag said. "And I'll see if there's any link between Harrison, the salvage team and the Navy yard."

"We've got to go back there," I said, swallowing a bite of pizza. "The Navy yard. Somehow, it's tied up with this whole thing, but I don't know how."

Sorren nodded. "We'll go back – together," he said, fixing Teag and me with a stern gaze.

He turned to look at me. "On a more mundane note, don't panic when your car disappears. Someone will be by shortly to take care of things. Can't leave it sitting around in that condition for anyone to notice." He paused.

"And I've been remiss," he continued. "You need more protection than that necklace can give you. All well and good that you and Teag have martial arts and weapons training, but that doesn't do much against magic. I need to find better defenses for both of you – magical ones."

"What does it want, the demon?" I asked.

Sorren looked down. "What Moran wants, we don't know yet, but we'll figure it out. But what the *demon* wants, that's easy." He met my gaze. "The blood of every living being in Charleston."

"This is the biggest thing we've been up against since Teag and I came on board," I said. "Can't the Alliance do more to help? I mean they can fix my car, but can't take care of a demon?"

Sorren leaned back in his chair and laughed before taking on a serious tone. "The Alliance isn't fixing your car, Cassidy. I am. I've had the need over the years to keep special services on retainer for just such emergencies. The Alliance isn't some kind of shadow military organization, or something like the CIA," he said. "That's not why it was created."

He crossed his arms. "Less than one hundred years before I was turned, a book was published, the *Malleus Maleficarum*. Have you heard of it?"

I nodded. The *Hammer of Witches* was one of the chief tools of the Inquisition, the defining book of the witch-hunter.

"There were demons moving unbound through Europe in the old days, as well as wizards of power who sought only their own ends," Sorren said quietly. "The threat was real. Unfortunately, the men who went to hunt the demons and wizards had their own agenda, or had already been corrupted by the ones they said they were hunting. Nearly all of the lives lost were innocents, while the real perpetrators went free."

I could hear the sorrow in his voice. The persecution and terror of the witch-hunters lasted for hundreds of years, taking thousands of lives.

"My maker, Alard, was a good man. He and others realized that allowing supernatural wrongdoers to go unpunished posed a danger to all of us, but the mortal authorities were not equipped for such a task. Alard was among the small group of vampires, wizards, shape-shifters, shamans, and immortals who made a pact to take on this burden."

Sorren was looking over my shoulder, as if he were seeing into the past. "Immortals have even less patience with bureaucracy than mortals. Those of us who are pledged to the Alliance hope to avoid another Inquisition by taking care of matters ourselves. We usually see to the needs of our own territories, calling on aid when needed. We catalog the problem artifacts, try to keep tabs on where they are, and safeguard pertinent information. Some help the Alliance by tracking and obtaining dangerous pieces. Others help by destroying malicious objects, or seeing to the storage of those that can't be destroyed. And we step in when groups and individuals use magic to cause harm."

He shrugged. "The Alliance has always been a loose construct of trusted friends and associates. People are brought into the group on the vouchsafe of one of the members, who is personally liable for their discretion and conduct."

He removed a ring from his finger and slid it across the table to me. The golden ring was quite old, set with a large garnet. It had been worn long enough that most of the engraving on its sides was gone.

"You'll see my memories, one of the first jobs I did for the Alliance, a long time ago," he said. "Antwerp, 1565, focus on the 'Black Dragon' so you don't get caught in other memories."

I nodded, and took the ring, repeating *Black Dragon* over and over again in my mind. The vision folded around me. I was somewhere else, some-when else. And I was seeing the scene through Sorren's eyes, hearing his thoughts, which was a little different from most of my visions.

*Alard withdrew a folded piece of parchment from his vest pocket and laid it out carefully on the cluttered desk. Carel, the man who owned the store that fronted for the Alliance, and his son Dietger clustered around it. I took a good look at the drawing. It was of a necklace with a pendant made from what appeared to be a cluster of small gemstones set in an unusual pattern.*

"That's the Verheen Brooch," Carel said in a low voice. "No one's seen it in over a hundred years. I thought it was lost."

"Not lost. Purposely hidden. The Alliance made a deal with the Verhoeveren family to be the guardians of the brooch once we finally tracked the thing down the last time it got away." *I heard a note of anger creeping into Alard's voice.* "The fools were supposed to keep it inside the magical wards and out of sight."

"What happened?" *Carel asked. He looked worried, too. Even Dietger appeared concerned. I was obviously the only one who hadn't been in on the story.*

"Their dim-witted granddaughter, Anique, found it after her parents died in that carriage accident a few months ago. I'd brokered the arrangement myself with the grandfather, and come back for good measure when he died to make my point to his eldest son. They understood how dangerous the brooch was. Obviously," *Alard said, disdain clear in his voice,* "the girl's parents never took her into their confidence. So we've got a debutante planning to wear the Verheen Brooch out in public at Lady Evelien's ball."

"The only thing more dangerous than wearing that... thing... is trying to sell it. Are you trying to get us all killed?" Dietger was angry now. I could smell his anger. Underneath it lay fear.

"I'm not going to sell the brooch," Carel replied calmly. "Alard and I are just going to make sure it gets into the hands of a responsible guardian, someone with the Alliance."

"If the brooch is so dangerous, why not just destroy it?" As soon as I'd spoken, I felt like I must have sprouted a second head. Everyone stared at me. It was my turn to feel righteously annoyed. "How come the mortals here know all about this, and I don't—even though I'm the one stealing it? You said this was a 'big' job. You didn't tell me there was a dragon involved."

Carel sighed and exchanged glances with Alard. "Perhaps we should all sit down. This could take a while. I'll fetch more tea, and blood."

"I'll get those, father." Dietger looked happy to leave the room.

"The Black Dragon isn't a dragon," Alard said. "He's a very old spirit, one that finds a new body to possess every lifetime or so. I don't think he ever was completely human. Someone imprisoned him long ago in the New World, but the damned Spaniards set him free in their quest for gold and silver, and brought him over with their loot. That idiot, Pizarro, never even wondered why the people he conquered had so many relics hidden and locked away. All he saw was treasure. Never occurred to him that it could be anything else."

"What was it, if not treasure?"

"*Oh, some of the pieces were decoys. But several of those beautiful breastplates and necklaces of gold, silver, and gemstones were magical. They were objects of power, and strong magic users had charged them with spells to keep what was bound beneath those towers bound forever.*"

"*And it's taken us several lifetimes to find those pieces again and get them back into the hands of people the Alliance trained to use them as intended,*" Carel said tartly as Dietger returned with the drinks, and a hunk of bread and cheese with ale for himself.

"*So this Verheen Brooch is an object of power?*" I sipped the blood. That kept me from watching the pulse beat in Dietger's neck.

"*And if the granddaughter is wearing it, that means the brooch has been taken out of the vault where it was sealing in something that really shouldn't get out,*" Carel finished.

"*Antwerp is built on a very old, very large, mound of earth. There are stories from the city's beginning about strange creatures exacting a terrible price for crossing the river,*" Alard said, picking up the tale.

"*Legend says that the city was made possible when a hero battled a giant and cut off his hand,*" Alard added. "*Hundreds of years ago, those dark creatures were imprisoned in the mound beneath the city, and in the deepest caves. Objects of power guard the entrances to that prison. In this case, the home of our debutante lies directly over one of the main shafts into the caves where the spirits are imprisoned. That's why we felt the need to ward it with the brooch. Now that the warding is compromised…*" Alard let his voice drift.

"*The Black Dragon may be able to escape,*" Dietger concluded.

*"Who, exactly, did the imprisoning? Who's the 'Alliance' you mention?"* I didn't like what I was hearing, and I liked less that Alard had obviously had just this kind of thing in mind when he turned me.

*"'We' are a loose coalition of vampires, shifters, magic users, and mortals who would prefer to keep the dark things buried,"* Alard replied. *"A similar faction imprisoned the Black Dragon and spirits like him. This sort of thing has been going on since before I was turned. I'm one of the elders now, and, unfortunately, these kind of responsibilities fall to me."*

*"What happens if they get out, these spirits?"*

Alard's eyes grew dark. *"Imagine beings whose hunger for blood is never sated. Things that are unwilling to slake their thirst from goats and deer. The Black Dragon and his kin feed off blood, but they also feed from life itself. They can drain a man's life without opening a vein. Can you picture what that would be like, loosed across the kingdoms? Even the Black Death would pale in comparison to the horror."*

*"So my job is to steal the brooch – and then what?"*

Alard turned away. I had a bad feeling that this job even made him nervous. *"We steal the brooch. Carel helps us get it into the hands of a trusted guardian. The Black Dragon stays buried."*

"Alard was your maker?" I asked when the vision let go of me. I gave him back his ring.

Sorren nodded, his expression unusually pensive. "He saved my life by turning me, taught me to be the best jewel thief in Belgium. He was my master – and my friend."

"If he's a vampire, then isn't he –"

"Destroyed," Sorren said, his accent creeping in,

thicker than I'd heard it in a long time. His eyes were clouded with sadness. "It was a long time ago."

"How long ago?" I asked quietly.

"Fifteen sixty-five," he replied without needing to think about it. "I was still young in the Dark Gift. Without Alard I was... adrift."

"I'm sorry," I said.

He shrugged. "It happened – in fact, it was the hunt for the Black Dragon that killed him, the vision you saw from my ring. Alard and his mortal partner Carel – who ran a store much like Trifles and Folly – died fighting a monster that never should have been set free. Carel's son Dietger and I took up as best we could after that, until..."

His voice faded away, but I took his meaning. Eventually, something had claimed Dietger as well, either the dangers of the job or old age. *How many mortal partners has he outlived?* I wondered. The loss still hurt him; that much was obvious. For all the history he had seen and all the abilities he had gained from his Dark Gift, I did not envy him the grief.

I looked at Sorren as if seeing him for the first time. He had been much younger in the vision, unsure and inexperienced. It was difficult to imagine him that way.

"And the Family?" I asked as I recovered my wits.

Sorren shrugged as he slipped the ring back onto his finger. "If you're expecting a magical Mafia, you're out of luck. The Family is a group of powerful individuals – immortals and mortals with magic – who run in the same circles and want what maximizes their own profit and position." He gave a wry smile. "You can see why such a group is hardly going to band together for any long-term purpose, since greed trumps loyalty. Short-term, yes – if the profit is big enough. But betrayal and squabbles get the best of them in the end."

"So what can the Alliance do for us?"

"Personal connections – very valuable for getting things done out of sight," Sorren said. "Money, if needed. Safe storage or disposal. Information. Hiding places. And the loan of specialized assets… supernatural artifacts, people with unique skills."

"You mean, like Teag and me," I said.

He nodded. "And a demon hunter."

I raised an eyebrow. "A real one?"

He chuckled. "A fake one would hardly help, now would it?" He nodded. "I've asked the Alliance to loan me Taras Mirov. He's good. And he's come up against Asmodius-level demons before and lived to tell about it."

"So that's it? We turn it over to him?"

Sorren shook his head. "Unfortunately, no. We've also got Moran to contend with. Taras will focus on the demon. Lucinda and I will take Moran. You and Teag are there for back-up."

I paled. "I'm not sure I can be much help."

Sorren met my gaze. "The Alliance doesn't have armies, Cassidy, or SWAT teams. Just a few volunteers. We'll be fortunate to have Mirov's help. The five of us are all there is."

# Chapter Fourteen

"I TOLD YOU we wouldn't stay in the car." Teag shot me a sidelong glance. Although his voice was pitched whisper-low, I knew Sorren would hear, but he didn't deign to comment.

We were behind the old house that Teag and I had spotted as a bad energy place near the old Navy yard. "I wonder if this place looked as bad when Old Lady Dennison ran it," Teag mused under his breath.

I shrugged. "From the pictures you found, this might be an improvement."

We'd had a full day (except for the part taking care of customers) to dig through Internet sites and property records on the suspicious buildings. The decrepit house had been a seedy rooming house, the stay-by-the-day kind of place favored by folks who were too down-and-out to even rent week-to-week.

Matilda Dennison was the last recorded owner. From the mug shot that turned up in a newspaper account online, she looked as hard-bitten as any of her clientele. Before she owned the rooming house, Dennison had been arrested for a string of petty crimes, and from the remorseless look in her eyes, I guessed that those arrests were just the times she got caught.

"You know, all those suspicious deaths in and around the rooming house make me wonder whether the bad juju was going on longer than we thought," Teag said. He eyed the dark, hulking structure. "Either that, or Madam Dennison was a poisoner."

"She wouldn't be the first landlady to think of it," Sorren said over his shoulder, proof that he'd been listening to every word. "Back in the 1700s, there was a couple hanged at the Old Jail for killing the travelers who stayed at their inn and stealing their goods."

He said it as casually as I might have commented that something happened ten years ago, but I recalled hearing about the incident from one of Drea's tour guides. Maybe for Sorren, nearly three hundred years felt like decades.

"Yeah, but we don't know where any of the latest killings actually happened," I reminded them.

"I like my theory – that there's just something wrong with this whole area," Teag said. "When it was a base, it had a higher than average number of suicides and violence. Anthony heard the developer is having problems getting new tenants because so many of the businesses who moved here are struggling. Loan defaults, bankruptcies, suicides. As I said – bad juju."

Sorren picked the locks and the door swung open. Maybe he really had been the best jewel thief in Belgium.

"Let's get off the street, shall we?" he said.

I stepped just inside the door. "Won't you come in?" Sorren assures me there are ways a vampire can enter without a formal invitation, but having one makes it simpler, and we were in a hurry.

After what happened the last time we were in the Navy yard, we came better prepared. Sorren wore his sword, which he said had been spelled against demon spawn by an Italian mage he had known in the 1700s. I didn't care where it came from, so long as it worked.

Sorren had also brought with him something that looked like an old fashioned reflector lantern. It was a rectangular brass lantern with a mirror in the back, but the bluish-black candle it held looked to me more like something out of a Voodoo shrine than a reading lamp.

"Take this," he said, shoving the lantern into Teag's hands. "And this." He dug a Bic lighter out of the pocket of his jeans and handed it over. "Don't light it until we need it."

Teag looked baffled. "I brought a flashlight. What do you mean, 'until we need it'?" he asked.

Sorren gave him a look. "You'll know." He turned to me. "Here," he said, and handed me what appeared to be an ornate walking stick, with a band of cloth wrapped around the middle. "Hold it by the cloth, since you're touch-sensitive," he instructed.

I turned it from side to side. "What does it do?" I asked, thinking that it looked too fragile to bash a demon or its minions over the head.

"If you need it, grip the wood and open yourself to the vision," Sorren said. "The cane will know what to do."

We followed Sorren into the front hall. His vampire senses were keener than ours, so he didn't need light, but we did. Once the door was shut behind us, Teag and I withdrew our flashlights, each fitted with a red filter to dampen the glare. It might keep us from attracting attention, but the red glow gave the run down building a rooming-house-from-hell look.

"I'm hoping vandals did this, because I sure hope the place wasn't quite this bad when Dennison was renting out rooms," Teag said.

I had to agree. It looked like a hangout for crack addicts and heroin hustlers – maybe both. The entryway smelled of old vomit and dried urine. Used condoms and hypodermic needles littered the corners. The walls were stained with substances I didn't want to identify.

My psychic gift told me that the people who had passed through this house had been in the process of dying. We all die, but the folks who found themselves at Dennison's Rooming House had been in a little more of a hurry, whether they knew it or not.

"What are we looking for?" Teag asked.

"A room, a spot on the floor, an object that feels like the bad stuff we get at Trifles and Folly," I said, guessing. "Something that might point to a reason old items are taking on dark power."

Teag played his light around the room. There was a rustle and a squeak, and I deliberately did not look down. My guess was that we'd scared off a rat. I was surprised that they hadn't bolted when Sorren entered. Vampires had that effect on a lot of creatures.

"Cassidy's description is close enough," Sorren said. "We're looking for a nexus, a point of power. It could be an object. Anything."

I took a deep breath and concentrated, feeling my senses flow out around me. It could be something used in the construction of the house, or even buried in the walls, given its long dishonorable reputation. But I didn't think so.

Bad things had happened in this house, lots of bad things. Killers had moved through these rooms. Some had been drug dealers and some of them were shooters, but the resonance of their remorselessness lingered. Violence and death…

If I stood completely still and listened, I could hear whispers and echoes. Some of the lost ones who moved through this space were hunting death. Their end was foreordained; all that remained uncertain was the means.

Fragments of conversations clung to the walls and the bare wood floor. Listening to any single one was like trying to hear a whisper in a crowded airport or a noisy subway. It didn't matter what they said. Hopelessness and abandonment imbued every word. Dennison's Rooming House had been the antechamber to hell and the bad mojo pervaded every nook and corner, every board.

Teag stayed as my wingman while Sorren checked out the upper floors. I knew he'd call for me if he thought he needed my gift. "I wish we knew what we were looking for," Teag said.

I took another step, drawn by something. When I looked down, I saw a button. Teag spotted it, too. "Be careful," he warned, worried after the visions I had the night before from Jimmy Redshoes' button.

I bent down and looked more closely at the button, which looked like it was from a man's casual shirt. I can read the history of all sorts of objects, but for some reason, buttons take me deeper. Maybe it's because buttons are worn close to the body, often against the skin. They give me a clear picture of the wearer, and often, what was going on around the person right before the button was lost. Before I could second guess myself, I picked up the button.

The room had changed around me. I was seeing what

the button's owner had seen, just before the button was lost.

*Light struggled through the grimy windows and tattered draperies. Faded, scratched wallpaper clung to the dented plaster. The room smelled of sweat and burned toast.*

*I felt the button owner's terror of something outside that scared him far more than the junkies and roughnecks that gathered at Dennison's. He was still breathing hard, barely outrunning a killer, worried that it was waiting for him the next time he went out.*

*I glimpsed what he had seen. He had been stealing from parked cars, breaking into houses, anything to get by. Along the line, he ran into something worse than a junkyard dog or a vindictive cop. Kevin, the button's owner, was scared to go back out on the streets. I saw what he saw: Moran, bending over a box of some kind. A dead body in a back alley, stripped of its skin. And a glimpse of a monster in the darkness that had caught his scent and would never give up until it caught him...*

*The scene shifted, and Kevin was back at the rooming house. A skinny man with eyes that were too wide and too deep set snarled at him and crossed the room to grab his arm. "What'd you find? Give it to me!" The skinny man yanked him backwards. He smelled as if he hadn't bathed in days.*

*"Let me go! You don't understand, it's coming." He protested, but Danny, the skinny guy, had a temper and wasn't letting go.*

*"You owe me, now hand it over." Danny demanded.*

*Several other men were in the living room, but no one looked up. They might have been too stoned to know a fight was happening, or maybe they didn't give a shit. One man was either dead or sleeping. Hard to tell which in a place like this.*

*"Let go!" Kevin yelled. Danny swung, but it put him off balance and he missed, letting Kevin pull free, ripping his shirt and popping buttons as he headed for the stairs.*

"Cassidy." I heard Sorren's voice in my head before I heard it with my ears. Whatever power he was using brought me back from the darkness, back to myself like a steel safety cable.

I clung to his voice. The tawdry rooming house and Kevin's terror faded and with every breath, I was Cassidy once more. When I opened my eyes, I saw Sorren bent over me, cradling my head and shoulders in his lap. Teag pried the button out of my fist and put it in the pocket of his jeans.

"Damn buttons," I muttered. I had a headache, but the shaky feeling that often came with a vision would last even longer. I took a deep breath. "Find anything upstairs?"

"Yes and no," Sorren replied. "From the amount of dried blood and staining, I'd say it's possible one or more of the killings took place here. I would not recommend you go nearer and was just about to suggest we leave, before I found you on the floor."

"It's almost as if the entire house is powered up. I'll be glad to tell you about it, but I really want to get out of here."

"I think that's a good idea," Sorren said. "I'm afraid your gift caught something's attention."

Before my vision, I would have said that the rooming house felt despairing. But something had changed. The energy was stronger now, malevolent, the sadistic glee of the predator.

The front door slammed closed. Overhead, I heard the heavy tread of footsteps in the empty second floor. Music came from somewhere in the house, the scratchy sound of a cheap radio. There were voices, too. Mumbling voices muttering threats and curses. Shouting voices, echoes of old fights, screams of terror. It sounded like someone was scuffling over our heads. Sorren had just confirmed no one was up there.

No one alive.

Even the smell of the place had changed, losing the musty odor of a long-empty shell, filling with the sharp, foul odor of unwashed bodies, vomit, blood, and wounds gone sour. I was really wishing we had included Lucinda in our little foray. I struggled to hold the flashlight in my left hand, the walking stick under my arm, and still touch my agate amulet, wondering if its magic could protect us here.

The house began to shake, caught in its own personal earthquake.

"Watch out!" Teag shouted, ramming into me and pushing me out of the way as the rickety chandelier in the parlor tore loose from its fittings and crashed to the floor, showering us with broken glass.

The shadows were moving. Shadow men rose from the floor as if they had sprawled there, awaiting the unwary. Gray ghosts materialized, shades of the unfortunate souls who had lost their way and their lives in the rooming house. Some I recognized from the vision, most I didn't, but the general sense of foreboding grew darker. We weren't welcome here.

The footsteps over our heads were moving toward the steps. They had changed, and now I could hear the scratch of talons and a heavy, dragging sound on the bare wooden boards. I did not want to see the creature making those noises.

Sorren and Teag and I were standing back to back. Sorren lunged for the door. To my astonishment, it would not open, though we had unlocked it. Cursing under his breath, Sorren tore it from its hinges and flung it aside.

It was night outside, but there had been a sky filled with bright stars when we entered. Now, the stars were gone, and so were the street lights and the outlines of anything beyond the doorway. Teag's car should have been right outside, but we might as well have been in the darkest part of outer space. I heard a strange chattering, and a clicking like the claws of a giant lobster out on the warped and battered wood of the porch. Something hissed just beyond the door.

Sorren drew his sword, and it glowed a faint, icy blue. "Get ready," he said, trying to watch the shadows and the doorway at the same time. I had the awful feeling that whatever was coming down the steps behind us wasn't as scary as what was in front of us.

Teag had jammed his heavy cop-style flashlight through his belt so it shone up, casting everyone's face in strange light. He held the lantern aloft in his left hand, the Bic lighter ready in his right.

I had a death grip on the walking stick, although I was still damned if I knew what it was supposed to do. For a moment, the darkness seemed to hold its breath, and then all hell broke loose.

Something big, with too many legs and big claws came down the stairs, fast. The shadow men rushed forwards, elongated arms reaching for us. The gray ghosts surged around us, and this time, I caught a glimpse of Kevin's face and Jimmy Redshoes, and five young men who looked like I should recognize them, but in the moment, their identities escaped me.

*The ghosts are protecting us,* I realized. *They're trying to hold back the bad guys.*

"Go!" Sorren shouted.

Two of the demon minions hurtled through the door, but Sorren was faster, slashing into them with his ensorcelled sword. Teag lit the blue-black candle, and it was like he switched on a search light, because a blinding flare of light illuminated a path to the car, driving back the shadow men.

"Run!" Sorren commanded, and we ran, staying as close together as possible.

"It's coming!" I yelled, as the thing on the stair reached the landing. The light from Teag's lantern only carved out the way ahead of us, leaving the rest of the room in shadow, so I couldn't see the creature. I was pretty sure I didn't want to.

More demon minions launched themselves at us as we ran for the car, but Teag's lantern and Sorren's sword made them draw back.

The thing behind us thundered closer, and it sounded as if sharp talons were ripping up the floorboards as it ran. Its breath stank like the bottom of a dumpster on a hot day in August, and something grabbed at the back of my shirt.

I pivoted, changing my grip on the walking stick as I moved, touching the wood and leveling its silver tip at the monstrosity in the shadows.

Fire blasted from the walking stick like an arc welder. It was too bright to watch, so I didn't get a good look at whatever was hot on our heels, but that was all right with me. The creature shrieked, and I glimpsed its many limbs flailing against the white-hot fire.

The vision overwhelmed me.

*I saw an aristocratic young man with blue eyes, blond hair and a slightly crooked nose, and recognized Alard, Sorren's maker. He was dressed like a dandy, but I saw the sheer force of will in his eyes, and knew he was much, much older than he appeared.*

*I glimpsed the walking stick in Alard's grip as three bat-winged monsters flew at him, ripping at his clothing with their long talons, striking with their barbed, whip-like tails, keening like banshees with an ear-splitting howl. I could feel his fear, but beneath the fear was confidence in his training and in the silver-tipped walking stick he brandished like a sword.*

*One of the bat-things lurched at Alard, raking his shoulder with its claws. Alard leveled the walking stick and spoke a word I did not understand, and the same blue-white blinding fire burst from the cane. It burned through one of the creature's wings before he swung it toward the others, cutting one of the monsters in half and blasting the third backwards with a hole where its distended chest had been.*

The vision winked out as Sorren threw me into the car and Teag floored the gas before Sorren was even seated, laying rubber as he peeled away from the cursed house.

"They're still watching," I said.

"True," Sorren acknowledged. "But they haven't followed."

"That can't be Moran's or the demon's focal point, because the shadows didn't seem to be able to leave the property," I said, forcing myself to be clinical to avoid collapsing in a twitching bundle of nerves. "But it has definitely become a lesser focal point – similar to the Foo dog."

"The shadow men are a nasty piece of work," Sorren admitted. "And they're gaining energy from whatever's behind this. But no, I agree that we haven't found the source."

"The guy with the button – Kevin – he thought he was being pursued," I said. "He witnessed one of the killings when he was returning to the place that he'd been stealing from."

"Did you get a last name?" Teag asked.

I shook my head. "No. But it's very possible that he died in the rooming house, so maybe that will narrow it down."

"I'll see what I can do. If I can't find anything online, maybe Anthony's sources can help," Teag said. He had inherited his ancient Volvo from his grandmother, and it creaked and groaned as it bounced along the crumbling roads of the abandoned Navy yard but kept on going.

"In the meantime, I'll ask Lucinda for her assistance," Sorren said. "The house as it stands is dangerous. That makes it Trifles and Folly's business to contain. Perhaps she can work a spell that makes sure its malice doesn't extend beyond the walls. Until we can get it exorcised."

Personally, I thought a wrecking crew might be even more effective, but I held my peace. Given the fuss I'd kicked up with the ghosts, I wouldn't imagine that they would take well to having a demolition crew on the premises. And after the demonstration we had seen, I feared the spirits that remained at Dennison's Rooming House could be a lot more dangerous than we knew. I didn't want to wish them on anyone.

"Kevin's ghost came back to protect us at the end," I said quietly. "So did Jimmy Redshoes, and other people I didn't recognize." I decided that I needed to see photos of the men who had been killed, determine whether they had been among our ghostly champions. "There were five young men whose ghosts looked familiar," I said, thinking aloud. "I don't know where I've seen them before, but I know I recognized them from somewhere."

"I'm on it," Teag said. "We'll figure it out."

We were silent for a few moments as Teag navigated the twisting roads as quickly as he dared. Finally, I looked down at the walking stick in my hands. My grip had shifted back to the cloth-covered portion of the cane, but the vision I had seen was still clear in my memory.

"This was Alard's?" I asked, looking at Sorren.

A shadow seemed to pass over Sorren's face, and he looked away. "Yes," he said quietly. "It served him well. I guessed that since you could see the memories in my ring, you could access the resonance in the walking stick." He gave a wan smile. "It's a powerful weapon.

"You'll forgive me if I'm a bit overprotective," he said, still staring out the side window of the Volvo. "I lost my friends once to a demon and its master. I'll be damned if I'll let that happen again."

# Chapter Fifteen

THE NEXT DAY was beautiful, and likely to be hot, so I enjoyed the relative cool of the morning and took Baxter on a longer than usual walk, resolutely trying to push the terror of the night before from my mind. Watching Baxter romp and pounce lifted my mood, and when we returned home I was even more thrilled to find my Mini Cooper, or at least a similar Mini Cooper, parked outside looking as good if not better than before our escapade. By the time we went back inside, I knew Baxter was tired enough that he would take a long nap until I came back to feed him at lunch.

I was tired after last night, so I swung into Honeysuckle Café for a dose of caffeine. There was a line, and both Trina and Rick were pulling shots of espresso as fast as the machines would go.

"Whadaya hear, Rick?" I asked.

He shrugged. "Nothing much." Without my having to order, he made my favorite skinny double latte and added a dollop of sugar free vanilla.

"Good to see you out and about, Cassidy!" Drea sidled up when I left the counter, clutching her own takeout cup and a bag with a muffin. Just then, a nearby table opened up, and by mutual agreement, we decided to play hooky for a few moments.

"What's new in the carriage tour world?" I asked.

Drea's smile twisted. She looked around the cafe to see if any out-of-towners were close enough to hear. "I was at the Business Booster meeting last night. There's talk about increased security, with all the deaths out by the Navy yard."

"That's a good thing, right?" I said, but inwardly, I worried. More cops on patrol could make it harder for us to get to the bottom of whatever was going on.

"Yes and no, Sugar," Drea said. "In theory, the boys in blue make our fair city feel safe. Spot a few from time to time and it's reassuring. See one on every corner and you start wondering what's going on."

I did know, and I hoped Drea would misunderstand my uncomfortable squirm. The police weren't the only ones working to keep Charlestonians safe. And right now, I felt like we were letting folks down.

"Have you heard any more about the deaths?" I asked.

"Only that Jimmy Redshoes was one of the dead men," she said, and took a long sip of her coffee.

"Oh no," I said, hoping I sounded surprised. "What happened?"

Drea shook her head. "No one knows. They found him out by the Navy yard, that's where he got his supplies for the do-dads he sold. There are some wholesalers over that way."

"Will there be a memorial service?" I asked. I didn't know anyone who disliked Jimmy.

"Nothing official, but some of us down around the Charleston City Market plan to raise a glass in his honor down at Nicky's tonight." Nicky's Bar was a locals' joint, a little too far off the tourist maps to get the out-of-towners. It was a favorite among the younger King Street and Charleston City Market area business folks.

"Count me in," I said. If Sorren intended to check out the other two sites Teag and I had scouted – and I'm sure he did – I figured I deserved a night off to recuperate. And with the crowd that usually gathered at Nicky's, I was bound to hear something interesting, maybe even something related to the deaths.

"Bring Teag, if he wants to come," Drea said. "Are he and Anthony still an item?"

I grinned. "Yep. It's over a year now. Looking good."

Drea glanced at her watch. "Yikes! We'd better go. I meant to be a little late, but now I'm *late*."

My muffin was gone, but I hadn't quite finished my latte, so I scooped up the empty paper bag, slam-dunked it into the garbage, and retrieved my drink. "I'll see you tonight," I promised, giving a wave as I headed off in the opposite direction.

I got to Trifles and Folly a few minutes before we were set to open at nine, just a couple of steps ahead of Teag. He looked a little flushed and I bet he had ridden his bike faster than normal.

"You'll never guess what I heard," Teag said breathlessly as I turned the key in the lock and went to disarm the security system.

"Jimmy Redshoes *was* the one they found dead in the Navy yard," I said.

"How'd you find out so fast?" he asked. "Anthony only heard when he got into the office this morning. And it was what we suspected with the button and all but..."

I waggled my nearly empty cup of coffee. "Drea."

"Figures," he said. "Just once, I'd like to be first with the scoop."

I chuckled. "You get your share of heard-it-here-first moments."

"It's so sad about Jimmy. Not that it wasn't for the other victims. But he hits a lot closer to home. I never paid a lot of attention to the trinkets that Jimmy sold. He was just part of the scenery."

Now that I thought about it, Jimmy Redshoes sold odd, and unusual pieces, the kind that might have been looted from someplace. *He always spun such fantastic tales about their history to get you to buy,* I thought. *His stories were too outlandish to be true, but they always made me laugh.* Now he was dead, and if I had a chance to make his killer pay, I would.

I headed for the back room to make a pot of coffee. The latte helped, but I was still feeling the effects of last night. Part of it was the crash after a mortal terror adrenaline rush. But the majority had to do with the cost of using my psychic gift in a major way. Drawing on that supernatural energy was exhausting, another reason I wanted time to recharge before heading back to the warehouse district.

"Speaking of which..." Teag said, following me to make a cup of tea in the hot pot. "I did a little poking around online. Look what I found out about unlucky Kevin."

He spread out several pages he had printed out on the counter. Right away, I recognized the photos of Kevin in two different online newspaper stories.

"Kevin Harvey – the guy whose button you found at the Dennison house, was a hustler who seemed to dream of going straight. He had a pushcart down in the park for a while, and he had even done a regular table at some of the local flea markets."

"What went wrong?"

Teag stirred some sugar into his coffee. "Kevin got busted for selling stolen goods. He managed to stay out of jail, but from what the article says, it ruined him."

"Anything else?"

"Kevin's murder was one of the things that helped finally shut down the boarding house for good. But get this," Teag added. "He's counted as one of the unsolved Navy yard killings."

"They're doing an impromptu gathering at Nicky's in lieu of a service for Jimmy. I think I'll go and see what I can learn. You still meeting Anthony tonight?"

"Yeah, hopefully it will be a 'non-eventful' evening so we can focus on a little romance." Teag laughed. I hoped so, too. It had been a little too eventful around here lately.

I WASN'T SURPRISED to find Sorren waiting for me when I got home from the service for Jimmy Redshoes. My first clue that he was present came when Baxter didn't yip himself silly when I came in the door. I had left a light on in the kitchen, and it was enough to see Sorren sitting on my couch with Baxter happily perched on his lap. Baxter looked bemused and glazed, and I knew Sorren had glamored the pup again.

"You know, that can't be good for Baxter, scrambling his little circuits like that," I chided. "You're going to give him brain damage."

Sorren chuckled, and stroked Baxter's silky fur. "I assure you, all I've done is given him the equivalent of a mild sedative. It causes no ill effects."

It certainly beat having Baxter bark until he was hoarse. "Cassidy, I hope you know by now that I would not harm you," Sorren said. "I'm well aware of how fond you are of the dog. And if it makes you feel better, one of my patrons in Belgium had a very similar little dog, and we got on together quite well."

*No surprise, if you glamored him every time you saw the pup,* I thought, but said nothing. Baxter certainly didn't look any worse for the wear.

"Have you been waiting long?" I asked. Maybe I should be freaked out about finding an immortal vampire waiting in my house, but it didn't seem any stranger than meeting him elsewhere, and Sorren didn't like to be seen places he was likely to be remembered.

"Just a few minutes," Sorren said. "Do you have any news?"

I caught him up on Teag's research about the man I had seen in my vision at the Dennison house, and the confirmation about Jimmy Redshoes. Sorren listened intently.

"There was something else," I added. "When I was leaving Nicky's Bar, I spotted a photo on the wall. Five young men in front of their ship, the *Privateer*, anchored down at the Battery."

I met his eyes. "The *Privateer* was a salvage ship. Teag showed me a picture of the ship and its crew. And I saw those same men among the ghosts that protected us at the Dennison house."

Sorren nodded as he thought over what I had just said. "Very good. I think there's a link between all the deaths, the haunted objects, and that salvage team. We just haven't found all the connecting pieces," he said.

"Did your source turn up anything?" I asked.

Sorren set Baxter gently on the ground. Baxter ambled over to me and scratched at my leg to be picked up. He licked me once, then settled down and went to sleep.

"Yes, but in the negative," Sorren replied. "No one's seen Corban Moran in decades. That's why I thought I had killed him. But apparently, he survived, and he's been in hiding. If we can find out what he's been doing, we should be able to figure out why he's surfaced here in Charleston, with a demon to do his bidding."

"Do you think the salvage team that disappeared has something to do with Moran?" I asked. "And with the sunken pirate ship?'

Sorren nodded. "Almost certainly there's a connection, and we need to find it soon."

"Did you find out anything else?"

"Moran's not the first to raise a demon in Charleston. There have been several, including Jeremiah Abernathy."

"Who?" I asked, searching my memory. The name sounded familiar, in a very bad sort of way.

"It was one of the cases the Alliance handled many years ago. Abernathy was a corrupt judge who profited from the pirates he hanged, whose loot he seized for his own," Sorren replied. "Abernathy was rumored to have made a deal with the Devil, though I doubt it was with more than a minor demon. He had gone to the rum islands, and made a pact with the dark magic there for wealth and power. But something went wrong."

"Like what?" I asked.

"No one knows for certain, but Abernathy's luck had a sudden turn for the worse," Sorren replied. "Can't say I minded. He was a foul creature, and deserved the end he got. We had to do some serious clean up after his dealings soured." He paused. "But now, after Mrs. Morrissey's comment about Abernathy doing business with the unlucky Captain Harrison, I'm beginning to wonder if he has something to do with what's going on now.

"Harrison's return from Barbados and the loss of the *Lady Jane* coincide rather neatly with Abernathy's run of bad luck," Sorren added. "We thought we had removed any tainted objects... perhaps there was something we didn't know about."

I frowned. "You think Harrison's pirate loot ended up with Abernathy, and that it was intended for him all along?"

Sorren nodded. "That's exactly what I think. And now, all these years later, a salvage team has disappeared diving for an old wreck. Right before Corban Moran shows up and men start dying."

"Abernathy's demon," I murmured. I looked up and met Sorren's gaze. "If something aboard the pirate ship would have given Abernathy control of a demon, and that item was lost in the shipwreck, then why didn't the demon get loose and destroy the city?"

Sorren gave me a look. "Check your dates. You'll find that right after Abernathy died, Charleston was struck with one of its worst Yellow Fever outbreaks. At least, that's what they called it at the time."

His answer chilled me. "Why didn't the demon keep on killing?" I asked.

He shrugged. "Different demons function under different rules," Sorren said. "Abernathy's demon could not remain here unbound, and he withdrew to the place between worlds where spirits dwell, waiting."

"Waiting for someone to find the item that was lost in pirates' shipwreck," I replied. "Something the salvage team found."

"Or was about to find," Sorren said. "We don't know – yet – how the item came to Moran. If the demon has been called back and is under Moran's control, for now, then somehow, Abernathy's artifact has been recovered. That makes it our business."

We were silent for a moment, then I found the courage to ask the question that had bothered me since the previous night.

"Why did you choose Alard's walking stick to give to me?" I asked.

Sorren was quiet long enough I didn't think he would answer. Finally, he looked down and shifted in his chair. "I gambled that the stick would work for you, as it worked for Carel," he said. "Carel had your touch magic. Alard received his walking stick from a powerful wizard, a good man who died in the service of the Alliance."

"But I'm not a wizard. I shouldn't have been able to call fire."

Soren gave a sad smile. "You didn't have to. The walking stick worked as an athame, a focusing tool. All you had to do was open yourself to the memories of those who used it before you. Their power, their magic, has become part of the cane. When you touched it, and let the memories flow through you, the walking stick did the rest."

I was going to need to spend some time thinking about that. "What now?" I asked.

"We'll need to find more weapons if we're going to keep investigating the hot spots you found in the Navy yard. The key we need to connect the pieces is out there; we just haven't found it yet." He gave me a resolute smile, and I saw the tips of his long eye teeth. "But we will."

I shut and locked the door after Sorren. Just then, my cell phone began to ring.

"Hello, Sweetheart!" My mom seems to have a sixth sense about when I could use a call. That was probably true, given the magic that runs in her side of the family.

"Hi, Mom. What's up?" Baxter was hopping around my feet. He always seems to get extra affectionate whenever I'm on the phone.

"Just got back from speaking in Denver and thought I'd give you a buzz," she said.

"Home for awhile?" I asked.

"Two weeks, then we're heading to Manitoba, then on to Toronto," she said. "It should be a nice break from the heat." My parents moved from Charleston up to Charlotte when I was in college. At the time, my father worked for one of the mega-banks, and the move was part of a corporate relocation. Then my mom got her big break and launched her speaking career based on 30 years as a psychologist, and once the money started rolling in from her seminars and events, dad was more than happy to retire from the corporate world and become her agent and event manager.

"How's the store?"

"Busy," I said. "You know – every day is a new adventure." Boy, and how.

"How about you? Are you okay? I've had the strangest feeling and I just had to call." Mom's voice had gone into her 'you can trust me, I'm a therapist' tone.

"I'm fine," I said, ignoring a flash of guilt. "Just a little tired." True enough.

"I had the oddest dream," Mom said. "I dreamed about Grandma Sarah baking in the kitchen at her house. Do you remember?"

I smiled. Grandma Sarah had her own type of powerful magic, an ability to heal people with her cooking.

"I dreamed that Grandma Sarah was baking a cake, and she was stirring the batter with her favorite wooden spoon. Then she stopped and looked right at me and said, 'Elizabeth, you need to remind Cassidy to use my spoon. I'm done with it and she needs it'." Mom laughed. "Isn't that odd?"

I swallowed hard, taking a meaning from Mom's dream that she couldn't have known. Sorren and I had just talked about helping me collect items that would help me channel white magic like Alard's walking stick – things that could serve as an athame or wand and connect me with the power of the previous owner. I went to my kitchen drawer and pulled out the worn, stained spoon and felt the essence of my grandmother's very strong, very pure white magic.

"I've got to go. But honey," Mom said, pausing. "Please be careful. I worry about you."

"I will be," I said, wishing I could figure out how to keep that promise. "Love you."

"Love you, too." The call ended, and I let out a sigh and reached down to pick up Baxter and cuddle him for a moment.

I looked around my house and smiled. It's not one of the biggest or most historic homes in Charleston, but it's perfect for me. In a relatively short period of time, I had made this place my own. On all the shelves and walls, there were photos, recent pictures, and snapshots from family vacations as I was growing up. Photos of my brother, aunts and uncles, cousins, and grandparents were tucked everywhere. And there were pictures of every dog I had ever loved, from the Cocker Spaniel I had as a kid right up to Baxter.

I paused for a moment and picked up one of my favorite photos. It was a picture of a beautiful blond Golden Retriever, and in the photo, it would forever be summer, with the sun shining on his fur and his tongue hanging out in a goofy smile. Bo had been my constant companion for nearly a decade. I still missed him. I smiled as I thought about how much he loved to fetch a ball, and how he loved almost everyone he met.

'Almost' because one night, when I had been walking him a little later than usual, a thief went for my wallet. I'd always figured Bo would hand over the family silver for a dog biscuit, but I had a surprise coming. Bo sensed the threat, and all of a sudden, my furry goofball turned into ninety pounds of snarling, no-nonsense protection backed up by a big dog bark and teeth that looked menacing. The mugger decided it wasn't worth it, and Bo got a steak dinner for his efforts. Even now, thinking about that time made me feel very loved and protected.

Remembering Bo and Grandma Sarah's spoon gave me an idea. I went into my bedroom and walked to my closet. Stretching up on tiptoe, I got a box off the top shelf. It was covered with pretty fabric, and it held some of my dearest treasures. Baxter danced around my feet as I carried it carefully over to my bed and sat down to open it.

If there's ever a support group for psychometrics, we'll probably all confess to being packrats of a particular type. We horde trinkets that are charged with powerful memories. I opened the box and smiled as I looked inside. There was a frayed friendship bracelet from my high school best friend, a shell from my favorite vacation, and tickets from some of the most awesome concerts I had ever attended, things that made me feel loved and happy whenever I touched them. But I was looking for something specific, and when I saw it, I had to swallow hard at the memories it evoked.

I reached in and pulled out a stained and dirty dog collar. Bo was my best friend and I wasn't entirely beyond suspecting that he might have also been an angel in a fur coat. As much as I loved Baxter, I would always miss Bo.

The metal tags jingled as I closed my fist around the collar, and I felt Bo's unconditional love and protection as clearly as I could see his wagging image in my mind. And I knew what I had to do.

I wound the collar around my left wrist until it was tight enough to stay on and still possible to buckle. Just being in contact with its vibrations made me feel protected and strong. With a sigh, I closed the box and put it back on the shelf, then I headed downstairs for a hot cup of tea.

# Chapter Sixteen

"I REALLY WISH we'd brought Lucinda with us," Teag muttered as we eyed the old Covington warehouse.

"Lucinda has a day job, remember? And while she's a friend and she's helping us, I'm not sure that she's an official part of the Alliance," I replied.

"Personally, I'd be okay with a private army," Teag replied. His right hand jiggled nervously in the pocket of his hoodie.

"What do you have in your pocket?" I asked

Teag sighed. "I filled both pockets with salt, just in case. And I stopped by the Rock Hound booth at the Charleston City Market and bought a chunk of agate and an onyx disk."

Now that I was paying attention, the pockets of his hoodie actually looked a bit heavy. *How much salt did he pour in there?* I wondered.

Then again, I had a dog collar wrapped around my left wrist, my agate necklace, Alard's walking stick shoved through my belt, and a flashlight in my pocket. On a whim, I had grabbed my grandmother's mixing spoon and pushed it up the jacket sleeve on my right arm so it was snug against my forearm. If Grandma Sarah thought it was important enough to send a message to me from the Great Beyond, I figured there was more to the spoon than met the eye. Teag had his heavy cop flashlight plus the lantern with a new blue-black candle. I didn't know what Sorren had with him, but I was hoping it packed a big paranormal punch.

"Can you feel it?" I asked. I stared up at the dark hulk that was the Covington-Simchak warehouse. The sense of dread and foreboding was overwhelming. Most people have a gut-feel aversion to supernatural bad places where power is strong. Sane people listen to those warnings and run in the opposite direction.

Not us. We were going inside.

"No one's here." Sorren's voice made me jump despite the fact that it was barely above a whisper. "And yes, I feel it. The energy here is very unstable. We need to be careful."

I could think of dozens of things I would rather be doing. Then I remembered the body of Jimmy Redshoes on the pavement. He deserved justice.

"You're sure it's abandoned?" I asked Teag. The cornerstone of the red brick Covington building said 1860, and it looked hard used. It sat glowering, almost sulking in the darkness.

A couple of security lights on other, newer buildings cast a glow that nearly reached the Covington warehouse, but the building itself was surrounded by shadows. The sense of dread intensified. It felt as if the building were daring us to enter.

"Officially at least," Teag replied. "Simchak Enterprises went bankrupt a year ago. They had problems for a while. It was bad enough to make you wonder if they were cursed or something."

*Or something,* I thought. "And before that?"

"The property has changed hands a suspicious number of times, often as part of a bankruptcy."

"What about the Covingtons?" I asked.

"They managed to keep the place in one piece during the Civil War by hiring a private army of goons to patrol it," Teag replied. "They had a reputation for dirty deals, which from what I could find, they earned fair and square. Do you know how they ultimately lost the building? A duel!"

For a while in the 1800s, dueling had been a real problem in Charleston. It was an amazing waste of life. I wondered if that long-ago duel played into the aura of betrayal and violence that radiated from the building.

"Anything that would give the warehouse supernatural energy?" Sorren asked.

Teag shrugged. "During the Civil War, most of the buildings in this area were used as morgues or to house prisoners of war, or even as makeshift hospitals." Dead soldiers, suffering prisoners, and wounded men in agony could certainly up the bad mojo for a site.

"One of the owners was shot by his business partner over some kind of fraud. Another owner lost the property in a card game, and committed suicide," Teag said. "This place has worse luck than the Hope Diamond. You name it – bitter divorces, underhanded dealings, old grudges. If this place is steeped in bad juju, it's earned it."

"Best we go inside before the police make their rounds," Sorren reminded us. "Step lively."

Vampire strength and centuries of practice breaking and entering have their advantages. Getting past the wooden barricades posed no problem, and in a few minutes, we stood in the middle of dark and exceedingly creepy empty warehouse.

"What do you sense, Cassidy?" Sorren asked.

I took a deep breath and turned inward for a few moments. I let the dread roll over me. Fear, pain, and loss roiled around me, as if they sprang from the very foundations of the old warehouse. I let them flow past me like the tide.

"So much sadness," I murmured. "The energy is jagged, unsettled. There have been so many disappointments and betrayals, the whole place is steeped in sorrow."

I paused. "There's something else. Very dark. Not fresh, it's been some time since it happened but... evil." I looked up. "Something very bad happened here. Powerful enough that it's affected everything, like it changed the DNA of the place or something. Worse than the boarding house..."

Sorren nodded. "That's why there are no rats," he said. He looked as if he were listening intently. "No rats, no mice, nothing but spiders and roaches. We must be very cautious. Expect the worst."

Spiders and roaches are drawn to dark magic, while nearly every other living thing runs the other direction. Figures.

We moved carefully around the old building. From the layer of dust, it didn't appear that anyone had been here for a while, though there were signs that vagrants had tried to stake a claim. Over in one corner, I saw some ratty mattresses, pieces of dirty clothing, and empty liquor bottles. They looked like they had been here for a long time. I couldn't imagine anyone wanting to spend the night here, no matter how high or drunk. The huge building was mostly empty, except for a few stacks of old wooden crates that looked as if they had been looted long ago. I shone my light around the cavernous space. The floor was littered with papers and garbage.

"What did the last owners sell?" I asked as my beam hit a couple of opened wooden crates.

Teag shrugged. "They took consignment shipments for other companies – and my bet is that not all of them were legal."

He went over to one of the large wooden crates. Some long-ago looter had already pried open the top and riffled through the packing material. "Industrial fasteners," Teag said, gingerly poking at the contents with a piece of wood he had found on the floor.

"Not a likely place for Jimmy Redshoes to get his merchandise," I said. We pried open another couple of boxes and poked through several more that someone else had already mostly looted. We found a mishmash of merchandise ranging from trucking parts to bolts to laboratory beakers.

While Teag and I searched the boxes and the northern side of the building, Sorren searched the rest. I walked over toward the mattresses, wondering if there might be anything that could link Corban Moran or the murdered men to the warehouse.

I kicked at an old newspaper on the floor. The date was over six months ago. That meant whoever had holed up in here did it before the murders began. I looked at the discarded clothing. Maybe there was a reason they didn't come back.

I shone my flashlight along the wall, and recoiled. "Y'all better come look at this,"

Sorren was beside me in a blur, sword in hand. Teag ran over a few seconds later. I pointed my light at the wall.

Hanging upside down against the stained bricks was the blackened, mummified body of a man. A dark, shriveled form had been nailed into the wall beside the body, and I realized with a lurch of my stomach that it was his skin.

A wooden basin lay under the dead man's skinless, rotted head. I guessed that the dried, black residue had once been blood.

A twisted, shrunken rope made out of something I couldn't identify made a circle on the floor in front of the murdered man. Teag glanced at the rope and blanched. "Is that what I think it is?"

Sorren nodded. "Entrails." I swallowed hard to keep from retching.

Placed at intervals around the circle were the remnants of four thick pillar candles. The wax had a dark red cast to it, as if blood had been mingled with the paraffin. Between the candles were shriveled bird talons. Crow feathers were tied in bundles, attached to crude stone carvings with twine that looked suspiciously like sinew. The shriveled bodies of rats and birds lay with the feathers, an offering to the power woken here.

Marked in dried blood on the dirty concrete floor were symbols that seemed to shift whenever I looked at them. My mind shied away from them, and the resonance, even at a distance, felt cruel and remorseless.

"We found one the police didn't," I said quietly.

Sorren nodded. "And now we know where Moran called his demon." He gestured to the occult items. "Killing the man raised power, and stored it in the blood. The runes used that power to strengthen the evocation. The circle protected the wizard, and the skin opened a portal to the Otherworlds."

"If he called the demon here, why isn't it still here?" I asked, although I was happy it had worked out that way.

"Moran called it and bound it, which puts the demon under his control – for now," Sorren said. "The real question is, how did a damaged wizard like Moran muster the power to evoke a demon, let alone control it?"

"Find out why the salvage team disappeared, and you'll have your answer," Teag said. "I have a couple of leads I'm chasing, so I should have some answers later tonight."

I started to get a headache, as if a storm were coming. When I looked up, it seemed as if the far end of the warehouse was darker than it had been, and I could smell a faint whiff of smoke.

"Teag," I said, growing more worried by the second. "When you were looking up deaths associated with the property, did you find any people who died in the warehouse?"

Teag was still poking through one of the wooden crates. "Yeah. There've been quite a few. Part of the warehouse caught fire in 1861 and a couple of workers burned to death. Two firefighters died putting out the blaze. Later on, one of the former owners hanged himself here. Then a night foreman was shot in a robbery."

He paused, thinking. "There were some workers who got backed over by trucks on the loading dock, and stories of forklifts running amok and killing workers. A year or so ago, some addicts broke in and overdosed. Why?"

"Because I don't think the people who died here ever left," I replied. I pointed toward the far end of the warehouse. The shadows were now completely opaque, and they were moving toward us.

Though the night outside was quite warm, the warehouse was rapidly growing colder. The shadows were coming closer and moving fast.

"I think we'd better get out of here," Sorren said. He stepped in front of Teag and me, but I wasn't sure what one vampire could do against what might be a legion of ghosts.

I'm a psychometric, not a medium, but since I was in contact with the floor of the warehouse, I was getting a pretty clear connection to the spirits that were manifesting. Faces appeared in the darkness, only to fade and be replaced by other forms. I heard the sound of footsteps approaching. Some sounded like the thump of heavy work shoes, while others were the slap of sneakers or the scuff of boots, enough to tell me that there were dozens of spirits heading our way.

Some of the spirits were curious. Others resented that Teag and I were among the living. I felt their anger like a cold wave. They had been brooding for a long time.

"I think your count is off," I murmured. "There are a lot more ghosts here than the ones you mentioned, and they're pissed." Teag lit his lantern, sheltering the flame of the lighter with his body.

"Run!" Sorren shouted. He reached into the messenger bag he carried and pulled out something that looked like a glass globe with a dim blue glow inside. He lobbed it over his shoulder toward where the demon summoning had been done. The orb shattered on the hard concrete and exploded in a blast of cold, white fire that flared high, burning without heat, consuming the corpse and the skin-portal along with the summoning circle.

Ear-piercing screams filled the cavernous space as the

cold fire consumed the portal, and a hurricane-force wind swept through the warehouse, raising a cloud of dust and dirt that stung our eyes and burned our skin, making it difficult to breathe.

The wind and dirt made it impossible to see where we were going. I lost track of where the door was, and the thought of that shadow horde waiting for us to blunder into range scared the crap out of me. In the wind, Alard's walking stick was more dangerous than helpful, and I had no desire to incinerate myself or my friends.

Behind us, the wind did its best to snuff out the cold fire, but the blue flames licked at the walls and scoured the floor, rising toward the high ceiling above us. It burned without heat, consuming the awful remnants of the sacrifice.

One of the wooden crates crashed to the floor with a boom like cannon fire. The crate exploded on impact, sending pieces of wood and a hail of bolts flying through the air, pelting us like shrapnel. Something hit the back of my head and I reeled. I could feel splinters through my jeans.

Another crate fell, then a third, thunderingly loud. It was only a matter of time before one of us was crushed or injured. My jeans and hoodie deflected the worst of what hit us, though I expected to be covered in bruises.

"This way!" Sorren shouted. The angle of the falling crates had given him the clue he needed to find our way through the wind toward the door.

As quickly as it came, the wind stopped, and I realized that the ghosts of the wronged dead stood between us and the exit.

I stumbled, and the ghosts closed ranks, cutting me off from Teag and Sorren. They turned to come back for me, and the cold wind gusted again, tipping the stack of crates right beside us.

Everything seemed to happen at once.

Instinctively, I threw my left arm up to protect myself. The ghosts lunged for me. Bo's tags jangled from the collar around my wrist, and suddenly the sound of an angry attack dog echoed from the stone walls. Bo's ghost stood between me and the vengeful spirits of the wronged dead, barking like a junkyard dog and baring his teeth, snapping and snarling.

The ghosts were still between me and the door, but they didn't try to get past Bo, buying me a few seconds to react. With my right hand, I leveled Alard's walking stick at the closest crate as it tilted crazily and began to career toward me.

I didn't know if Bo's ghost would disappear if I tried to focus on the memories that activated Alard's walking stick, but there wasn't time to worry about it. I willed myself to concentrate, opening myself to the resonance of the walking stick, fearing that at any moment, the ghosts would close around me.

Fire burst from the silver tip of Alard's cane, striking the crate that was headed straight for me. The crate burst apart with a crash, and the blast of fiery power threw the fragments backwards, showering the ghosts with a rain of burning embers.

I tried to run, but the ghosts forced me back. Crates were tumbling everywhere. I saw Sorren throw Teag out of the way, only to be buried by the falling jumble of splintered wood and the hail of bolts, clamps, and sundry metal fasteners. I didn't dare blast the crates now for fear of incinerating Sorren and Teag. I shoved Alard's walking stick through my belt.

"Sorren!" I screamed. Teag thrust his lantern with its blue-black witch's candle at the ghosts and they shrank back, clearing a path to the door. He grabbed me by the shoulders and threw me toward the opening; diving to follow me, he rolled and was back up on his feet. I landed hard, but Teag grabbed my arm and dragged me to my feet, hauling me toward the door. Behind us, I heard Bo's ghost holding our attackers at bay.

A thunderous roar reverberated from the walls as we ran the last few feet to the door. I was bleeding in a dozen places from where bits of wood and metal had clipped me, and Teag had a nasty gash on the side of his head, plus at least as many injuries as I did. I wanted to turn to look for Sorren, but Teag had a hold on my sleeve, dragging me forward.

I knew Sorren was immortal, but he had also told me that he could be destroyed. A stake through the heart would immobilize a vampire of his age, but decapitation would be fatal. It wasn't difficult to imagine pieces of flying wood impaling him or some odd piece of metal shearing through his neck. I had no idea whether ghosts could attack the undead directly, and my loyalty warred with my common sense because I wanted to run back in to see if I could help. Teag must have sensed my conflict, because he kept a tight grip on my arm.

A piece of one of the falling crates clipped me in the head and I went down on one knee. Bo's snarling ghost wavered and winked out. The angry spirits surged forward, tearing at our clothing, grabbing fistfuls of hair, scratching at us with bone-sharp fingers that left bloody welts down my arms and back.

"We can't leave Sorren in there!" I said, staggering to my feet and stumbling as Teag refused to let me fall. The ghosts were right behind us. Teag shoved me through ahead of him, and the darkness closed around him, pulling him backward.

"Cassidy! Run!" Teag yelled.

I wheeled back toward the warehouse. I was not giving up.

"Get your dead fucking hands off of him!" I shouted at the darkness, lunging back through the doorway. One hand closed around Teag's arm and the other grabbed a fistful of his hoodie and despite the way my vision reeled from the throbbing welt on my skull, I pulled for all I was worth, bracing my feet against the doorframe.

The vengeful dead fought me, hungry for another sacrifice. I was swearing like a sailor under my breath, channeling my fear, anger, and desperation to save Teag. Icy cold tendrils were shredding Teag's hoodie and shirt, and he screamed in pain as sharp, skeletal hands scraped the flesh from his back.

I acted on instinct. My right hand came up, palm out, straight-arm, and a blast of yellow-golden light barely missed Teag's ear. Its power threw me backward into the parking lot and dragged Teag with me, since my hand had a death grip on his hoodie. I stared in horror, afraid that the warehouse was about to go up in flame, but it was power, not fire that streamed from my outstretched palm. Like the force fields I had seen in science-fiction movies, the golden light held the ghosts at bay. I felt my grandmother's presence more strongly than at any time since her death. Grandma Sarah was a loving woman, but when someone she loved had been wronged, she could be fierce.

The burst of light gave us the chance to scramble backward until we had put most of the lot between us and the warehouse. The golden light winked out. I sat back on my heels, staring at the warehouse in despair.

"We left him in there." I was never going to forgive myself.

"He's almost six hundred years old, Cassidy. I'm sure he's been through worse things than this," Teag said, but I could tell from his voice he didn't really believe his words. Teag was pale, and bleeding in enough places that he looked as if he'd been mugged. My heart was thudding, blood pounding through my veins in aftershock. If Sorren still existed, he wouldn't have any trouble finding me.

The street of warehouses seemed deafeningly silent. I froze, waiting to hear sirens, but if the Covington place ever had a security system, it was deactivated along with the electric service. I glanced around, but the run-down warehouses nearby barely had outdoor lights that worked, let alone security cameras. I didn't know what was worse: thinking the cops might show up at any second with guns drawn, or being utterly alone out here in the dark with no back-up.

"What do we do?" I asked, staring at the warehouse. "He could be hurt. We can't just leave him in there."

"Vampires heal super-fast."

I shook my head. "Not if something impaled him. If he's been impaled through the heart, he won't turn to dust, but he can't move."

"Fortunately, that did not happen."

Sorren emerged from the far side of the Covington building. He had worn jeans, a dark t-shirt and a black lightweight jacket for the night's endeavor, and it looked as if he had rolled in sawdust. A deep gash on his forehead soaked one side of his face and the collar of his shirt in blood, but the wound was healing even as I watched. His hair was dark and matted, testimony to other injuries I could not see. One sleeve of his jacket was torn at the shoulder, and he had put the knees out of his jeans. His sword still hung from his belt. A gash across the front of his shirt and a bloody wound beneath it vindicated my worry. The crates had not struck him through the heart, but they came close enough.

Teag let go of my arm and we ran over to Sorren. The only thing that kept me from throwing my arms around him in relief was concern that I might hurt him. He held himself more stiffly than usual, and I realized he was walking with a bad limp. I wondered if he had broken bones, and whether a vampire's skeleton healed as rapidly as skin and tissue. Sorren managed a wan smile.

"Your concern is deeply appreciated," he said, and then glanced up at Teag. "As is your good sense in keeping her from running to the rescue." He held his arms away from his body as if to present himself for my inspection. "As you can see, I am still here."

Covered in blood, his clothes tattered and his hair matted with dirt and sawdust, he looked more like the victim of a bomb blast. One glance made it clear that no mortal could have survived his injuries.

"You were under the crates when they fell," I said.

Sorren nodded. The moonlight was enough for me to see that just in the time since he had made his appearance, the gash on his face was nearly healed.

"And it was a good thing you were not," he replied. He went to take a step and his leg buckled under him. I reached forward to steady him, but Teag beat me to it, helping Sorren to the ground.

Teag put his hand on Sorren's shoulder and knelt

down beside him. "You need to feed. You're hurt and it's almost dawn. Let's not make this one of our usual arguments – we don't have time," Teag said, holding his arm in front of Sorren's mouth. I had seen this before.

Unfortunately, we'd had a couple of bad encounters that had given Teag and Sorren the chance to hash out this feeding thing. The good part was since that first time, Sorren treated Teag with a whole new level of respect and there was no question now that he was 'family'.

The fact that Sorren didn't argue let me know just how badly he was hurt. He bit into Teag's wrist, and took several gulps of blood. Then he drew back, leaving two neat, small punctures that were already healing. There were just a few small flecks of blood on Sorren's lips. "Thank you," he murmured. Up close, I could see the tautness in Sorren's face and guessed that the pain was excruciating.

Even such a short feeding seemed to give him strength, but Sorren faltered when Teag and I helped him stand.

"Sorry. Bones take a bit longer to heal," he said. With Teag under one arm and me under his other, we helped Sorren stand and moved as quickly as possible toward where we had left the car.

I glanced at my watch. Dawn was only a few hours away. "Can you get to your safe resting place?" I asked. I didn't know what other threats lurked in the Charleston night for vampires, but if there were other would-be predators – human or supernatural – that were looking for prey, I doubted very much that Sorren would be up to the fight right now. "Let us take you back to the shop."

To my surprise, Sorren nodded. "I was thinking the same thing," he admitted. The gash on his face had healed without a trace, and I guessed the same would be true for his scalp wounds, but from the way he slid into the back seat of the car, I could tell that every motion hurt. Teag and I shook out our jackets and splinters rained down on the road. I felt prickly all over, and I figured we had been peppered with tiny bits of wood and packing material.

"There's a package of hand wipes under the seat. You'd better wipe the blood off your face. If we get caught, you look like death warmed over," I said, and winced at the utterly tactless, if true, description.

"Indeed," Sorren said, but I could hear amusement in his voice. "It would not do to attract attention."

Maybe it was my imagination, but I felt eyes on us until the car was outside the Navy yard perimeter. *Could the supernatural reaction at the Covington building have activated ghostly activity at other locations?* I wondered. If the demon could make objects with a bad history into maliciously haunted weapons of magical destruction, I figured it was possible.

It didn't seem smart to stick around long enough to find out. I made sure I was driving the speed limit, and I knew my headlights and tail lights worked, so there was no reason for anyone to stop us. Even so, I didn't really start to breathe until we were back on King Street.

Downtown Charleston was nearly deserted at this hour. I hoped that held for police patrols as well. I reminded myself that as the owner of Trifles and Folly, I had every right to be at my own shop any hour of the day or night, but I also knew that any cop worth his badge would wonder about three people showing up in the dead of night looking like they'd been in a gang war.

A glance in my rearview mirror told me that Sorren was

even more pale than usual. The wet wipe had removed the blood from his face, but there was no getting around his blood-soaked hair and stained clothing. Teag and I were cut and bloodied, our clothing torn, and we were bruised and covered in splinters and grime. No matter how hard I tried, I wouldn't be able to come up with an even halfway plausible explanation for our appearance. I hoped it wouldn't be necessary to give one.

Just to be on the safe side, I pulled into the alley behind the shop. Going in the front door was almost certain to attract attention. In the car, Teag gave Sorren his hoodie, which I hoped would obscure his features as well as his appearance from any of the security cameras keeping vigils over my neighbors' rear doors.

Teag stayed slouched in the car as I opened the door to the shop and let Sorren in. I hoped that meant anyone watching the tape would assume that if two figures entered, it would be Teag and me. No one knew Sorren, and we tried to keep it that way. Those questions were better avoided.

"I can make it from here," Sorren said. He smiled at me. "Thank Teag for me, and thank you for being willing to rescue me. It was foolhardy, but brave."

"Good partners are hard to come by," I replied. "No one will bother you if you need to be down there for a while to recuperate."

He moved toward the steps to the shop's basement where he had a hidden windowless room. I could see that he was still limping. "Don't worry – when I'm ready, I'll let myself out. Good night, Cassidy. Be careful."

I locked the door behind me and got back in the car. Teag didn't sit up until we were out of the alley, just in case. "Think he'll be okay?" Teag asked.

I shrugged. "As you said, in almost six hundred years, I imagine he's seen worse. He said to tell you 'thanks'." We rode most of the rest of the way in silence, exhausted.

"Do you think other victims were killed at the warehouse?" Teag finally asked as we pulled up in back of his apartment.

I frowned, then shook my head. "I don't think so. We didn't see evidence of other murders and I didn't get any sense of them. I think Sorren was right – that was where Moran summoned the demon. Maybe he's got a reason not to go back there. One thing's certain: if those ghosts could have gone outside the building, I'm quite sure, with as angry as they were tonight, they would have done it."

"Then that means that somewhere else has got to be the site linked to the killings, and to whatever it was that the salvage crew found." Teag said. I could hear the weariness in his voice. Now that the life or death drama was over, the adrenalin crash had taken a toll on me as well. I couldn't wait to crawl into bed.

"Maybe," I replied. "All I know is, if it's more dangerous than the warehouse, I vote for bringing more back-up."

# Chapter Seventeen

JUST MY LUCK: the next day was bright and clear, not too hot, and a perfect day for tourists to explore the Historic District. Teag and I were exhausted from the previous night. It had taken me an extra half an hour and a whole container of concealer to cover up the visible evidence of the fight at the warehouse. My entire body was bruised, and I was covered with cuts, scratches and nasty-looking claw marks.

Teag wore a long-sleeved shirt despite how hot it was, and he moved like his back hurt. I remembered how the ghosts had shredded his shirt and the skin beneath it, and I winced just watching him move.

It figured that for the first time all week, we were slammed with customers almost from the time I opened the door in the morning.

"How long did it take to get all the sawdust out of your hair this morning?" Teag asked *sotto voce*.

I rolled my eyes. "Who says I got it all out?" Sawdust was still sprinkled all over my bathroom floor from my attempts to get it out of my hair, my clothing, even my eyebrows.

"Did you get rid of all the splinters?" I whispered.

Teag sighed. "No, and I swear I've got them everywhere – and I do mean, *everywhere.*"

"TMI!" I protested, but I could relate. When I took off my clothes, fine splinters poked through the fabric of my jeans, my hoodie, even my socks. My whole body itched, and no amount of lotion had helped.

Business was so brisk, I didn't even have time to run out and pick up lunch, so we ordered pizza delivery and grabbed bites in between customers. All the while, my mind kept going over everything that happened at the warehouse. I was sure that the next step was finding out more about the missing salvage crew. There might be more unknowns, but that seemed to be the logical next step.

Since I was functioning on only a few hours sleep, I promised myself that the elusive clues would surface once I got some rest. In the meantime, I tried to keep myself alert with conversation, coffee and a few trips to the washroom to splash cold water on my face when my energy began to droop.

As the customers browsed, I wondered whether Sorren was still recovering in the lightless safe room beneath the shop. It wouldn't be good for business if customers knew we had a vampire in the basement. I finally gave up worrying, and figured that Sorren would heal and feed again on his own schedule.

In between sales, I surreptitiously began making notes on a list by the register of key points we knew about all the haunted objects. The day sailed by, and I gauged how time passed by how full the coffee pot was. Finally, I was down to the dregs, of the day, the pot, and my energy level.

Five o'clock rolled around, and the last customers chose their treasures, paid the bill, and ambled off in search of dinner. I followed the last shopper to the door, chatting about restaurant recommendations – hard to go wrong with Charleston's fantastic options – and turned the lock when I closed the door behind her. With a sigh of relief, I flipped the sign from 'open' to 'closed' and sagged against the door frame.

"I swear today was forty-eight hours long," I said. I let my head rest against the wood and immediately regretted it. There was a goose egg the size of a large marble under my hair where one of the bolts had hit me. Every muscle ached, and my head throbbed.

"You're just out of practice," Teag teased. Despite his teasing, he had dark shadows under his eyes and looked haggard. He moved stiffly, and I knew he probably hurt as much as I did.

"How badly was your back scratched up?" I asked.

Teag grimaced. "I have welts everywhere from all the stuff that fell on us. My back looks like a tiger used it as a scratching post. Anthony had to work late last night so he didn't come over, but I'm going to have to think of how to explain this that doesn't include breaking and entering."

Anthony's position as a lawyer meant that Teag couldn't always be completely forthcoming about our activities. We both thought Anthony suspected that we sometimes bent the rules, especially about things like trespassing, and intentionally did not press for details to avoid conflict with his conscience and his law license. "You could always say we went to play paintball as a teambuilding activity," I chuckled. "Leave him his plausible deniability."

"That explains the bruises, but not the scratches." He paused. "I guess I can say I fell on one of those serrated gratings." Teag sighed. "That's the only thing I dislike about what we do. I hate not telling Anthony the whole truth."

"He's safer not knowing," I replied.

Teag gave a lopsided smile. "He could handle it." I could see from his expression it was time to change the subject. "So... what were you working on every time the customers walked away to browse?"

I walked back to the paper I had next to the register and waved it at him. "Looking for points of similarity between the haunted items. Any thoughts?"

He chuckled and walked over to the table where he usually served clients and withdrew another scribbled list. "Great minds think alike I guess."

"Come up with anything?"

"Maybe. I'm thinking the location we didn't get to," Teag said. "I checked out the address, and it's some kind of self-storage company, now defunct." He paused. "Remember, Rebecca said the Foo dog statue had been in storage? Nothing new on the salvage crew though, I was too tired last night to follow-up."

"We have some work to do," I agreed. "Is Anthony expecting you for dinner?"

He shook his head. "Unfortunately, no. He's still tied up with that big case and that means sporadic late nights for a while. Good for me being able to keep odd hours without having to explain, but lousy in the relationship department."

My last semi-serious relationship had been with a young doctor at St. Francis hospital, and the love affair had foundered because of his long, unpredictable hours.

I sincerely hoped that Teag and Anthony could adjust and make it work. "Does that mean you're available for dinner?"

"Works for me."

"Want to pick up take-out and then see what we can find out about the missing salvage team? Maybe we can see if there is any connection to the storage unit," I suggested.

"My thoughts exactly."

Teag paused. "Should we check on Sorren? I mean, shouldn't we do something more to help him recover his strength?"

I raised an eyebrow. "I think you did your part. He'd tell us if things were dire."

Teag shrugged. "I don't know. He looked pretty ragged when we got back."

I agreed, but since Sorren had never stayed in the safe room before, I had no prior experience to go on. "Tell you what. It's still early. The sun hasn't even set yet, so he's not awake. Maybe we can stop by after supper and at least knock on the door and see if he needs something."

With that, we finished closing up for the night and slipped out the back. It was a beautiful evening, so we decided to walk a few blocks to Forbidden City, our favorite Chinese restaurant. It was busy when we got there, and I was glad we weren't trying to get a table.

Fortunately, the owner, Jay Chau, likes us. Jay saw us in the doorway and waved. "Long time, no see!" he said, crossing the room to give me a hug and shake hands with Teag.

"Business looks good, Jay," I complimented, looking around the packed dining room.

He gave me a broad wink. "Thanks to friends like you, it stays busy. Give me a moment, and I'll get your reservation ready," he said in a voice that would carry to the two parties that were waiting for a table.

"Just take-out tonight, Jay," I said. "Been a long day and we're ready to crash."

"Too bad," he said with a grin. "I had the best table in the house for you. Keeps your backs to the wall. You'd see everyone who comes in."

"You've been watching old mobster movies again, haven't you, Jay?" Teag joked.

Jay shrugged, palms up, as if to say 'busted'. "I can't help myself. *Scarface* was on late night cable, followed by *Wise Guys*. They're my favorites."

From a certain angle, Jay had a slight resemblance to Al Pacino, if Pacino was about thirty-five years old and Asian. He played it up with a penchant for wearing black, and on weekends, he sometimes even sported a pin-striped suit.

"Are those your folks?" I asked, with a nod to a well-dressed older couple whose table was heaped with far more food than I could imagine them eating. It looked as if the entire menu had been brought out, though the man and woman were rail thin.

"Yep," Jay said. "And you know what? Now that Forbidden City is a big success, my father claims my career switch was originally his idea."

As the only son of immigrants, Jay had followed his parents' prodding and gone to medical school. He'd hated every minute of it, and dropped out, following his dream of running a restaurant. Originally, his parents hadn't been thrilled.

"How's the food truck doing?" I asked as Jay handed out menus.

He grinned broadly. "Very well. You've seen it?"

"It's hard to miss a truck painted with a huge Chinese dragon on the side," I said with a smile. "Not to mention the big kite you put up when the truck sets up shop."

"Let me give you a minute to decide, and I'll be back to take your order," Jay said. Jay always went out of his way to give us the VIP treatment, and I think he also enjoyed a chance to chat a little with friends.

"Don't go. I'm too tired to think," I said, closing my menu. "I'll have my regular."

Teag put his menu on top of mine. "Me too."

Jay was back in a flash with our orders, and we headed back to the store. Sorren didn't answer our knock, so we drove back to my house. Baxter was thrilled to see us and even happier for a few pieces of stir-fried broccoli, which he considered a treat. Go figure.

We ate first, since we were both starved. I opened a bottle of wine, and poured us each a glass. We pushed the dinner dishes out of the way and pulled out the lists we had made.

"What have you got?" he asked.

"All the pieces had some kind of tragedy in their history," I said, looking at the first item on my list.

Teag nodded. "True. But given the age of the stuff we sell at the store, there have to be loads of other pieces with a sad story associated with them and they aren't haunted."

"That we know of," I replied, and Teag shrugged to concede the point.

"None of the pieces that came from Trifles and Folly seemed haunted when they were in the shop," he added.

"But they reacted in the presence of a strongly haunted item, like the Foo dog," I agreed.

"We don't know what link – if any – exists between

the men who were killed near the Navy yard and the haunted objects," Teag said, consulting his list.

"If our guess is right and Jimmy and Kevin were buying – or stealing – items from places in the Navy yard, maybe even the self-storage place, we don't know whether any of their objects have been haunted."

"Which means that there could be incidents happening that we haven't heard about," Teag replied.

I gave him a look. "The only reason we know about the haunted objects is because Rebecca knew my reputation and a bunch of items were all together at Gardenia Landing. Trinket was an accident." The idea that there could be other haunted items whose owners had no idea what to do was really frightening.

"Think about it. Who is the average person going to call if they bring home a new antique and everything goes haywire?" Teag said.

I responded with the obvious answer. "Ghostbusters."

Teag raised an eyebrow. "Seriously. You know folks in Charleston. The first inclination is to keep everything hush-hush."

Teag was right. Charleston valued propriety. "They're just going to put up with it," I said.

Teag nodded. "Exactly. But if we can figure out what's behind it, maybe when we deal with whatever is at the Navy yard, it will take the juice out of any other items. I think we ought to see if any of the objects we know about came from the storage place at the Navy yard."

"And we also need to figure out how the salvage team is connected to the Navy yard," I added. "I have a feeling they're at the heart of this whole thing."

Teag grabbed my laptop and started to work his Weaver magic. While he worked, I cleaned up the kitchen and put the leftovers in the fridge. Baxter had already eaten his kibble, and he curled up under Teag's feet.

"Old articles about the crew of the *Privateer* aren't hard to find," he said. "They were among the top wreck-finders several years running. They were good, and they were careful."

"Can you find anything about how they disappeared?" I asked.

Teag studied his screen. "That's where it all gets sketchy," he said. "Accounts don't agree. Some say their ship was headed out of Antigua when it disappeared, and others say Barbados. The Coast Guard spotted them a hundred miles off the Charleston coast." He shook his head. "There are even a few sightings days after the official reports say the ship disappeared."

"Someone with magic could arrange confusion like that," I said, leaning back against the counter and taking a sip of my wine.

Teag nodded. "A wizard like Corban Moran, even damaged, could make people doubt their senses, see things that weren't there." He scrolled through more screens, frowning.

"Was there any indication what treasure they were after when they disappeared?" I asked.

That took a little more digging, and some of Teag's magic to crack a few password-protected sites. He cracked his knuckles, then sat back with a grin.

"They were after the treasure of the *Cristobal*, a Cuban pirate ship that sank off the South Carolina coast a hundred and thirty years ago," he said. He was silent for a while as his fingers flew across the keyboard.

"That's interesting," he said, hunching toward his screen. I came around to stand behind him.

"What?"

Teag frowned. "When I went out on the Darke Web to see if there was any mention of the *Cristobal*, I got more hits than I expected." He twirled a pencil as he thought. "Seems there's been a lot of conjecture about just what the *Cristobal* was carrying when it sank. Salvage teams like the *Privateer* might have been after gold, but the wizards and conjurors on the Darke Web were after more practical treasures."

"Artifacts?"

He nodded. "Magic's thick like molasses down in the Islands," he said. "Just as dark as molasses, too, polluted by all the slavery and death. I recognize the pseudonyms of the people who were interested." He looked up at me. "They aren't the Alliance's kind of people."

"The Family?"

Teag shrugged. "I'm sure they'd have liked to get some powerful dark artifacts, but if they were part of this crowd, it was through proxies."

"Seems like the trouble started before the *Cristobal* even left port," he went on. "There were several suspicious fires on the docks that day, and three men were found dead under mysterious circumstances." He raised an eyebrow. "The *Cristobal* was in such a hurry to leave port that the harbor master made a note of it." He frowned. "What's interesting is that no one's sure just why it sank."

"I thought it went down in a storm?"

Teag made a face. "It did – but it was a freak storm. The most reliable witness was a sighting from the *Lady Jane*, a merchant ship. They saw a ship they believed to be the *Cristobal* sailing into a bad squall. Whoever kept the duty log noted that the storm seemed to come out of nowhere and dissipate just as quickly. They logged that they tried to find survivors, but only found a few floating crates after the storm passed."

"Magic," I said quietly. Teag nodded. "And it ties back to what Rebecca said about Harrison's ship – the *Lady Jane*."

He leaned back again and laced his fingers behind his head, wincing as he touched a sore place from last night's fight. "What if our theory is right, and one of the artifacts that sank with the *Cristobal* could strengthen a man's hold over a demon?" he asked. "What if that's why Jeremiah Abernathy wanted it so badly – badly enough to hire pirates to bring it to him?"

"If it's true that he raised a demon – and Sorren was in Charleston back then, so I'm betting he's got the story right – then I'd say that if Abernathy thought his grip over the demon was slipping, he'd be willing to do anything to hold onto it."

Teag stared at his screen as if he could will it to provide the answer. "I'll keep digging," he said. "Both on Abernathy and on the crew of the *Privateer*. The salvage crew wasn't based in Charleston, but they did a lot of business here. Maybe someone who knew them has a piece of the puzzle."

"Come to think of it, Mrs. Morrissey mentioned Jeremiah Abernathy when I told her I was going to stay at Gardenia Landing," I said. "I think it's time I go pay the Historical Association a visit."

Just then, Baxter came tearing out of his bed under the desk, snarling and yapping like a hell hound. Teag set the laptop aside and we both got to our feet warily. Alard's walking stick and Grandma Sarah's mixing spoon were on the counter where I'd left them this morning. I grabbed both of them, hoping I didn't need to use the cane. I had no desire to burn down my own house.

"See anything?" I asked. Teag had gone around the left side of the downstairs, looking out windows, while I circled on the right.

Teag shook his head. "Nothing out of place," he said. Baxter barked frantically, baring his teeth.

"Someone's out there," I said, spotting a movement in the shadows.

"If it's Moran, he's not wearing his hat," Teag replied.

I put my hand to the agate necklace, and felt nothing. *Damn.* Last night had probably drained it of all its protective mojo, and we had gotten home just before dawn, so cleansing it in the moonlight wasn't possible, even if I had been awake enough to think about it.

Sorren was in no shape to rescue us. Lucinda was out of town. We were on our own.

The lights went out.

Lucinda had warded the house, and Sorren assured me it was strong magic. Maybe so, but the warding apparently didn't include the power lines. We waited, listening. Baxter was giving a deep-throated growl. Too deep, in fact, for it to be Baxter. I looked up, and saw that he had been joined by Bo's ghost, who was barking like a rabid guard dog. Oddly enough, Baxter didn't seem to be fazed at all by the spectral ghost dog, and the two of them staked out positions watching the front door.

Outside, I heard the wind begin to howl on what had been a quiet evening. I moved over to the window, keeping myself out of the sight of anyone outside, and saw that despite the noise, none of the shrubs close to the house were bending, and none of the shutters banged. The air about six feet out from the house had an odd iridescence, and I wondered again just how Lucinda had placed her magical protections.

*What will the neighbors think of my glowing house?* I wondered, then debated whether they would even be aware of the magical struggle going on.

"Do we call the police?" Teag asked.

"And tell them what?" I asked.

As I watched, opaque darkness rose on the other side of the opalescent protective field. It warred with Lucinda's warding, making it impossible for us to see the garden or the street. The darkness seemed to absorb light, and it was clear that Lucinda's magic was fighting against it. If the shroud of darkness could snuff out her protections, I didn't want to know what it would do to us.

This was a lot more excitement than I ever wanted. Teag felt his way down the wall and back into the kitchen to where he had left his jacket and messenger bag, then dug out the lantern and its blue-black candle along with his lighter. Its cleansing light flooded the room, out of proportion to the size of the candle.

"Are you crazy?" I shouted. "He'll see us!"

Teag shot me a grin. "Yes, I am. No, I don't think so." With that, Teag rushed toward the front door and flung it open. I was a step behind him, walking stick in my right hand, wooden spoon in my left.

Teag's lantern shone a brilliant glare that made the garden and the entire side street bright as day. Alard's walking stick remained dark, but the same coruscating light that had shone from the spoon-turned-athame rolled out from the piazza, past the brick garden wall and beyond, a protective, powerful surge of power.

Teag's magic candle and my white light strengthened Lucinda's warding, and the opaque darkness began to flake away, like paint off a crystal ball. The wind died abruptly, and the electricity came back on. The opalescent light faded, and Teag's candle was just an unremarkable flickering flame. Baxter sat on his haunches, looking confused. Bo's ghost was gone.

"Do you think whoever it is will come back?" I whispered, afraid to trust the apparent victory.

Teag shrugged. "Who knows? I mean, we don't even know who sent that. Moran? The demon?"

I'd reached my limit for the night. Teag looked worried, peering out through the night to where his Volvo was parked. He would have to go outside of Lucinda's warding to get to his car, and drive a mile or two before he got back to his own warded space. Too risky, in my opinion.

"Come on," I said. "You can sleep on the couch tonight. Let's do some more digging online. I'll pour us both another glass of wine."

# Chapter Eighteen

"CASSIDY, DEAR! So good to see you! And how is that adorable little Baxter?" Mrs. Morrissey looked up when I entered the Charleston Historical Archive the next morning, and gave me a big smile.

"Baxter's doing fine," I told her. "Thanks for asking."

She glanced at me over her glasses. "What brings you over here early in the morning? Did you come to find out more about the B&B?"

"Not today," I said. "Got something else to look up. And I brought you a hazelnut latte," I added, holding out my good-will gift. I happened to know Mrs. Morrissey had a weakness for good java.

"That's so sweet of you!" she said. "Thank you!"

I marked my name on the sign-in sheet. Just for good measure, I signed Teag in, too. The Archive liked to be able to document how many people used its services. That information came in handy when it was time to ask for grants and donations, and Mrs. Morrissey listed Trifles and Folly among their staunch supporters on a prominent plaque on the wall. Teag had been known to use his Weaver talent from time to time to help Mrs.

Morrissey hunt down odd bits of local history, so we ranked high on her list.

The Charleston Historical Archive was housed in a beautiful home South of Broad. Families with names like Rutledge, Calhoun, and Gadsden had called the house home at some point in their lives, signers of the Declaration of Independence, governors, senators, pivotal figures in the run-up to the Civil War, wealthy land owners, and politicians.

The home's final private owner, Claudia Drayton, had been an heiress whose family tree mingled the bluest blood in South Carolina. Claudia's will left her beloved home and its furnishings to the City of Charleston on the provision that it become the city's permanent historical archive. Mrs. Morrissey was Claudia Drayton's granddaughter. She was also one of many dowagers in her social circle who volunteered time and donations to further the Archive's work.

"Anything I can help you with?"

Mrs. Morrissey liked to be helpful, but she also liked to be in the know. I could see that twinkle in her eye, and I intended to shamelessly encourage her. I'd learned from past forays that a trained librarian will stop at nothing to get to the bottom of a juicy research question.

"I'm looking for information about a piece of property out in the old Navy yards," I said. "There's a hint that a piece that came into the shop may have a connection to the history of that land. And I've got to admit, I don't know much about the area out there."

Mrs. Morrissey nodded, and I could practically see the wheels begin to turn. "Well, now. That strip of land has quite a history," she said, and the corners of her mouth quirked up in a smile. "In fact, it's been part of some of the biggest scandals in Charleston's history."

For a prim society matron, I detected an unmistakable delight in her voice at the idea of digging up dirt. I suspected that, at heart, Mrs. Morrissey was my kind of lady.

"Point me in the right direction," I said.

Mrs. Morrissey looked around the Archive's first floor, which was empty of people except for the two of us. "I can do you one better. I'll be glad to lend you a hand," she said.

She led the way. The Historical Archive was a mansion converted to its new purpose without completely losing its character as a home. Mrs. Morrissey's office still looked like the parlor of a wealthy family, complete with couch and arm chairs in case donors dropped by for tea.

The Board Room was really the former dining room, which still boasted a Chippendale table and chairs, and a full set of Waterford crystal. Having helped out at fundraisers over the year, I knew that the 'good stuff' was pulled out for VIP receptions.

A sweeping grand staircase rose from the front hall to the upstairs, where the bedrooms of the second and third floors had been converted to house collections of rare books and artifacts. The front entrance to the home boasted a foyer large enough to be considered a room of its own. I noticed that today the entranceway boasted a new collection, something I hadn't taken the time to examine when I had entered.

"Using the foyer for exhibit space?" I asked.

Mrs. Morrissey laughed. "Our new Board chairman pointed out that we have such an extensive collection of interesting items, it's a shame not to have more on display. So we've started to create more small exhibits and we'll rotate them every few months. It's good for publicity, and maybe it will help donations, too!"

I made a quick glance around the foyer. 'Healers and Helpers' was the title, and the exhibit managed to pack a lot of fascinating objects into a small space. One case held an antique doctor's bag and vintage nurse hats, plus memorabilia from Wayside Hospital, a long-forgotten Civil War-era facility. On the wall hung what looked like a shaman's staff, and beneath it were bags of dried herbs, tinctures and teas along with a card that talked about root medicine and folk cures. Pictures of old ambulances, now-defunct hospitals, and even the long-gone Charleston Medical College hung on the walls.

I glanced in passing at a huge oil painting on the wall across from the stairs as Mrs. Morrissey headed up. Something about it caught my eye, and I resolved to have a good look before I left. Then I hustled to keep pace with my hostess, who was already a few steps ahead of me.

The stairs opened to a wide second-floor gallery. Mrs. Morrissey swept past several rooms. A flash of red in one of the rooms made me pause.

"Do you have a new exhibit?" I asked, unable to resist sticking my head into the room.

"We will as of Monday," Mrs. Morrissey replied with a touch of pride in her voice. "'Ramblers and Rogues' has been several years in the making. It's a nod to some of our city's more notorious residents."

She walked into the room and gestured for me to follow. "Come on. I'll give you the ten-cent tour." We walked in and she flicked on the lights. "Do you like what we've done with the room?" Mrs. Morrissey asked, obviously proud of the outcome. Large, colorful red banners hung against the walls, each with different inset larger-than-life portraits of men and women from by-gone years. Throughout the room, encased in glass cases, were all kinds of objects. I strained for a better look.

"I love it," I said. The graphics on the banners had punch and looked modern and inviting. A bundle of individual audio headsets hung near the door, awaiting the first visitors.

"It's part of our capitulation to modern sensibilities," she said with a sigh. "The only way to get people interested in history, it seems, is to get their attention with the salacious and outrageous, and hope that a little knowledge seeps in around the edges. Even the History Network and the Discovery Channel seem to be going that way."

"Is it working?"

She grinned. "Like a charm. We've already pre-sold a full house for opening night for the exhibit."

"Ooh... show me!" I begged

Mrs. Morrissey flipped another switch. The television monitors came to life, and the display cases glowed. Over the speakers in the corners of the room, I heard the strains of a song on an old-time music box.

"It's a walk on the wild side of our fair city," she said, and I could hear the enthusiasm in her voice. "Black sheep, pirates, duelists, gamblers, ne'er-do-wells, and poisoners," she said with a sweeping gesture that took in the whole room and its contents. "Most of them are the stuff of local ghost tours, but we wanted people to realize that they were real people who were part of the city's history."

I felt a tingle down my spine and took a step backward, remembering what had happened when I wandered through the 'Plagues and Pestilence' exhibit at the Lowcountry Museum. Maybe the sneak peek wasn't such a good idea. Still, I thought, it couldn't hurt to look from the doorway, and maybe I would get an idea that would help with the Navy yard problems.

"Who's that?" I asked, pointing at a portrait of a dark-haired woman whose beauty was tempered by the coldness in her eyes.

"Lavinia Fisher, Charleston's most famous poisoner and quite possibly the country's first serial killer," Mrs. Morrissey replied.

I'd heard the story many times of how Lavinia and her husband John poisoned the guests at their tavern outside of town and stole the dead men's money. They hadn't been caught until hundreds of travelers had gone missing. John had ultimately confessed, but Lavinia had been unrepentant, insisting she be hanged in her wedding gown and jumping off the gallows on her own accord to cheat the hangman of his due. Sorren had talked about her on more than one occasion. He'd had the dubious honor of being one of Lavinia's guests, the one who got away. Her cold eyes seemed to follow me, and I took another half-step backwards as I saw the mannequin next to the portrait wearing an antique wedding dress.

"We've got some of Blackbeard's gold, a watch belonging to a notorious Civil War spy, pistols from some of the city's most infamous duels, and this," she said, standing next to a glass encased object in the center of the room. "Come see."

Against my better judgment, I edged into the room

until I was close enough to make out the object in the case. I made very sure not to touch anything.

"Jeremiah Abernathy's 'judgment' coin," she said triumphantly, pointing to the case, "and his 'decision cane', the one he supposedly used in all the murders." For being a proper society matron, I was concluding that Mrs. Morrissey had a wild streak.

I startled at the name. "You've heard of Jeremiah?" Mrs. Morrissey asked, delighted.

"Actually, he's associated with the story I came to talk to you about," I said, intrigued against my better instincts. I leaned closer, careful not to make contact.

"That's why having his items is such a coup for the museum," she replied. "He's such a colorful character, I think this might put him on the map of memorable historical bad guys. Maybe even get Hollywood's attention." She pointed to a large oil painting on the far wall. "We've even got his portrait."

I followed her gaze. The man in the portrait had been painted in his best suit, a style nearly a hundred and fifty years old. He had an arrogant tilt to his jaw, thin, merciless lips, and cold gray eyes.

"We think we may have an item that was associated with him," I said. "Can you tell me more?"

"Jeremiah Abernathy was a corrupt judge who ran a whiskey and gambling empire in Charleston's wild days," Mrs. Morrissey said. "Rumor has it, he was the illegitimate son of one of the rice planters and a Creole slave, but if that's true, Abernathy never claimed his Creole heritage. He was known – and feared – for his ruthlessness. He hanged a lot of pirates, some of whom might have been business competitors."

I peered into the case. A gold coin lay in the spotlight.

Next to it was a worn ebony cane with an elaborate silver handle and a lead tip, much like the one Sorren had lent me from Alard.

"Jeremiah Abernathy didn't like people who refused to pay their debts. He had the protection of powerful people in the city, and he operated with impunity by his own rules, which were enforced by his private squad of strong-arm men," Mrs. Morrissey said with more relish than I thought a woman of her standing really should be according an old-time criminal.

"When someone tried to cheat him, Abernathy would have them brought before him in his private 'court'," she recounted. "Usually, if stories are to be believed, the offender had already been worked over by Abernathy's men, so the real question was, would they die easy or die hard?"

My eyes widened, more at her choice of words than at the concept. Mrs. Morrissey went on enthusiastically. "Abernathy would take his cane and thump it hard on the floor three times to convene his 'court'. He would make his accusation, and allow the panicked victim to plead and bargain for his life." She raised her eyebrows.

"Very few men who were brought to Abernathy had any leverage to bargain for mercy. By the time they got low enough to renege on a debt to him, they had already squandered their fortunes," she added. "He would thump that cane of his again to indicate that he was about to give out his sentence."

Her voice had dropped, and I found myself leaning in, hanging on every word. "And?"

Mrs. Morrissey grinned. "He would take his coin, which he claimed the King of Spain gave him, and he would toss it three times. Heads, the victim died. Tails, the victim lived. Best two out of three determined the poor wretch's fate."

I stepped back from the case. My imagination could supply what it must have been like to kneel before Abernathy's court, life hanging in the balance as the coin flipped and landed. I didn't need my gift kicking in to confirm those images. "What happened to him?" I asked, sounding a little breathless.

"Times changed, and some of Abernathy's protectors fell from power. The government began to look into some of Abernathy's business deals. It all ended in a blaze of gunfire when federal agents raided Abernathy's stronghold. One wing of his mansion exploded with all the illegal whiskey. Abernathy burned alive, thumping his cane, and swearing that he would return to get vengeance on those who crossed him."

I shivered. "That's some story," I said, looking askance at the glass case. I was growing more uncomfortable by the moment the longer we stayed in the exhibit room, and my intuition was telling me to get out now. I made a show of glancing at my watch. "Oops – we'd better get up to the stacks before I need to go back to the shop."

"Well, at least you got a taste of the exhibit. Be sure to tell your friends." Mrs. Morrissey touched the panels at the door. The music box fell silent and the spotlights went dark, but I couldn't keep from glancing over my shoulder to make sure nothing was following us.

On the mansion's fourth floor was a huge ballroom that once hosted fetes that attracted a who's-who for South Carolina and the entire Southeast. Now, the ballroom was home to the 'stacks', rows of dark wooden bookshelves that housed the majority of the Archive's books. Between the shelves were large library tables for reading, along with computer terminals for online research.

"Now, dear, what is it you wanted to know?" she asked.

"There's a rumor that Jeremiah Abernathy hired pirates to bring something back for him from Barbados aboard a ship called the *Cristobal*," I said. "The *Cristobal* sank off the Carolina coast." I gave her my most innocent, winning smile. "I'm trying to find out what might be known about that incident."

"Ohh," Mrs. Morrissey said, her eyes shining. "What do you have of his?"

*A demon,* I thought. "We might have a letter related to the *Cristobal* situation, but we're not sure yet whether it's genuine." I hated to lie, but I was certain she really didn't want to know the truth.

"Let's see," she said. She hummed as she selected large, cloth-bound books off the shelves and set them on one of the big reading tables. "Computer searches are easier on my back," she said. "But some of these old books haven't been digitized yet."

She looked up. "You also mentioned the Navy yard. Was it something related to Abernathy?"

I shrugged, palms up. "I'm not entirely sure. Did Abernathy have any connection to that area?"

"If you want, Cassidy dear, go ahead and get the computer working on loading the 'real estate' records page on the Archive site," she said, with a wave of her hand toward the terminal

I got to work as Mrs. Morrissey began to flip through the huge old books. A glimpse told me they were maps and surveys of the greater Charleston area, and from the yellowed paper, I was guessing the most recent volumes were from the 1800s.

"All right," she said finally, dusting her hands together. "Let's see what's in the records." She motioned for me to join her at the reading table.

"This is a reprint of some of the earliest maps of the area, and they show who laid claim to which pieces of property," she said. "That land where the old Navy yard is has seen more than its share of trouble over the years. The location made it a good sheltered port, and the pirates were quick to take advantage of it, all the way back to old John Rouge – Red-eye John."

I leaned over, scanning the page. A black-and-white sketch of a hanging caught my eye. "I gather something went wrong?"

"Eventually, the deal he had with authorities fell apart, and in 1715, the Royal Navy attacked Red-eye John's haven, killing most of the pirates and burning their homes, saloons, brothels, and ships. Red-eye John was captured and hanged." She gave an impish grin. "The stories said he cast a curse on the city, and that his spirit called out to Blackbeard for revenge. Blackbeard laid siege to Charleston a few years later."

I peered at the book and the map. "Does anyone know where, exactly, Red-eye was hanged?"

Mrs. Morrissey pointed to a spot on the map. "Right about here, according to legend." It was within the bounds of the old Navy yard, but I'd have to look more closely to see if it matched any of the old buildings we'd scouted. I laid a pencil with its point next to the spot on the map and took a photo with my phone for Teag to examine later.

"Any ghost stories about Red-eye?" I asked.

Mrs. Morrissey laughed. "Oh my goodness. You know Charleston – there's a ghost around every corner!

Yes, there have been stories about ol' Red-eye. Some folks claimed they could smell something burning out in that area, when nothing was on fire. Others say they've seen the ghost of a man hanging in mid-air, then suddenly plummeting, like on a gallows."

I felt a chill go down my back. "Anything else?"

Mrs. Morrissey consulted her sources. "Rumor had it that after Red-eye was hanged, they found bodies in shallow graves. Might have been some of his victims. 'Course, he wasn't the only pirate to drop anchor in that area."

She gave me a sidelong look. "You know, there is even a rumor – never substantiated, you understand – that the founder of Trifles and Folly had some dealings with privateers."

Sorren had told me that story the last time he was in town, only it was no rumor. He remembered Dante fondly – and my ancestor Evann, who was Sorren's partner back then. "Imagine that," I said noncommittally.

"That's a prime piece of land," I said. "I can't imagine it was too much longer before someone laid claim to it legitimately."

"Oh, that happened soon enough. Before that point, there were more pirates, more raids, and more hangings." She flipped a few more pages. "Then along came Edwin Sandborn, whose father had a prosperous rice plantation upriver. Edwin thought that if he could start his own shipyard, he would save on docking fees and make a profit off the nearby plantations."

She raised an eyebrow. "There were also rumors that Edwin's family was also doing some smuggling along with their rice shipments." She managed a very proper smirk. "You know smuggling is in our blood in this city."

"What happened to Edwin?"

Mrs. Morrissey leaned against the table. "Some people say he got in trouble trying to elope with the daughter of one of the other rice planters. Others say he tried to elope with the buried treasure of one of the other plantation owners. One foggy spring night, someone shot him dead as he sat at the desk in his office. After that, the dockyard fell into disarray and eventually was sold." Again, I marked the spot on the map with the pencil point and snapped another photo.

"What happened to the land after Edwin?" I asked.

"The property has changed hands a number of times – unusual, since so many of our commercial properties remain in the same family for generations," she replied. "And every time, there was a whiff of impropriety. Most ventures ended very badly – bankruptcies, mental breakdowns, embezzlement, murders."

"Have you ever heard of a man by the name of Corban Moran?" I asked, typing the name into the computer to see if I would stumble on anything that had eluded Teag's hacking. I wasn't surprised when the search came up blank.

Mrs. Morrissey frowned. "Moran?" She shook her head. "Do you mean Corwin Moran?" She walked over to the shelves and pulled down another book, skimming through the pages until she found what she wanted.

"Is this who you meant?" she asked, setting the book on the table. "He was a smuggler – pirate, really – in the years soon after the Revolution." She shook her head. "Awful man, even by pirate standards. Killed so many men, some people thought he had made a deal with the Devil," she added.

*Not the Devil,* I thought. *Just a demon.*

"He burned to death in a fire," she said. "At least, that's what the stories say." She pointed to a sketch in her book of Corwin Moran. I was certain he was the man I'd seen in the broad-brimmed hat, the man who had returned to Charleston to raise Abernathy's demon.

Just then her phone rang, and I did my best to look completely absorbed checking my cell phone as Mrs. Morrissey took the call. She looked up when she was done. "I'm sorry, dear. I've got to go over to the Chamber of Commerce and straighten out some details for the reception they're holding. It's part of our latest fundraiser. You're welcome to stay here and use the computer – I shouldn't be more than half an hour."

I checked the time. "Are you expecting anyone?"

Mrs. Morrissey nodded. "That's why I hesitated about going over to the Chamber. One of the professors at the University is dropping by to discuss a lecture we're planning for the Fall Luminaries Lantern Tour schedule."

"I love those tours," I said, thinking silently how I wished Sorren could lead one of the sessions. "They make you feel as if you're right there, like you've met the people."

Mrs. Morrissey brightened. "That's the whole goal – to give reality TV a run for its money and get more people engaged in history." She gave me a conspiratorial wink. "After all, every good historian knows that history is the *original* reality show.

"I've got an expert on African myth and folklore who's supposed to be here sometime this afternoon, and I know that if I step out for a moment, she'll show up while I'm gone."

"I don't mind waiting," I said. "Once you get back, I can finish up in the stacks and still get to Trifles and Folly in time to finish out the afternoon."

"Bless you," Mrs. Morrissey said. "If anyone else shows up, tell them I'll be back soon. I won't be long." She left me with instructions not to let anyone else in and to let the phone go to voice mail and hustled out the door.

It wasn't until she was gone I realized I had just volunteered to be alone in a museum. Damn.

# Chapter Nineteen

I WALKED INTO the foyer and took the opportunity to look at the 'Healers and Helpers' exhibit, being careful not to touch any of the cases or objects. I figured I was safer with objects that had been used to heal and protect rather than with pieces that had belonged to killers and rogues.

I walked over to appreciate a beautiful oil painting that hung on the opposite wall. It was a painting of a long-ago ball that had been held in the Drayton House's ballroom. Judging by the clothing of the people in the painting, I guessed the period to be mid-1700s. The women were resplendent in their long dresses with massive skirts of silk and satin, and the men looked prosperous and satisfied in their knee breeches and brocade waistcoats.

I had seen the painting many times, but I'd never had the time to study it. To get a better view, I walked up a few steps so that it was on eye level. The artist's main focus was on the mansion's current owners at the time, who were in the center of the action. But he had also captured the likenesses of many of the other notable guests, some of whom I recognized from Charleston's history. One image caught my eye, and I let out a slight gasp. Off to one side, trying to look inconspicuous, stood a thin blond man with light skin and high cheekbones. His sea-gray eyes seemed to meet mine and a startle of recognition thrilled through me. Sorren.

My mind was still reeling from surprise when I heard the faint sounds of an old-fashioned music box.

I froze, straining to listen. The music box had been part of the 'Ramblers and Rogues' exhibit. Mrs. Morrissey had turned it off when she turned out the lights.

From above me, I heard a thump, a sharp sound of metal on wood. Exactly what a lead-tipped cane might sound like pounding against the wooden floor.

*Thump. Thump.*

Jeremiah Abernathy had convened his court once more, more than a century after his death.

There was no way in hell I was going to go up those stairs. I began to back down the steps carefully, doing my best not to make any noise. Mrs. Morrissey had not mentioned any ghostly activity. Then again, between the age of the house and the notoriety of many of the artifacts the Archive housed, perhaps she had come to take haunting in her stride.

I heard a coin fall and rattle on the floor.

I eyed the door, wondering how badly Mrs. Morrissey would be disappointed if I locked it behind me and high-tailed it back to the store. I could tell her that Teag came down with acute appendicitis. Or that the shop was being invaded by aliens (sometimes, that didn't seem far from the truth).

The coin fell again.

I could feel my heart thudding. *Get a grip, Cassidy*, I

chided myself. *It's probably a recording on a timer, or a glitch in the wiring. I didn't touch anything. There's nothing to worry about.*

Something clinked at the top of the stairs. As I watched, a coin rolled off the top step and fell to the next, impossibly remaining on edge. I stared in fascination and horror as it fell from stair to stair until at last it tumbled from the bottom step, spun for a second, and landed flat at my feet.

*Heads, you die.*

I had backed all the way down the stairs, and now stood in the foyer. A glance at my watch told me that Mrs. Morrissey wouldn't be back for at least twenty minutes. Once again, I weighed my options. I could leave and lock the door behind me, but that would mean breaking my word to Mrs. Morrissey and putting the archive in a bad light with the expert who was due to arrive any minute. I decided to ignore my thudding heart and stay where I could keep an eye on the stairs and the door at the same time.

From the empty second floor, I heard the unmistakable sound of a man's boot step.

My hand went to the agate necklace at my throat. Last night, after Teag and I had chased off whatever attacked the house, I had placed the necklace in the moonlight to recharge it. I hoped that would be enough to let Jeremiah Abernathy and any of the other rogues know that I was not someone they wanted to mess with.

Unfortunately, I had neither Alard's walking stick nor my grandmother's wooden spoon, though Bo's collar was still twined around my left wrist.

*Too bad it's too warm to have worn my jacket. I'm pretty sure Teag filled the pockets with salt,* I thought.

Then again, I had no idea how I would have explained it to Mrs. Morrissey if she found me standing in a circle of salt.

*Maybe Abernathy's ghost is just putting on a show,* I thought. *After all, he seemed like the bullying type.*

Upstairs, I heard more footsteps. I decided Abernathy could walk around all he wanted, so long as he stayed on his own floor.

The music box was still playing. I heard a woman's laugh, and remembered the display dedicated to Lavinia Fisher, the serial killer. She was not someone I wanted to meet in person. I hoped she and Jeremiah would keep to themselves upstairs and leave me alone.

The temperature in the foyer plummeted. When Mrs. Morrissey had shown me through on the way upstairs, it was comfortably cool. Now, it was as if I had stepped into a refrigerator, enough to raise gooseflesh on my arms. Not a good sign of things to come.

Upstairs, the heavy footsteps sounded again, closer this time. Before, they had been muffled, as if someone were moving around the exhibit room. Now, the steps were in the upstairs hallway, and coming toward the landing.

I was torn between keeping my eye on the top of the stairs and moving closer to the door to the outside. Maybe I could stand on the Archive's wide piazza and welcome Mrs. Morrissey's visitor out there, I thought, crossing to the door in a few quick strides.

I turned the knob. The door wouldn't budge. The deadbolt had been unlocked when I came in, and Mrs. Morrissey had only locked the handset when we went upstairs, I was sure of it. I knew for a fact that I had only locked the handset after she left, since I didn't have a key to the deadbolt. But no matter how I turned the knob or clicked the button in the handset, the door refused to open.

"Maybe it sticks," I muttered to myself, grabbing the knob with both hands and pulling. Nothing happened.

Behind me, the footsteps were getting closer to the top of the stairs.

I was sure the Archive must have a back door, and I thought about checking the kitchen, but that would mean going past the main stairs. I could get trapped in the back of the house if Abernathy's ghost actually descended to the first floor, and I had no assurance that the kitchen door would open. For all I knew, it was locked with a deadbolt, too. I couldn't count on getting out that way.

I pulled my cell phone from my pocket, and stared at it in outright amazement. Though I was right in the middle of the Charleston Historic District and only a few blocks from my store, the display said 'no signal'. I tried to call Teag, although I had no idea what he could do to help, but the call wouldn't go through. Shoving my cell phone back into my pocket, I grabbed for Mrs. Morrissey's desk phone, but when I raised the receiver to my ear, there was no dial tone.

Jeremiah was playing with my mind.

My watch said I still had at least ten more minutes before Mrs. Morrissey got back, and that was assuming she would be on time. I'd never run an errand to the Chamber that quickly, and I wasn't counting on punctuality.

The foyer had grown even colder, and when I glanced up to the top of the stairs, I realized something had changed. Before, I could glimpse the ceiling and a little of the walls of the upper floor. Now, the top of the stairs was completely dark, darker than it should be in the middle of a spring afternoon in a building that had plenty of windows. Much darker than it had been just moments ago. And as I watched, the darkness swallowed the top step. I heard the scuff of boots and the thunk of a walking stick.

Jeremiah was coming.

A knock sounded at the door, and I turned for an instant to look in that direction.

In that moment, Jeremiah struck.

The darkness tumbled down the stairs like floodwater, roiling and rolling as if it had weight and substance. Every fiber in my body screamed a warning. As the darkness flowed closer, even without touching it I knew it was unclean, filthy with hatred and the need for vengeance, polluted with cruelty and a casual disregard for light and life.

Bo's ghostly form appeared in front of me, snarling and snapping like an insane guard dog. But Jeremiah wasn't afraid of ghost dogs, and his darkness slammed Bo's spirit out of the way.

Jeremiah was a man who wouldn't let anything stop him from getting what he wanted, even if that meant bending a demon to his will. The darkness inched toward me, backing me up against the wall, hungry for my warmth, my life. Tendrils of darkness clutched at me, just like the shadows in the Covington warehouse, and I felt the cold take my breath. Bo's ghostly barking seemed far away. The agate disk struggled to hold back the evil and I could tell its power was fading fast.

Since running was out of the question and there was no good place to hide, I looked around for a weapon, something to fend off the darkness. I saw the shaman's staff hanging on the wall and dove for it, grabbing it down just as the darkness lifted me off my feet and threw me across the room.

I hit the opposite wall hard enough to knock some framed pictures from their places. I banged my head, striking one of the spots where the falling crates had nicked me the night before, and the world swam.

In the tide of darkness, I could hear Jeremiah's boots coming down the stairs, closer every minute. I forced myself to climb to my feet, trembling against the unnatural cold, frightened and angry and determined to give him a fight.

I closed my right hand around the shaman's staff. The wooden staff was wrapped with layers of colored string dyed in shades of plum, dark orange, blue, and green. Feathers, bits of metal, bone, and shell hung from leather ties, and a hunk of agate had been set into the top of the pole and securely wrapped with sinew. The staff felt comfortingly heavy in my hand, and I could feel the tingle of remembered power as my palm closed around the worn ash handle.

Instinctively, I flung the staff out in front of me like Moses parting the Red Sea, a futile, gut-level gesture. And as I leveled the staff at the darkness, memories flooded through me as my gift roared to life. I could feel all the shamans and seers who had possessed the staff generation after generation, feel their lives and memories wash over me and fill me, and their power roar through me.

I closed my left hand around the agate necklace, and Bo's ghost appeared again, lunging at the darkness, barking loudly.

Out of my arsenal of new 'weapons', Alard's walking stick spewed fire, and Grandma Sarah's wooden spoon sent out an opalescent protective field, but the shaman's staff was different. I didn't have either the walking stick or the spoon with me, but the staff had power of its own. I felt a force of will, the determination of a people who had faced great hardship and overcome it. I felt the long-ago shaman's magic, power and defiance, and it gave me strength to hold the staff against the dark onslaught.

I could feel the darkness resisting, fighting the staff, unwilling to yield. Memories continued to pour through me, binding me to the staff. I had no idea how to control the staff's power or do more than hold the darkness at bay.

The door to the outside slammed open, shaking the glass in the windows. I felt the magic before I caught a glimpse of Lucinda's face; it was wild like a hurricane and powerful as a storm at sea. Lucinda was chanting in a language I did not understand, but the power behind her words thrummed through my body and resonated with the magic in the staff.

Lucinda swept into the foyer, and out of the corner of my eye, it was as if another image was superimposed over her face, a bent old man with a straw hat who smelled of pipe tobacco. Outside, I could hear the frantic barking of dogs.

Lucinda stretched out her hand toward the stairs, and powerful magic flowed from her, ripping the darkness asunder. The shadows recoiled, disappearing back up the steps until once again I could glimpse the ceiling and hallway wallpaper. Abruptly, the music box fell silent.

I did not move. I was shaking, still holding the shaman's staff outstretched, trying to remember to breathe. It took a few breaths before I could lower the staff. The images in my mind reverberated with Lucinda's magic as if her power and its magic were of old acquaintance. I felt its reverence for the spirit I glimpsed of an old man who tipped his hat and vanished. Gratitude threatened to overwhelm me. I did not want to imagine what would have happened if the darkness had taken me.

"Thank you," I said. My voice was trembling. "How did you know I needed you?"

Lucinda's laugh was warm and full. "I didn't know, child. I had an appointment with Mrs. Morrissey. I should have been here twenty minutes ago, but everything seemed to go wrong. That's when I knew I had to hurry, because it felt as if something was preventing me from coming. And when I came up on the piazza, I could feel the power of that darkness and I knew someone was in trouble. So I just did what I do."

Now that I had a moment to collect my wits, I realized that Lucinda wore a business suit, instead of the flowing skirt and shawl she had on when she had warded my home. "You're the professor Mrs. Morrissey said was coming, the expert on African myth and folklore," I said, belatedly putting the pieces together.

"The same," she said with a wide smile. "Dr. Lucinda Walker, College of Charleston Humanities Department, at your service." She winked at me. "You didn't think I spent all my time blessing houses in the dead of night, did you?"

I was still so rattled I wasn't sure what to think. "I'm glad you had an appointment today. I don't know that I could have held off Jeremiah by myself for very long."

"Humph. That shadow wasn't going to get close to you when you were using my grandmother's staff."

I looked from Lucinda to the staff that was still clutched, white-knuckled, in my hand. Slowly, I held it out to her, and she took it reverently, then kissed the agate stone and murmured something I did not hear, something that sounded like a blessing or endearment. She carefully replaced the staff on the wall in its holder.

"Your grandmother's staff?" I echoed.

Lucinda nodded. "I loaned the items for the root worker exhibit, some from my family and some from around. I'm the eighth generation to do root magic in my family. It's an ancient and proud tradition."

Knowing Mrs. Morrissey was due back any moment, I gave Lucinda a quick recap of what had happened. She nodded as if such a story was the most natural thing in the world.

"Spirits like Jeremiah Abernathy were bad news when they were alive, and they're no better after they're dead," Lucinda said when I finished. "He could have thrown you for a turn if he had gotten to you. And that Lavinia Fisher was pure evil. You sure don't want to mess with her."

"I thought I saw an old man, with a hat. He smelled of pipe smoke."

Lucinda smiled broadly. "Ah, that's Papa. Papa Legba, one of the most powerful Loas. I asked him for protection when I knew there was evil inside and someone needing help."

"Please tell him thank you for me," I replied. "I'm glad both of you showed up when you did."

"I'll bring him some rum and sweet potatoes and tell him they're from you," Lucinda promised. "I'll make an offering tonight, and add a few gifts of my own. I tell you true – I felt better for both you and me when I knew Papa was with us." Together, we hung the pictures back on the wall that had fallen when Jeremiah's spirit attacked.

"I see you've met." Mrs. Morrissey's voice startled me. She had come in the open door behind us, and looked a little flushed from the heat outside. "I hope I didn't keep you waiting."

"I just got here," Lucinda said. "And Cassidy and I were just making introductions."

Mrs. Morrissey looked at me. "Thank you for watching the office while I was gone. Did you need to go back up to the stacks today?"

I managed to repress a shiver. "I think I'd better get back to the shop," I said. "Thank you for your help." I paused. "With all the old items in the Archive's collection, have you ever seen ghosts here?"

Mrs. Morrissey nodded. "Hard to find an old home in Charleston that isn't haunted," she replied. "But I've never felt frightened, at least, not until we created the Rogues exhibit." She managed a wan smile, but I could see that something had rattled her. "To tell you the truth, it gives me the creeps. I'll be glad when those pieces go back into storage."

My HEAD WAS still spinning as I headed back to Trifles and Folly. A water main break was tying up traffic, so fewer tourists than usual milled around the streets window-shopping. Even so, several people were browsing in the shop when I returned, and so I headed behind the counter to answer questions and help them find what they were looking for. Conversation with Teag would have to wait.

The shoppers made their purchases and left the store. Teag shot me a victorious grin.

"That was a five hundred dollar sale."

I gave him a tired smile in return and sat down at the stool behind the counter. "I made a three hundred dollar sale – and was menaced by the ghost of Jeremiah Abernathy."

Teag's grin faded. "At the Archive? Damn. Are you okay?"

I nodded tiredly. "I am now – thanks to Lucinda."

"What was Lucinda doing at the Archive?"

Teag listened intently as I recapped what had happened. I filled him in on what I had learned in the stacks before the ghostly attack, and finished off with a detailed description of the incident in the foyer – complete with Lucinda's dramatic entrance and scholarly alter-ego.

"I'm beginning to think it's not safe for you to go anywhere alone until we get this straightened out, Cassidy," Teag said, worry clear in his voice.

I sighed, fearing he was right. "That goes for you, too," I reminded him.

"Something happened today that gave me an idea," I went on. "We've usually encountered my gift with items that have strong negative energy. Maybe because those tend to be the problem items. But when I grabbed the shaman's staff that belonged to Lucinda, its power connected with my gift. It helped keep Jeremiah at bay. Like the walking stick that Sorren lent me.

"I think it would be a good idea to start a new collection of weapons," I said, leaning back against the wall and closing my eyes. "Maybe get some kind of paranormal spook bazooka or something. It would be nice not to feel as if I've been wrung dry."

"Hold on a moment." I heard Teag leave the front of

the shop, and return a moment later. He pressed a cup of coffee into my hands. "Drink up. I made it just the way you like it. You look like you've been through the mill."

"I feel like it," I agreed, and sipped the coffee. "Thanks."

"No problem," Teag replied with a grin. "I've been waiting to tell you about what I found out while you were gone. Of course, your story is more exciting."

"Lucky me. Have you heard anything from Sorren?"

Teag went to retrieve a piece of paper from the office, and gave it to me. "I found this on your desk this morning," he replied. The paper was written in long-hand, in a style of penmanship all but forgotten in today's text message society. Bold, swift strokes filled the small note in a decidedly masculine style. *Feeling better. Stepped out for a bite. See you soon.*

"His idea of a sense of humor?" Teag asked.

I chuckled tiredly. "Appropriately macabre, don't you think? But it means he's up and around, and if he feeds well he should be good as new in time for our next outing."

"Outing," Teag echoed. "You know, that word sounds a lot more fun than what happened at the warehouse. An 'outing' should involve a picnic lunch and a sunny day at the park, not killer shadows and falling crates."

I chuckled. "I'll keep that in mind." Another sip of coffee fortified me. "So tell me the rest of your news."

Teag leaned back against the counter. "I called Alistair over at the museum," he said. "On a hunch that the salvage guys who disappeared might have had some pieces on exhibit over there." He grinned. "And it turns out, they did."

I sipped my coffee as he warmed to the tale. "Alistair only knew the main man, the salvage team's owner and research director, Russ Landrieu. Tulane graduate, worked on the expeditions to find the *Titanic* and the *Hunley*," he added. "Pretty well-respected guy, knew all the big players in the sunken treasure business. A couple of the team's adventures made it onto the History Channel."

"Did Alistair have any scoop for you?" Alistair McKinnon, Curator of the Lowcountry Museum of Charleston, was as well connected as Mrs. Morrissey, both to Charleston's donors and to the pulse of what was going on the city. Trifles and Folly often loaned pieces to the museum for use in period displays or tableaus.

Teag nodded. "Back when the *Hunley* was found, everyone was fascinated with shipwreck explorers." I remembered. The *H.L. Hunley* was a Confederate submarine that had been missing for more than a hundred years before it was finally re-discovered and painstakingly salvaged. It had been the talk of Charleston for months, and made national headlines.

"Alistair wanted to round out their shipwreck exhibit with some lesser-known finds, and he contacted Landrieu. Landrieu and his team were happy to provide artifacts, photos, video – even some personal effects like jackets and diving gear."

"You're not going to suggest that we go over to the museum, are you?" I asked testily. I had always considered the Historical Archive safe – before today – because it was mostly books and clippings. The museum, on the other hand, had artifacts. Artifacts tended to trigger my gift, with embarrassing consequences. Teag and I had attended an exhibit at the museum a few years back on antique china settings and silver items, which had seemed like a safe excursion. We took a wrong turn, and I ended up in the 'Plagues and Pestilence' exhibit on all of Charleston's many epidemics. The impressions and resonance overwhelmed me, and I passed out cold. I hadn't been back since.

"We don't have to go today," Teag said. "But Alistair told me that Landrieu had gotten back in touch with him about nine months ago to tell him that they were going after a really interesting old wreck."

"The *Cristobal*," I said. Teag nodded.

"Landrieu emailed Alistair some of his notes and research, trying to interest the museum in giving the expedition a grant, and possibly doing an exhibit on the pieces they brought up."

"Alistair still has the notes?" I asked, sitting up straighter.

Teag grinned. "He sure does, and he's willing to show us. We've got an appointment for tomorrow, right after the shop closes."

"Let's make sure we can defend ourselves this time," I replied. "Just in case Jeremiah Abernathy or Moran and his demon decide to pay us a repeat visit."

# Chapter Twenty

THE LOWCOUNTRY MUSEUM of Charleston took up most of a block on the edge of the Historic District. It included the original old home where the museum had its start, and had grown into a modern building underwritten by its patrons, who added onto the building every few decades.

It was after six when we parked Teag's old Volvo in the lot. Alistair had agreed to meet us even though the museum was technically closed. Personally, I was relieved. Going into the museum made me nervous enough without being afraid I'd have an audience for any bad reaction. I hadn't quite lived down the incident at the Academy Theater, and I didn't want to give anyone more to talk about.

"Alistair said to meet him by the side door," Teag said. "That way you don't have to go through the public exhibit space to get to his office."

I gave a wan smile. I knew Alistair remembered the last time I'd visited. Whether he suspected that I had a psychic gift and not just a 'delicate constitution' I had no way of knowing.

"Cassidy! Teag! So good to see you," Alistair greeted us, holding the door open so we could enter the locked staff entrance.

"I love the new silver exhibit," I said. "The photos online are gorgeous." I swore off visiting the museum in person, but I was a donor so I had online access to all the new programs.

Alistair smiled. "That's one of my favorites," he said. "Although really, I don't think the photos do it justice."

He led us down a long hallway to his office and gestured for us to sit down. The museum prided itself on putting its budget into acquisitions and traveling exhibits, not administrative overhead, so the office was functional but not fancy.

"Teag told me all about your interest in the *Privateer* salvage team," Alistair said, walking around his desk to pick up a small stack of paper and a leather journal.

"Russ Landrieu was very excited about their last expedition," he added, a note of sadness in his voice. "He was certain they had found the *Cristobal*, and he thought this dive might be their big break. I think he was hoping for some good headlines, maybe a TV show, and patrons to fund more diving," he said, and sighed. "Of course, that isn't what happened."

The more we looked into the history of the *Cristobal*, the more I was certain the *Privateer*'s crew had been murdered, likely by Moran. But we were still speculating on the motive, and we didn't have a confirmed link between Moran and Landrieu. I wouldn't have put it past Moran to let Landrieu's crew take the risk and do the work, only to steal the cursed treasure once it was retrieved.

Alistair held the papers out toward us, and Teag took

them, handing off half of them to me. He began to flip through the journal. "Have you read all of this?" Teag asked.

Alistair shook his head. "I meant to, but we got busy, and then when the *Privateer* went missing, I filed the papers away, because the exhibit was obviously never going to happen."

I thumbed through the papers. I saw nautical coordinates, sketches of what the *Cristobal* looked like in its prime, and some blue-sky notes on what the exhibit might include.

Holding the papers, I could sense Landrieu's excitement, his optimism, and his passion for diving. Landrieu had big dreams, and Alistair was correct that the diver had thought the *Cristobal* could be his team's claim to fame.

But as I riffled through the notes, I could feel a shift in Landrieu's mood. The optimism became tempered with worry, and then a tinge of fear. I looked over to Teag. "Find anything?" I asked.

Teag shrugged. "We'll need to read through all this carefully, but there are a couple of places where Landrieu says he thinks he's being followed, maybe by a rival salvage crew." He looked to Alistair. "Did he say anything like that to you?"

Alistair nodded. "I didn't really think much of it at the time, but later, after the *Privateer* went missing, I wondered."

"I know it's been a while, but do you remember exactly what Landrieu said?" I asked.

Alistair looked at the ceiling, deep in thought for a moment. "He said that people would be surprised by the treasure, that it wasn't just a bunch of gold doubloons," he said, remembering. "He'd stumbled on some old log books, and he was certain that there was a one-of-a-kind piece the *Cristobal* had been carrying in secret." He frowned. "Landrieu even hinted that it might be cursed."

He laughed nervously. "Of course, I didn't take that seriously at the time, but later on, when the ship disappeared, I thought Landrieu had been right about the curse."

"Was he afraid of competitors?" I asked.

Alistair nodded. "He swore me to secrecy, and I didn't think he'd told me anything very revealing. That's also why he gave me the journal and the papers, for safekeeping." He shook his head. "Landrieu said he thought someone was shadowing them, trying to get ahead of them. I noticed that he was carrying a gun." He paused. "He said he was approached by a man with a disfigured face who offered him a million dollars if he and his crew would forget about the *Cristobal*."

"And Landrieu refused?" Teag asked.

Alistair nodded. "With these explorers, it's not about the money. It's the thrill of finding what's been lost and getting bragging rights." He shrugged. "And if the wreck was really as good as Landrieu thought, they might well have made more than a million with a TV show, grants, that sort of thing."

I wondered if, for all his talk of curses, Landrieu had any idea of the danger of what was down in the *Cristobal*'s cargo hold. "May we take these with us, to study?" I asked.

"Just sign them out and bring them back," Alistair said. "I figured you would want to go over them with a fine-tooth comb." He met my gaze. "I would love it if someone could figure out what happened to those fellows. They seemed like a nice bunch of guys, doing what they loved."

"If Landrieu and his team dove near Charleston, did they have an office here?" I asked, handing the papers to Teag.

Alistair shook his head. "They were very frugal. Saved all their money for their dives. Although when they were working here in Charleston for several months at a time, they did take a storage unit to stow their gear."

*Storage again!* It was like an alarm going off in my head as I tried to focus on the here and now.

"Anything else?" Teag asked, slipping the papers and the journal into his messenger bag.

Before Alistair could answer, I leaned forward. "Do you know anything about a man named Jeremiah Abernathy?"

Alistair leaned back in his chair. "Abernathy? Sure. In his time, he was notorious." He frowned. "What does ol' Jeremiah have to do with the crew of the *Privateer*?"

I smiled in a way I hoped was disarming. "I was over at the Historical Archive and saw their new exhibit, and Mrs. Morrissey said that there were rumors that Abernathy had some kind of cargo aboard the *Cristobal* when it went down."

Alistair grinned. "You're good at your research. I've heard that rumor, too."

"Any truth to the scuttlebutt that Abernathy had an interest in the occult?" I pressed.

Alistair nodded. "Actually, yes. Jeremiah had a lot of enemies, and he took precautions. He had plenty of bodyguards, lots of guns, and a network of informants, but even that didn't make him feel safe. He was quite a superstitious man, and toward the end of his life, he was worried about curses. He surrounded himself with all kinds of amulets and good luck charms." Alistair shrugged. "Obviously, they didn't work."

He leaned forward and grinned conspiratorially. "We have some of Abernathy's things. Want to see? "

I weighed the frightening thought of going into the museum's stored collections area against what we might learn, but my anger over the deaths of Landrieu and his crew made up my mind. "Lead on," I said, even though Teag gave me a skeptical look. I just shrugged, hoping for the best.

We followed Alistair down the long hallway toward the stairs to the collections level below. The lighting was dimmed, since the museum was closed and most of the staff had gone home. My senses were on full alert, and I felt jumpy. That might be from being in a museum surrounded by hundreds of artifacts with strong emotional resonance. I was certain that many of them also had supernatural mojo. I was hoping that was all there was to it, but just in case, my hand went to the agate disk necklace I'd faithfully recharged in the moonlight.

Alistair unlocked a keypad and let us into a large room. It reminded me of the stacks at the Archive, except that where those were filled with books, this area had long metal shelves in rows as far as the eye could see, all filled with historical 'stuff'. Boxes with cryptic markings. Jars filled with discolored formaldehyde and pallid, preserved things best left unexamined. Glass-lidded cases filled with butterflies, taxidermied birds and small mammals, and other oddities.

It was cooler down here, and I folded my arms around myself. In part, it kept me warm, but it also brought

Bo's collar closer to me, a reassuring presence. I had debated about whether or not to bring the walking stick and the spoon. I couldn't figure out how to explain the elaborate, antique walking stick to Alistair, nor did I want to be responsible for setting the museum on fire. The wooden spoon was up the right sleeve of my light jacket. I glanced at Teag, and saw a bulge in his jacket where he carried Sorren's lantern.

We walked along the wall rather than among the tall rows of shelves. Hanging from the wall were dozens of large mirrors of every size, style, and era. Some sported elaborate gold frames, while others were set in carved wood or precious stones. The convex and concave mirrors gave an eerie, funhouse appearance. The mirrors ranged from small enough to fit over a vanity to the size of a door, and as we passed by, they reflected our images in a way that made me keep thinking I saw something out of the corner of my eye.

"Here we are," Alistair said, turning sharply. The long rows had breaks every so often that worked like cross-streets, and Alistair headed down one of these sections, while Teag and I tried to keep our bearings and make sure we knew how to get out.

Several of the rows we passed had large glass cases full of elaborately dressed dolls. Down another row, I saw the same cases filled with ventriloquist dummies. I remembered the museum's recent exhibition of antique children's toys, and saw more cases filled with wind-up cars and trucks. Everywhere I looked, the rows were filled with interesting items. I wished we could stop to look, but at the same time, I didn't want to find out by mistake which ones would trigger my gift. I hoped we could make it out without causing a scene.

Alistair stopped between two rows, got his bearings by looking at the row numbers, and headed confidently toward a large wooden box. He lifted it down from the shelf and carried it a short distance to a large table.

"These were some of Jeremiah Abernathy's personal items, donated after his death by the local authorities," Alistair said. "Apparently, he was in enough trouble that no one ever came forward to claim his effects."

I moved closer to see, and Teag looked over my shoulder. I saw a gold pair of cufflinks, a silver flask, gold-rimmed spectacles, and a knife with an antler handle. Even without touching them, I felt the same resonance as I had at the Archive's exhibit: cold, violent, remorseless… and frightened.

"You said Abernathy was in trouble. Did his luck wane at the end?" I asked.

Alistair nodded. "Oh yes. Not long after the sinking of the *Cristobal*, in fact. Deals gone bad, associates who turned on him or turned him in, problems with the police, and with the federal government." He shook his head. "For all the power he once had, Abernathy died violently in fire and a gun battle. Toward the end, he was hounded by his fellow criminals, the authorities, and some say the supernatural."

*Losing control of your demon will do that to you,* I thought. Something toward the bottom of the box caught my eye.

"See something, Cassidy?" Teag asked.

I noticed that there were several photographs in the bottom of the box – old tintypes with faded images. Teag reached in and pulled the pictures out, holding them for me to see.

One of the old pictures showed Jeremiah Abernathy

standing next to a tall man in a hat. Corban Moran. Moran's face and skin hadn't withered in this photograph, and he appeared to be a man in his early forties. But I knew from Sorren that looks could be deceiving. Still, we had the link we needed.

Moran knew Abernathy, and almost certainly knew about the demon. Both Abernathy and Moran came to ruin when the *Cristobal* sank. Moran, a damaged immortal, showed back up just when Landrieu's dive team was about to recover the *Cristobal* treasure. Moran had approached Landrieu, who turned him down. Now Landrieu and his men were missing, probably dead, along with at least half a dozen more unfortunates sacrificed to feed Abernathy's demon. And now, I thought I had the piece that linked all the rest together.

"We should probably let you get home and have dinner," I said, conscious of the time and the fact that Teag and I still had to get back without running afoul of a pissed off demon, the demon's minions or Moran. Just another night in paradise.

Alistair had just replaced the box on the shelf when we heard the 'clunk' of an electrical breaker. Half of the lights in the collections room went out. A second later, we heard another 'clunk' and the other half flicked off.

Emergency lights cast a dim glow, but shadows stretched between the long corridors and their tall shelves. Alistair looked more annoyed than alarmed. "Well now, that's unusual," he said. "I'll have to have a word with building maintenance. Come on, I can still see well enough to get us out of here."

We took a few steps and halted as strange sounds carried over the gloom. From one direction, I heard the scuffing of feet, but the footsteps were light, like a small child. From the other direction, we heard the unmistakable sound of a metal key winding up a spring. And from right in front of us, hidden by shadows, came the sound of hundreds of wings flapping.

"Run," Teag said, grabbing my arm. Alistair hesitated for just a second, and then led the way at a faster-than-dignified pace.

The emergency lights gave off just enough of a bluish glow that we weren't completely blind, but like driving at twilight, our eyes weren't functioning at their best, either. I glimpsed movement in the shadows to my right. Whatever was out there wasn't much taller than our knees, but moving quickly.

"Get us back to the main hallway!" I hissed to Alistair.

From the left came the sound of dozens of music boxes, each playing a different tune, all at the same time. The buzz-click of mechanical joints moving and the shuffle of metal feet on the tile floor echoed in the huge room. I could hear the halting din of metal drums played by tin marchers, the wheeze of old springs wound too tightly, and the grinding hum of wind-up cars and tanks. Something had brought the old toys to life, and set them after us.

"Those are dummies down there," Teag yelped, pointing to the right. "Ventriloquist dummies, and they're moving by themselves!"

An impossible flock of birds began to dive bomb us. They flew fast enough to get up a good speed, flocking down the long aisle, intent on closing the gap with us. Passenger pigeons and Carolina parakeets, birds I'd seen in the glass cases, but that no one had seen in flight for over a century because each and every one was dead, taxidermied, and extinct.

Whatever propelled them kept them flying until they reached us, then the dead birds fell from the air, pelting us with their stiff, lifeless bodies.

"The dummies are gaining on us!" Teag warned. I was too busy swatting long-dead birds away from me, getting scratched by their sharp beaks and talons.

Tinny old-time music and wind-up buzzing grew louder as the army of old toys marched and rolled toward us. Paint peeling, dented and bent, their advance was incredibly creepy, and they were moving much faster than they should have been able to go.

The dummies and the toys rounded the corner, pouring into the main cross-hallway. If there had been any doubt that some sentience was controlling them, their single-minded pursuit removed it. The hallway where we had entered was just ahead, and in the huge mirror at the end of our corridor, I could see the toys were gaining.

Something hit me from behind, scrabbling at my back, pulling my hair, kicking against my spine. Solid and hard, it rammed against my skull with enough force that I saw stars. I wheeled, slamming the ventriloquist's dummy against one of the metal shelves, trying to scrape it off as it clamored for a hold on my clothing.

Bo's ghostly form appeared, barking at the dummies and metal toys, running at them to draw them off or force them back. Unfortunately, his spirit mojo wasn't a match for the very solid, scary-real attackers coming our way.

Metal toys skittered beneath my feet like rats, making it difficult to get my footing. I kicked at them, still trying to knock the dummy off of me. Teag and Alistair were doing the same thing, kicking at the wind-up trucks and bears and soldiers that rammed at their ankles as more of the ventriloquist dummies snatched at our pant legs.

I heard glass smashing, over and over again, and then the overwhelming smell of formaldehyde. Far down the corridor, lost in the gloom of the emergency lighting, things were sloshing and slurping their way toward us, those pallid, wet misshapen specimens I had glimpsed on our way in.

We reached the main hallway, but where the mirrors had brightened the space with their reflected light as we entered, now they were wreathed in shadow. Shapes moved in the mirrors, things that weren't really there until you looked at them out of the corner of your eye, things that didn't want you to see them, not until they were close enough to strike.

Those things were getting closer, lurching and halting their way toward the surface of the mirrors. I didn't want to find out whether they would stop there or not.

I swung my leg hard against one of the shelves, trying to get rid of one of the dummies that had wrapped his arms and legs around my shin. It put me off balance, and I fell against the shelving, sending a rain of objects down from above. I threw my arms up over my head to protect myself.

Bo's ghost was still barking up a storm, growling and snarling in the direction of the formaldehyde creatures. He hadn't had much effect on the dummies or toys, but whatever the sloppy-wet things were, they seemed to slow their approach.

Teag had started kicking the dummies out of his way, and I remembered that he told me he played soccer in high school in addition to his martial arts training. His aim was good, and he had some serious power behind those kicks – he sent dummy after dummy skidding down through the advancing mass of wind-up toys, silencing some of the nerve-jarring racket.

Alistair looked terrified at the attack and appalled at the realization that he was going to have to damage museum property to escape. But when one of the dummies chomped its wooden jaws down on Alistair's shoulder, he howled with pain and rammed the dummy against one of the room's steel beam columns.

The wet, sloppy sounds were coming from the way we had entered, as well as the snap-snap-snap of flaccid suction cups drawing their long-dead owner down the tile. The smell of formaldehyde was overpowering, and I was afraid we would either pass out from the vapors or burst into flames.

"It's flammable!" I shouted to Teag as I saw him dig in his bag for the candle and lantern. That approach was out, unless we wanted to go up in a big fireball and take the museum with us.

I couldn't muster the concentration to focus on the spoon-athame I had up my sleeve thanks to the hordes of attacking toys and the crazed dummies that just wouldn't take 'no' for an answer.

I spun around, trying to scrape another dummy from my back, and brought more things sliding and crashing down around me. Teag had grabbed something that looked like a harpoon, and I realized that it really was a harpoon, snatched from off one of the shelves. Alistair had a cast-iron frying pan, and he was setting about himself like a crazed duffer, sending the dummies flying and smashing a path through the wind-up toys.

I looked around in panic, and spotted a shelf full of old, neatly tagged axes and farm implements. I was less afraid of what visions I might see from the ax I grabbed than I was of what would happen if the dummy clinging to my back managed to head-butt me one more time. The problem was, swinging at my own back with an ax wasn't going to help me, and the dummy already had one stiff wooden arm around my throat. A moment later, the other arm wrapped around from the opposite side, and the dummy started to squeeze, hard, all the while chattering with its hinged jaw as if it were laughing at my attempts to breathe.

With my right hand, I swung the axe around my legs as I sputtered for breath. The blade bit deeply into the large head of another dummy, and I kicked the body free, bowling down a dozen of the wind-up toys. With my left, I pressed the agate necklace against the dummy's hard wooden hands as I tore at it to free my throat. As soon as the agate connected with the wood, the hands came free, and I shook the dummy loose, sending him flying.

"Cassidy!" Teag shouted, running toward me as best he could through the chaos. He stabbed at another dummy heading my way, sticking the sharp tip of the harpoon into the mannequin's chest, then flinging him away.

I could tell that Bo's barking had changed direction, but I was too busy fighting for my life to look.

"The mirrors!" Alistair yelled.

Teag and I wheeled. The shadowy figures that I had glimpsed in the background of the mirrors had gotten much, much closer. Some of them pressed up against the glass from the inside, while others ran their hands over the surface, looking for the way to open the doorway to our realm. A few of them were already slipping through the glass, climbing out to come our way.

Teag hurled his harpoon at the nearest mirror, shattering it. No shadow emerged. The doorway was closed.

I hurled my ax at the next mirror, ignoring the groan from Alistair as we smashed another precious furnishing.

"It's those mirrors or our necks," I yelled. Alistair stepped closer to the next mirror just as its shadow reached the glass, closed his eyes, and swung his frying pan, sending the mirrored fragments flying.

I grabbed the nearest solid object I could find and used it to smash the next mirror.

At the far end of the main corridor, opposite where we had come in, I saw the dim glow of an 'EXIT' sign. We'd still have to run the gauntlet of half of the mirrors, but we would be going in the opposite direction to the sloppy sloshing noises and the growing number of shadow men who were leaving their mirror portals.

I stumbled, and this time, a cascade of fabric tumbled down on me, snaring my feet and making me fall. I came up, gasping, fighting my way clear, and realized that I had brought a tangle of old quilts down on me.

The axe had been neutral, with no resonance when I touched it, but the quilts that surrounded me had strong auras, stitched through with the protectiveness and love of their long-ago makers. That gave me crazy hope as I struggled to my feet.

"Come on!" I shouted to my embattled friends. "We're going to get out of here."

I held out the quilt. "Get under here. Now!" Teag and Alistair looked baffled, but caught between the slip-slop of the formaldehyde monsters and the silently approaching shadow men, they were ready to try anything. Bo was in full attack-dog mode, and while he was holding off the shadow men and the wet things for now, I knew it wouldn't last for long.

Alistair anchored the quilt on one side of me while Teag caught up with us. I held the agate necklace in my left hand, and held out my right arm with the spoon-athame, palm out.

The coruscating, pearlescent light flared from my palm, wrapping us in its protective cocoon. It resonated with the energy in the quilt, and the antique bedspread took on a faint, opalescent glow. As Teag took hold of the quilt on the other side of me, I felt the power grow, as if he magnified whatever had been imbued into the fabric and embroidery.

"It's working!" Teag cheered. "This quilt was stitched with some strong stuff, Cassidy. It's almost militant about protecting us."

"Keep moving toward the exit," I said through gritted teeth.

We made it halfway down the corridor before two of the ugliest *akvenon* minions I'd ever seen skittered out from the gloom, blocking the doorway.

"Shit!" I muttered. Teag said something more colorful. So did Alistair, but in Latin. The gist of it all was that we were totally screwed.

The steel fire door behind the *akvenon* shrieked as it ripped from its hinges. A blast of white light blinded us, striking the *akvenon* and splitting them open like lobsters bursting over an open fire. The next blast went streaming over our heads toward the shadow men and the oozing formaldehyde creatures behind them.

"Don't –" I managed to yell before the white fire hit the fumes and a loud flash-bang exploded behind us.

Sorren and Lucinda stood shoulder-to-shoulder in the doorway. Lucinda had the staff from the Archive in her hands, holding it like a flame-thrower. Sorren grabbed us, dragging us out of the way as foul-smelling clouds of smoke billowed toward us.

"The collections!" Alistair despaired, reaching back as if he could save his precious antiquities.

Halon gas nozzles switched on, dampening the fire. Alistair looked stricken, and I felt awful.

Sorren knelt down in front of Alistair. In the distance, we heard sirens. We had to get out of there, quick.

"You went into the archives to put back an artifact, and smelled gas leaking," Sorren said in the same voice he used to glamor Baxter. Alistair stared at him, wide-eyed, utterly lost in Sorren's gaze.

"You tried to escape, but the air was bad and you nearly passed out," Sorren added. "Just as you reached the door, the blast came. It knocked you off your feet and tore the door off its hinges."

"Yes. Yes, I remember."

"You never saw us," Sorren said with a sad half-smile. "You were alone at the time."

"Yes," Alistair replied. "I was alone."

The shadow men and monsters were gone, and we'd just destroyed priceless artifacts. As happy as I was to be alive, I grieved for the irreplaceable history that had been lost.

Corban Moran was going to pay, big time.

Alistair was going to be all right, although the museum might not be. I really hoped Alistair wouldn't lose his position over the damage. I was shaking with pent-up fear and anger. Sorren hustled us away from the building.

"Teag's car –" I protested.

"It's been moved, honey," Lucinda said, resolutely striding away from the scene of the damage.

"The security cameras in the museum –"

"Have been altered," Sorren replied. "It will look like a power failure."

"How –" Teag began.

"I sensed where you'd gone," Sorren said. "And I feared that Moran would interfere. Lucinda and I came as quickly as we could." He looked apologetic. "I'm sorry it wasn't sooner."

"We learned a lot," I said, still light-headed from our close brush with death. "Most of it can wait. But I think we've got what we were looking for," I said. "Teag's got the journal and papers from the salvage crew, and Alistair added the missing piece."

I looked at Sorren and Lucinda. "Storage," I said. "That's what they've all got in common that we haven't had time to investigate. Now we've just got to figure out why it matters."

"I'll see what I can find out through my channels," Sorren said. "And I've requested a demon hunter's assistance, but he hasn't arrived yet. In the meantime, take advantage of the break to recuperate. Once we have more information and our demon hunter, we'll be ready to move."

# Chapter Twenty-One

"YOU SAID THE last site we didn't get to was a closed storage facility, right?"

Teag nodded. "Yep. The place was called Stor-Your-Own and it closed about six months ago."

"What a coincidence," I said drily. "Landrieu and his salvage team put their dive gear in storage when they were in town. And from the journals, it says the storage facility is in the old Navy yard, fairly close to the warehouse where Moran called the demon. The whole Navy yard is on land Jeremiah Abernathy used to own, back when he controlled the demon."

"We also know the Foo dog was in storage, and if we can find out where, maybe that's the connection with the suddenly-haunted antiques," Teag replied. "Maybe storing something with bad resonance near a demon activates the juju."

"That's something we need to find out. And it wouldn't hurt to see what you can dig up about Stor-Your-Own's history and owners. It's convenient that it went belly up right at the time Moran surfaced."

"Let's do our digging from a safe distance this time,"

Teag said. "After what happened in the warehouse and the museum, I'm not thrilled about just going into another haunted building to poke around."

I held up both hands in surrender. "No arguments here. My bruises have bruises."

"Now that you mention it, I remember a couple of the folks I called mentioning storage."

I chewed my lip for a moment, thinking. "If we could prove that even some of the problem pieces were at one time stored at the facility in the Navy yard, then we would know it's something about that particular site that activated them."

"It wouldn't hurt to do some digging into the business records, too," Teag mused. "Why did it go out of business? Who owns it now? Did something happen to any of the previous owners? There's a reason it's just standing there empty."

Teag grinned. "Sounds like we've got a full day in front of us tomorrow. Monday is usually one of our busy days."

I sighed. "True. But Maggie said she'd come in to make up for the hours she missed. Part of me hopes we don't get a lot of customers so we can work on this, and the other part of me really wants to pay the electric bill."

"I agree," Teag said with a laugh. "But I know you, Cassidy. And I know you won't let this drop until you get to the bottom of it."

I finished my drink, thinking about what Teag said. At least a dozen men were dead, including the salvage crew and Jimmy Redshoes. And if Moran had his way, that would be just the beginning.

\* \* \*

MAGGIE WAS BACK, and seemed fully recovered. For someone who was semi-retired, her near-boundless energy made me feel like a slacker. Her gray hair was cut in a trendy, chin-length bob, and she confided that she liked the cut because it kept her hair out of her face when she was doing her daily yoga. She was slender and dressed in a style I thought of as 'Woodstock-esque'.

"Good to have you back, Maggie!" I said with a grin. "Glad you're feeling better."

Maggie beamed. "Good to be back, Cassidy. I don't get sick often, but it seems like when I do, it hits twice as hard. Believe me, I'm glad to be on my feet again!"

"Are you up to watching the front for a little bit?" I asked. "Teag and I are working on an acquisition."

Maggie waved me off. "Happy to do it. It's been too darn quiet all by myself at home. Take your time. I've got it covered."

While Maggie handled the customers, Teag took his laptop to the break room and I went into my office to make phone calls.

"We heard back from Debra and Rebecca and the lady with the funeral vase," I reported after some time on the phone. "And you were right – all the pieces were stored at Stor-Your-Own at some time in the last year."

"Mrs. Butler doesn't remember the name of the storage unit, but she's going to check her records," I said. "And before you ask, Trinket Ellison said the same thing. She believes the opera glasses were in storage for a little while after her mother's death while the family sorted things out, but she didn't make the arrangements herself, so she has to check."

"I suspect the Ellisons have people for that."

I nodded. "Knowing the Ellisons, their people probably have people for that."

"How about Rebecca? She said she bought the Foo dog statue at an estate sale," Teag said.

I nodded. "Uh huh. And she also said that the sale was fun because there was so much to see, between what had been in the house and what had been tucked away *in storage*."

Teag crossed his arms and his ankles and gave me a happily smug look.

"What?" I asked, rolling my eyes.

"What do you mean?"

"That's your 'I-know-something-you-don't-know' pose. Spill."

"From what I can find online, Stor-Your-Own definitely has a checkered past," he said. "And that's just from what's in the public record. I haven't hacked anything yet."

"Yet."

He grinned. "Want to know?"

I rolled my eyes, and he laughed. "So, Stor-Your-Own finally closed for good six months ago, but it's had problems almost since the beginning. The owner died last year, left a total financial mess for his widow. She's been in and out of court, skirting bankruptcy and lawsuits, and so selling the storage facility probably hasn't been at the top of her to-do list."

"Lawsuits?"

Teag nodded. "The guy who owned it, Fred Kenner, wasn't a real stand-up sort of guy. There've been allegations of money laundering, as well as suspicions that he turned a blind eye to drug dealers renting units."

"Lovely."

"Isn't it?" Teag agreed. "Kenner had a lot of shady dealings. He'd filed for bankruptcy before, then moved to a new city and started over again. He had a slew of names, and some off-shore accounts."

"Why own a storage facility?" I asked.

"It's cheap to build, and it doesn't take a lot of work to bring in steady cash," he replied with a shrug. "Think about it. Most people put their stuff in storage and don't come back for months, maybe years, and all the while, their monthly rental goes right into your bank account. All you need is an office manager to sign up new accounts and occasionally sweep the floor. Easy money was Fred Kenner's watchword."

"How long was Stor-Your-Own in operation?"

"Kenner converted an empty shipping facility into a self-storage facility about three years ago. And for the first couple of years, it seemed to operate in the black. Then Kenner got in trouble with some kind of pyramid scheme, and started pulling cash out of other, more legitimate, investments."

"In other words, he was desperate enough to make a deal with a demon – or with Moran, who's the next best thing," I said.

"Bingo."

I leaned back in my chair. "Okay, so the storage facility has been there for three years, but the deaths only began about six months ago. What changed?"

Teag shrugged. "Good question. And my guess is, Moran. Kenner's world started to fall apart at about the same time the murders started. He was always a shady dude. He beat a rap for tax evasion, and the workers at one of his businesses sued him for not paying them for overtime. But he managed to get away with it until a year ago."

"So his luck changed?"

Teag nodded, twirling a pencil as he thought. "He was under indictment for fraud. His real estate investments took a big hit when the economy soured, and he owed money to the wrong people. He had gambling debts. The Feds were looking at him for insider trading, and if they had nailed drug dealers using the facility, the government could have seized the property under the racketeering laws."

"Sounds like a perfect storm," I said. "And right about that time, Landrieu and his team disappear, Moran summons his demon, and the killings start."

"And Kenner might have been Victim Number Two," Teag said. "They found his badly mutilated body inside the storage unit security fence right when all the shit was about to hit the fan around his business dealings."

He looked up. "They charged the office manager, Flora Beam, with the crime. Her attorney claimed insanity and so she's locked up in a psychiatric facility."

My blood ran cold. "When?"

"If my dates are right, Fred Kenner died about a week before the murder near the Navy yard," Teag replied. "Which means he might have been the first death after the sacrifice we found."

Something Teag had said jiggled a memory. "You know, when I had the vision at the Dennison house, I caught something about Kevin stealing things from his stash. Do you think he meant the storage facility?"

Teag shrugged. "It's possible, although he might have been dumpster diving."

"What about Jimmy Redshoes?" I asked. "Do you remember the kinds of things he sold? They were more like what you'd find in a yard sale than from a street vendor, because he almost never had two of the same thing. What if he supplied his merchandise by breaking into an abandoned storage facility?"

Teag frowned. "Could be. But if it was abandoned, wouldn't the tenants have cleared out all their things before it shut down?"

"Maybe some of them did," I speculated. "But if Kenner was such a shady character, and the facility closed up on short notice, maybe some of them didn't get word in time. Or maybe they never got the notice. You said it yourself," I continued, "people who store things often don't pay any attention."

"That makes sense," Teag replied. "That's why there are those reality TV shows about selling unclaimed items."

I nodded. "But if Kenner was dead and his estate's been tied up in litigation, they might not have been able to sell things off, or maybe no one's even gotten to dealing with it yet."

Just then, the phone rang and Maggie grabbed it before I got there. "Cassidy," Maggie called, "call on line one."

I greeted the caller and listened to the voice on the other end. "Thank you so much. I really appreciate your going to all that bother." I turned to Teag with a Cheshire-cat grin. "That was Mrs. Butler. Says the linens were stored at Stor-Your-Own until about six months ago."

Teag fist-pumped the air in victory. "Gotcha!"

I poured a new cup of coffee and leaned against the break room counter. "We still don't know why the bad juju seems to be picking up momentum," I said. "The murders are happening more often, and it's only been recently that there are reports of haunted objects causing problems."

"Landrieu thought he was being stalked," Teag said. "We know Moran approached him. I wouldn't put it past Moran to make Landrieu and his team disappear if they got in his way."

"Meaning that once Landrieu located the *Cristobal*, and Moran had recuperated from the damage Sorren did to him, Moran got rid of Landrieu and retrieved what he wanted himself."

Teag nodded. "As far as the objects go, maybe Moran's demon-binding artifact needed time – or exposure to something – to gain strength," he theorized. "So the objects started out normal, and then got contaminated as the energy in the storage facility strengthened."

"Could be," I agreed. "Trinket said that no one else had reported having an incident with the opera glasses."

"It makes sense," Teag said. "The people who owned the haunted items had them for years without anything freaky happening. Then there's a move, a death, a need to clear out space, and the pieces go into storage for a while. And when they come back, they're not the same."

I frowned. "Then why wouldn't the malicious magic register when the pieces came to us at the store?" I mused.

"Maybe some power at the storage unit made the pieces vulnerable, but the magic didn't show up until it was triggered – by something, or someone," Teag ventured.

"I'd love to get my hands on Stor-Your-Own's files to find out who else had things stored there about the time everything started to go bad," I said. "And I'd really like to talk to Flora Beam and see what she knows." I met Teag's gaze. "If her boss made a deal with a demon, she might have every reason to have gone insane." *And more than a few reasons to kill Kenner,* I thought.

"I told you, I haven't started hacking yet," Teag said with a mischievous grin. "If the storage facility had information online, I should be able to get in. As for Flora, let me work on Anthony. If we play enough angles, we're bound to come up with something."

THE NEXT MORNING, Teag and I were heading to a rural area on the outskirts of Charleston to visit the Wendover Psychiatric Hospital. Anthony had taken the morning off to go with us, and he had already used his connections to gain permission to talk with Flora Beam.

"If there wasn't the possibility of this connecting to those murder cases, I wouldn't be doing this," Anthony said, for about the tenth time.

"You're the one who told me about the deposition," Teag said. "Flora Beam was declared mentally incompetent to stand trial because she raved about demons and ghosts and claimed that she had to kill Fred Kenner because he was possessed."

I knew that Teag had spent the afternoon online, using his magic and the darker recesses of the Internet to get a look at the court records regarding Flora's testimony. It wasn't hard to see why the judge ruled her unable to stand trial, with talk about demons demanding blood sacrifices, malicious ghosts, haunted objects and supernatural menace. But to Teag and me, Flora was dead-on. What she said she witnessed would put any normal person around the bend.

"I saw photos from the trial," Teag said, turning toward Anthony, who was driving. I sat in the back.

"Not many people ever showed up on Flora's side of the courtroom. But there was one man who was there every day. Fifty-ish, balding, looked like he might have been ex-military. Any idea who he was?"

Anthony shook his head. "Probably a friend or relative. There wouldn't be a record of who attended if they weren't part of the proceedings."

Teag had shown me the photos, and we both agreed the older man's consistent presence raised questions. Was he a loyal friend, sticking with Flora despite the awful testimony, or one of Moran's people, sent to keep an eye on things?

Anthony coached us on how to get past security. Teag and I had dressed up, looking like paralegals in our spiffy business suits. It was interesting watching the up-and-coming young lawyer in his element. Teag just grinned, proud of his partner.

The interior of the psychiatric hospital tried to be homey looking, in a high-security institutional kind of way. Meaning that the room where individuals committed to the hospital could have supervised visits had upholstered furnishings instead of hard plastic prison chairs, but the couches, tables and chairs were all bolted to the floor.

An aide brought Flora out to meet us. I caught my breath. Teag had shown me the employee photo in the Stor-Your-Own database that had been taken when Flora was hired. She had been a plump, grandmotherly looking woman with gray hair, cheerful blue eyes and a welcoming smile. In the photos from the trial, she had looked understandably haggard from stress. But now, with her baggy state facility jumpsuit, handcuffs and the ankle manacles that hobbled her, she looked emaciated and haunted, like someone who has stared into hell and found something staring back.

"Hello, Flora," Anthony said in his kindest tone. "We have some questions for you about what happened at the storage unit."

I met Flora's gaze and saw madness there, but I also saw intelligence. *Maybe the madness was a form of self-defense,* I thought. *Maybe it's how normal people deal with finding out there really are monsters under the bed.*

"I said everything I mean to say," Flora replied. She didn't sound belligerent, just weary. No doubt she had done her best to warn people of the danger, alert them to the real source of the problem, only to have her testimony disregarded out of hand and her reports mocked.

"Have you ever heard of a man named Corban Moran?" I asked.

Flora slowly turned to look me in the eyes. "Best you forget you ever heard that name."

"Did he do business with Fred Kenner? Was he around the storage facility?" I hoped Flora would trust me, woman-to-woman. I saw wariness in her expression, along with the longing to have someone, anyone, believe her.

"Yes," she said. "To both questions. And when he showed up, all hell broke loose."

"What about Russ Landrieu?" Teag asked. "Did he and Moran cross paths?"

A pained look came over Flora's face, and she began to rock back and forth in her chair. The aide started toward us from where he waited by the door, but Anthony shook his head and the man withdrew.

"Oh, Lordy. Oh, Lordy," Flora said. "Yes, Mr.

Landrieu and his folks used to come by when they went out on their boat. Nice fellow. Always waved when he came in or out, paid his bill on time, never caused any trouble. When I found out he was a celebrity with all those treasure dives, I asked him for an autograph. He seemed to get a kick out of that."

For someone who had been portrayed as a raving lunatic at the trial, Flora was calm and well-spoken. *Then again, so are most serial killers,* I reminded myself. Intuition could be mistaken, but I didn't sense that Flora was dangerous. If Kenner really had been possessed, she might have done us a public service in getting rid of him, although I suspected Moran had done the killing and let Flora take the fall.

"What about Landrieu and Moran?" I prompted. Flora's mind seemed to wander, and I wondered if she couldn't remember, or didn't want to.

"The last time I saw Mr. Landrieu, he and his team came out to get their things. He told me that this was the 'big one', the dive that was going to put them in the big time," she said. She rocked back and forth as she talked, and her palms ran up and down her forearms, self-soothing her way through memories that had caused her plenty of trouble.

"Mr. Moran was there," Flora recalled. "And they had a big argument, him and Mr. Landrieu. I was up in the office, so I couldn't hear what it was about, but I could see them arguing on the surveillance cameras." She shook her head. "That was a bad thing to do. You don't want to argue with Mr. Moran."

"How did Moran know Kenner?" I probed.

Flora shivered. "Moran's trouble," she whispered. "And Mr. Kenner didn't need more problems. I figured

Mr. Moran loaned him money, since Mr. Kenner had a lot of people looking for him to pay them." She leaned forward. "I don't mean bill collectors – they called, too. I mean guys who would throw a brick through your window when you were late with your payment."

"Did Moran store anything at the units?" I asked.

"You don't want to know," Flora said, and I saw her gaze grow distant, as if she was retreating into herself.

I leaned forward. "Yes, I do. Because the thing that killed Mr. Kenner is back, and it'll keep on killing until we know enough about Moran to stop him."

Relief warred with the need to shield herself from what she had seen. "You believe... about the thing I saw? The demon?"

I nodded. "I've seen it too, Flora. We both have. We're going to stop it, but we need to know what you saw – what you *really* saw."

We had read her deposition, but it was clear that the claims she made seemed so far-fetched that the attending psychologist and lawyers had taken it with a grain of salt. It was also possible that Moran had somehow managed to tamper with the evidence. I wanted to hear it straight from Flora's lips.

Flora drew a deep breath and closed her eyes. "All right," she said. "But it ain't pretty."

"I know," I said. "But we need to hear it. All of it. Please, don't leave anything out. It's important."

Flora's arrest paperwork said she was sixty-two, but she looked at least ten years older since the trial. Outside of work, Flora had volunteered with the local garden club, collected canned goods for the food bank and helped out at her neighborhood animal shelter. Nothing in her past would have suggested she would be convicted of murder, especially of such a gruesome killing. Now, as she mustered the courage to revisit her story, I saw strength in her features that even madness could not erase.

"Mr. Kenner wasn't a mean man," Flora said. "He was just weak. Took the easy way. Money got tight and trouble came. He got scared. Didn't know what to do. Then Moran showed up with lots of money. Mr. Kenner was in so deep, he'd have bargained with the devil himself."

She gave a short, harsh laugh. Kenner had done just that. "For a while it got better. Moran took some units down in Building Four, and kept to himself. Mr. Kenner told me to stay clear of his units, and I did. But then it got bad, real bad."

"Bad, how?" I asked.

Flora shut her eyes and wrapped her arms around herself, but I could see a determination in her features to keep on talking. "I started seeing things, hearing things when I'd close up at night. I thought it was just my eyes playing tricks on me, but it kept happening."

She let out a long breath. "Mr. Kenner started to act real strange, got mean as a junkyard dog. His eyes went funny, like he wasn't in there anymore." She shivered. "I didn't watch many horror movies, but it was like something got in his head and made him someone else."

She shook her head. "Not my imagination. Ghosts. Haints. And creatures that shouldn't be. Like on TV, except real." She was quiet for a moment, still rocking back and forth. "Then one day, I heard something that sounded like a man moaning, like he was gonna die. I went looking to see if someone got hurt, and I come around the corner and see Mr. Moran and this monster, and a whole lot of blood."

Her voice got soft. "So much blood. Blood everywhere. And Mr. Moran looked at me, and his monster looked at me, too. Ugly as sin, with big sharp teeth like a shark and skin like a lizard, like what it might be if you crossed a man with a crocodile. And it was covered in blood."

"Where was Mr. Kenner?" Teag asked gently.

Flora opened her eyes and met his gaze. "He was where the blood was coming from. They killed him. They… took him apart. I ran." She shook her head.

It was the same story she had told the court, the story no one believed. She hadn't killed Fred Kenner, but what she saw had damaged her. Maybe she was safer in here. I counted her as one more of Moran's victims, someone else to avenge. And I had one more question left to ask.

"There was a man who came to the trial," I said. "Who was he?"

Flora nodded. "Clockman," she said. "He tried to warn me. He knew… He knew…"

The aide tapped Anthony on the shoulder. "Your time's up," he said. "I need to take her back to her room."

Anthony, Teag and I rose. I leaned over toward Flora. "Thank you," I murmured.

She seized my hand so suddenly, Teag jumped and the aide moved in to protect me. "Stop him," she begged. "Stop him."

The aide interposed himself, removing her hands from mine and hustling her away. I stared after her. Stop Moran. Stop the demon. Silently, I made her the same promise I had made to Jimmy Redshoes. We'd make it right. Come hell or high water.

# Chapter Twenty-Two

ANTHONY HAD TO go back to the office, so he dropped Teag and me off at the store after we were done interviewing Flora. Teag headed to his place, with a promise to do magically-enhanced Internet research in order to follow up on the information Flora had given us. I was looking forward to having a quiet evening at home.

I knew when I walked up to my door and Baxter wasn't barking that Sorren was there. Sure enough, he and Baxter were sitting on the couch together in the dark. He lifted Baxter down to the floor and my little Maltese scampered over to greet me.

"You're going to scramble his circuits if you keep glamoring him," I said.

"If it counts to ingratiate me, I fed him." Sorren's face was halfway in shadow, but from what I could see, he seemed to be in much better shape than the last time I had seen him.

"How are you?"

He shrugged. "I've been worse. Immortality often means you can't die, even when you want to."

There wasn't really any response I could make to that, so I let it go. "Any news from your sources?"

"People in my circles tend to move around a lot. Not all of them embrace modern conveniences, like cell phones. I have left messages. Whether or not we hear in a timely matter is hard to say. Over the centuries, one's view of timeliness changes."

"I saw an oil painting at the Historical Archive," I said. The meeting with Mrs. Morrissey seemed like forever ago. "There's a man who looks a great deal like you."

A ghost of a smile flitted across his face. "I tried to be inconspicuous."

I chuckled. "Do you remember when it was painted?"

Sorren nodded. "It's a curious thing about immortality. Mortals forget so much, yet live such a short while. We live so long, and forget nothing." He met my gaze. "I've come to believe that's part of the curse."

"Is immortality a curse?"

Sorren's expression grew pensive. "Sometimes I think so. Other times, not. I haven't decided yet."

"What do you know of white magic?" I decided an abrupt change of topic was appropriate.

"You mean, like you've been able to call on, using the stored memories in an object as a source of power?"

I nodded. Since I was self-taught when it came to my touch magic, I was always eager to learn. I hadn't had a chance to discover what Uncle Evanston knew, and most of the time when Sorren was in town, there was too much going on for a lesson. I'd been making it up as I went, and I was coming to the conclusion that might not be a good thing.

Sorren paused. "I was fortunate to have Alard as my maker. He mentored me in the Dark Gift. Those whose makers are not so generous, or who lose their makers too young, are not so lucky."

He shook his head. "Your ancestors were able to pass the store down from one generation to another with enough overlap to 'train' the incoming owner of Trifles and Folly. You were born with your gift, but how to use it doesn't come naturally. Unfortunately, your Uncle Evan didn't have the chance he'd hoped for to show you what to do."

"The family said he had a heart attack," I said quietly. "But that's not true, is it?"

Sorren and I were long overdue for this conversation.

Sorren pressed his lips together and then shook his head again. "In a manner of speaking. His heart stopped abruptly."

"Because someone – or something – killed him."

He nodded. "Yes."

"Tell me."

Sorren looked at me, and I saw the full sorrow of the centuries in his eyes. "Evan had your heart for adventure. And like you, he was a gifted psychometric. He inherited the store from his father, who also had your gift. But he had the chance to work with his father for a decade before the store fell to him."

"Did any of my ancestors – the ones who owned Trifles and Folly – die of disease or old age?"

Sorren shook his head. "No. Although members of your family believe otherwise."

I felt like the world around me was spinning. Baxter pawed at my leg to be picked up and I lifted him into my arms like a fuzzy little anchor to reality. Sorren's words took my breath away, but at the same time, they weren't a complete surprise.

"What happened to Uncle Evan?"

Sorren looked past me, as if he were reliving the memory. "We went looking for a particularly dangerous item, a watch that could enable the wearer to 'jump' into the skin of another person. The search took us to an old lunatic asylum in West Virginia," he said quietly.

"Psychiatric hospital," I corrected without thinking, then remembered that six hundred year-old vampires weren't always politically correct.

He shrugged. "Words change, but not the beliefs of those who confine people.

"The Alliance wanted to return the watch to a safe storage place," Sorren continued. "We were up against a very powerful enemy who wanted the watch for himself. I fought the enemy, and Evan went after the watch. He was supposed to just keep it out of the line of fire but he touched it –"

"And all the lives of everyone who had touched it coursed through him at the same time."

"Yes." Sorren nodded and then paused. "Perhaps if he were younger or stronger... but it was more than his heart could take."

Sorrow lodged in my throat. Having been possessed by moments of other people's lives, I did not want to think too hard about the power that had overwhelmed Evan.

"He picked me to inherit the store. I remember the first time I met him. I was a little girl."

"What do you recall?" Sorren asked.

I thought back. "He gave me a bracelet," I said quietly. "And he asked me what I saw."

"What did you tell him?"

I smiled, remembering that long ago day, my seventh birthday. "I told him a story about a dark haired girl with curls in a white dress who liked to chase ducks. He listened as I told him all about her." I looked up and met Sorren's gaze. "It was a test, wasn't it? To see if I had the gift."

Sorren nodded. "Yes. He was very excited when he came back. He was so thrilled that someone in a new generation had the talent. Sometimes the magical gift skips a generation, and even then, Evan had an eye on retirement."

I stroked Baxter's soft fur. "But he didn't get to retire."

"No, he didn't. And I mourn him, as I mourn all your ancestors, back to the first Evann, who opened this store when South Carolina was barely a colony." I heard the sadness in his voice.

"So there's no retirement plan," I said, but the humor sounded forced.

Sorren looked at me and chuckled. "Cassidy – I am a very wealthy man. I take care of my own. I have never left one of my partners without support."

I returned his gaze. "Trifles and Folly isn't the only store like this, is it?"

He shook his head. "Over the centuries? No."

"And now?"

A faint smile touched his lips. "There are several sister shops scattered around the world. All managed by someone with a gift that enables them to identify – and intervene – when dangerous objects come onto the market. From there, the Alliance takes over, as it does here."

"I want to find more things I can use to protect myself. I'm tired of getting knocked flat on my ass every time we go out."

Sorren nodded. "I agree. Your Uncle Evan was quite good with a number of weapons, both mundane and magical. You and Teag need protection."

Just then, the phone rang, and I jumped. I could tell from the caller display that it was Teag. "Just talking about you," I said with as much cheer as I could muster. "What's up?"

"Is Sorren there?"

"Yep."

"Mind if I come over? I've got some more information – and something to show you."

"Sure," I said. "I'll put out some cookies. Come on over."

I looked up as the call ended. "I'm glad Teag called. If we're going to decide what to do next, he should be part of it."

Sorren nodded. "That's fine. Lucinda should be here in a few minutes as well."

Teag made it in record time. "Good evening," he said cheerily.

"I think that's supposed to be my line," Sorren said, with an utterly deadpan delivery. It was so unexpected that I did a double-take. Maybe the fear of facing down the big bad darkness made me a little punchy, because I laughed harder than the joke was worth.

Teag grabbed a soda from the fridge and came to sit down with us in my living room. A moment later, the doorbell rang, and I welcomed Lucinda into the room.

"I know you say you don't read minds," I said, "but I had just been thinking that we really needed to invite Lucinda into this before we take the next step."

"That's just common sense," Lucinda replied. Tonight, she was dressed in a form-fitting black cami and a crinkled, loose cotton skirt. I glimpsed silver necklaces with the *veves* of several powerful Voudon Loa. Her hair was held back with a headband. It was quite a departure from the buttoned-down business suit-wearing professor.

"Good. I'm glad we agree," I said.

"Now that Lucinda is here, we can get to one of the reasons I dropped by tonight," Sorren said. "You wanted to be better able to protect yourself," he said with a look in my direction. "I brought you something that will help you do that."

Sorren took a piece of amber from his pocket. It was circular, about the size of a stuffed mushroom, and the smooth surface had been carved with runes. He held it up between his thumb and forefinger.

"Do you know what this is?" he asked.

Teag frowned, thinking. "It's a spindle whorl," he said, finally making the connection. "They were used to weight the spindle and help twist fiber into thread."

Sorren nodded. "They used to be quite common. Long ago, people understood that there was magic in the process of weaving and spinning. It's not a coincidence that it's said that someone 'spins' a spell. Teag's beginning to understand it, although he's more prone to spin data than wool. Spinning whorls were thought to possess magic."

All traces of humor left his eyes. "This was a gift from a Viking Seior to my maker," Sorren said. "I've seen its power."

I looked to Sorren and then to Lucinda. "I thought the Seiors died out back in the Dark Ages." I've always loved mythology, and reading old legends and folktales has been a hobby since I was a kid.

Sorren gave a half-smile. "I assure you, Secona is very much alive."

Mentally, I did the math. If Sorren was five hundred

and some years old and Secona had given the whorl to Sorren's maker, then both the staff and Secona were very, very old. Well, damn.

"What does it do?" I asked. The thought of taking up the centuries-old spindle whorl of a Viking witch and wise woman gave me pause.

Sorren's smile was encouraging. "I don't know what it will do for you. Why not try touching it and see how it speaks to you?"

I could think of about a millions reasons why that might not be a good idea, but practicality won out. If we were going into a dangerously haunted facility to face down a demon, then I needed a better way to defend myself.

I sighed and nodded my assent. "Okay. Pass it over. Probably better if I do this sitting down."

The whorl was a beautiful piece of amber. Its rich, clear color drew me down into its depths, into the one-of-a-kind bubbles and imperfections. I knew enough about weaving from Teag to know that a whorl weighted a distaff, which was a pole around which thread or yarn was coiled. Legends all over the world revered the distaff as a powerful and sacred tool for gaining divine guidance, cursing enemies and seeing into the future.

I had no idea how such an ancient magical item might react to my touch. Lucinda came to stand on one side of me as Sorren brought me the whorl.

"Honestly, Teag's the Weaver," I said. "It might be more in line with his Gift."

"And perhaps at another time we'll test that but Lucinda has something else for Teag," Sorren said, giving a nod to Teag. "But you need something now. See how Secona speaks to you," he urged.

"Hold on," I said, setting aside the spoon that was inside my sleeve. I thought about unclasping Bo's collar, but left it wrapped around my wrist. I took a deep breath and held out both hands, palms up, to receive the whorl.

*The amber felt warm and smooth on my palms, and the whorl was heavier than I expected for its size. I sensed the incredible age of the whorl and the disillusionment that came with long existence. So much gone, never to return…*

*Power thrummed through the amber. Every magical working leaves a residue. Magics great and small had been done with this whorl, and the echo of those spells clung to the smooth resin. She who wielded this piece had great magic. I remembered the name, Secona, and I saw a blonde woman wearing a blue cloak with a headpiece of black lambskin trimmed in white rabbit. A gem-inlaid mantle covered her shoulders and fell to the bottom of her skirts. Strings of glass beads hung around her neck, and a large leather bag was attached to a belt at her waist. She wore ermine gloves and carried a distaff set with a brass and stone top. She was old and very powerful, and across the ages, I sensed that she was looking at me, taking my measure.*

*In my vision, Bo was at my side, a large and powerful guardian presence. He gave a wag of his tail and sat down, letting me know that the woman was not a threat.*

*I felt my psychometric gift connect with the power of the whorl, and the vision of another place and time overwhelmed me. I saw rough-looking men clad in tunics and furs. They were tall, broad shouldered with red or blond hair. I saw them loading longboats with* dragon figures on the prow, and I knew that I saw a Viking war party.

I did not understand their language. I didn't need to. I saw the raiders' preparations through the eyes of a woman who moved among these men as an equal and was accorded the respect due a queen. She spoke and the men hastened to do her bidding. They brought her swords to bless and she spoke words of anointing over them. The tallest and strongest of the raiders, the man to whom all the fighters deferred, sought her counsel and listened gravely to her words.

Wives and mistresses watched the boats sail from the shore, but Secona accompanied the warriors. I could feel the magic in her whorl, feel it channel power between the heavens and the sea, sense the energy that it drew from the world itself and fed back to her gift. Secona had made the whorl that I held in my hands, and it preserved a piece of her memories and her power, maybe even her consciousness.

Centuries flickered and passed in a blur. Power grew stronger, deeper. Secona endured. Among the unfamiliar images, I glimpsed a face I knew. Sorren looked unchanged, but the world around him was that of centuries past. I felt a bond, sensed her fierce protection, and once again, power surged through the amber, cleansing and restoring as it passed.

My eyelids fluttered open, and I felt unsteady, though I had not moved from my seat. Lucinda put a hand on my shoulder as Sorren carefully removed the whorl from my hands.

"I saw… centuries," I murmured.

Sorren and Lucinda exchanged a telling glance. "I'd say the whorl will accept her," Lucinda said.

Sorren slipped the whorl into a small velvet bag and handed it to me. "Please keep this with you, Cassidy, from now on until we find an object better suited to you. Your gift makes you valuable – and vulnerable."

I saw an old sadness in Sorren's eyes. Over the centuries, he had worked with many human allies to do the Alliance's work. I knew for a fact that he had worked with at least ten generations of my own family. *How many mortals had become his comrades?* I wondered. *Maybe even his friends, and what did it cost him to lose them to the dangers that went with the business?*

I shook my head, trying to clear my thoughts. It was difficult to shake off the impressions I had read from the whorl, and the power I had touched still tingled in my fingertips. "I still don't know what I'm supposed to do with it."

"And you won't, until you're in the moment," Lucinda said. "Magic is like that."

That was a little more seat-of-the-pants than I liked, but I had to admit it was probably true. I took a deep breath and laid a hand over Bo's collar to calm myself, and I picked up Baxter when he danced around my knees for attention.

"Cassidy and I did some snooping," Teag said.

Sorren looked like he was about to launch into a reprimand, but I raised a hand to forestall his comments. Sorren and Lucinda listened as we recounted our visit to Flora, our calls to the former renters, and the stranger Flora had nicknamed Clockman.

"I don't think there's any question that the storage unit is where we'll find Moran and his demon," I summarized. "What I want to know is how we're going to deal with them when we find them." I met Sorren's gaze. Even now, I think my willingness to stare him down still surprised him. "Do you think we can stop them, and end the killings? And will getting rid of Moran and the demon put the haunted objects right again?"

"Yes, I think they can be stopped, and yes, I think that will end the killings and most likely stop the hauntings," Sorren replied, but I sensed a cautionary note in his voice. "The difficulty comes in the number of attempts it takes to find the right approach, and the price to be paid."

I didn't like the sound of that at all and I was guessing Teag didn't either from the way he tightly folded his arms.

If this had been a movie, I imagine that right then, there would have been a loud clap of thunder or the lights would have suddenly gone out, or the wind would have blown a shutter loose. When the moment passed and absolutely nothing startling happened, it seemed anticlimactic, as if the director had missed his cue.

"We can even the odds as much as possible by bringing in help," Lucinda said. "That's one reason Sorren asked me to join you. As you saw at the Archive, I have skills," she said with a hint of a grin. "In Voudon, you're never alone, and I'll bring my family ghosts and ask the Loas to lend us a hand."

She leveled a conspiratorial look that seemed designed to lift my spirits. "And I have asked my sister seers to send me their power. You'll see. We'll give Moran and his demon a run for their money."

I suspected that both Lucinda and Sorren were far too experienced at these kinds of things to be cocky about the odds for success. Still, Lucinda's confidence and the revelation that we had more back-up than I expected did cheer me up a little. I looked to Sorren.

"What are you bringing to the party? Legions of the undead? An Alliance hit squad?"

Sorren looked askance at me. "The undead would not be of help, even if I could summon them."

"Alliance hit squad... I like that." Teag volunteered.

I rolled my eyes. "I didn't mean it literally. I meant, what tricks do you have up your sleeve to increase the odds that we all make it back in one piece?"

"I've heard from the demon hunter. That's as close to a 'hit squad' as I can come. He'll come to my house tonight," Sorren said. "I'd like all of you to meet him. It would be good to do our planning on safe ground."

He gave a wan smile. "As for 'tricks up my sleeve,' my only magic is the Dark Gift," Sorren added. "My maker left me a few magical relics. You held one of them in your hands. I apologize for the oversight in not having collected it sooner." He paused. "The whorl did not accept Evan. Perhaps Secona favors you."

"You said that your... maker... received the whorl from a Viking witch," I said. "Is she a vampire too? If she's immortal, can you get her to help us out?"

Sorren looked away, and his expression was unreadable. I saw sadness, regret, and other emotions I could not place. "Secona has slipped farther and farther from the mortal realm with every passing century – more so than the rest of us. She was not a vampire. She is... other. I have not seen her in several lifetimes. The last time I asked for her intervention, she did not heed my call."

He didn't need to add that Secona's lack of help had caused a tragedy. I could see that in his gaze. It was also apparent that, however long ago the betrayal had occurred, the memory still hurt him deeply.

"Well then, who needs her?" I said, trying to brush past an awkward moment. "We'll figure it out as we go."

"Teag," Lucinda said, "I have something for you." She reached into her purse and withdrew a head wrap that was red and white. On it, I saw the veve for Ogoun, one of the more helpful Voudon Loas.

"Please, accept this as a gift and wear it," Lucinda said. "I have asked the blessing of the Loa on it, and since you have weaving magic, I believe that the cloth will speak to your power and give you strength."

"I would be honored," Teag said, accepting the piece of cloth as if he were holding a sacred object. "And I will definitely wear it. I'll take all the help I can get." After a pause, Teag gave Sorren an embarrassed smile. "Don't suppose you found any magic blades I could use?"

Sorren laughed. "I'll see what I can do."

Teag's Filipino martial arts tradition meant he could fight with blades, and use just about anything as a weapon. He was dangerous enough with regular knives, but if we could locate something that would tie into his Weaver magic, he could be awesome.

My gaze wandered back to the head wrap Lucinda had given Teag. I hadn't expected to learn much about Voudon in Charleston – we were far from New Orleans. But Sorren had told me about how Mama Nadege – Lucinda's ancestor – had brought her customs with her when as a slave more than one hundred and fifty years ago, her mistress had brought her from New Orleans to Charleston. Mama Nadege's spirit had never left Charleston's shadowed alleys.

I was sure she was not the only secret practitioner of those rites. Once I was alert to the traces of Voudon, now and again I spotted the beautiful, complex drawings

– *veves* – that were used to invoke the Loas. Lucinda had passed along a powerful gift, since some Voudon practitioners wore head scarfs and 'aprons' in the colors sacred to their favored Loas when they attended rituals and ceremonies. I was betting that's where Teag's scarf had come from and I hoped that the Loas were inclined to listen to petitions for our safety.

I looked at the others. "I don't know about the rest of you, but I'm hungry. Let's go in the kitchen." They followed me and found seats around my table. I pulled a bag of cookies out of the pantry and put them on the table.

Teag laid out an aerial photographic map of the facility. "I printed this out," he said. "And digging into the information I could find on Stor-Your-Own, I turned up some interesting tidbits."

Sorren leaned over to get a better look at the map. "Do you have an idea of where the disturbances are localized?"

Teag nodded. "Here's the office," he said, pointing. "There's a fence around the whole compound, but with the electricity turned off, the gate won't work, so we'll have to cut our way through the fence.

"There are four buildings." He continued. "One of the buildings is the shell of the original brick warehouse. The others are newer pole barn buildings built when the storage facility was set up."

"So someone gutted one of the old warehouses that had been used as a morgue and a prison, and turned it into storage units," Lucinda mused. "Lovely."

I shrugged. "You know Charleston – everything gets re-used. I mean, if you can't sense the resonance, why would you waste a perfectly good building?"

Teag pulled out another sheet, a printout of a diagram

Flora had probably used to orient new tenants. "Here's a map of Building Four," he said. "It's the one where Flora said she saw 'bad things' happening." He raised an eyebrow. "According to what Flora said, it's where Russ Landrieu had his storage unit, and where I suspect Moran and his demon are doing what they do."

Teag pulled some papers out of the messenger bag he had slung across the back of a chair. "Believe it or not, most of Stor-Your-Own's information was online. The court executor hired another storage company to help notify renters after the murder and closing to help wrap things up and they weren't so great on security. They left the door wide open for me."

He paused. "Using the information in those files, I called the tenants who hadn't paid their rent at the time Stor-Your-Own closed," he said. "I found out that three of the people were dead. Three others had gone missing. The only thing they all in common was that they had rented at Stor-Your-Own right before it closed down."

He sighed. "Some of the calls were dead ends – phones disconnected, that sort of thing. But the people I did reach all told me that they didn't collect their things because they were afraid. They had seen things at the storage buildings that scared the hell out of them."

He gave us all a pointed look. "Bad luck clings to that place like stink on a skunk. When I looked up the other two late-rent people, I found that one of them has been in a coma from an unidentified disease for the last four months, and the other is in prison. From everything I read about what happened, it seems like a very normal, devoted and hard-working man suddenly snapped one day and killed his family and his neighbors without any explanation."

"That's some powerfully bad mojo," Lucinda remarked.

He nodded. "People said the place was freezing cold when the units were supposed to be climate controlled. They saw shadow men and heard terrible noises. Lights wouldn't stay on or constantly flickered. And every one of them said a terrible feeling of despair hung over the place."

The four of us exchanged glances. "Looks like at least a few of Stor-Your-Own's tenants had some run-ins with ghosts," Lucinda said.

Teag nodded. "And it makes me wonder about the other folks, and whether their bad luck started when they rented their units. Maybe they were more susceptible to being influenced by whatever's out there."

I looked at Teag. "Speaking of which, thanks to Sorren and my grandmother and Bo, I have several 'charms' to help me focus and control positive energy. What about you? We need to make sure you're going to be safe. Do you have anything beyond Lucinda's gift?"

Teag chuckled, and removed his hoodie. Underneath it was a finely-woven scarf that hung around his neck and went down to just above his waist. I could see the runes woven into the scarf, both in the texture of the fabric as well as in the colored pattern. A long thread hung from one end.

"I've been working on this for a while," he said. He followed my gaze. "That's a 'spirit line' to allow the spirit of the woven piece to leave the piece. I've woven intentions and protective magic into it."

Then he reached into his pocket and held out a handful of different-colored threads. "Weaving lines," he said. "I can store my magic in the knots and patterns, and draw on them as we need them." He gave a self-conscious smile. "Sorren found me a good teacher." He shrugged. "I needed something to do in my spare time."

Lucinda smiled, looking at the workmanship in the scarf. "Very nice," she said. "I can feel its magic. Very strong."

"What magic have you learned that you can use?" Sorren asked with concern.

"Not nearly enough given what we're up against," Teag said. "It's mostly defensive. I can use the knots to anchor my spirit and dispel attacks of illusion, fear, and magic. I can also bind others if I can get them to look at the weaving. Well, I could also tie someone up so they couldn't get loose – but they'd have to sit still. Sorry, I know it's not much."

Lucinda approached Teag and placed her hand on his chest. "Child, don't discount your gift. You're early on your journey but your power and spirit are strong. Can you also anchor Cassidy if needed?"

"Sure, I'd probably need to be able to touch her, but I can do that."

"You must remember that if Cassidy gets caught in a vision. Being able to limit her involvement could save both of you," Sorren said. "We should expect our adversaries to use our weaknesses. Cassidy's talents are much more widely known than yours. Moran will try to use her magic against her." He stood.

"I need to go prepare for our demon hunter. I'll see you all later tonight."

# Chapter Twenty-Three

I'D NEVER MET a demon hunter before. I'd seen movies, so I guess I was thinking of someone who looked like a cross between Van Helsing and Blade. Taras Mirov didn't.

Mirov was about five and a half feet tall and muscular. He didn't look like he worked out at the gym. His kind of build came from a grueling military regimen and hard physical labor. Mirov had sandy blond hair, cut short. His eyes were light blue, cold and unreadable. I put his age at early thirties, give or take a few years. He wore an olive green jacket and fatigues with a black t-shirt and heavy lug-soled boots.

"I'm here to take care of your problem," he said when Sorren met him at the door. Mirov's English was good, but his accent was thick. He carried himself like a soldier. Hard to change old habits. He shrugged out of a battered backpack as he entered. I couldn't see any weapons on him, but I was betting he was armed to the teeth.

It was close to ten o'clock, and we had driven out to Sorren's house in the country, a short way beyond the city limits. It was one of many homes he owned around the world, he had told me, acquired through third parties that kept his name – and therefore questions about his age – out of the public record. The house was newer than antebellum, but not by much. By Charleston standards, it was small as former plantations went. The fields held thoroughbred horses, not crops. A small but very loyal and discreet staff meant Sorren was insulated from the day-to-day management, making it easy for him to stay out of sight.

In the time I'd been working with Sorren, I'd only been to the house once or twice. It was old and grand, decorated simply and tastefully. Comfortable, but with very few personal touches. I wondered if Sorren didn't go in much for knick-knacks, or whether over the centuries, things become a burden and mementos hold too many memories. Or maybe, this was just a safe-house and his real home was elsewhere.

There were some questions you just didn't ask your vampire boss.

Sorren showed Mirov in to the living room, where Teag, Lucinda, and I were already seated. Mirov did not wave or make a move to shake hands. All business.

He did, however, accept a cup of tea. Sorren had made it the Russian way, in the large antique samovar that sat on the dining room table. It was a gesture of respect, and it made me see Mirov as more than just a hired gun.

"Your trip was uneventful?" Sorren asked, taking a seat and gesturing for Mirov to sit down.

Mirov shrugged. "Fortunately, yes. Eventful is usually a bad thing," he said, allowing a faint smile.

Sorren made introductions and recapped what we knew thus far. Teag, Lucinda, and I added our details. Mirov listened intently, not speaking until we had all finished.

"So you're not completely sure yet where the demon's made his nest?" he asked.

Teag unrolled the map of the old Navy yard. "The bodies have either been found near or within the grounds of the Navy yard, or were men who had some kind of connection to that location. And we've got evidence that Moran was using one of the buildings at the abandoned storage facility, so that's our starting point, and probably the demon's lair." He shrugged. "I just don't want to assume anything until we have evidence."

"It also aligns with the coordinates the Alliance supplied of where we've seen a spike in supernatural activity," Sorren supplied.

"And that entire area has had enough death, misfortunate and betrayal to give it monumentally bad mojo," I said.

Mirov chuckled. "Bad mojo? I would say so."

Up close, Mirov reminded me of a stray dog that had been in too many fights. Lean, wary, constantly ready to react, with the scars to show for a life on the rough side. Mirov's hands and arms had a number of old cuts and burns, plus something that looked like a nasty bite. The puckered skin of a severe burn went down his neck and peeked out at the collar of his shirt. His short hair barely covered another old scar, a large one, on his scalp.

"Can we get into this Navy yard for another look?" Mirov asked, studying the map.

"Yes we can, but whether we should or not is another matter," Sorren said. "The police have stepped up patrols because of the number of bodies found."

Mirov looked mildly amused. "I'm not worried about your police."

"It would be inconvenient if you were spotted, or detained," Sorren noted.

Mirov shrugged as if that outcome was unlikely.

"I've been into the area twice with Teag and Cassidy," Sorren said. "Both times, we were attacked and had to fight our way out. The violence escalated between the two attacks. I don't think you'll be able to get in and stroll around without attracting attention, and that will tip Moran and the demon off. We could lose our chance."

"The fact remains, we haven't located the demon's nest with certainty. You think it's in the storage facility or somewhere close. But that's four large buildings – and there's not much room for error unless we can pinpoint his location. It's already risky to go to him in his home territory," Mirov said. "Better for us if we can draw him out into the open." He shook his head. "The area is too big to go in without knowing his location. Too much room for error."

"I'll go," Sorren said. "I'm faster and stronger, and harder to destroy." He gave Mirov a lopsided grin. "You're good, Taras, but you're still mortal."

Mirov gave another shrug. "Fine by me. Get an address, and we can pull down satellite pictures at street level." He smiled. "I love the Internet."

"I'll check the area around the storage unit," Sorren said. "Confirm the layout, check for any recent activity." He must have seen my look of concern, because he shook his head.

"No, I'm not going to try to enter any of the buildings… I don't want to alert them too early," he added. "But if we're going to war, we need to know the lay of the land."

Mirov leaned forward. "When do we strike?"

Sorren frowned. "When we feel we're ready. Soon, but not quite yet." He paused. "Did you bring what I requested?"

Mirov nodded and opened his backpack. He took out several items wrapped in cloth and tied with twine. As I looked closer, I saw that the twine was unusual, made of many-colored strands, and each knot was sealed with wax. I glanced at Teag and he nodded. The bindings were magical.

Teag moved the map aside, and Mirov laid the wrapped pieces on the coffee table.

"Go ahead," he said. "Unwrap them. See if the objects will accept you."

He slid two of the packages toward me and two toward Teag, then watched us, waiting. I glanced at Sorren, who nodded reassuringly.

The first package I picked up was wrapped in a piece of suede. I snapped the wax seal and felt a tingle of magic. The twine fell away, and the suede opened to reveal a ring with a tiger's eye stone.

"The ring affects your inner sight," Sorren said. "It gives you greater control about what you see and when you see it. It can bring you clarity, and allow you to shut down your sight if you don't want to be affected by visions."

Handy, that. I took a deep breath and picked up the ring, expecting to be floored by a vision. It felt warm in my hand, and I felt a glow of well-being and strength. Warily, I slipped it onto my finger. Then I closed my eyes and focused on the ring, willing it to keep me from seeing visions. Before I could second-guess myself, I put my hand down on the second package and felt... nothing.

After an instant of panic, I centered myself and willed for clarity. My senses were flooded with impressions of the second object. I saw faces of the object's former owners, places far away and long ago, and a sense of danger averted. I asked the ring to dial the sensations back to normal, and the visions subsided.

"Off hand, I'd say it likes her," Lucinda said, grinning.

"Now the second one," Mirov said with a glance.

I had already experienced some of the impressions this object had to give me. This item was wrapped in old silk. I felt a frisson of magic as I snapped the wax seal, lifting the jet and gold bracelet out of its antique covering. The jet felt cool in my hands, but it gave me a sense of strength and safety that made me want to clutch it and hold on tightly.

I braced myself, and slipped the jet and golden bracelet onto my wrist. My magic felt purer, stronger than before. I did not receive visions of the bracelet's past wearers, only a feeling of security, like I was wrapped in strong, protective arms.

"Jet protects you from negative energy, and it will call power to your other, defensive magic," Lucinda said. "A very nice complement to your other tools."

"Thank you," I said to Taras for bringing the items, and then to Sorren, who had chosen them. I looked expectantly to Teag. It was like magical Christmas morning, and I wanted to see what was in his presents.

Teag looked self-conscious and a little scared as he reached for the first of his two packages. He touched the seal and drew back suddenly, shaking his hand. "Damn! That felt like it shocked me!"

Sorren nodded. "That means you have an especially strong connection."

Teag regarded Sorren with a wary look, and tried again, snapping open the wax and unwrapping the craft paper and then the canvas on the heavy package. When he folded back the canvas Teag caught his breath. The Espada Y Daga, a sword and knife set used in Eskrima, lay before him in ornate, rune-inscribed scabbards.

"Wow," was all Teag could muster as he reverently reached out to touch the scabbards. "They have power?" Teag asked in confirmation as he lifted the sword and scabbard and carefully slid the blade free.

"Yes, both the sword and dagger were spelled against the supernatural when they were forged," Sorren said. "The scabbards have magical runes. They cleanse the blades and remove any lingering taint. The set belonged to a dear friend, Grandmaster Castillo, who used them in service to the Alliance until his death."

"Tell me he died of old age," Teag said with a wary look.

"Sadly no," Sorren replied. "He was killed by a dark witch. But he died with valor and gave us the victory through his sacrifice. And while the blades aren't tied directly to your Weaver magic, they're powerful and do fit very well with your fighting skills."

Teag reached for the second package, which was wrapped in newsprint. He broke the seal and lifted out a carved wooden circle the size of his palm, with hemp cords of varying length knotted to the ring. At first glance it looked like a Native American dream catcher that had yet to be finished.

"What is it?" I asked.

Teag handled it reverently. "I've seen things like this in books about Weaving magic. You weave the cords to create a spell within the circle," he said. "Kind of like a hand loom for magic. It's a way to create powerful spells quickly." Even from here, I could feel the stored power in its twisted threads.

"Until you're trained in creating your own, this one will serve you." Sorren said.

"Hemp also helps with vision and clearing a path," Lucinda added. "Knot it as you invoke power, and it will store that power to refresh you when you tire. Keep it close at hand, and you'll be able to find your way even in the dark."

"I don't know what to say. Thank you. If it weren't for the whole demon thing, I'd agree with Cassidy that it feels like Christmas," Teag said with a grin.

"Thank you," I said, looking to Sorren.

Sorren nodded. "Lucinda made suggestions, and I asked Taras to bring me the pieces from one of the Alliance libraries."

I was about to ask a question when my cell phone rang. I glanced down and recognized Maggie's number. It was extremely unusual for her to call this late, so I got up and walked a few steps away to answer.

"Cassidy – have you seen what's on the news?" Maggie said, foregoing any greeting. She sounded upset.

"Maggie, what's going on?" I asked.

"Turn on TV! They've found another one of those mangled bodies – and this time, it's right in front of the store!"

I caught my breath. Lucinda's wardings would have kept harm from coming to the store itself, but leaving a body so close was a warning, if not a provocation to fight. "I'll check the news," I said, trying to stay calm. "Thanks for letting me know."

"Do we open up tomorrow?" she asked.

I wondered what kind of messages would be on my answering machine at the house. "I don't know," I admitted. "If we don't hear from the police, I'd say so. If anything changes, I'll let you know." I ended the call and slipped my phone back in my pocket. Only then did I realize that the others were staring at me expectantly.

"There's been another demon murder," I said. "And this time, the body was dumped in front of Trifles and Folly."

Vampires watch TV, as it turns out, and subscribe to cable. Sorren turned on the TV and we all gathered to see the newscast. Police tape crisscrossed the area in front of the store, cordoning off a section of sidewalk between the curb and the door.

I sighed and put a hand over my eyes. I was likely to have an answering machine and email box full of questions, condolences and friends asking 'WTF?'

"Do they know who the victim is?" I asked.

Teag already had his smart phone out and was searching the Web. "Officially, no," he said. "Give me a minute."

"Male, approximately forty years old, Caucasian, the ID they're running is Chris Turner," he reported. He looked up. "Last known address, the men's shelter out by the old Navy yard."

"Let's wait for the crowd to clear," Sorren said quietly. "Then we need to do a little investigating of our own."

Hours later, when the police had finished up for the night and the gawkers and news crews had gone home, downtown Charleston was dark and silent. Teag and Mirov and I drove past the store once in his car to make sure everything was calm. Sorren followed in Lucinda's car. We figured that if anyone reported us,

Teag and I could say that we came by to check on the store and brought Mirov along as a bodyguard. Sorren and Lucinda would just be a couple out for a drive Normally, the area around the shop is considered to be a 'good' neighborhood, and some of the restaurants and bars a few blocks down are open late, so foot traffic after midnight wouldn't seem completely out of the ordinary.

Teag, Mirov, and I pulled around to the back of the store, warily watching the shadows. Sorren and Lucinda parked in the alley behind us. Mirov insisted in getting out first. He had a very modern SIG P225 in one pocket and a nasty-looking broadsword in a scabbard at his hip. All he needed was a long duster coat and he would have looked like he was right out of Hollywood central casting.

Mirov jerked his head in the direction of the store to give us the all-clear. Teag and I were wearing all our protective charms, and I still wished I had a gun like Mirov's. Guns don't work on demons, but they do just fine on the humans under a demon's control.

As soon as I stepped out of Teag's Volvo, I could feel something very wrong. The air itself felt tainted, and the energy of the space was twisted and foul. I closed my hand around the ring, willing clarity, and when I opened my eyes, I could see a very faint glow around Trifles and Folly – Lucinda's warding, still holding strong. I let out a sigh of relief. Awful as it already was, it could have been worse.

Mirov was moving down the alley slowly, making sure our way was clear. We came up the side street, and I was afraid someone would spot his sword and gun, but no one passed by. Sorren and Lucinda were waiting in the shadows in front of the store. I noticed that Sorren was also wearing his sword. I was really hoping we didn't have to explain any of this to the Charleston police.

"What do you make of it?" Sorren asked Lucinda. Lucinda was wearing her very large shoulder bag, which I had learned carried a multitude of Voudon necessities. She walked slowly toward the crime scene tape, careful not to touch anything. Lucinda raised her face to the wind, and lifted her hands, palms up, to the sky. I saw her lick her lips as if tasting the air, and she drew a deep breath. Finally, she approached the front of the store, stopping a few paces back from the façade. She stretched out a hand, and in response, her warding shimmered at her touch. It looked as if streaks of black soot marred the otherwise golden light.

Lucinda began to chant under her breath, and the sooty taint gradually faded, leaving the warding energy clean and strong. Lucinda stepped back, admired her work, and spoke another word of power. The warding became invisible once more.

Next, as Mirov and Teag watched for trouble, Lucinda ducked under the police tape, approaching the dark stain on the sidewalk that remained despite the crime scene technician's best clean-up. Lucinda chanted again, and withdrew a Kretek clove cigarette from her bag. She lit it, and the smell of its distinctive smoke hung on the night air. I knew that smoke purified, and that tobacco smoke was used to open communication to the spirit world, while cloves produced visions. I noticed that Lucinda kept a hand under the Kretek, not wanting to leave the ashes behind. Magic was safest when you left nothing for your enemies to find.

I made a fist with the hand that wore the ring, willing myself not to go into a trance. One of us was enough.

I walked back and forth, looking for found objects, anything that the beings who did this might have dropped. Part of me hoped I would find something that could help us stop Moran and the demon. The other part of me really didn't want a vision from anything that either of them ever touched. To my relief, I didn't find anything, but that wasn't a surprise. The cops had already been over the area, and I doubted our enemies were that sloppy.

Lucinda began to sway back and forth, humming an unfamiliar melody, her eyes shut, face upturned. After a few moments, she took a deep breath, opened her eyes, and murmured her thank-yous to the Loas.

She ducked outside the police tape and turned to Sorren and me. "Like the other murders, he wasn't killed here, just dumped," she said, her voice tight with anger. The smell of cloves clung to her clothing like an aura. "That's why there wasn't as much blood as you'd expect, considering." Considering that the body had been flayed and then torn apart, bones broken and joints shattered, before the killing blow was administered.

"Did it leave a revenant?" Sorren asked.

Lucinda shook her head. "Not anymore. I freed the spirit and its energy. And in a moment, I'll get rid of the nasty psychic sludge the killers left behind."

Although the whole thing had taken less than ten minutes, I was getting antsy. I could see that Mirov was fidgeting, looking decidedly uncomfortable.

"We need to get out of here," he murmured. His accent seemed thicker, and I wondered if that happened under stress.

"Not long," Lucinda said, with a glance toward Sorren. "I think you want this space cleared."

Sorren nodded. "Just be quick."

Lucinda reached into her large bag and withdrew a bottle of rum, a piece of chalk, a horseshoe and a handful of iron nails. She used the chalk to mark a *veve* on the horseshoe and laid it front of the stained pavement. Then she walked in a circle outside the police tape, sprinkling the ground with rum and dropping iron nails as she hummed and sang. When she had finished the circle, she retrieved the horseshoe and the nails and handed them to me, along with the rum.

"Put the horseshoe near the front door and the nails near the back door," Lucinda instructed. "Sprinkle a little of the rum on the sidewalk outside the warding at both doors."

She turned to Sorren. "We're through here." The five of us walked around the block to the alley.

"What about security cameras?" I asked nervously, torn between glancing up to see which cameras might have captured our image and not wanting those cameras to have a full-face shot of me.

"Not a worry," Lucinda said. "Your demon hunter friend zapped them with something that fried their circuits."

I was glad he hadn't zapped the security lights in the alley behind the shop. They weren't bright on the best of nights, and tonight my nerves were jangled enough, I would have preferred the kind of lights they use for nighttime football games.

I was very aware of the shadows as we walked toward the cars. The alley smelled of old garbage and mold, urine and dirt. Just then, every security light in sight suddenly went dark.

I heard the scuttle of claws against pavement, and a

low, guttural growl. The *akvenon* ran like hunchbacked, reptilian Mastiffs, as big as a large man but with teeth like a crocodile and skin like a snake. Horrible, curled claws protruded from their feet, and powerful hind legs propelled them with nightmare speed.

"Incoming!" Mirov shouted.

I looked up to see three *akvenon* minions, heading straight for us, in between us and our cars. The scuttling noise grew louder, and three more of the minions closed on us from behind.

Mirov stepped up to meet the three demon spawn hurtling down the alley toward us, while Sorren moved to get between us and the others approaching from behind. Lucinda stood with Mirov, while Teag and I took our positions a pace behind Sorren, ready to do what we could.

"I liked fighting them better when I could hit them with my car," I muttered. Tendrils of mist curled around my ankles, coalescing into Bo's ghost dog form. Bo lowered his head and stalked forward, growling. I wasn't sure he could do anything to the *akvenon*, but I didn't figure it would hurt to have all the help we could get.

"One for each of us," Teag replied. "That's better odds than we had last time."

"Get ready," Sorren said grimly. "Cassidy – draw on the memories from the new artifacts and see if you can call the kind of power you summoned at the Archive."

There was no time to point out that I had absolutely no idea of how to do that. Instead, I planted my feet firmly, stretched out my right hand with the spoon-athame up my sleeve, and opened myself to the memories of the spoon and the spindle whorl, the ring, and the bracelet. Alard's walking stick hung from my belt loop, just in case. Lives and centuries spun around me, gathering in a cloud of power, and with a shout, energy coalesced in my body, coming to a focus in my outstretched palm, and blasting toward the *akvenon* with a torrent of power that stung my hand.

These new artifacts enabled me to call an energy stream that wasn't flame but packed a wallop when it hit the target, unlike Alard's wand which spewed real fire, and my grandma's spoon that projected a force-field.

The stream of energy caught the *akvenon* at the front of the pack full in the chest like an explosive charge, blowing a hole through his ribs. The *akvenon* gave a death shriek as its form began to unravel, decomposing into shadow before it vanished entirely.

The energy stopped abruptly, and I felt as if I had just run a marathon. *Why don't magic objects ever come with instructions?* I thought. *It would have been nice to know I only get one shot before I have to 'reload'.* Grimly, I grabbed Alard's walking stick, since it looked as if the spoon-athame and the souped-up power it got from the jet bracelet needed time to recharge.

Sorren went for the second *akvenon* with his sword, his speed and vampire strength easily a match for the creature. Bo's ghost harried the third minion. Teag bent down to pick up a rock the size of his fist from the gutter and let fly. The rock struck the third minion right between its slitted reptilian eyes. He lobbed off two more shots, smacking the *akvenon* in the head both times. Every time it tried to advance on Sorren, Teag forced it back again. At this rate, he should pitch for the Yankees.

The rocks had kept the minions at a distance, but that wasn't going to last forever. Sorren already had his sword in hand, and Teag drew his new short sword and dagger. Warily, they advanced on one of the *akvenon*, while I took aim at the other.

Sorren went left. Teag went right, and I sent my shot down the middle. Sorren had immortal strength and speed, making him a match for the creature. Teag wasn't immortal, but he was damn good. Years of martial arts made him quick on his feet, able to make lightning-quick strikes and get back before the monster's claws could strike. He had blades in both hands, but the minion underestimated what Teag could do with his feet. Eskrima had taught him blade work; Capoeira taught foot fighting and acrobatics. Put them together, and he was lethal as he swept the minion off its legs, then followed with a kick that could break bones. By the time the minion came back for more, Teag was ready with his blades. I wished I could watch, but I had my own *akvenon* to fight.

I leveled the walking stick at the *akvenon* and used the ring to focus my thoughts, managing to blast a torrent of fire that blackened the monster's tough skin. The creature recoiled, then charged me again. I concentrated harder, hoping to get fire that was hotter, longer in duration. I heard a popping, sizzling sound and an ungodly shriek, and the *akvenon* exploded into charred bits that disintegrated and vanished.

Mirov's Sig popped once, then twice, its suppressor muting the sound of the shots. The rounds slowed the *akvenon* rushing him, but didn't stop it. Mirov was cursing under his breath in Russian as he jammed the gun in his belt and took up his sword two-handed and went after the monster.

Lucinda had a short wooden staff in one hand,

something else she had pulled from her huge tote. It was festooned with crow feathers and charms bearing the *veves* of the Loas. She called out a word of power and leveled the short staff at the *akvenon* like she did this kind of thing every day. A wave of power blasted the creature back, slamming it into one of the other *akvenon*. That slowed them down, but didn't stop them.

Mirov pivoted out of the way of the *akvenon*'s sharp claws and brought his sword down hard on the monster's neck, severing its head. With a cry, he ran at the next minion. He slashed low, severing one of the thing's legs, then brought the blade point down, through its chest. It was already disintegrating into shadow when the third minion sprang forward, slashing at him with its claws.

Mirov blocked the creature with his sword as his left hand grabbed for something under his jacket. Silver glinted in the moonlight as he flung a knife-edged throwing star at the beast. The star blade caught the *akvenon* in the neck, spraying the alley with its ichor. Mirov wheeled, bringing his sword down with his full strength, impaling it from one side through the other. The creature jerked and spasmed, flailing with its deadly claws, and Mirov twisted the blade. With a screech, the *akvenon* bucked against the blade and then dissipated into darkness.

The air smelled of ozone like after a lightning storm, and my palm was red and blistered. Mirov was breathing hard, splattered with the beast's black blood. Lucinda kept her short staff aloft, watching the shadows for another attack. Sorren and Teag had finished off their opponent and walked back to rejoin the group. Their clothing was streaked with ichor, and Teag was sweating, but they looked unharmed.

"Let's get out of here," Sorren said. "There's no good way to explain this to the police, and we can't stop a demon from inside the Charleston jail."

# Chapter Twenty-Four

EVEN THOUGH IT was Wednesday, we were too busy in the store for Teag and me to talk about anything but business all day. I hadn't even had time to check the package Sorren had left on my desk. When the time came to close up, I sagged against the wall and closed my eyes, letting out a long breath. "Be careful what you wish for," I said. "That was the busiest we've been all week."

"At least we can pay the bills," Teag noted, looking on the bright side.

I had been so busy, I hadn't had a chance to check the voice mail on my cell phone. I recognized the number and put it on speakerphone.

"Hi Cassidy," Mrs. Morrissey's voice chirped from my voice mail. "I did a little more digging on the Navy yard. Turns out that, during the Quake of 1886, there was an old warehouse in that area that was used as a temporary morgue for the victims of the earthquake. It gets worse," she added. "Back in 1858, there was a Yellow Fever epidemic. It hit Charleston so badly, some churches lost half their membership within a week. Guess where they brought the bodies to try to contain the contagion?" She paused. "Most of those buildings were on land that sooner or later ended up belonging to Jeremiah Abernathy.

"I hope you don't mind the long message, but I thought you might want to know. Stop by any time. I always enjoyed helping Evan, and I'm glad to help you, too."

I put the cell phone back in my pocket, deep in thought. *How much had Evan taken Mrs. Morrissey into his confidence?* I wondered. *Did she have an inkling about what we really did at Trifles and Folly?*

Teag had overheard the message. "More evidence that we're looking in the right place," he said. I slipped my phone into my pocket.

"Did you get a chance to hack any more of the Stor-Your-Own files?" I asked. I was dying to know who Clockman was and how he fit into the picture.

Teag nodded. "After we got back from seeing Flora and dropping you off, Anthony and I had a bit of a row."

I looked at him, worried. "Bad?

He shrugged. "Not fun. He's resigned himself to ghosts, but Flora's talk about demons, and the possible connection between what we're dealing with and the murders, has him really freaked out. He's worried about both of us."

"What did you tell him?"

Teag looked uncomfortable. "I told him that the shop worked with a secret European organization that looks into supernatural threats, kind of like NSA for ghost hunters. CSI: Undead. Torchwood. He can figure it out." He sighed. "And then I told him it was all part of a new Homeland Security partnership and I couldn't say more."

I didn't know whether to hug Teag or burst out laughing. "Wow," I said. "Just… wow. You're good. That's the most inaccurate truth-telling I've ever heard." Teag looked a little sheepish, and I grinned. "Hey, you were brilliant. And honestly, aren't you glad he doesn't want you to get eaten by a demon?"

"It's kind of sweet, yes," Teag replied drolly.

I happened to glance out the window, and I saw a figure in the shadows across the street. Teag seemed to sense the shift in my mood, because he sobered immediately. "There's someone out there," I said.

"Moran?"

I shook my head. "Not tall and skinny enough. I'll go to the front door. You go around the back and see if you can catch whoever-it-is by surprise."

He nodded. "I'm on it."

I moved to the door, keeping out of sight of the big glass windows in the front of the store. Then I counted to one hundred to allow Teag to get into position before I threw open the door.

Our stalker was gone.

"No one there," Teag said, shrugging. Neither of us wanted to go beyond Lucinda's wardings.

"Maybe we're jumping at shadows. Ready to see what Sorren left us?" I asked. We had come into the office that morning and found a small package on my desk with a note from Sorren. The note said that it was something he had found scouting 'the location' and I should look at it when Teag could help. I took that to mean that Sorren thought it would pack a psychic wallop and so I should have Teag around to anchor me.

"Absolutely," Teag replied. "I thought we'd have a chance to look at the package much sooner. I never expected to be so busy today." Teag walked with me to the office after making sure the door was locked and 'Closed' sign was turned.

Sorren had left me a paper bag, folded and tied with a string.

"Do you want me to open it, just in case?" Teag asked.

"Sure, but I'm not getting any vibes," I answered. Teag wasn't as sensitive to objects as I was, but if it was really bad, he'd know.

"Sorren's sense of humor?" Teag asked as he removed a worn, muddy baseball cap from the bag.

"He said he was going to see if he could verify the location of the activity for Mirov. It could be nothing and it could be bad, real bad," I said.

"But if you read it... I could practice my grounding on you. And if it's real bad, I can pull you back quickly. Lucinda and Sorren thought that ability would come in handy."

I stared at the hat in his hand for a moment. There were about a million ways this could go wrong, or at least become highly unpleasant, but if we could figure out how to bring down Moran and his crew, a little discomfort was worth it.

"Give it here," I said with a sigh.

"Better sit down, just in case," he warned. "Let me prepare my cords and I'll put my hand on your shoulder."

He didn't have to convince me. We closed the office door. Teag made a hot cup of tea with plenty of sugar and had it ready to revive me if the vision was too intense. I sat down and took a few deep breaths. Then I held out my hand for the hat.

Teag placed the hat in my hand and I felt the reassurance of his hand on my shoulder. The hat was unremarkable, a cheap gimme cap, with the logo of a hardware chain on the front. It was filthy, torn and probably one of thousands produced at some factory in China. But when the fabric of the hat touched my skin, I felt that tingle.

The person who dropped this hat hadn't been evil. But he had been terrified. I wrapped my hand around the cap and let my eyelids flutter closed, focusing on the vision. The store faded around me, and my inner sight took over.

I WAS IN *a dark corridor. Scared. Mildew and dust and a faint odor of moth balls hung heavy in the air. My flashlight cast a glowing circle that jittered from my shaking hand. I was inside one of the storage facility buildings, clutching a box in one hand, as I tried to hold both it and the flashlight. I fumbled to put a lock back on one of the storage unit doors.*

*Something was coming. I felt it. I heard something shuffling along the tiled floor, maybe something being dragged. It was the kind of sound that gave any sane person the urge to run, and that's what I was trying to do, just as soon as I got that damned lock back on the door. Damn! I should have brought my gear... didn't think it was quite this bad.*

*The sound was closer. I looked up, staring into blackness. I set the lock and pocketed the keys and eyed the distance between where I was and the doorway.*

*I tucked the box under one arm like a football player and led with the flashlight, like a frightened quarterback. My running footsteps echoed, but the shuffling noise was still behind me, and getting closer. I pushed my way outside through a broken door and out into the night air, and I picked up speed. I wanted to look behind me, but I'd seen too many horror movies or maybe I'd looked back on a previous trip, because I kept my eyes focused on the hole in the fence, and the safety of the high grass on the other side. I'm getting sloppy. I should have been prepared.*

*The air ahead was muggy and warm. But behind me, there was an arctic blast that raised my hackles. Whatever was chasing me hadn't stopped at the door to the storage building like it always had before. I'd figured on the chase, called it a calculated risk. Out here, I thought I was safe, although I knew that nowhere inside the fence was really safe. Considering how dangerous the rest of the Navy yard was, I guess it was all relative.*

*I was almost to the fence when I felt something tugging at my shirt. Terror gave me the adrenaline for a last burst of speed, and I tore free. I was scrambling under the fence, desperate to get through when the metal caught my hat and cut my scalp.*

The vision disappeared.

I came back to myself a little quicker than the last time and calmer. I was leaning back, breathing hard as if I had been the one doing the running. My heart pounded in my ears, and I felt a sheen of sweat on my forehead and arms. Teag was standing next to me, his hand still resting on my shoulder as he daubed my face with a cool washcloth.

"I'm back," I said. I took the cloth and pressed it against my temples. After a moment, I took the hot cup of very sweet tea into my hand, and took a few sips, willing the sugar to revive me. "That helped," I said.

"I've never been this clear after a reading. We may have hit on something. It was very similar to when I used the ring."

"Glad to be of service," he joked in his most serious 'butler' voice.

"Were any of the people you called from the storage facility men?"

Teag nodded. "Three of them, but only one phone number still worked. I got an older guy who told me to stop harassing him and hung up. Never even got a chance to say hello."

"That could be the man I saw in the vision." I recounted what I had seen, while Teag listened with concern.

"You don't know how old that vision is," Teag said. "But it could mean one tenant is brave – or desperate – enough to go in there after whatever he left behind."

"It wasn't the first time he'd gone inside," I said, sorting through the images. "He had a plan and a route, but something surprised him. I don't think whatever's in there ever went beyond the building after him before."

"That means it's getting stronger," Teag replied. He made a cup of tea for himself and came back with a package of cookies from the Honeysuckle Café. "It also makes the storage facility different from the other sites we've been to."

"We figured that," I said, nibbling on a cookie. "The murders are feeding the demon, helping it gather strength. Let's call the man from Stor-Your-Own again and see if we can go over to visit him. If he knows his way around, maybe he'd be willing to guide us in – especially if it means he might be able to get to his things more safely in the future."

"What could he want badly enough to take the risk he's been taking?" Teag asked. "Something he thinks he can't live without."

Teag dialed the man's number again, and this time, someone answered.

"I don't want to answer a survey and I don't want to donate money," a gravelly voice said.

"Mr. Pettis! Wait! I need to talk to you about Stor-Your-Own," Teag said. The line was silent. After a moment, we heard rustling, so we knew he hadn't hung up on us.

"What about it?"

"We're trying to help tenants who couldn't remove their items before the facility closed be able to get them out safely."

"Yeah? What's it gonna cost me?" Obviously, Mr. Pettis was nobody's fool. On the other hand, he was desperate enough to go into a dangerously haunted abandoned building to get something he needed.

"We're not asking you to pay anything," Teag said in his most soothing, affable voice. "After all, those items belong to you. We'd like to see you get them back."

"You're kinda late, aren't you? Place closed down six months ago."

In the vision, I hadn't seen Mr. Pettis's face because I was experiencing the scene through his eyes. But his voice reminded me of the man in the neighborhood where I had grown up, the one who was always yelling at the kids to stay off his grass and who never gave out Halloween candy. The kids called him a grump and a troll. It wasn't until I was in high school that I found out the guy worked nights and then spent all day taking care of a bedridden wife. Maybe Mr. Pettis had a similar story.

"We'd like to get a statement from you about your claim to what's in the storage unit, and our rules say we have to take the statement in person," Teag said. "May we stop by your house?"

"How do I know you're not going to rob me?" Obviously Mr. Pettis seemed to believe that a strong offense was a good defense.

"I can validate the information from your storage unit application," Teag said, grabbing the folder. He read back details like payment dates, check numbers, and Mr. Pettis's address. "Flora seemed to think you were pretty special," he added, and I raised an eyebrow. Teag's magic deals with data, but he's got strong intuition and sometimes he'll pull something out of thin air that amazes me.

"Oh she did, did she?" Pettis said, but this time, he chuckled. "Well, I thought Flora was pretty special too. She had time to talk to me. Not many people do." He was quiet again, and Teag let him think.

"Come on by in the next hour and we can talk. Don't be late – I don't stay up past nine and it would be best if you're gone by dark."

Teag grinned. "Thank you, Mr. Pettis. We'll be brief – and we'll see you in about thirty minutes." He ended the call and looked at me with a triumphant grin. "We're in! Let's go talk to Pettis, and then get something to eat. When I go home, I'll get on the computer and see what I can find about him. There are databases out there that bail bondsmen and collection agencies use to skip trace. I'll do some more digging."

Teag wrote down the address from his notes. We locked up, and headed over to find Mr. Pettis.

The Pettis house was in a modest section of Charleston,

far from the mansions South of Broad or on the Battery. The neighborhood might have been new in the 1940s or 1950s, but it looked hard worn.

"His name is Chuck," Teag said as we pulled up. "Chuck Pettis. Age fifty-five. High school diploma, went into the military, saw action in the Middle East. Married once, widowed about five years ago. Two children, but they live out West."

The house had a bare-basics look to it. We headed for the front door. I pretended not to notice that Chuck was watching from behind the curtains.

Teag knocked at the door. It opened just far enough for Chuck to look out through the gap of the safety chain. "We're the ones who called about Stor-Your-Own," Teag said. He'd combed back his skater boy hair for the appointment and donned a jacket. Chuck looked him over and gave me a critical glance before he grunted and closed the door.

Teag and I exchanged a confused glance, then I heard the chain sliding in the lock and the door opened.

"Don't just stand there," Chuck rasped. He stood to the side so we could enter.

I have never seen so many clocks in my life.

Chuck Pettis was obsessed by time. Clocks of every description covered the walls: old wooden school clocks, grandfather clocks, factory time clocks, antique pendulum clocks. Clocks filled the bookshelves, covered the mantel above the fireplace, and sat on the table. Antique Baby Ben alarm clocks in silver and brass, big, little and miniature were tucked in every corner, on windowsills and atop the TV. In the living room alone I counted at least half a dozen cuckoo clocks.

All of them were running. None of them were set to the same time.

The ticking was louder than my heartbeat. The house seemed to vibrate with the swing of each pendulum. And suddenly, I knew what Chuck had been carrying in my vision. Clocks.

Chuck's graying hair was cut short around a bald pate. He had a hawk-like nose, and his thin lips were set in either a grimace of pain or an expression of perpetual disdain. He was too thin, and his faded shirt seemed to hang on him. There was intelligence in his green eyes, but it was canny, shrewd, more the look of elusive prey than the glint of a predator.

Chuck was afraid of something. Really afraid.

"You've got a lovely collection of timepieces," I said. It was true. The clocks spanned more than a century, from 1800s industrial models to the 1950s. Chuck had the best collection I had seen outside of a museum. None of the clocks were electric. And there were more in the other rooms.

"I like clocks," Chuck said, but his gaze slid to the side, and I knew he was either lying or not telling the whole truth.

"Thank you for letting us come over," Teag said.

Chuck motioned stiffly for us to have a seat on the slip covered, swaybacked couch. "What do you want to know?" Chuck was back to being his gruff self. He plopped down in an old recliner like a king on a throne.

"What can you tell us about Stor-Your-Own, Mr. Pettis?" Teag asked.

Chuck eyed us suspiciously. "You two lawyers?"

I shook my head. "No. But we are investigators, trying to get the items back to their rightful owners." Another half-truth. We *were* investigating. And we wanted to get any dangerous supernatural items back where they belonged. But as I looked around, I wondered why on earth Chuck would risk the supernatural dangers of the abandoned storage facility – not to mention arrest for trespassing – over more clocks.

"I never got a notice in the mail," Chuck said suddenly. "About that Stor-Your-Own closing down. That's not right. I paid them good money for my rent there. Never caused any problems. Paid on time, too."

"Did they call you?"

Chuck motioned toward the kitchen, where I saw an old-style black phone on the wall. Anywhere else, I would have thought it was ironically retro. Here, I bet it came with the house. "I don't just jump up and answer every time the danged thing rings, you know. Damn telemarketers. Call all the time during dinner or when I'm watching one of my shows. Then I get out there, and they hang up."

"Did they leave a message?" I asked.

Chuck fixed me with a look as if I were daft. "Got no patience for one of them answering machines. Someone wants to talk with me badly enough, they'll track me down, eventually."

I had the feeling that not many people tried.

Using my left hand, the one with Bo's collar wrapped around my wrist, I let myself touch the worn upholstery on the couch.

*The images that came to me were like old Polaroid photos, the colors faded by time. I glimpsed two children, both younger than ten years old, playfully chasing each other with cardboard-tube swords. A dark-haired woman looked on, with a smile of maternal patience. It was the same room and the same furnishings, but with one important difference: there were no clocks.*

Bo's collar seemed to insulate me from the visions, making me more of an observer than someone present in the scene. I shifted my hand, and this glimpse had fast-forwarded in time.

*The house was quiet. The dark-haired woman I had seen before was several decades older, and she looked careworn and sad. Even so, there was a sense of frayed security about the scene, a feeling of comfortable habit, of constancy and familiarity. Still no clocks.*

I leaned back, but the cushions, flatted by long use, gave more under my weight. This was one of Chuck's favorite places to sit. The vision I saw was more recent.

*Regret and loss weighed on me. Sadness – and fear, of the empty hours, of the long nights, and of what bleak future lay in store.*

And in this vision, I saw the clocks.

"– so I go there and find the gate locked," I heard Chuck conclude. If Teag had noticed that I spaced out, he didn't show it, and Chuck seemed so intent on convincing Teag of his position that he wasn't paying any attention to me.

"I can certainly understand why that would have been upsetting," Teag replied.

"Is your unit filled with more clocks?" I asked.

Chuck seemed to suddenly remember that I was there, and his eyes narrowed. "Not sure it's anybody's business what's in there," he snapped.

I gave my best disarming smile. "I'm not trying to pry. It might help us with the insurance people if we could show that whatever you have in storage isn't harmful in any way."

Chuck frowned. "Harmful? No. Not of much interest to anybody except me, I suppose. And you're right, little lady. I've got clocks. Lots of them."

"You have a beautiful collection," I said, and Chuck seemed to soften a bit at the praise. I was about to say something else, but one of the cuckoo clocks began to strike the hour, fifteen minutes early.

"Mr. Pettis –" I began, only to be silenced by the shrill ring of a large Baby Ben alarm clock. I jumped at the sudden racket. Before I could gather my wits, one clock after another went off, each striking a different hour. To my astonishment, Chuck Pettis jumped to his feet with a wild expression on his face. He ran to each clock in the order they had struck the hour, and wound them with an urgency as if his life depended on it. For the pendulum clocks, he withdrew a huge ring of winding keys from a clip on his belt and selected just the right one for each to keep them going.

Teag and I exchanged baffled expressions, assaulted by the cacophony of bells and chimes. Suddenly, the house was silent once more. As if nothing unusual had happened, Chuck returned to his worn recliner and settled into his seat.

"You were saying?" he asked.

There were so many questions I wanted to ask, but I didn't want this wary man to shut down and kick us out. "That's quite a performance your clocks put on," I said.

The ghost of a smile touched the corner of Chuck's thin lips. "Isn't it? Like a choir, each one with its own voice." There was a wistfulness in his voice I hadn't expected, as if the clocks had become stand-ins for the companions who had deserted him.

I had the sense there was more to the clocks than just a love of punctuality, more than a collector's fondness for precision mechanisms. "You have so many beautiful clocks, and you say that what is stored at Stor-Your-Own isn't particularly valuable. So why do you risk going in to get more? It's in a pretty rough neighborhood."

Fear glinted in Chuck's eyes. "Who told you that I'd been in there?"

I leaned forward, hoping my sincerity came through loud and clear. "We have an eyewitness who saw you come through the fence. The last time, you lost your hat, isn't that right?"

"What are you going to do, turn me in to the police?" Chuck demanded, and I could see that his fear was fueling his sudden anger.

I shook my head. "No. You're only taking what belongs to you. But we do need your help."

"Oh yeah?" Chuck asked skeptically. "I knew it. You're planning to rob the place." He reached between the arm of the recliner and the seat cushion, and I was pretty sure he had a gun down there.

"No! Nothing like that. We're trying to stop whatever it is that's causing all the problems," I said, speaking in a rush to keep him from drawing a weapon on us. "We know about the shadows, and we also know that they weren't always there. We want to make them go away so that you and the other tenants can go in safely to get your things. So that people stop dying."

"Why should I believe you?"

I felt a nudge of intuition and ran with it. "Because we were friends of Jimmy Redshoes."

That seemed to take the wind out of Chuck. He withdrew his hand from the seat cushion and sat back.

His bravado was gone, and he looked suddenly older. "Ah, that was too bad, what happened to him. I was sorry to hear about it."

"The police think it was a drug deal gone bad," Teag said.

Chuck's eyes flashed. "That's not true!" He let out a long breath. "I knew Jimmy long ago, before he got into a peck of trouble and kinda lost himself," he said quietly. "He was a good kid, never hurt anyone. Life just messed him up and he couldn't get straightened out. Jimmy didn't rent a unit at Stor-Your-Own. Didn't have the money to pay for that. But it wasn't the best managed place, even before it closed. Flora did what she could, but she couldn't keep an eye on everything. Jimmy would sneak in and stash his things in one of the units no one was renting."

Chuck sighed. "Towards the end, there were a lot of empty units and nobody was keeping track. Jimmy didn't have anywhere safe to put his things, like winter clothes when it was summer." He raised his face and met my gaze as if challenging me to argue. "More than once, I kept Flora distracted so Jimmy could get in or out without anyone noticing."

"Hell's bells, I paid a king's ransom for my unit – overpriced garage, that's what it was. I figured Jimmy wasn't hurting anything. When things started to go bad, I tried to warn Jimmy. Told him I'd go in with him to help him move his things so he didn't have to go there anymore. I even told him he could keep some things in my shed out back."

Chuck shook his head. "Me, I can take care of myself. I saw combat. I know how to protect myself. But Jimmy... Some men come back from soldiering stronger. Some can't live with themselves. Others get mean. And guys like Jimmy, it's like there's something inside that breaks and won't get fixed."

I hadn't expected a soliloquy like that from Chuck, and it made me re-think my first impression. He was certainly a crusty guy, but something in him had loved the children and the dark-haired women I had glimpsed, even if he wasn't one to wear his heart on his sleeve. And it was obvious that something had touched him deeply about Jimmy Redshoes, a fellow soldier who never completely came home from war.

"I have a feeling that you know what really killed Jimmy Redshoes," I said quietly. "And I promise you, we'll believe you if you'll tell us what you've seen."

Chuck looked torn, then he swore under his breath and crossed his arms across his chest like he was daring us to break our word. "Ghosts," he said. "Haints. Spirits. Doesn't matter what you called them. Something bad came in when that tall guy with the shriveled face showed up."

*Moran.* "What do you mean?" I asked.

"I don't know his name. Everything was just fine until he showed up and then it all went to hell in a handbasket. He brought the evil with him."

Chuck was angry. He stared at us as if he expected us to call the county mental health authority, and when we both nodded, he looked surprised.

"What building did the guy with the shriveled face use?" I asked.

"Building Four," he spat. "Polluted the whole place. Mark my words – Jimmy Redshoes would still be alive if it weren't for him."

"If you have a storage shed, why did you keep your clocks at Stor-Your-Own?"

Chuck uncrossed his arms and leaned back in his chair. "Because the shed's full. So's my garage. But the clocks out there don't work anymore."

"I'm not sure I understand," I said. "Why do you need so many clocks? What's so important that you would go into such a dangerous place to get more?"

Chuck let out a long sigh. "I have to keep them running. If they stop, I'll die."

I must have looked baffled, because he went on. "The night I took my wife, Emma, to the emergency room, the night she died, there was an old woman sitting out in the hallway. She didn't seem to be waiting for anyone, just sitting and knitting, and staring. She told me that time was running out, and that I was going to pay for my sins when the clocks wound down."

"What sins?" Teag asked gently.

Chuck looked up, and glanced toward a black and white photo on the wall. It was a picture of a much younger man wearing an army uniform from the 1990s, and I recognized Chuck.

"I did things, in the war, that I'm not proud of," he said. "Special Forces. Black Ops. Doesn't matter that I was under orders. I shouldn't have done them. Emma didn't hold them against me, but I'm sure God will. I won't rest easy when I'm dead, and I won't see Emma again, I'm sure. So I don't want to go any sooner than I have to."

"That's why you have to keep getting more clocks," I said, meeting his gaze

He nodded soberly. "Wind-ups are dependable, but I can't let them run down. Nothing runs as well as those old-fashioned Big Bens, but they're hard to find, which is why I stockpiled them in my storage unit. The new ones break too quickly. And I don't dare use electric clocks – what if the power goes out? But even the old clocks wear out after a while. Then I've got to get more."

"After the last time, I don't want to go back," Chuck blurted. Then he pointed to the table in the kitchen, where several clocks lay in various states of disassembly. "But I'm going to have to go soon. I lost a couple more clocks. Over the years, I got pretty handy fixing little stuff, but nothing lasts forever. I can't fix those."

"If we agreed to help you get your clocks out, would you show us the best way in and out, where you saw the shriveled face man, anything else noteworthy? I have a map," Teag asked. "We think we know how to get rid of the shadow men and the ghosts – and we can help you move your clocks somewhere safe."

Chuck looked wary, but I could see the struggle in his eyes. He wasn't sure he could trust us, but we were holding out the two things he wanted the most. Finally, he nodded. "It would be better if I took you. The best paths change depending on the haints. You need me."

Teag and I glanced at each other. "We're not sure it would be safe for you and don't want to put you in danger. We've also got a couple more people who're part of this," I said. "We need to work around their schedules too – we'll need to check with them before we can give you an answer."

Chuck raised an eyebrow. "I can take care of myself. You got muscle? That suits me."

I chuckled, thinking how Sorren might feel about being described as 'muscle', but decided it wasn't an altogether off-base description, and certainly fit Mirov. "Something like that," I said. "And we'd have to go at night."

I could see that Chuck didn't like that, and I didn't blame him. But Sorren was a vampire, and broad daylight just wasn't a possibility. To my surprise, Chuck gave a curt nod. "Night's best for staying out of the way of the cops over at the Navy yard. They might not admit to believing in ghosts, but they don't like it over there after dark, either."

"I'll call you as soon as I have an answer," I said.

"Where can I store my clocks?" Chuck asked. "I don't have a lot of money."

"Let me look into a couple of options," Teag said. "I'll see what I can find."

"I'll be ready," Chuck promised. "It'll be nice having some back-up for once."

He walked us to the car, and I was surprised when he grabbed my arm. "I told you I was Special Forces," Chuck said. "The Black Ops unit I was part of, they weren't your usual crew. We de-fanged things that were alien or dark magic." He met my gaze. "I hope you know what you're doing, because that's what we're up against, at that godforsaken place."

I nodded. "Yes it is. And we mean to put things right."

We left Chuck with assurances that we would be back in touch, and he watched from his window as we drove away.

"What's Anthony doing tonight?" I asked.

Teag sighed. "Preparing for his big presentation tomorrow. I hope it goes well. But either way, I'll be glad when this trial is over and he can come up for air. We haven't gotten to spend much down time together lately."

Anthony's loss was my gain. While I was crazy about Anthony and thought he and Teag were amazing together, having Teag at a loose end because Anthony was working late had certainly made our skullduggery easier to manage.

"Let me know when Anthony finally has some free time, and I'll juggle the schedule around so the two of you can take a long weekend," I said. It was only fair, given the amount of off-the-clock time Teag put into Trifles and Folly's 'other' business. Sorren made sure Teag and I were paid well for the risks we took, and we both appreciated it, but money only went so far when it came to erasing the stress of being chased by ghosts and menaced by monsters. On the other hand, a few days on a sunny beach was the cure for a multitude of ills.

# Chapter Twenty-Five

WHEN I GOT home, I found yet another bundle tied in brown paper lying in the middle of my kitchen table. I recognized Sorren's handwriting on the note: *this should help put the pieces together for you.*

"Another one?" Teag asked. With Anthony working late and me not having a social life at the moment, we had picked up takeout again, along with the papers and journal Alistair had given us at the museum.

I sighed. "Want to bet what's inside provides a wallop of a vision?"

I held my hand just above the package, sensing its supernatural strength. Dark, but maybe not an all-out spooky. If luck was with me.

Teag held up Russ Landrieu's journal and papers. "You know you're going to need to take a look at these, too, once I've read through them."

I nodded, resigned to the fact that it was going to be one of those kinds of nights. "Let's eat first, please? I deal better with the visions when I'm not hungry, and besides, the food's getting cold."

I eyed the package the whole time we ate. Even from

a distance, I could tell that whatever was in the box had been party to a tragedy.

When we had finished our meals, I couldn't put it off any longer. I took a deep breath, and then slid the package over in front of me. Teag watched, alert to help out if my vision caused trouble.

"Do you want me to anchor you again?" he asked.

"No, let's try it without you or the ring and see how it goes." I raised an eyebrow. "If I have trouble, feel free to jump in."

The wrapping paper gave me an insight into Sorren's mood. Handling the brown paper and the twine, I sensed his worry. He was concerned for Teag and my safety, and justifiably uncertain about how we were going to stop Moran and his demon. While I would have liked to have read total confidence, just to shore up my own nerves, I knew Sorren's worrying was a good thing. It would make for caution, and with luck, we could handle our demon problem without more deaths. *With luck*. That was the tricky part.

I pulled the twine loops apart and peeled back the paper. Inside was a broken piece of weathered wood and several yellowed pages from a ledger. I frowned, exchanging a glance with Teag, who shrugged.

I laid my hand on the broken wood. Immediately the comfortable surroundings of my kitchen disappeared, and I found myself onboard a wooden sailing ship in the midst of a terrifying storm at sea.

*The deck was drenched, and waves pounded the clipper as winds tore at its sails. Rough seas made the ship rise sharply and then fall out from under the feet of the men who scrambled to keep her under control against all the forces of nature.*

"Captain Harrison!" one of the sailors shouted. "We're taking on water."

Captain Harrison turned from throwing a pouch into the water. He knew he wasn't going to come home from this one. The captain was a man in his late fifties, and I recognized his face from family pictures I had seen at Gardenia Landing. The man who built Gardenia Landing, the sea captain whose fortunes waned when he did business with Jeremiah Abernathy.

"Put all the men we can spare on the bilges," Harrison ordered. "Get the rest in place to man the sails. With luck, we'll make it through this."

Harrison eyed the sky, and I followed his gaze. Their ship, the Lady Jane, was fighting for her life, and her captain knew it. But as I followed his worried gaze skyward, what I saw troubled me far worse than even the violence of nature.

The horizon had a greenish glow, like foxfire. Lightning streaked down from black clouds, striking the heaving surface of the sea, and some of those streaks were green as well. A miasma hung over the sea, a foul haze that stank of dark magic. Harrison saw it too, and I could see he was afraid.

Harrison fingered an amulet that hung on a chain around his neck, and I saw that it was a medal of St. Nicholas of Greece, the patron saint of sailors. Harrison knew the dangers of the sea, and he looked like a man to hedge his bets.

"Looks like the storm that took down the Cristobal," one of the sailors said to another.

"Not natural. Mark my words: it's a hexed storm. We won't see shore again," the other replied.

*Harrison looked as if he wanted to reprove the man, but I could see he feared the sailor's words were true.*

*"I don't like the look of the storm, sir." It was Norris, one of his officers, a man who had served aboard one ship or another since he was just a boy. "It's not natural."*

*Harrison shook his head. "No, it's not."*

*Norris met Harrison's eyes. "The cargo we picked up from the* Cristobal, *the pieces you delivered to Mr. Abernathy – d'ya think they were cursed?"*

*Cursed, I thought, but not in the way Norris expected. Magic had taken the* Cristobal *to the bottom of the ocean, along with artifacts Jeremiah Abernathy desperately needed to control his demon. If Harrison had picked up some of that cargo and delivered it, Abernathy might have decided not to leave any loose ends, people who might have noticed what was in those waterlogged crates.*

*"Aye," Harrison replied. "Or maybe it's divine justice for my being fool enough to do business with the likes of Abernathy. I should have known better."*

*Harrison's position as a ship's captain was the legitimate side to his family's shipping business. Smuggling was the underside of that trade, and what kept a difficult industry profitable. Rum, tobacco, stowaways, and other illegal cargo paid the bills and the enormous cost of upkeep. That meant trading with an unsavory set of partners, the type a gentleman would commonly deny. From that standpoint, bringing back some flotsam for Jeremiah Abernathy must have looked like a bonus, free money for scooping up some pieces from the* Cristobal's *wreckage.*

*Then Abernathy decided to eliminate witnesses.*

*The sea churned beneath the ship, with waves rising high into the air, then crashing down onto the deck* with force enough to splinter masts. Each wave that pounded the Lady Jane's deck swept sailors overboard. Desperate men lashed themselves to the rail. Even then, the sea cheated, sending wave after wave of suffocating, freezing seawater to nearly drown those that were not swept away, or break their bodies when their lifeline kept them rigid against its force.

Harrison made his way back to the bridge. Another wave swept across the Lady Jane's deck, and Harrison nearly lost his grip on the railing. He was soaked to the skin, teeth chattering against the wind. The green mist shrouded them from seeing anything, isolating them on the vast, roiling sea.

The water picked Harrison up like an empty bottle and flung him down the deck, smashing him against the base of one of the masts. He struggled to his feet, dragging himself up against the wind, and held on as another wave rose high over the deck and slammed into them once more. Men, rope, tools and anything not nailed to the boards stood a good chance of being thrown into the churning sea.

Resolute, Captain Harrison dragged himself along the railing. His right leg sent blinding pain through his body whenever he put weight on it. He was certain it had broken when he smashed against the mast. Staggering and limping, using his arms to haul himself down the rail, Harrison again made it to the steps, staying on his feet as the ship pitched.

Just as Harrison reached the top of the steps, an ear-splitting crack of lighting sizzled through the driving rain, striking the top of the Lady Jane's tallest mast, splitting it like a dry twig. The mast exploded, sending a deadly rain of wood chunks and knife-sharp splinters *flying through the air. A dozen men fell, struck in the head or chest with the heavy wooden debris. More men staggered as long splinters pierced their bodies, driven through their skin like nails.*

*The huge mast creaked and groaned a death cry as it toppled, bringing its sails with it, crushing men beneath the massive post, sweeping them overboard with its yardarm or tangling them in the heavy, soaked canvas of its sails.*

*The wind keened through the remaining masts, and the air buzzed with the charge of the nearby lighting strikes. Harrison staggered into the bridge, facing his terrified officers.*

*"We're taking on water," his first mate said. "You can feel it in the way she handles."*

*Harrison nodded. "Not surprised," he replied. "She's not as young as she used to be." It went unsaid that neither was Harrison.*

*"Do we head for the lifeboats?" one of the officers asked.*

*"In this storm?" another challenged. "Might as well throw yourself into the sea."*

*Harrison kept his eyes on the sea, and on the green flashes of ungodly lightning that flared and crackled down around them. He had the look of a man steering into hell at high speed, and if the officers around him had hoped for salvation, one look at his expression stripped them of all hope.*

*A wall of water rose, towering higher than the ship's remaining masts. The wave swept the* Lady Jane *up with it, then dropped her into a trough as the huge wave came crashing down. The drop broke her keel, and the wave smashed what was left of her masts. The* Lady

Jane *went quickly into the icy depths, shrouded in a green, ghostly fog, its cursed captain holding onto the wheel with a death grip as the sea claimed him for its own.*

"CASSIDY! WAKE UP! You're shivering like you've been in the arctic," Teag said. The vision left me, and I was sitting in my kitchen once more, but the cold of the merciless sea clung to me. My teeth were chattering, and I folded my arms across my chest, running my hands up and down my upper arms to warm myself.

"Before you ask, yes, having you anchor me made a big difference. And in the future, you are more than welcome to do it anytime you're willing."

Teag gave me a pitying look and went to the living room to retrieve an afghan from the couch. He wrapped it around my shoulders and went to make me a hot cup of tea. I accepted it gratefully, holding the cup in my hands and letting it warm me as I let the horror of the vision slip away.

"Why is it you never get to see cute puppy dogs and happy bunnies?" Teag wondered.

"I do," I said, barely stopping my teeth from chattering. "I don't generally need assistance with those visions." That was the bright side of our work at Trifles and Folly. Most of the pieces we handled were boringly normal, without any resonance at all. Some held the echoes of joy and wonder, like souvenirs from bygone trips, well-traveled luggage, silver and crystal that had been wedding presents or were part of holiday celebrations for many years. Touching those items was one of the best parts of my job.

Teag poured a cup of tea for himself and sat back as I told him about Captain Harrison and the ill-fated *Lady Jane*.

"So Harrison came upon the *Cristobal* either as it foundered or shortly afterwards, soon enough to scoop up crates and barrels that floated to the surface," Teag said. "I'm guessing here, but I'd bet that either Harrison had done some smuggling for Abernathy before this, or knew enough about him to think he'd pay for goods from a pirate ship."

I shrugged. "For all we know, the crates might even have been addressed to Abernathy."

Teag nodded. "Could be. So Harrison delivers the goods – but only part of what was actually onboard the *Cristobal*."

"The rest went to the bottom with the ship."

"Abernathy and Harrison concluded their deal, and Harrison took his ship back to sea," Teag said. "But then Harrison sails into a strange storm, just like the *Cristobal* did. In fact, it's so much like the freak storm that sank the *Cristobal*, Harrison gets suspicious, but it's too late. Abernathy – or Moran, or the demon – decide Harrison is an inconvenient loose end. Conjure up a nasty storm, and sink the evidence," Teag said, making a spiraling gesture like water going down the drain.

"I think that's exactly what happened," I said.

"What about the ledger?" Teag asked. I reached for it, but he grabbed it away.

"Rest," he said with a warning look. "I can read as well as you can." I sat back, happy for the reprieve.

Teag frowned as he scanned down the faded ink and old-style penmanship. "Offhand, I'd say it's Captain

Harrison's log book," he said. "Just pages torn out – but it happens to be the day they saw the *Cristobal* sink."

"What does it say?" I resisted the urge to want to see for myself. The horror of the *Lady Jane*'s wreck was still too close.

"I can see why Harrison and his crew were frightened by the storm that sank them – aside from the normal human reasons to not want lightning to strike your ship or big waves to wash you overboard.

"Harrison's notes say he and the crew spotted a ship flying a Spanish flag on the route between Barbados and Charleston, between Bermuda and the coast. It was a good distance ahead of them, but clearly in sight." Teag looked thoughtful as he studied the next portion of the log.

"Harrison says that they had crossed paths with the *Cristobal* before, and recognized it, even at a distance. Clouds came up 'unusually fast' his notes add," Teag continued. "Here's what he says: '*The air took on an unusual color, like the green glow of a certain fungus, a sickly, diseased color like a rotting corpse. The mist gathered all around the* Cristobal, *so we could scarcely make out the tip of her tallest mast. Clouds gathered, and bolts of lightning began to strike all around the ship, but nowhere else. All around the* Lady Jane, *the sky was clear and we had calm winds. This discrepancy was noted by my men, who commented on it at length and many took out charms or good luck trinkets and prayed for deliverance.*'" Teag met my gaze and raised an eyebrow. "There's more. '*I ordered our course changed so that we did not steer into the same unlucky conditions as the* Cristobal. *Yet I wished to see if assistance would be needed.*'"

"For a pirate ship?" I said with a snort. "More like he hoped there would be cargo to loot if things went wrong."

Teag nodded. "I thought the motives sounded very noble. '*We saw lightning strike the* Cristobal *in several places, and the sea was wild beneath her. One huge wave and one deafening peal of thunder later, and the* Cristobal *vanished from our sight.*'"

"Just like that," I murmured.

"Apparently so. Matches what I found on the Darke Web."

I thought for a moment, sipping my tea. "Abernathy and Moran wanted what was on the *Cristobal*," I continued. "Somebody hired a wizard to sink the ship. We'll probably never know whether that person was Abernathy's enemy or someone with a grudge against Moran or the crew of the *Cristobal* themselves. Whoever it was wanted to make sure Abernathy didn't get what was onboard the *Cristobal*, but sinking the ship didn't completely fix the problem. Some of the items washed up anyway. He couldn't have guessed that Harrison would happen upon the wreckage and see an opportunity."

"Then Abernathy and Moran got rid of Harrison, figuring that eliminated a witness," Teag said. "And they might have wanted to go back after the wreckage right then, but something else must have gone wrong. Moran disappeared and Abernathy wasn't strong enough to control the demon himself, so his fortunes soured and the demon caused a fair bit of damage until Sorren and the others could banish it."

"But they didn't destroy the demon, and they didn't manage to banish it permanently," I said as I absently reached down to stroke Baxter's fur.

"Which meant that once Moran recovered, he had a reason to come back to Charleston and bring the demon back, and he'd want the items from the *Cristobal*, to strengthen his control over the demon," Teag added.

I nodded. "That accounts for the deaths near the Navy yard." I glanced to Teag. "Could it account for the cryptomancer? The one someone was looking for on the Darke Web? Maybe Moran needed help breaking a code on the artifacts from the *Cristobal*."

"Very likely. And if so, then the odds are good that the cryptomancer is one of the dead men," Teag said.

"Anything useful from Landrieu's notes?"

"Nothing as interesting as what Harrison describes. Most of Landrieu's journal has notes about the dives his crew took – looking for the *Cristobal*, and other wrecks. Water condition and tides, longitude and latitude – the kind of stuff you'd expect." He sighed. "Now and then, Landrieu goes on about how he hopes the *Cristobal* find will put his crew in the big leagues. But it all starts to change about three weeks before the dive."

"Oh?" I shifted in my chair and unwrapped myself from the afghan, finally warm.

"Landrieu was afraid he was being followed. Some of their equipment got vandalized, and he started to get the feeling someone was warning him away from the *Cristobal*." Teag shrugged. "Landrieu thought it was a rival dive team. And he sketched the man he saw."

Teag held up Landrieu's journal. I was not surprised that the pencil sketch showed a tall man with a withered face partially hidden beneath a broad-brimmed hat.

"Why didn't Moran just let Landrieu's team salvage the *Cristobal* and steal the stuff from them after the hard work was over?" I asked.

"What if, over time, something about the magic changed?" Teag speculated. "Or maybe Moran got paranoid, and was afraid that whoever had the artifact might get control of the demon?"

"You've told me what the journals say. Does your magic tell you anything else?"

Teag thought before he replied. "It makes Landrieu's feelings about the dive tangible. Excitement, and then suspicion, and at the end, fear. I think Landrieu knew something bad was after them. He just didn't realize how bad."

"So Moran called up some kind of dark magic to destroy Landrieu and the crew of the *Privateer*. Did you think he was paranoid enough to believe Landrieu was working for Sorren?"

Teag shrugged. "It's possible. Moran and Sorren have a history. And from Moran's point of view, Landrieu was going after something he wanted. He might have thought Sorren put him up to it."

Until now, Baxter had been happy to curl up under the table around our feet. Without warning, he jumped up and raced out to the front door. His bark was so loud and shrill, I thought my ears would bleed.

Since the 'front' door on my Charleston single house really looks out on the piazza and garden, I had to go to the side window to see the street. Chuck Pettis was out there, and he was facing down an *akvenon* minion.

I didn't take time to think about it. I threw open the door and ran the length of the piazza.

"Chuck! Hurry!" I shouted.

The *akvenon* swiveled to glare at me, and from its baleful look, I knew that Teag and I were the real reason it was stalking my street. Chuck glanced at the open door and made a run for it, moving faster than I expected. The *akvenon* followed, growling and snapping at his heels. I suspected that the creature didn't really want Chuck: it wanted a way into the house to get at Teag and me. It was about to get a surprise when it hit Lucinda's wardings.

And if Chuck wasn't on the up-and-up, he'd be just as surprised.

Chuck sprinted for the door, with the *akvenon* close on his heels. The demon minion sprang at Chuck, launching its squat, misshapen body into the air. I ran forward, but Teag caught me by the arm before I could step beyond the warding.

Chuck wheeled, leveling a boxy device that looked like a souped-up TV remote control at the *akvenon*, and stood his ground. I expected to see a flash of a laser or hear an ear-splitting squeal. I heard nothing. But the *akvenon* did.

The demon spawn minion dropped to the ground, shaking violently. Its squashed head swiveled one way and then the other, as its lantern-jawed maw snapped in fury at the air.

Chuck didn't prolong the standoff. He gave the minion one last blast from his weapon and practically dove across my threshold.

It didn't take the *akvenon* long to react. Howling and snarling, it reared up on its clawed feet and bounded for the doorway like a mutant Doberman. I slammed the door, waiting for the bulky minion to come crashing through the glass. Instead, it hit Lucinda's warding. An amber glow flared and disappeared, knocking the creature back ten paces and putting him flat on his demon ass.

Chuck looked from the warding to Teag and then to me. "Who the hell are you people?" he asked. "And what the hell is an *akvenon* minion doing outside your house?"

# Chapter Twenty-Six

I FROZE. IT wasn't like I could deny what had just happened. Chuck had run for his life from a snarling demon minion, which bounced off a Voudon mambo's protective warding like a marble off Jell-O. So I decided that a good offense was the best defense.

"Why were you stalking me?" I demanded. Teag was next to me, and he casually fell into a defensive posture.

Chuck rolled his eyes. "I wasn't stalking you – not really. I wanted to check you out, the way you checked me out. You don't think I fell for that cockamamie story you gave me, did you?"

"What's in your hand?" Teag said. Up close, the gadget really did look like a remote control, but the *akvenon* sure hadn't liked it.

Chuck smirked. "EMF disruptor. Kind of like pepper spray for spooks. They give off an electromagnetic field. This scrambles their signal."

"That's not exactly off-the-shelf technology," Teag observed, raising an eyebrow. He would know. Between the supernatural Darke Web and its mundane competitor, he had a pretty good idea of what kind of equipment was out there, legally or not.

Chuck shook his head. "Military. I told you – I was Black Ops, the *real* Black Ops dealing with the stuff that lives in the shadows, that ain't from around here – and I mean Earth, not the old Commie Block countries or the Middle East. Terrorists, they're the least of our worries. Hell, all they can do is kill you. The stuff we chased could eat your soul for breakfast."

He could have been lying, but I didn't think so. Question was, did that make him an ally or a rival?

"You certainly can't go back out there right now, so you might as well come in," I said, exchanging a glance and a shrug with Teag.

"I'll go clear off the table," Teag offered, which meant I should stall Chuck while Teag hid Sorren's package and the journal from the museum. Baxter had been barking like a maniac, but as soon as Chuck was safe inside, the little fuzzy turncoat toddled up, sat down and gave our unexpected guest his most adorable expression.

"Well aren't you quite the watchdog!" Chuck said, and to my amazement, bent down and scratched Baxter behind the ears. I still wasn't sure how far we should trust Chuck, but that went a long way toward convincing me he was a quality person. That and the fact that he made it past Lucinda's wardings.

I glanced past Chuck to see Teag nod the 'all clear', and put on my best hostess smile. "Let's go into the kitchen."

On the way, I realized that there was a new sound, faint but unmistakable. Chuck was ticking.

"Teag – he's wearing a bomb!"

I swept for Chuck's legs as Teag went to pin him

down. Thing was, Chuck was former military himself, and he didn't go down without a fight.

"For the love of God! I don't have a bomb!" Chuck said. "Get the hell off me! It's watches. Just watches!"

Before I could stop him, Chuck ripped back the front of his jacket. I braced myself, expecting to be blown to bits. A heartbeat later when I hadn't exploded, I looked down to see the jacket Chuck was holding open.

Beneath Chuck's jacket, he wore a vest covered in wristwatches. The timepieces had been taken off their straps and sewn in rows onto the vest so that they covered the fabric completely. From the sound of it, they were all wound and operational.

Teag let out a low whistle. "I haven't seen that many wristwatches being worn by one person since a guy tried to sell me a cheap Rolex in the New York subway."

We let Chuck up, and climbed to our feet. Chuck shoved the EMF disruptor in his pocket and glared at us. "I told you, if the watches ever run down, I die. That's the other reason I tracked you down. You're my best bet for getting the rest of my clocks out of that godforsaken storage unit and getting rid of that damned demon."

Flashing lights outside caught my attention, and I went to the window. "Uh oh," I said. "There's a police car outside." I paused. "You two stay here. I'll handle them."

I straightened my hair, put on my most innocent smile, and headed toward the door. Lucinda's warding shouldn't affect the police, but just in case, I stepped out onto the piazza and walked toward the door to the street.

"Can I help you, officer?"

The cop looked at me, and I knew he was trying to see behind me, onto the porch. "We got calls that someone was attacked by a vicious dog?"

I managed to look annoyed. "Did that pit bull get out again?" I shook my head. "I don't know who he belongs to, but he's always getting loose. Big dog, all white, huge teeth. He chased a man down the street, but they're both gone, now."

The cop made a note in his book and nodded. "If you see the dog again, give Animal Control a call. They'll catch him and we'll fine the owner."

"I'll let you know if I see anything," I promised, certain Animal Control did not want to deal with a demon minion.

"Have a good evening," the cop said with a nod, and headed back to his car. I watched him pull out, and then went back inside.

"I'll make some more tea," Teag was saying as I returned to the kitchen.

I gave Chuck a level glare. "Now, where were we? Did you say, 'demon'?"

Chuck gave me a no-bullshit glare. "You know damn right I did. If you didn't, you wouldn't have protections set by a Class 1 Practitioner."

"A what?" This time, the confusion wasn't feigned.

Chuck rolled his eyes. "You guys ever hear about how Hitler wanted to collect supernatural objects? You know, like in *Indiana Jones*?"

Teag put the kettle on to boil and came over to listen. I nodded in response.

"Yeah, well over the years, he wasn't the only one. Every two-bit dictator and narco lord thinks he'd be so much more bad-ass if he just had a demon or two on his payroll. Or an old Egyptian artifact that makes enemies turn into cockroaches. You get the picture. Well, we were the guys they sent in to steal that shit back."

"I've heard about soldiers going in to save cultural treasures and artwork," I said. "I've never heard about them being airlifted in to snatch crystal balls."

Chuck's smirk returned. "Do you think the government gave a crap about artwork? What do you think was so valuable about those 'cultural' treasures?"

*Magic.* It made sense. Benign or dangerous, magic was powerful, and whoever controlled the artifact controlled the magic. The Alliance couldn't be the only group out there trying to get dangerous objects out of circulation. On the other hand, the Alliance destroyed or bound the objects. Governments were likely to want anything with special powers for themselves. So did groups like the Family, which employed the likes of Corban Moran. So hard to tell, sometimes, who the real good guys were.

"What happened to the items after you 'liberated' them?" Teag asked. I figured he had come to the same conclusions I had.

Chuck shrugged. "You know how everyone talks about Area 51? The place where they think the government hides all the UFOs out in the Nevada desert? The stuff we stole went to a place like that, only they still don't talk about it." He crossed his arms over his chest, daring us to contradict him.

"Is that who you're working for? The military?" I asked. That could pose real problems. I didn't much fancy being locked up in a secret facility until government researchers figured out what made me tick, and I figured Sorren would be even less thrilled about the prospect.

Chuck shook his head. "Nah. I don't trust those guys. They said they were locking the stuff up but, they work for the politicians, you know?" He leaned forward. "So why are you so interested in going into a place any sane person would leave the hell alone? I don't think you're urban explorers, and I don't think you're ghost hunters. Someone paying you? What's in it for you?"

I exchanged a glance with Teag. I really wanted to say that if I told him, I'd have to kill him, but that was a little too close to the truth. "We work for a global organization that gets dangerous objects off the market," I said carefully. "It's kind of a public service. The objects are either destroyed or bound so they can't hurt anyone. They don't get funneled into anyone's arsenal."

Chuck gave me a look like I was the biggest sap in the world. "Huh. I used to believe that kind of thing, too. But it's a nice thought."

I wasn't going to argue with him. "Something brought you here, Mr. Pettis. I don't think you were entirely surprised to run into a bad spook. So why did you come?"

For all Chuck's curmudgeonly manner, there was something very vulnerable about him. Whatever he had seen in the service had scarred him, broken a piece of him, and now that the wife and children I had glimpsed in my vision were gone, those old horrors weighed on his mind.

"I want my clocks. That's part of it. But some of it's for Jimmy," he said, and I knew he meant Jimmy Redshoes. "I saw what killed him, Jimmy and the other men." He lifted his chin defiantly. "I knew better than to try to tell the cops. Hell's bells, they'd have locked me up and probably charged me with the murders if I told them I saw a demon flay those men." He leaned forward. "But I think you'll believe me. I think you already know that."

"What do you bring to the party, Mr. Pettis?" I asked. I really wished Sorren was here to glamor the guy and find out if he was telling the truth, although my gut said he was, through a tilted perspective.

"The guy you want is named Moran. Tall, thin guy with a puckered face. Hides under a hat, but he looks like he pruned up in the sun," Chuck said bluntly. "Jimmy Redshoes and Kevin Harvey, they used to come into Stor-Your-Own and loot the units that were abandoned. They left my stuff alone, and I left them alone. I understood. You gotta do what you gotta do to survive these days."

*Kevin Harvey.* That was the name of the man I'd glimpsed in the vision at the Dennison house. "That's where they got the things they sold," I said. Chuck nodded.

"I also knew those guys who dove for treasure. Russ and the guys from the *Privateer*," Chuck said. "Nice folks. Something fishy about what happened to them. I think Moran had something to do with it."

Chuck's instincts were too spot on for his own good. His Black Ops background dismissed the notion that he was naïve. I suspected that he was a sterling judge of character in figuring that we weren't the kind to kill him for knowing too much, and that he likely had a touch of his own magic.

"You were going to tell us what you bring to the party?" Teag reminded him.

Chuck gave a world-weary smile. "I know all the ways in and out of Stor-Your-Own. I've been going in and out since it closed, and I'm alive to talk about it – which is more than I can say for any of the others. I know the layout. It's not what you might have seen on a map," he said with a look that told us he figured we had done our homework.

"The place has gone to hell in a handbasket over the last six months," he said. "Sinkholes. Debris from the last hurricane that took off some of the roofing. No electricity. That makes the building darker than the back of the moon, and you've got to navigate in and out before something eats you."

He gave me a pointed glare. "I know where Moran and his demon make their nest in that place. I know their habits, and I know how to get around them." He jabbed a thumb at his chest. "I'm your guide. All I want is my clocks."

Chuck was bat-shit crazy around the edges, but if he'd seen the action he said he had, he was entitled to it. He had a point. To my knowledge, Sorren hadn't scouted the interior of Stor-Your-Own, and we sure as hell weren't going to. I didn't doubt his claim that he had been going in and out successfully for months, managing to stay alive when so many others hadn't. What I didn't know yet was whether or not he was in league with Moran.

"Your proposal is interesting," I said. I glanced at the vintage Longines watch on his wrist. "Let me hold your watch for a moment."

Chuck looked taken aback, and then he simply stared at me. Slowly, he removed his wristwatch, a real antique beauty. I held it in my hands, pretending to study its face. I saw flashes of the same memories I glimpsed at Chuck's house: *the dark-haired woman, now dead.*

*The children, now grown. His loneliness and defiant independence. The guilt over things that had occurred under orders during the war. I saw flashes of his happiest memories, and fragments of the things that haunted his dreams.* And when I was done, I knew a few more things. Some of them involved precognition, Chuck's hidden, burdensome talent.

Chuck's belief that he would die without the clocks was genuine. Not necessarily true, but definitely something he believed without reservation. Blame PTSD. I did.

Chuck's government connections were severed abruptly and bitterly long ago. He wasn't going to rat us out to the NSA.

I glanced up to Teag, who gave me a nod. Teag's ability to weave information includes perception. He's an insanely good judge of character. Chuck made the cut.

I realized Chuck was staring at me as I handed back his watch. "You're psychometric," he said matter-of-factly. "Of course you are. That's how you know which pieces are dangerous."

I thought about arguing, but instead I just shrugged. "We've all got our gifts. We can't all see into the future." I met his eyes. He looked startled, then his gaze slid away. He knew I'd made him.

I had no idea how I was going to explain this to Sorren, but I trusted both my gift and my gut. "If you want a chance to make Moran pay for killing Jimmy and Kevin – and for everything else – we'd be glad to have you as our guide."


I TOLD SORREN about Chuck and his unusual background, as well as my read of his trustworthiness and my invitation. Sorren had been understandably skeptical, and had asked that he and Mirov get to meet Chuck before plans moved forward. It was a reasonable request, and I couldn't fault Sorren's caution, even if it dented my pride a bit to be second-guessed.

"Look at it this way," Teag said as we waited in Trifles and Folly for the others to show up. "Sorren's been doing this for a lot longer. Maybe once you've been at it for a couple of hundred years, he'll let you pick members for the team without him."

"Very funny," I said, but he had a point. I was still new at this. And I hoped my choice had been a good one.

Sorren and Mirov arrived before Chuck. Sorren had recently fed, because his pallor was gone, and his light complexion was a touch ruddy, as if he had been out in the wind. In low light, he could easily pass for mortal. Mirov, dressed all in black, looked like a hit man out of a Cold War movie.

"You're taking a risk by involving an outsider," Sorren said. "I'm not convinced we need him."

"You were going to go check out the storage facility." I said. "Did you have the chance to go?"

Sorren nodded. "But I didn't go past the fence. The energy stinks of demon and death. It's definitely where the demon is nesting, and if the demon's there, odds are so is Moran."

I leaned back in my chair. "Then that's a big plus for bringing Chuck with us. He's been in and out of there fairly often since it closed, so he knows what's normal and what isn't," I said. "He says there's damage from the last couple of storms, plus lack of maintenance, and he knows how to get around it. Plus, he's certain he knows where Moran and his demon are holed up. Up until now, he's mostly avoided them. But he's desperate enough to get his clocks, he offered to guide us."

"He's one more liability," Mirov added, clearly unhappy about my invitation. "We have no idea how he'll react under stress."

I arched an eyebrow. "He's been 'reacting under stress' for six months now. Teag checked out his story – he really is ex-Special Forces, former Black Ops. He saw combat. Plus I'm ninty-nine percent sure he's clairvoyant."

"He comes with his own weapons," Teag volunteered. "And he didn't freak out when the minion came after him."

"For all we know, he could be working for Moran," Mirov said.

"That's why I read his watch," I replied, starting to get annoyed. "He's frightened of Moran, and repulsed. He genuinely grieves Jimmy Redshoes. He wants a chance to avenge Jimmy and Kevin. And he left the Army on terms that soured him on the military and cut off his old ties, so I don't think he's going to turn us in."

"He won't," Teag said. "I hacked into a couple of military databases. Chuck was reprimanded for insubordination and given a dishonorable discharge for leading a mutiny against his commanding officer."

"Why?" Mirov asked, his eyes narrowing.

Teag gave a 'gotcha' grin. "According to testimony, Chuck tried to talk his superior officer out of the mission, because he had a premonition it would go terribly wrong. The officer refused to listen. Chuck wouldn't back down, and took a swing at the guy. Chuck ended up in the brig, and the officer led the mission."

"What happened?" I asked.

"The men walked into a trap. All but a handful died. The commander survived and pressed charges." He grimaced. "If Chuck hadn't taken a swing at him, he might have gotten off with a lesser punishment. As it was, he was court martialed, served time in Leavenworth, and given a dishonorable discharge."

"No wonder he's bitter," I said.

"He'll know more than he should about what we do," Sorren groused.

I leveled my gaze at him. "Then glamor him. If you can use mind control on Alistair, you can handle Chuck."

Just then, Chuck knocked at the locked front door of the shop. I wasn't about to ask anyone to come in the back door after what happened the last time we used the alley.

Chuck wore the same type of outfit as I'd seen him in before: olive green jacket (ticking), fatigues, and combat boots. He had a new gimme cap covering his bald head, this time from a trucking company. I saw a Glock in a holster on his belt, and I was guessing he had his 'remote control' and possibly other spiffy tools hidden about his person.

"Thanks for coming," I said, letting him in. "Come on back. We're in the kitchen." He grunted a greeting. I figured he was nervous, as well as just curmudgeonly.

Teag offered Chuck a cup of tea, but Chuck shook his head and stood at one side of the small table, eyeing Sorren and Mirov. "I'm here," he said. "What did you want to know?"

"Cassidy says you're willing to guide us into the storage facility," Sorren said. He was standing out of direct light, leaning against the counter.

Chuck regarded him for a moment, then nodded. "I said I would."

"Why?" Mirov asked. He was at the end of the table, dark, glowering, and intimidating. I suspected it was intentional.

Chuck didn't scare easily. "Moran and his attack dog killed my friend Jimmy, and I figure he was behind some other people disappearing. People I liked. I spent ten years getting rid of scum like him when I was in the Army. It rubs me wrong, and I'd like to do something about it – and get my clocks."

"Attack dog?" Sorren asked, raising an eyebrow.

Chuck gave a sarcastic smile. "What else do you call a demon that comes when you whistle?"

I could see that Chuck's attitude and his knowledge were making an impression on Sorren, and I suspected he was using his heightened senses and long experience to size him up. I had the feeling that Chuck was sizing up Sorren as well.

"What do you know of demons?' Mirov scoffed. "Comic books? Movies?"

"I was with a team that fought a lamashtu in Iraq," Chuck said without batting an eye. "Lost two men, came out with four, bound the demon and turned it over to a local holy man to get rid of," he added. "Gave me this." Chuck pulled up his sleeve. A deep gash ran from his shoulder to his wrist.

"Go ahead," he said, leveling a challenging look at Sorren and Mirov. "Touch the scar. If you've got an ounce of magic, you'll know I didn't get it cutting my lawn."

"Anything else?" Mirov questioned, not yet convinced.

"We put down an Adromalech-level demon in South Korea," Chuck replied. "Nasty. His minions spit a mix of acid and poison. I got this for a souvenir," he said, and bent his head so that we got a good look at the puckered burn on his neck. "I spent two weeks in the base hospital. Almost died before they figured out how to knock out the infection."

He glared at them. "And I'll say it again: go ahead. Touch the scars. If you're what you claim to be, it'll be clear that I'm telling the truth."

We appeared to have a testosterone stand-off between Chuck, Sorren, and Mirov. I rolled my eyes.

"Folks, we've got a demon on the loose and at least a dozen dead men. Chuck can get us in, and get us around the obstacles," I said. "Personally, I think we need all the help we can get."

"Give me a moment," Sorren said. "I'd like to speak with Taras." Sorren and Mirov moved into my office and closed the door.

Chuck looked at me and raised an eyebrow. "The blond one. You know what he is?"

I deliberately misunderstood. "Belgian?"

Chuck glowered. "Vampire."

"How did you know?"

Chuck snorted. "Used to work with three of them, back in Dragon Unit. Me and the other guys used to donate blood to the company medics so they'd have a supply. Let them bite me more than once, in a pinch, when they got hurt bad."

Despite my first impressions, I found myself liking Chuck. He was cantankerous and headstrong, but he stood up for his friends and for what he believed. That was a rare trait. I couldn't blame Sorren and Mirov for their caution, but I was convinced Chuck belonged in our group, along with Lucinda.

Sorren and Mirov emerged from their discussion. Mirov glowered, but I couldn't tell whether he had been overruled or whether that was his normal expression.

"You're in," Sorren said abruptly, moving to stand directly in front of Chuck. Chuck lifted his chin to the challenge in Sorren's voice, but he did not try to meet Sorren's gaze.

"Be clear on this. If you betray us, or cause harm to come to one of mine, you will not survive." Sorren's expression made it clear that the warning was not idle.

"I'll hold up my end," Chuck snapped. "I'll get you in and out. Just make sure I get my damned clocks."

"When?" I asked.

"Tomorrow night," Sorren replied. "There's nothing to gain by waiting any longer, and the longer we wait, the more likely it is that Moran will change his plans and we'll lose our chance."

"I borrowed my brother's old panel van," Teag said. "It's beat up, but it runs well. And it's nondescript, just a hard-used white van." He grinned. "He won it in a card game, and it's had a lot of owners – it would be tough for anyone to track it back to him, or us. That should be good to get Cassidy, Chuck and me to the Navy yard."

"Lucinda and Taras and I have our own transportation," Sorren said. "We'll meet you at Stor-Your-Own."

"We'll be there," I said. "It's about time Stor-Your-Own and the dead men got to rest in peace."

# Chapter Twenty-Seven

I was dressed for mayhem. Since I'd taken over Trifles and Folly, my all-black wardrobe had expanded, and not in the little-black-dress way. I'd found it prudent to acquire black jeans, black shirts, a couple of black hoodies, and shoes with really good traction. I even had my own lock picking kit, and had the best jewel thief in Antwerp as my mentor. This wasn't what I had anticipated when I majored in Antiquities in college.

Maybe I should have been concerned at how often breaking and entering seemed to come with the job. But I knew the danger that the objects we were dealing with presented, and the risk of getting caught seemed far less frightening than what the demon could do.

Teag was dressed in all-black as well, looking a bit like a raven with his sharp features and dark eyes. I spotted his magical stole before he zipped his hoodie closed, and I saw the headscarf tied over his dark brown hair beneath his hood. In my mind, we looked like burglars, but I guess we could tell people we were on our way to a Goth outing.

"You've got the head wrap and the stole," I noted. "How about the hand loom and swords?"

Teag nodded. "Yep. And I brought my fighting staff, too. Did you bring your lucky charms?" I knew he was trying to keep the mood light, but from the way he drummed his fingers on the steering wheel, I also knew that he was nervous. So was I.

"I've got them," I replied. Bo's collar was wrapped around my left wrist. I had a very strong sense of his presence, to the point of finding several of his hairs on my shirt, a shirt I had purchased after his passing. It could be that dog hair lingers forever in the carpet, but I chose to take it as a message of support from beyond the Rainbow Bridge.

The amber spindle whorl was in my pocket. I had carefully removed it from its velvet bag so that I could get skin contact with it as soon as I put my hand in my pocket. I had the ring and the jet bracelet. And of course, I wore my agate necklace, purified and recharged in the light of last night's moon. In the right sleeve of my hoodie, I had Grandma Sarah's mixing spoon. I had Alard's walking stick through a belt loop on my left hip.

I spotted a bit of cloth sticking out of Teag's pocket. "Did you bring something extra?"

"Just something I thought about at the last minute," he said. "I used to buy little things from Jimmy Redshoes once in a while, just to help the guy out. Sometimes, he would sit and whittle while he was waiting for a customer to come by, and he would sell some of the things he made."

Teag reached into his pocket and pulled out a carved wooden bird, then replaced it and zipped his pocket shut. "That was one of the last things I bought from him before he died. Since whatever's haunting the storage facility probably killed Jimmy, I just had the feeling he'd want to go with us, at least in memory."

Memory, as I knew, had a powerful magic all its own. "I think he'd like that," I said.

Teag pulled out a short length of rope, knotted with nine knots. "The knots are a way of storing power," he explained. "It's part of a Weaver's gift. I can use it to get a second wind, or give one of you a 'recharge'." He paused for a moment to steer. "I've got the hand loom pre-woven. It's on my belt, so I can get to it fast if I need it." As I was beginning to learn, magic is very personal, and items of power are not always what they appear to be.

He glanced at me. "Let me anchor you if the ring isn't enough. We don't have much experience with the new pieces Sorren and Mirov gave us. You don't need to get a full-fledged vision in the middle of a battle and go down for the count."

He wasn't going to get an argument from me on that.

It was after ten on a weeknight, and there wasn't much going on. Once we left the historic district, traffic thinned out, and by the time we made our way to Chuck's neighborhood, we went blocks without passing another car.

The streetlight near Chuck's house was dark, and there were no lights on inside his house when we drove up. "Think he lost his nerve?" Teag asked as we drifted to a stop by the curb. I looked around nervously.

Then I spotted a figure moving out of the shadow of one of the tall trees in the front yard. I recognized the man's gait before I saw the face, and knew that Chuck was up for the night's work.

I opened one of the van's back doors from inside and Chuck jumped in. "Go!" he said, finding a spot on the floor and a hand-hold to keep himself from sliding around. I got back in my seat and Teag pulled away, making sure to stay well within the speed limit.

I glanced back at Chuck. He wore a knit cap pulled down over his head and the collar of his black Eisenhower jacket turned up to partially hide his face. I wasn't surprised that his jacket was ticking. Dark pants and work boots meant he was ready for action.

"Thanks for the ride," Chuck said. I could see a mix of emotions in his face: excitement, fear and maybe even a bit of hope that after tonight, his need to steal back his own clocks would be over. "I'm glad you got this arranged soon. I lost another clock today."

That would account for some of the fear I sensed, although any rational person would feel worried about the night's agenda. "We'll get you some new ones tonight," I said. "And once we've gotten rid of the demon, we'll move the rest somewhere safe where you can get to them easily."

"I kind of have a routine for going in," Chuck said, zipping his jacket closed. "Like we used to have when we were going into a firefight. Soldiers are superstitious. When we come out of our first battle alive, we figure that we must have done something right, and after that, we try to do everything just the same before each fight, just in case."

He dug into a small pouch that hung on a lanyard beneath his vest. From it, he drew out a photograph. Chuck held it out for me to see. It was a picture of the same dark-haired woman whose essence I had sensed when I was in his house, and the same children, at about the age I had glimpsed them in my vision.

"That's Emma," Chuck said, and I noticed that a woman's wedding ring also hung from the lanyard.

"She's gone, but sometimes, I think she's still watching over me, you know? Those are my kids when they were little. Scott's a truck driver out West – doesn't get back to visit much. Diane's married and has kids of her own." He tucked the photo back into the pouch and slipped it under his vest.

Chuck fixed me with a glare. "I'm glad you people aren't any of those ghost hunters like on TV. God, those shows make me crazy. I started watching them, thinking I might learn something."

He made a disdainful gesture. "And what did I see? A lot of lousy video in bad lighting with everyone going, 'Hey, did you hear something' or 'Wow, did you see that?'" He shook his head. "Bunch of wusses, the lot of them. They hear a couple of thumps and a whisper or two and they almost crap their pants. Take them somewhere like Stor-Your-Own, they'd be begging for their mommies."

Teag stifled a snicker, and I had to smile. Teag and I both watched those paranormal investigator shows as a guilty pleasure. We often compared notes the next day, laughing about the overblown reactions.

I had met a couple of ghost hunters who were the real deal, and some urban explorers who had seen things they couldn't explain. "Some of them do know what they're doing," I said. "Their producers are on their backs to make it look exciting, or they'll get cancelled."

Chuck made a rude noise. "Yeah, well in my book, they're all phonies. And what's worse, they make it look easy to go up against the spooks. The worst that ever happens on those shows is that a door slams shut." He met my gaze. "We know what happens when Moran's demon catches up to someone."

We fell silent for the rest of the ride. In a few minutes, we got to the Navy yard entrance. Teag had intentionally kept the hood on his jacket down to avoid a second look from any cop who found hoodies suspicious. A couple of times, I thought I felt a tingle of magic as we passed some spots along the way, and I remembered that Lucinda had said that her friends had agreed to cast spells for our protection. I was grateful for the assistance.

Teag drove on, slouched in his seat like a tired handyman. *Nothing to see here, officer. Just finishing up a long day of work.*

I grabbed a bag next to my seat. Sorren had gotten us night-vision goggles. That kept us from shining our flashlights around like a beacon for the demon. I handed a pair to Chuck, who didn't need any instruction on how to use them. I put mine in my lap and hung on to Teag's until we got where we were going.

Thanks to Sorren's reconnaissance, Teag knew to pull the van into the parking lot of the business adjacent to Stor-Your-Own, belonging to an abandoned shipping company.

Teag had put an old license plate on the van and splattered it with mud. We turned and walked toward the street, then cut across in the shadows of a row of trees and made our way behind the dumpster to the Stor-Your-Own office.

I stopped in front of the door, and looked down. "Salt," I said quietly, and Teag glanced toward the ground and nodded. Someone had poured a thin line of salt all along the outside of the office wall, and it looked as if it ran to the fence, and maybe beyond.

"Do you think it goes the whole way around?" Teag asked.

"Could be," I replied. If so, Lucinda's friends had been busy. Salt was a protective barrier, and if magic had been added to the mix, then it might keep the shadow men and the *akvenon* from following us – but it wasn't going to stop a demon.

"Let's get inside." Sorren, as usual, had come up on us noiselessly, with Mirov a step behind. Lucinda was with them. I noticed that she was carrying the shaman's staff from the Archive. Mirov and Lucinda were also wearing night vision goggles. Sorren didn't need them.

She smiled when she saw that I was looking at the staff. "I told Mrs. Morrissey that I needed it for a special event." I thought I saw a faint glow from inside the large agate set in the top of the staff.

"You'd better let me go first," Chuck said. He had brought a small pair of wire cutters, and made an entrance for us through the chain link fence.

Now that we were in the compound, I saw the old original brick warehouse more clearly, the one that had the long, bloody past. Even without going inside, I could feel a brooding heaviness that clung to the building. I wondered whether that was new since the triggering of the supernatural power. I doubted it; the building had too much history.

Three other metal pole buildings filled the area inside the fence. Chuck's clocks were in Building Three. He was pretty sure Moran and the demon were in the brick warehouse, Building Four.

"Watch your step," Chuck said. "There are places where the asphalt is split, and other places where it's buckled. Easy to turn an ankle or worse. Once we get inside, watch where I walk. Some of the roof fell in with the last big storm. It's a good thing there's no power – bunch of electricity lines are down."

Chuck had insisted that he grab half a dozen clocks from his storage unit before we did anything else. Sorren agreed to remove the rest of his stash to another location after the demon had been handled. I was afraid that our delay would tip off Moran to our presence too early, but then again, I wasn't in a hurry to face the demon, either.

It seemed crazy to bother with the clocks when we had a demon to kill, but Chuck pointed out that in case things got out of hand – meaning that we blew up the entire compound – he wanted to make sure he got enough clocks to give him time to put his affairs in order before the rest ran down. Since blowing the place up wasn't out of the question, and Chuck really thought he would die without his clocks, it made sense from a certain point of view.

Chuck led the way, with Sorren and Mirov behind him. Lucinda insisted on being last, which put me behind Sorren and Teag behind me. I had one of those heavy, military-type flashlights on a carabiner on my belt loop, just in case. I had no desire to be trapped in the dark with a demon, night goggles or not.

The closer we got to the storage buildings, the more uneasy I became. I had been careful to wear my hiking boots because the lug soles had good grip for running, and the rubber insulated me to an extent from contact with the ground. I had found out the hard way that I could 'read' the ground if there was enough emotional resonance.

Even so, the collective memories of the storage facility vied for my attention, like distant voices just out of range. So many stories were tied up in the items people stored here. People made all kind of excuses for why they hung onto things they didn't need, but often, the truth was simple. Storage units held the objects that were too disturbing to keep close at hand and too emotionally important to get rid of. I felt echoes of sadness, longing, and faint hope. So many people had come and gone through this space, both recently and in the Navy yard's troubled past. The lug soles couldn't completely insulate me from the power of the resonance.

I glimpsed different emotions as I passed every unit, like feeling a draft of air conditioning on a hot day walking past open doorways. A few of the units were neutral or even happy, but most of the units gave off a sense of resignation and transience. Some of the units stood open, like gaping maws, their steel roll-down doors askew. Trash and leaves had blown into the vacant units that faced the outside. Empty boxes littered several of the units, and I got the distinct feeling that the renters had cleaned out their things in a hurry.

"Cassidy?" Teag gave my arm a gentle shake. "Are you in there?"

I nodded and took a deep breath. "Yeah, I'm here. There's just a lot of very strong resonance – much more than I usually get from just walking through a site."

I took a step and Teag pulled me back sharply by the arm. "Watch out!" he cautioned, and nodded toward where I had been about to walk.

A sinkhole yawned down into darkness. It had been hidden by the shadows cast by the other buildings. It looked deep, and I didn't want to think about how far down the bottom might be. Not far from the sinkhole, the asphalt had cracked nearly down to the road bed, then buckled so that the crack gaped open and jutted several inches above the surface of the street. It seemed as if the compound itself had somehow conspired to make it as difficult and dangerous as possible for anyone to enter.

"Mind your step," Chuck cautioned. This time, a piece of sheet metal roofing lay twisted on the path. Chuck led us around the obstacle, kicking roofing nails and other debris out of his way. Chuck wasn't taking any chances. He had his gun in his right hand, and his EMF disruptor in the other. He said he had fought demons with his Black Ops unit. I hoped he had stolen some of that equipment and brought it with him. He was a good guide, moving confidently through the rubble and wreckage.

The green glow of the night vision goggles made the abandoned facility even creepier than it would have been, which was saying something. I liked not making a target of ourselves, but at the same time, broad daylight wouldn't have been bright enough for me.

Neglect was apparent as we walked closer to the buildings. Charleston's heat and humidity make for a constant war against mold, mildew, and bugs. Since we're on the Southeastern coastline, hurricanes and nasty storms are regular visitors. The summer's brutally hot temperatures tend to fade paint, weaken wood and soften asphalt. Although Stor-Your-Own had only been out of business for six months, it was clear from looking around that it had not been properly maintained for some time.

*Were people so utterly deaf to natural energies that they could spend time in and around these buildings and not feel the evil?* I wondered. I thought about Flora, whose job required her to walk through each building several times a day to clean up and monitor the site. *And it cost Flora her sanity.*

Chuck led us to Building Three. "In here."

Stepping into the darkness, I felt as if I had been buried alive. One hand went to my agate necklace, while the other felt for the whorl in my pocket. I closed my hand over my ring, concentrating on dampening my gift, and took several deep breaths. The darkness released its grip on me. The collar on my left hand felt warm, and I could feel Bo's protective presence near me.

Lucinda was murmuring a quiet chant as we moved further into the gloom. A moment later, the door slammed shut with a boom that echoed through the large, empty building.

By the time Stor-Your-Own closed down, the renters said the whole place felt creepy, as if the demon's taint had activated all the old ghosts, the dark resonance of objects stored there, and the tragic history of the land beneath our feet. So while the demon's nest might be in Building Four, every building was dangerously haunted, and the threat level was higher than ever before.

We had come into the building by a side door, and it put us at the end of a long row that ran the width of the warehouse. Cobwebs shrouded the corridor like something out of an *Indiana Jones* movie. Heavy, clingy webs hung down from the ceiling in sheets, and they rippled as the air stirred around us. The surface of the floor seemed to move, covered with roaches. Calling them 'palmetto bugs' didn't make them any less ugly.

I really wanted a flame thrower, anything to make the spiders keep their distance. Maybe it was Sorren's presence, but the spiders retraced their lines, into the shadows of the high, open rafters. No telling what was up there, watching us.

"My unit is over here," Chuck said. "Careful where you step."

Sorren and Mirov used their swords to cut us a path. The stone at the top of Lucinda's staff glowed, and its faint light kept the spiders back. Roaches skittered around our feet. They didn't seem bothered by the glow. Then again, they'll survive nuclear war, so I don't imagine they're afraid of much. Their shells crunched under the soles of our shoes with every step.

As I looked around, I saw that there were several side corridors opening off this aisle, and along all of them were the roll-away steel doors of the individual storage units. Most of the doors had been left open by their previous tenants. A few hung half shut, as if they were jammed on their runners. They loomed like dark caves. Anything could be waiting in there.

Chuck's unit was about a third of the way down the corridor. By the time we reached it, we had passed three intersecting hallways that stretched off beyond the range of our goggles. From inside his jacket, Chuck unfolded a canvas backpack that looked like it could hold a lot of clocks. He was quick with key in the lock on his storage unit door.

The steel door clanked as it rolled up on its runners. The sound rolled through the building like thunder. Chuck revealed his cache – a unit stacked almost floor to ceiling with boxes of Baby Ben alarm clocks.

"Be quick about it," Sorren said.

Within a couple of minutes, Chuck had stuffed his bag full of clocks. He riffled in a faded and stained duffle bag that was near the door, pulling out several pieces of government-issue equipment that I doubted he picked up at a scratch and dent sale. He slipped the items into his pack or pockets without explanation, then locked the door and shouldered into the backpack.

"Show us the way," Sorren said. I could tell his patience was wearing thin. Every moment we lingered was more opportunity for the demon in Building Four to figure out ways to keep us from getting where we wanted to go.

"Over here," Chuck said. "Down this way."

I figured it was a toss-up as to where we were safest. Inside the building, we had its resident spooks to deal with, but the demon might not see us coming. Outside, we were more likely to be spotted, and there was no guarantee there wouldn't be just as many homicidal ghosts, bloodthirsty *akvenon* minions or spirit-sucking shadow men waiting for us.

"Do you feel it?" I murmured to Lucinda. "There are *things* all around us, watching. And I don't think it's the spiders." The storage building was oppressively silent. Darkness stretched in all directions, and with the night goggles, it was harder to tell shadows from shadow men. Even so, I had the feeling that the darkness just beyond our goggles' range down the side corridors was full of spirits, energy and supernatural *somethings* – none of it good.

"Uh huh," she replied, and I heard her say something under her breath. The smell of pipe smoke wafted past us. I could hear her singing softly but I could not make out the words.

"It's trying to goad us into running," Chuck said. "It likes us being scared." I could hear the defiance in Chuck's voice. He didn't like being pushed, and his anger and headstrong nature gave him the power to overcome his fear.

As we moved further into the darkened building, it grew colder, much colder than anything without air conditioning gets in the summer in Charleston, even at night. The feeling of being watched was overpowering. The smell changed, too. When we first entered, the building smelled of dust and mildew and stale air. Now, the scent had changed. It reminded me of a mausoleum I had once gone into with Sorren, retrieving another artifact. The smell of dust mingled with death, rotted fabric, and moldering wood. The resonance was stronger the deeper in we went, too. Left-over emotions and memories clung to the empty units: dashed hopes, abandoned dreams, interrupted plans.

It was worst near the units that still had locks, the ones that were still filled with their owners' cast-off possessions. I swear the stuff in those units knew it had been left behind and resented it. People don't pay to store trash. The things they put into storage they either mean to come back for, before life interrupts, or feel that they can't let go of, even if they don't want it around.

Even if they don't know it, the objects have a hold on them: memories, guilt, obligation. Sometimes, that hold is supernatural. I had the feeling that was the case with much of what was left in these units. I wish I could have told the owners that you can't abandon bad mojo. It will wait for you, find you, and track you down. The abandoned units were brooding, and like a drunk in a bad mood, they were looking for someone to take it out on.

Our plan was simple. Find the demon. Fight the demon. Kill the demon.

The devil was in the details.

Sorren, Mirov, and Chuck had discussed strategy at length, with Lucinda, Teag and I chiming in with ideas. Our biggest problem was that we didn't know exactly where the demon's nest was. Chuck was certain it was Building Four, but even that was a big place. There were lots of places to hide. We were counting on Lucinda and me being able to narrow it down when we got close to the building, so that we didn't go in a door that put us right on top of the demon, but didn't enter so far away that the demon had a chance to prepare.

Assuming, of course, that the demon didn't already know we were coming.

The air felt heavy, the way it does before a storm. The darkness seemed more opaque, and the feeling of being watched intensified. Not just watched – resented. Every instinct told me that I needed to run the other way. We kept going.

I was glad Sorren was up front with Chuck. I knew that Sorren could see just fine in the dark without needing goggles. Lucinda was still chanting and singing in a low voice, and I caught another whiff of pipe smoke.

Out of the corner of my eye, I caught a glimpse of motion in the shadows. Teag saw it, too.

"Spirit lights," he murmured. "Very faint, but definitely there."

"The spirits know we're coming," Lucinda said, her voice roughened by the chanting. "They know."

Somewhere inside the building, I heard footsteps on the concrete floor. They stopped, and then to the right, I heard the screech of something dragged across the thin metal siding on the walls of the units. Down the length of the corridor, the latches on the closed doors began to vibrate as if the compound were shaking in an earthquake.

Behind us, one of the open storage unit doors crashed down, then another, and another, starting at the far end of the corridor and rolling toward us like a tide. I felt a surge of power flow past us, sending the doors nearest us slamming to the floor. I knew the steel panels didn't slide that easily on their runners. Something was making its displeasure very clear.

We got to the end of the corridor. I was starting to glimpse faces in the shadows, gray figures of the ghosts of this cursed land. The figures shifted in the gloom, at times becoming more defined, then dissolving into nothing. I couldn't make out the details, but I knew who they were. Hanged pirates. Wronged businessmen and hardluck women. Victims of Jeremiah Abernathy's court and Moran's demon. Too many restless souls, too much blood-soaked ground. The demon's power drew the spirits, gave them energy, but they were here before the demon came, and some of them would be here after the demon was destroyed. Too much blood had been shed for me to think we could exorcise this unhallowed ground in just one night – or maybe ever.

Sorren turned to the rest of us. "We go out this door, cross a driveway, and go into the door on the end of Building Four. That's where I need everyone's senses on alert." He looked at me and then at Lucinda. "Chuck says he's seen activity at the northern end. That's the opposite corner, a straight shot." He raised an eyebrow. "Once we go in, it's on."

The storage unit was not the ideal place to confront a demon. Problem was, there isn't really a good place. We might have lured the demon out, using one of us like bait, but that introduced so many variables – and the possibility that a passer-by could get caught up in the firefight – that we took that idea off the table early. Going to the demon on its home turf was suicidal, no matter how many movies show the hero fighting a dragon in its lair. What makes a great movie doesn't usually play well in real life.

We had debated the alternatives. If we went into the old warehouse mid-building, we could be right on top of the demon before we got our bearings. And if the demon sensed us – a very likely possibility – it would be over before it began. I would have preferred it if we could have made a circuit of the building to locate the demon, but odds were, if we located him he would also locate us. I figured he already knew we were here. He was confident, waiting for us to come to him. I just hoped we could turn that confidence against him.

We crossed the short expanse of asphalt between buildings, staying low and keeping to the shadows. Even so, I felt watched. I wasn't sure which was worse: being outside and exposed or going into Building Four where we knew a demon was waiting.

We got to the building and Sorren bent to pick the lock on the door, but it was unlocked, and swung open at a touch. Just as I feared: we were expected.

# Chapter Twenty-Eight

WE OPENED THE door to hell.

The old warehouse stank of death. The air was heavy with the smell of blood and the stench of rotting flesh. It was a compliment to compare it to a charnel house, because the bodies here weren't treated with respect and certainly weren't embalmed awaiting proper burial. It smelled worse than a slaughterhouse, unless the meat being cut up happened to be weeks old and left out in the sun to rot.

Blood streaked the walls and steel doors of the warehouse. Blood pooled on the floor. Gobbets of things best unidentified were dried on the walls where they had been flung in an orgy of gluttony. Maggots churned in masses that heaved under their own weight. Even the spiders and the roaches had quit Building Four. *Abandon hope, all ye who enter here...*

Mangled soldiers had breathed their last within these brick walls. Prisoners of war had prayed to die. Slaves had toiled here under the lash. Workers had died here, under unconscionable conditions. Epidemic victims had seen fevered visions. And on the land beneath the building, pirates had been hanged and buried while their bodies were still warm.

Their spirits were still here.

But in the shadows all around us, as blue-white orbs hovered and dodged, I glimpsed more recent spirits, ghosts for whom death was still a shock. Jimmy Redshoes. Kevin Harvey. And the five-man crew of the *Privateer*, still following their captain, Russ Landrieu, beyond the grave.

There were others as well. Fred Kenner, Stor-Your-Own's murdered owner. I saw faces I knew only from their obituaries, the drifters and vagrants who had been fodder for Moran's demon. They stared at me from the shadows, as if there was something I could do to end their torment. I felt no threat from them.

Moran and his demon were threat enough.

Our night vision goggles cast the interior in foxfire shades, a sickly green luminescence. The ghosts weren't alone in the darkness. Shadow creatures prowled in the hollow sockets of the empty units, misshapen, distorted energies that had never been men, creatures that fed on terror. Here in the presence of their master, they did not bother masquerading as human. Their true form showed in grotesquely elongated limbs, twisted forms, and lantern-jawed heads. They were just waiting for orders.

At every cross-corridor, Lucinda put a barrier of salt and iron nails, trying to seal off those hallways so nothing could come behind us. It was a nice idea, but I wasn't counting on it working. A glance down those corridors told me they were littered with garbage and abandoned possessions. Apparently, Moran and the demon had made themselves at home. Lucinda lagged behind us, chanting softly to herself, calling on the Loas for protection and help.

The air stank of bile and sulfur, rot and shit. Now that we were halfway down the corridor, we could see that the demon had rearranged the place to suit himself, battering down the thin metal panels that separated the individual units to make the back third of the corridor one large den.

The blackened skins of the murdered men hung on the walls like trophies. Symbols of power were daubed in blood above and below the skins. The bones and decaying carcasses of small animals littered the floor: stray dogs, feral cats, unlucky rats, and rabbits that ventured too close to a demon starved for blood. In the center of the area, on a low wooden table, dozens of candles burned in a tawdry shrine.

"Come to finish me off?" A deep, mocking voice echoed through the storage building.

Corban Moran stepped out of the shadows. Without his hat, I could see his shriveled features clearly, quite a difference from the man I'd seen in the photo with Jeremiah Abernathy. Sorren had left him for dead. Moran may not have died, but the cost of that encounter was clear.

"You are supposed to be dead." Sorren's voice was low and dangerous. I was watching two predators face off against each other, and I hoped Sorren was the biggest bad-ass on the block.

"You certainly tried." Moran's tone was thick with contempt and hatred. "I knew Abernathy's demon was still unbound, and I knew no one had ever brought back the most powerful artifact from the *Cristobal*. I needed that piece to recover my power."

"And you killed the salvage team that almost beat you to it," Sorren said.

Moran shrugged. "It's a dog-eat-dog world." He smirked. "I tried to buy them off, tried to scare them off. They wouldn't leave it alone. Now they're dead and I have the artifact."

He held up a crystal sphere the size of a bowling ball. Inside was a blood-soaked mummified goat's head. "The Baphomet Orb," he said, holding it like a trophy.

I shivered. I'd found a reference to that artifact in one of Uncle Evan's old journals. A Baphomet Orb was difficult and dangerous to make, and thankfully rare. It gave the owner power over a demon called by name. The orb held the head of a goat severed under a full moon, soaked in the blood of a murdered man, into which a candle made with fat rendered from a hanged man was placed and burned, then the whole thing was bound in strips of human skin and encased in glass, sealing in its power.

"It won't bind the demon forever," Sorren warned. "You're a fool if you think you can control that thing for long."

"I don't need forever," Moran replied. "I just need longer than I had left."

"And what's in it for the demon, besides what's left of your soul?" Sorren asked. It was like the rest of us weren't there, the continuation of an old pissing match. I didn't need magic to feel how much the two hated each other.

"I promised him the city for his taking," Moran said with a grand sweep of his arm. "That should keep him well fed and return my full magic – and then some."

"You followed Cassidy," Sorren accused.

"I figured she'd lead me to you," Moran replied with a sneer. "You've always been soft about your pets. I wanted to kill her like I killed the others and leave her for you to find – a reminder of the old days."

Our group subtly shifted positions. Moran was only part of the threat. Mirov was scanning for the demon, and Chuck was close to him. Lucinda had moved up near Sorren to handle Moran and his magic. That left Teag and me for the minions and shadow men, and any vengeful ghosts or other nasties that might be waiting for us.

Even so, we weren't really ready for it when all hell broke loose.

I can't describe a demon's shriek, because words don't suffice. But if you put a live horse through a wood chipper, and lit a lion on fire, and put the two awful death cries together, you might be close.

The demon had a skull like an ibex, with long, black horns that curved backwards. Red eyes gazed balefully. It stood on powerful hind legs, with a muscular body covered in coarse, matted dark hair like a musk-ox and feet like a vulture, its dark claws fouled with old blood. It was clearly and grotesquely male, and naked except for lanyards of withered, severed fingers and the skulls of animals, some still with rotting bits of fur.

It rose from the shadows behind Moran like a nightmare god, bellowing its awful shriek, and it went straight for Sorren.

Sorren sidestepped with vampire speed, and Mirov was right behind him, sword in one hand, Sig in the other. Two rounds burst from the Sig, catching the demon full in the chest. To my utter surprise, the shots drove the demon back a step, as a silvery powder blossomed from the wound in the monster's matted hair.

The beast screamed in fury and went after Mirov. Chuck pulled something that looked like a sawed-off shotgun from beneath his jacket, flipped a switch, and thrust it at the monster, hitting him with the green fire of a supernatural stun gun. The demon staggered, and in that instant's pause, Mirov came in slashing and stabbing, scoring deep gashes that bloodied the demon's filthy hair. It swept a clawed hand at Mirov, knocking him out of the way, and went after Chuck, who was swearing under his breath as he jabbed his stun pole at the demon again, green fire crackling.

I didn't get to see what happened next, because four *akvenon* minions skittered from the darkness, snapping their teeth. They came at Teag and me with high-pitched shrieks that echoed deafeningly from the metal and brick. Teag gripped his sparring staff and fell into a defensive stance. He didn't wait for the minion to come any closer. He gave a war cry and ran at it, his staff moving almost too fast to see, landing blow after blow while remaining out of the minion's reach. He pivoted on one foot, sending the second *akvenon* slamming against the wall with a Capoeira kick.

I leveled Alard's walking stick at the two *akvenon* coming at me, and drew a deep breath, clenching my fist over the focus ring as I slid my hand along the smooth wood. Fire blasted from the tip, temporarily blinding me with my night vision goggles. The *akvenon* screamed as the flames engulfed them, blackening their scaly hides, and they fell back, but I knew one shot was not enough to stop them for good.

The orb had disappeared from Moran's hand, replaced by a wicked-looking sword in his right and an old-school wand in his left. I looked again, and realized his athame was the preserved severed front paw of a black cat. This guy was seriously mental.

Lucinda struck first with a streak of white light from her shaman's staff. Moran blocked it with his wand-arm. He spoke a word of power and angled the cat's leg athame at her, sending back a blast of power that sent a wind through the corridor, raising a storm of dust that stung our eyes and made it hard to breathe.

Lucinda brought her staff down to the ground with a thump, and Moran's power reversed itself, roaring back at him and snuffing out the candles on the altar. Sorren charged in, using his strength and immortal speed to get inside Moran's guard as he battled Lucinda.

Lucinda chanted louder. I heard banging and scratching from the depths of the old building, and overhead, it sounded as if the building were being whipped by gusts of wind that whistled through the roof.

Fear shivered down my back, and I drew a deep breath. I let one hand touch the amber whorl in my pocket. I felt Bo's presence more strongly than I had since his passing, and his ghost took shape, standing guard beside me.

*Fear makes the wolf bigger than he is,* Grandma Sarah used to say, and for good measure I caught a faint whiff of cinnamon sugar. I took courage from the vision, knowing she was watching out for me, sensing her magic in the spoon-athame inside my sleeve.

I saw two glowing red eyes appear out of nowhere, right before a shadow figure lurched toward me, arms outstretched.

Several things happened all at once. I heard the snarl of an angry dog and the snap of teeth as Bo's ghost launched itself at the attacker with all the fury of a rabid Rottweiler. I lashed out with my right hand, palm out, as if to push the shadow man away, and felt my grandmother's magic fill me, moving down my arm and through my skin in a burst of golden light that left my palm and struck the shadow figure in the chest. The attacker was no match for Bo and my grandmother, and the apparition winked out.

One down, more to go. Defeating one shadow man did not make the others give up. They came at me like a wave, and darkness enfolded me, smothering and confining. I was so cold that I was shivering, and the shrieks and cries of the long-dead echoed in my ears. Shadow hands tore at my clothing and grabbed at my hair. I could hear Teag fighting through the shadows to make his way toward me.

Bo snarled and lunged, and the white light flared once more from my right hand, but this time, the shadows had regrouped and while some fell back, others dared to inch closer.

Teag's hand came down on my shoulder, and I felt him anchor me, dampening the fear and cold, sending me energy. I tightened my grip on the spindle whorl in my hand, feeling the cool, ancient amber against my skin. Cold white fire streamed from my outstretched hand, and in my mind I pictured Secona, seer to the Vikings, in all her power. The shadow men shrank back, dissolving into mist as the white fire punched through them. This time, they vanished, but I figured they weren't gone for good.

Mirov and Chuck had their hands full with the demon. Mirov's dark jacket and shirt had been torn away from his shoulder, and a bloody gash ran from shoulder to collar bone. Chuck also had taken a swipe from the demon's claws, which had cut into his scalp, matting his hair and collar with fresh blood.

The demon was trying to keep both Mirov and Chuck in its sight, and they were making that difficult. Chuck had abandoned his stun gun stick. He had his Glock in one hand and a strange glowing ball in the other.

Mirov's Sig boomed again at close range, a shot that would have torn a hole through a mortal's chest. The bullet struck the demon in the head, tearing into its thick hide, sending a spray of black, stinking ichor that splattered Mirov and Chuck. The demon staggered.

Chuck lobbed the orb in his hand. It shattered as it hit the demon's back and exploded, opening the skin of the demon's back, sending the demon reeling toward Mirov, who held his sword leveled for the killing blow.

The demon careened into Mirov, whose blade sank hilt-deep into the monster's chest. For good measure, he fired another shot from the Sig, point blank. Chuck hit the demon from behind with a silvery, studded orb thrown with his full strength. The studded orb burst into a screeching flare of energy, and the demon shrieked in response, flailing in anger and pain. I bet they were part of Mirov's arsenal, something he'd shared with Chuck, because I didn't think silver nitride bound with magic was in the Black Ops pack of dirty tricks.

Mirov was still too close, without time to get clear of the demon's powerful talons. The claws raked him across the face and chest, but he emptied the rest of his clip into the demon, blowing away much of its face.

Chuck shot the creature in the back, putting a bullet through the spot where a heart should have been. When he'd emptied his gun, Chuck shoved it into his belt and threw another of the studded silver bombs, something

I bet was like the EMF jammer he had used on the minions.

Moran was looking worse for the wear, but so was Sorren. I wondered if using his magic before he was back to full strength cost Moran, because with every volley of magical power, his disfigurement grew worse. He was much more withered than the first time I had seen him, but his eyes blazed with hatred and his mouth was set in a grim take-no-prisoners expression. I knew that he and Sorren intended to battle this to the death.

Moran still stood in the middle of the demon's nest. Behind him, I glimpsed the Baphomet Orb on a table, and figured it was what he was protecting. The demon had no problem ranging afield from its lair, nor did the minions, unfortunately.

Sorren was cut and bleeding in a dozen places, but he came back again and again and Moran's damaged immortality was no match for Sorren's vampire speed. Moran blocked the attack with a force-curtain of black mist. Lucinda sent a blast of white light from her staff, straining against the mist until the curtain vanished, giving Sorren another opening to swing his blade and slash Moran across the ribs.

Teag came up behind Lucinda and placed one hand on her shoulder while he worked to loosen another knot in the circle loom he wore at his waist. I could practically see the energy flow from Teag into Lucinda, see her gain strength like water to a wilted plant. She murmured thanks, and Teag swung back to me, just in time to face a new threat.

More of the *akvenon* minions were heading our way. Bo's ghost lunged at them, and with each new wave of attackers, that worked once or twice. I sent a blast of fire from Alard's walking stick, but these minions scuttled fast enough that the worst of the blast missed them.

"A little help over here!" I yelled to Teag.

Teag held his staff in the crook of his arm, reached in his pocket and withdrew a tangled mat of colored threads. He stretched it between his fingers, and thrust his hand out toward the closest minion. The *akvenon* tumbled over as if caught in an invisible net, its clawed feet scrabbling to get free. The mat of threads in Teag's hand crumbled into dust.

The walking stick's magic was taking a toll on me, so I shoved it through my belt and grabbed Secona's whorl in my left hand as my right hand closed around the ring. I focused on the ring and drew power from the jet bracelet, willing the images of power imprinted on the whorl to spring to life. Long-ago magic from long-forgotten battles sprang to my hand, flooding outward in a cascade of brilliant white light that bowled the *akvenon* over and flung them back to slam against one of the thin metal walls.

Mirov had replaced his Sig with long silver throwing shivs. He and the demon rounded on each other, both bleeding from more wounds than I could count, both a little shaky on their feet, and both utterly intent on destruction. A deep gash ran from Mirov's left eyebrow to his chin, and a slash to his right thigh left him limping.

Chuck looked worse for wear as well. I wasn't sure what he still had left of the weapons he'd grabbed from his bag of tricks, and I didn't know how much longer he could last.

Chuck dove toward the demon, this time with a bigger version of the EMF disruptor I had seen the night he had fought the minion at my house. He gave the demon a good jolt, enough to distract him while Mirov sent two of the silver shivs spinning toward the demon.

One lodged in the demon's throat, and another struck him in the belly. Both sank deep into the demon's body, and the monster roared and twisted, its red eyes slitted in pain and rage.

Teag secured the head wrap more tightly and gripped his fight staff as we braced for a new onslaught of *akvenon*. Four more minions came at us this time, and the shadow men pressed forward, coming at us from all directions.

Teag and I were fighting back to back. He had been able to use his threads to force-net two of the minions, but that didn't stop the shadow men. He put his hand on my shoulder and loosed another hemp knot. It kept me on my feet, but I wouldn't be able to take much more of this. I knew the head wrap held some of the power of the Loa Ogoun, a fierce warrior, and I figured Teag was in need of some otherworldly support right about now, too. Teag let go of me and drew his short sword. Staff in one hand, blade in another, Teag's Eskrima training was getting a good workout.

Moran seemed to be throwing everything he had left at Sorren and Lucinda. I had enough on my plate with the minions and shadow men, but the magic they were trading back and forth lit up the inside of the old warehouse like the Fourth of July. Sorren's sword was red with Moran's blood, and I could see dark vampire blood on Moran's blade. It was a toss-up on who could stay on his feet longer.

"Incoming!" Teag shouted, as the minions ran at us. Teag had expended all his magic except for the protection of the embroidered flat scarf and his blades.

I hoped it would be enough, because I was almost out of tricks myself. While the magic in the walking stick and the spoon-athame and the whorl wasn't really my own, summoning the energy to use my gift to touch the memory of that power drained me more than I'd realized.

Bo kept barking, trying to keep the shadow men at bay. One of the minions skittered in fast and launched itself at Teag. Teag used his staff as a lever to leap up and land a kick to the minion, sending it flying into the darkness across the room. The other minion came at me, knocking me to the ground. I screamed as its claws slashed into my shoulder, and on instinct, my hand came up, and blasted it with the whorl's white-hot power at point-blank range.

The *akvenon* squealed and hissed like a crab on a hot griddle as its thick-scaled skin peeled away and its rancid flesh began to burn. I gagged on the stench and got my feet up, slamming into the minion and hurling it as far away from me as I could.

One of the shadow men caught Teag just as he got his feet under him, and grabbed at his shirt, shredding it down the back. Teag whirled, striking with his staff, but the pole went right through the shadow man. Swearing under his breath, Teag backed away as the shadow man's long fingers sank deep into his left arm, raising deep cuts that welled bright with blood.

"Get back!" I shouted, and Teag dropped and rolled as I got off a shot with the bright force of the athame.

It pushed the shadow man back, but more were coming, and as I struggled to my feet, I despaired of making it out alive.

Dozens of shadow men rushed toward us, and I knew I was going to die. But just as they were about to reach for us, a cold, damp tide of fog rolled in, rising between us and the shadow men, and in that mist I saw the faces of the men Moran had murdered for his demon. Jimmy Redshoes, Kevin Harvey, Fred Kenner, Russ Landrieu, and his crew and the nameless vagrants whose murders no one had noticed. They rose like a wall between us and the shadow men, shoulder to shoulder, surrounding us, holding the worst at bay – for now.

Sorren looked almost as bad as when we had been attacked at the warehouse. His hair hung lank around his face, he had the pallor of a corpse and he was bleeding in more places than I could count. He seemed to be baiting Moran to come at him, diving back and forth, tempting Moran to venture further out from his place in the middle of the demon's nest.

Mirov, too, seemed to be drawing the demon to him with a sudden round of frantic attacks. Chuck bellowed a Rebel Yell and leaped onto the demon's back, bringing a military-issue bush knife down with all his might. Chuck struck again and again at the demon's spine as Mirov slashed and thrust with his sword.

Chuck was covered with black ichor and his own blood, but I could see the determination in his face. He leaned forward and slashed his blade across the demon's throat as Mirov lunged, sinking his sword deep and drawing it down in a move that would have eviscerated any living creature.

Moran loosed a blast of white light at Sorren, and I realized as Sorren screamed and fell back, skin blistering and charring, that it was simple daylight conjured as magic that might be our undoing.

Lucinda saw an opening and rushed past Moran, scooping the Baphomet Orb into her arms and dodging back, carving a clear path with an exceptionally strong flare from her staff.

Moran raised his arms to the ceiling. With a sizzle and snap, the overhead lights in the building suddenly pulsed on, with a surge that sent sparks flying from the overloaded lights. Bulbs popped, and the smell of burned wiring filled the air. In the momentary flash, we were blinded, and I knew Moran was moving in for the kill.

I couldn't see, but I could hear. The minion came at me, clicking and snapping, hurtling through the air. The ghosts couldn't stop it, and my eyes hadn't adjusted yet. I felt Bo's ghost brush against my left leg, so I dove to the right, clutching the whorl in one hand and the ring in the other for clarity.

The minion's sharp claws ripped through my left shoulder and I gasped. Blood flowed down my arm, and it hurt like hell. The minion's feet clattered on the concrete floor, and I heard Bo barking like a hellhound. As my vision slowly returned, I used Bo's barks to maneuver out of the minion's way. It meant I dodged the worst of the blows, but not all of them. By the time I could see again, blood was running down my face from a cut on my scalp, my right thigh had a gash that was going to need stitches, and I had only narrowly missed being clawed down the belly.

I thrust out my right hand, shoving the *akvenon* away and blasting it with magic at the same time, choosing the white-fire of the whorl to do the most damage. It shrieked and writhed, withering from the point-blank hit of magic. Teag's staff came down hard on its skull, crushing bone, and with a sweep, he kicked it out of the way with a move that should have been in the World Cup.

He swung his staff in an arc, knocking another minion off its feet and slamming down the staff on its back. He had his short sword in his right hand, and as the third *akvenon* leaped at him, Teag got under it, bringing his blade up and through its belly as I scrambled out of the way. The *akvenon* screeched, impaled on the ensorcelled blade, and ichor gushed over Teag's sword. He jerked the blade free and the minion fell to the ground. He swung his staff, batting the writhing body back at the other three approaching *akvenon*. They fell on their bloodied companion, ripping it to shreds, temporarily forgetting us.

Teag gave me a hand up. His hand was warm and slick with blood, and I could see that in the few seconds we had been blinded, the minions had taken a toll on both of us. "Some night out, huh?" he joked. His face was streaked with sweat, blood, and ichor, blackened from the dust that covered everything.

Lucinda stood in the intersection of the corridors, staff upraised, head thrown back. Her body was twitching and bucking as if ridden by an unseen power, and I smelled the scent of pipe smoke, stronger now. It seemed to me that another power overtook Lucinda, and I saw the image of a gnarled old man in a straw hat, leaning on a cane.

Behind Lucinda, it looked as if the rest of the storage building ceased to exist and an infinite well of blackness had opened up, blotting out everything else. Somehow, I knew that this blackness was different from the shadows and darkness that had clutched at me in the unit. This was the darkness between stars, the darkness of the grave and what lay beyond. And in that moment, my limited knowledge of Voudon gave me the name for what I saw.

Papa Legba, Master of the Crossroads, the Loa who held the keys to the afterlife, possessed Lucinda, and it was into his arthritic hands we would send the demon back where it came from.

Moran screamed and pointed his wand at Lucinda, shrieking curses at her. But the power Lucinda had called encircled her, and the harm Moran intended rebounded, striking him full force. He fell back, coughing up gobbets of blood, as began to shake and scream as if he were being shredded from the inside out.

Sorren dove forward and swung with his full vampire might, severing Moran's head from his body. Moran's body continued to buck and twist, grabbing for Sorren blindly, animated by unholy magic.

Mirov glanced away for just an instant, and in that second, the demon struck. One clawed hand dug deep into Mirov's shoulder, ripping his left arm from his body. The demon jerked forward, sinking its teeth into Mirov's neck. Mirov spasmed, managing to thrust one more silver shiv into the belly of the demon before the creature gave a vicious shake, breaking Mirov's neck and throwing him clear.

Lucinda's chanting rose above the chaos of the winds, and I clung to its sound for sanity. I stared at the double image of Lucinda and Papa Legba like a drowning man searching the horizon for rescue. The staff rose, and the agate gem flared a brilliant, red light that swept across the corridor and the unit, clearing the area like a blast wave.

I fell flat on the ground, and the shadows and energy that had pulled at me were swept backwards with an irresistible force. Lucinda/Papa Legba raised the Baphomet Orb to the sky, then hurled it into the maw of primal darkness that loomed behind them. It exploded like a supernova, sending a pillar of fire up through Building Four's rusted tin ceiling, rising into the night sky.

Lucinda stood at the intersection of two corridors. A crossroads. I reached into my pocket and grabbed the vial of dirt and kufwa dust and hurled it to the ground just behind where Lucinda was standing.

Cold, cleansing wind swept through the storage unit, sweeping past us with a rush, and in the frigid air, ghostly hands reached forward, grabbing hold of the demon and holding him tight as he struggled, howling his rage. The winds snatched up Moran's bucking and writhing headless body, heedless of the dark blood that surged from the stump of his neck, impervious to his grasping, bony hands.

The ghostly jailers dragged Moran, his minions and the shrieking demon toward the portal. Just as he tipped into the abyss, Chuck reached into a pocket and lobbed what looked like a grenade into the darkness after the demon. There was a flare of blindingly white light, a deafening boom, and the acrid smell of chemicals.

Abruptly, the portal closed. The shadow men disappeared.

The vision of Papa Legba lingered a moment longer, and the smell of pipe smoke replaced the stench of the demon, wafting through the brick building. The old man beckoned toward the ghosts that still stood sentry around Teag and me: Jimmy and Kevin, Fred, and the others. Like weary refugees, they turned toward Papa Legba, drifting toward the place where he stood. When they reached him, they and the Loa vanished. In the distance, we heard a dog bark three times. Wind, sound, and shadows disappeared.

"What the hell did you throw at the demon?" Teag asked, staring at Chuck.

Chuck's jacket was covered with blood and ichor. His gimme cap was long gone, and sweat beaded his forehead. His clothing was shredded and he stood like he'd broken some ribs.

"Just a little Willie Pete," he said with an exhausted grin. "White phosphorous grenade. Couldn't use it before without killing the rest of us, but in the right spot, it makes a nice flash-bang."

I thought there really should be some kind of response to that, but I was too exhausted to think of it. I sagged against Teag, as the adrenaline rush faded and I let a different kind of darkness sweep over me.

# Chapter Twenty-Nine

"WE WON, DIDN'T we?" I woke to find myself in my bed in my own house, with Baxter snuggled by my side. My arms had fresh bandages and I could feel more gauze on other body parts, beneath the covers. The drapes were pulled closed, but the nightstand lamp cast the bedroom in a warm glow.

"Mostly." Sorren was sprawled in an armchair, looking more disheveled than I'd ever seen him. One glance at the glimmer of light beneath the closed curtains told me it was daylight, but my vampire business partner had not gone to ground.

"It's dangerous. You should be in the basement," I murmured, and the words sounded slurred even to my own ears.

"I'll be fine as long as I don't go outside. How are you?"

I looked at Sorren, and realized that the gashes had healed from last night's battle. He had cleaned up and discarded the ripped and soiled clothes for a t-shirt and shorts, and if it weren't for his pallor, he might have looked like a college student with a bad hangover.

Except for the eyes. Those were ancient. And right now, it was clear that he was worried about me.

"I've felt better." Baxter woke when he heard my voice, and wriggled up onto my chest where he could lick my face and my nose. I hugged him, and he snuggled against the dog collar on my left wrist as if he were cuddling up to an old friend. They say dogs can see spirits. Perhaps he and Bo had made friends.

"The doctor gave you something for the pain when she patched you up. You've got some stitches and bruises, but you'll heal quickly. You just need rest."

More memories of the battle returned, fighting their way through the drugs. "What about the others?" I asked.

"Chuck will be fine. I took him home and made sure he got patched up as well. He was the surprise of the evening," Sorren said with a tired smile. "Your instincts were good. In fact, I think we'll keep him on our friends list, like Lucinda." He paused. "And I left him a key to a unit at a different storage facility, one I'm certain won't be closing any time soon. There's a note with the key assuring him that he will find his clocks moved to the new unit by midnight tomorrow."

"What about Teag?"

Sorren let his head fall back against the chair. "Teag's got a couple of broken ribs, some nasty gashes and plenty of bruises, but he'll be fine. A pretty remarkable young man; he more than held his own. Anthony kept close tabs on the doctor and is quite adamant about taking care of our boy personally. He'll make sure Teag gets his rest."

"Surprised none of us needed the hospital." I managed to get out before a yawn took me.

"I have very good doctors on call. There's not much they can't handle, and they're extremely discreet and trustworthy," Sorren assured me. "They'll continue to check in on you, Teag, and Chuck until you're fully mended." He chuckled. "Don't be surprised if Anthony stops by to fuss over you. After he got over the shock of seeing Teag covered in blood and demon ichor, he was very concerned about you." Sorren closed his eyes and smiled. "Teag swears that Jimmy Redshoes was his guardian angel. He says Jimmy's ghost pushed him down and kept him from getting sliced up by one of the shadow men."

"I believe it," I murmured. "Jimmy and the ghosts held the line for us. Once a soldier, always a soldier."

"Perhaps," Sorren said quietly, and I heard something in his voice I could not identify.

"Is Lucinda OK?" I asked. "I saw Papa Legba… she channeled him."

Sorren chuckled. "Lucinda is as gifted as her foremothers. It's no small feat to call a Loa of that power. I suspect Lucinda will need some time to recuperate, but she took the least damage of any of us."

That left one more person, and I was afraid I already knew the answer to my question. "Did we lose Mirov?"

Sorren nodded. "He fought bravely. An instant's distraction – that's what it comes down to in these fights. I took care of the body, and let the Alliance know."

I didn't have much chance to get to know Mirov, but his death made the dangers of our work soberingly clear. "So it's over?"

Sorren nodded. "Yes. Getting rid of the demon closed the conduit to the spirit energy that was spilling over to the objects and energizing the Navy yard. It doesn't get rid of the area's bloody past: that will always make it a hotbed for supernatural activity. But it should end the killings and dampen the hauntings. The minions and the shadow men are gone, too."

"Too late for Jimmy Redshoes," I murmured, fighting the draw of sleep.

"Not entirely," Sorren said. "Papa Legba holds the keys to the afterlife. He helped the ghosts who wanted to go pass over and move on. They're at rest." If I heard a bit of envy in his tone, I decided not to mention it. Perhaps final rest sounded good, now and again, to a being that had lived as long as Sorren.

Baxter had settled onto my chest and gone back to sleep. I stroked his fur and felt happily adrift.

"I suspect the Navy yard will always have its ghosts, but it should have fewer – and less dangerous – ones now," Sorren added.

I felt pleased in a warm, woozy way, as if I'd had a little too much wine. If I had to guess, I suspected Sorren had worked some of his vampire magic to help me sleep and heal. And right now, that was okay with me.

"Go ahead and rest, Cassidy. I'll stand guard," Sorren said. "It's not like I can leave, now that the sun's up," he added with a lopsided grin. "And besides, your cellar's a bit damp. Just think of me as your own dark guardian angel."

"Thanks," I murmured.

"And when you're up to it, there's a new crate for you at Trifles and Folly," he said matter-of-factly. "Turned up in an estate auction. Quite a few things from 1918. That was an interesting year."

*World war, flu pandemic. Yep, that was bound to be an interesting box.*

And the funny thing, as I drifted back to oblivion, was that I was already looking forward to the adventure.

# Author's Note

THANKS FIRST TO my agent, Ethan Ellenberg, to my editor, Jon Oliver, and to all the folks at Solaris who have been wonderful to work with over the years. I'm very excited about this new adventure, and looking forward to explore where it will take us.

Authors have a funny way of using fiction to filter real life experiences and turn them into something different. This novel, and the short story *Buttons* that inspired it, arose from a particular set of circumstances and events, without which the story would not have developed as it did. It's been a very interesting process seeing what my subconscious made of things, embellishing and embroidering and changing pieces around to end up with something distinct, yet rooted in the original. For that reason, it's also been a different kind of book for me to write, which was fitting, considering that we were venturing into new territory.

My partner and husband, Larry Martin, has come to play an increasingly important role with the books over time. He is my primary beta reader and first editor, with an eye for finding typographical errors and continuity issues. Over the years, he has become an excellent plot brainstorming partner, and he played an essential role in bringing this book to life. The books are stronger because of his involvement, and I am happy that a life partnership has developed into a creative partnership as well. Watch for us to co-author a new Steampunk novel, *Iron and Blood*, in 2015.

Charleston, South Carolina is a real place. Some of the landmarks and a few of the historical figures in this book do exist, and some (but not all) of the historical events were real. But the characters and their shops are all a work of fiction. So for example, if you go to Charleston (and I hope you do, because it's a lovely place to visit), you can see the real Charleston City Market and walk down King Street, but you won't find any of the businesses or restaurants I've mentioned by name. The old Navy yard is real, but not the history I invented for it (so far as I know). Any resemblance to real people or actual businesses is completely coincidental.

Many people in Charleston will tell you that the ghosts, however, are real. My ghosts are fictional, but that's because Charleston has enough of its own already. But don't take my word for it. See for yourself.

Want more about Cassidy, Sorren and Teag?
Check out my *Deadly Curiosities Adventures*
e-book short stories on Kindle, Kobo and Nook!

# About the Author

**Gail Z. Martin** writes epic and urban fantasy, steampunk and short stories. She is the author of the Chronicles of the Necromancer series, the Fallen Kings Cycle series and the Ascendant Kingdoms Saga series of epic fantasy books, as well as the Deadly Curiosities urban fantasy world and coming in 2015, *Iron and Blood*, a steampunk novel, co-written with Larry N. Martin. Gail is a frequently contributor to US and UK anthologies. She also writes two series of ebook short stories: *The Jonmarc Vahanian Adventures* and *The Deadly Curiosities Adventures*.

Find her at:
www.ChroniclesOfTheNecromancer.com,
on Twitter @GailZMartin,
on Facebook.com/WinterKingdoms,
at DisquietingVisions.com blog
and GhostInTheMachinePodcast.com.

She leads monthly conversations on Goodreads: https://www.goodreads.com/GailZMartin

and posts free excerpts of her work on Wattpad: http://wattpad.com/GailZMartin.

When she's not writing, Gail also enjoys reading, cooking, watching anime and Dr. Who, and hanging out with her husband, kids and dogs.

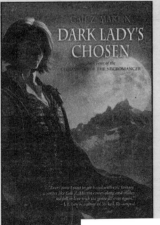